T0367581

His Heart I Hold

AIKEN A. BROWN

HIS HEART I HOLD

iUniverse books may be ordered through booksellers or by contacting:

iUniverse
1663 Liberty Drive
Bloomington, IN 47403
www.iuniverse.com
1-800-Authors (1-800-288-4677)

ISBN: 978-1-4917-7662-9 (sc)
ISBN: 978-1-4917-7663-6 (e)

Print information available on the last page.

iUniverse rev. date: 9/9/2015

CONTENTS

His Heart I Hold

In a Brother's Eyes: the Brant McLachlan Story (2005) introduced us to a small town in Mississippi and a family so relatable that they became part of our own. We were captivated by Brant's charm, drive, personality and his relationship with his life-long love. *His Heart I Hold* is a unique love story that explores not only the strength of the human spirit and the fragility of the human heart, but the definition of love itself.

Jennifer and Christian's story is one of love born of tragedy. When Brant's life was cut tragically short, Jennifer lost her husband, and Christian lost his brother. They never imagined falling in love, but, as they navigated their way through shared loss, a friendship caught fire, and while Jennifer struggled with the idea that she could ever love another, Christian battled deep feelings of betrayal. Together, they learned lessons of selflessness, loyalty, respect, empathy and understanding that helped them ultimately define love and the beauty of its complexities, while realizing one common truth… it's his heart they hold.

It's been a decade since they told us Brant's story, now Jennifer and Christian McLachlan share their story… in their own words.

In a Brother's Eyes: the Brant McLachlan Story (2005)

Set in the Deep South, *In a Brother's Eyes: the Brant McLachlan Story* takes place in a small Mississippi town where Friday night high school football is king, families stick together and true love is supposed to conquer all. *In a Brother's Eyes* is a Southern novel that focuses on the traditions prevalent in the South: its obsession with football, its strong sense of religion, its close-knit communities.

In a Brother's Eyes tells a story of triumph on the football field, but it is primarily a love story. It tells the story of a small, country town and their love affair with a high school quarterback whose outgoing personality and natural charm causes a town to fall in love with him, a family to adore him, and people to root for him even after he makes a decision that will threaten to destroy his relationship with his life-long girlfriend.

In a Brother's Eyes is an emotional roller coaster ride full of laughter and tears. Throughout the course of the novel, Brant McLachlan's love for Jennifer Smith faces the ultimate test and leads to an emotional struggle that begs the question...does true love always prevail?

IN A BROTHER'S EYES: THE BRANT MCLACHLAN STORY

CHAPTER ONE

Have you ever met someone who could always make you smile... make you laugh? Have you ever just sat around and thought to yourself... *wow, I wish I was like him... I wish I was that talented or maybe that funny or that outgoing?* Have you ever known a person who was so special that you wished you could be just like him, if even only for a day? I have, and, growing up, he lived just across the hall from me.

Every sport bears the names of those who have achieved greatness. Baseball has Babe Ruth, Hank Aaron and Willie Mays. Basketball claims the one and only Michael Jordan. Stockcar racing is synonymous with names like Petty and Earnhardt. Hockey has Wayne Gretzky; golf has Tiger Woods, and boxing has Muhammad Ali. Football is no different; it has its heroes, and everyone knows their names, their stories. However, there is one story that has been left unwritten, and that's the story I want to tell. Though he'll never be remembered as a great NFL quarterback, Brant McLachlan changed the face of professional football with the spirit of a nineteen-year-old and the bright smile of a young man living out a little boy's dream.

I'm Jordan McLachlan, and, with the help of my parents, friends and a loving community, I have compiled a story that is very close to all our hearts. It is a story of courage, desire and a confident grin that will never be forgotten. Everyone has a favorite athletic hero, and I am proud to tell you the story of my hero... my little brother, Brant McLachlan.

A wise person once said, "yesterday is history, tomorrow is a mystery, and today is a gift from above, that's why they call it the present." Several years ago my family and I learned that lesson first-hand.

It was said of my brother Brant when he was only a freshman at North River High school in Cummins, Mississippi, that he would never play a day of college football. His unreal natural ability compounded by his unobtainable desire for perfection had people in our small, country town excited about producing our first professional athlete.

Cummins, population around 1,800, is located just south of Meridian, Mississippi. It's a close-knit community where neighbors go out of their way to help one another and gossip spreads like wildfire at the corner, country store. It's small town life at its finest, and though it would always be the place he called home... everyone in our close-knit community knew that one day Brant McLachlan would outgrow Cummins, Mississippi. There would come a day when you entered Cummins and were greeted by a sign that proudly welcomed you to Cummins, Mississippi: HOME OF BRANT MCLACHLAN. Brant's dreams became the dreams of a town... his success, Cummins' success.

Brant is the youngest of my parents' four boys, six minutes younger than Ethan and fifteen minutes younger than Christian.

That makes me the oldest. In fact, I'm thirteen years older than the triplets. My mother was young when I was born, and, being a dedicated career woman, it took her a long time to decide she was ready to have another baby. When she did get pregnant with her long-awaited second child, she, my father and I were all in for a surprise. Mom wanted a little girl, but Dad and I prayed hard for a little boy. Though I'm sure I would have been thrilled to have a little sister, Dad and I really had our hearts set on a boy. We wanted someone to play football with, someone to wrestle with, and someone who would never interrupt Saturdays spent in front of the television watching college football with a dance recital or a piano lesson. We prayed for a boy, promising to spoil him rotten if God would just hear our prayers, and our prayers were answered... times three. I was the proudest big brother alive when my three baby brothers entered the world, thus forever, each in his own way, changing my world.

Brantley was, from the first day that I held him, the light in my eyes. He was born with a head full of blond hair and a smile just as bright. As he grew his hair only got blonder and his smile wider. It gave him a happy-go-lucky appearance that fit his personality to perfection.

He was good at everything he ever tried to do, and it was always easy to see that this kid would hold the world in the palm of his hand.

Football was Brant's passion. A competitive fire burned deep within his soul, and he could never get enough of the adrenaline rush that football provided. But, football, PlayStation, *Chutes and Ladders*... you name it, and Brant wanted to win. He was a competitor, and in a Southern town where Friday night, high school football was king, Brant McLachlan was small town royalty.

Football was his future, but there is no doubt in my mind that music could have been. Brant *never* stopped singing. You couldn't name a song that he didn't know... not a country music song anyway. Alone, in a crowd, in the car, or on the football field, Brant moved from one song to another, singing a verse here and a verse there with no thought of who was listening or if *anyone* was listening at all. Mom encouraged him to pursue music, not only because she considered it less dangerous than a career in football, but because she knew that the stage was invented for people like Brant. He was a born performer. Brant never wavered though, and when he said that the football field would be his stage, we all knew that he was right.

Football was engraved in Brant's brain. He lived it twenty-four hours a day, seven days a week, three hundred and sixty-five days a year. It seemed that from the time he could speak, "Super Bowl ring" was in his vocabulary. When he was little, he would take my class ring off my finger and pretend for hours at a time that he was talking to the press about his multiple Super Bowl victories.

Brant and school never quite got along the way that our mother might have hoped. Brant never gave school the time that it required, but that, by no stretch of the imagination, means that he didn't know what work and dedication were about. Every morning Brant was up with the sun, so he could jog five miles and make it home in time to shower and get to school on time. He dreamed up new offences during math, English and history. After school he practiced with the team for two and a half hours. When practice was done for the day, Brant came home and worked unrelentingly on precision passing. It was once said of a professional pitcher that he possessed such phenomenal control that if you asked him to hit a stop sign with a baseball from sixty feet away, he would ask, "*S-T-O or P*?" That's how good my brother was with a football. From the time he was a little boy, he might as well have had the words I'M GONNA BE FAMOUS ONE DAY written across his forehead in big, bold letters for all the world to see.

While the rest of the nation may have been oblivious to the talent we were hiding on the less than spectacular football fields of a slow-paced, Southern town, the people of Cummins couldn't wait for the day when we would unleash our hometown prodigy to go and make a name for himself and for our town.

My brother Ethan was always the intelligent type, but never too showy about it or critical of others because of it. He was fairly athletic; he enjoyed football, but his interest was always medicine. Our mother was a doctor and our father a football coach, so for Ethan to take an interest in sports medicine seemed only like the most natural of unions.

Ethan read constantly, and he knew much more information than he ever felt the need to share. He is the only guy I know who could, or who ever cared to, practically recite "All Summer in a Day," a short story by Ray Bradbury. Why he ever took to committing it to memory, I don't know, but believe me when I say we gave him grief about it. Never was any boy more intrigued by "The Monsters are Due on Maple Street" or *The Firm* or *The Lords of Discipline*, "Birches," and "The Road Not Taken" than Ethan was. He loved novels, short stories and poetry; it was a passion that he and I shared. Despite my similar love for literature, Ethan's attempts to include the rest of the family in book discussions usually failed. He said "William Faulkner" and Brant heard "Marshall Faulk," and the conversation usually ended there. My Dad, my brothers and I always picked at Ethan because, in so many ways, he was so different from the others in our male-dominated, football-obsessed house.

Growing up, Ethan always had a genuine thirst for knowledge, but he handled it in such a way that he never seemed strange or unusual, the way people of such a high intellect often strike me. Basically, what I guess I'm trying to say is… my brother is highly intelligent, but he's no geek. In fact, I think that it was the way that Ethan always talked about literature and about how authors were able to leave so much behind when they were gone and could no longer tell their stories that inspired me to write this book. He taught me to write from my heart, and he gave me the desire to see this project through, though he never said a word about it.

Of my three younger brothers, Christian was always the most like me. He is extremely athletic and was above average in the classroom, but not the best in either area. He is tall and well built with brownish-blond hair, a mixture of Ethan's brown and Brantley's blond.

Some see Christian's as a lifetime spent in the shadows of Brant's athleticism and Ethan's intelligence, but I don't see it that way at all. He is the most well-rounded member of our family, and he adds something to it that superior intellect and lightning fast feet never could.

As far as character is concerned, Christian is one of the strongest people I know. He learned at an early age that there is always gonna be someone out there better than you are, so if you want to make your dreams come true you have to be willing to work harder than the other guy. Everyone has heard the story about the guy who bragged about surviving the great Mississippi flood. When he got to Heaven, he was bragging to God about surviving the great Mississippi flood, and God just said, "that's great... meet Noah."

Having constant reminders of superiority so close by, kept Christian striving, determined to make a name for himself as a collegiate athlete. He learned that jealousy was a feeling that would tear so much apart, so much that was worth holding on to; and he was a better person for it.

Writing Christian's story would be a task worth taking on. I could easily write a book about each of my brothers, but sooner or later I'm sure that my readers would get tired of hearing me brag!

As I mentioned, my mother is a doctor. She is actually the Chief of Staff at North River Hospital outside of Cummins. We may not have a Sonic or a McDonald's within a forty-mile radius of town, but the hospital just outside of town is the second largest hospital in Mississippi and easily one of the best hospitals in the South.

Growing up as the preacher's only daughter in Cummins, Mississippi, where all the Baptists, for the most part, attend the same Baptist church, Mom had her share of worthy suitors, but, when she was fifteen, she fell madly in love with North River High School's freshman quarterback, and they have been together ever since. The church was the basis for their marriage, and it remains that way today. My brothers and I never met our grandfather, but I haven't missed a day of church as long I can remember.

My father, that quarterback that Mom fell so hard for, spent twenty-five years coaching high school football at North River. He coached me, and he coached my brothers. Dad's coaching played a major part in making Brant the player that he became, and it formed a special bond between the two of them that few fathers and sons ever have the opportunity to enjoy.

Dad played college football for the University of Alabama, but, though he was drafted, he never played professionally. He played for the Bear, though I have never in my life heard him refer to his old coach by his nationally recognized nickname. He never lets us forget how great of a man he thinks legendary Coach Paul "Bear" Bryant was. "Sacrifice, work, self-discipline, I teach these things to my boys, and they don't forget them when they leave," he quotes when he reflects on the old days. My dad tells football stories like they're war stories. He is the only military-loving, grateful patriot I know who can make a Super Bowl sound more intense than a world war. For him and, thus, for us, football was a way of life.

Hot, humid summers in the South mean longer days, a vacation from school, families sharing ripe, juicy watermelons on their back porches as they talk about their days, trips to football camp and plenty of time to reflect on the upcoming fall football season.

The summer after the triplets' junior year of high school is one that our family, our friends and our town will never forget. It was a summer when we wondered not what professional team that Brant would sign with or how high he would go in the draft, but a summer when we wondered if he would ever play another game of football at all.

CHAPTER TWO

It was two days after North River High School's final bell of the year had sounded, signaling the beginning of summer. I had just decided to move back into my old room at my parents' house while the construction of my own house, less than a mile away, was being completed. The process of building my own home had proven to move slower than anticipated. To intensify matters, the buddy I had been living with for the past two years was getting married that July and needed me out as soon as I could find a place to stay.

I got my brothers out of bed early, and we spent the morning moving me back home. We all had trucks, and I didn't have that much stuff, so the move only took one trip.

When we were done hauling my bed, chest of drawers, desk, stereo system and a couple other boxes full of clothes and other junk up the stairs at the house, we decided to go for a drive. We didn't have any plans, but we never had any trouble finding things to entertain us during the summer. Most likely, we would have ended up at the lake and gone for a swim to cool off.

It was a sweltering summer day. Brant was driving his blue Z-71 ahead of me. Christian and Ethan followed in their red and black trucks that were identical to Brant's. Their trucks were gifts from our parents, and the boys loved driving them.

In fact, Brant's truck was his favorite toy. It had big tires and a chrome toolbox. There was a giant Dallas Cowboys star on the back window and a No Fear sticker on the bumper. A plethora of CDs filled the console, and there was usually a half-full Dr. Pepper in the cup holder.

Brant was driving way too fast as usual. He had to be hitting close to a hundred miles per hour when the rest of us, none of whom are nearly as fearless, were left eating his dust. The triplets grew up sitting on Dad's lap, steering his truck or our four-wheeler on the dirt roads along the outskirts of town. Driving wasn't new to them, but, on this day, we would learn that no one, no matter how confident or how good of a driver he is, should ever take advantage of what a vehicle can do.

Like I said, Brant's truck was his toy. He was running wide open, the windows were down, the radio was blaring Garth Brooks, and Brant was keeping with the beat on the steering wheel, never dreaming that in the next moment his world would be turned upside down.

We were probably the only cars for miles. I knew Brant was going too fast, but it seemed like harmless fun along the backroads of Cummins. In fact, he made it look like so much fun that the other three of us were doing all we could to keep up with him. Then, in the blink of an eye, a large dog bolted from the woods. My breath caught, and I slid to a screeching halt as Brant jerked the steering wheel, swerved, and narrowly missed the dog, who yelped as he bolted back toward the brush.

I watched in horror as Brant's hands worked, fighting to regain control of the truck. I closed my eyes tightly as the truck crashed into an upcoming guardrail. Opening them again, forcing myself to watch, I saw the truck skid into the ditch, then turn over on its roof, pick up speed, slide back onto the side of the road, then flip again before careening down a grassy hill as if it were a bouncy ball, flipping end over end with ease.

Never in my life had I been so afraid. I imagined myself having to tell my parents that Brant was dead, and I quickly pushed the thought from my head. An overwhelming sense of shock shot through my body as Christian, Ethan and I jumped from our trucks and stared at one another in a moment of sheer terror.

As soon as Brant's truck came to rest, I took off running down the hill as fast as I could. I jumped over the ditch and fought my way through the high grass. "Go get help," I cried back to my brothers. They were running after me, their eyes glazed. "Get help!" I demanded them.

Ethan grabbed Christian's arm. "Call 911," he instructed calmly.

"I don't have my cell phone," Christian panicked. "Where's yours?"

"At home," Ethan gulped. He grabbed Christian's shoulders. "Chris, listen to me," he said as he took control of the situation. "Go get in your truck and drive back to the Country Mart... call 911... tell them what happened... tell them to hurry."

Christian nodded and sprinted back toward the road as Ethan hurried to catch up with me.

We screamed Brant's name as we ran, helpless to do anything more. I was running as fast as I could toward that totaled, blue truck, though in my mind I didn't ever want to get there; I was too scared of what I would find when I did. When I finally got to the bottom of the hill I began to shake with fear, and I had to fight to steady my hands.

Guilt consumed me. Brant always drove recklessly around town. I knew it, and so did everyone else, but never once, at least not with any hint of sincerity, had I ever told him to slow down. The local sheriff's deputy had occasionally pulled Brant over for exceeding the speed limit. He would give him a little talking to, wish him luck on Friday night and send him on his way, but he never gave him a ticket. Most of the time he only smiled, waved, and gently scolded Brant with a wag of his finger as he sped by.

Looking out for my little brothers was my life, but, on this day, I felt like such a failure. My body was reacting, but my mind was in a daze. I adored the kid in that truck, and I couldn't imagine trying to go on living without him. I knew I couldn't sleep at night knowing that there might have been something I could have done to protect him.

All I could think about was the little boy who used to sit on my lap while he played Nintendo or ride on my back when he got tired of walking at Disney World. I could see him watching me play football, his eyes wide as he studied the quarterback and soaked in his every move. I could see his smile, and I could see his bright, innocent blue eyes all in a flash.

The truck had landed right side up, though, in my opinion, it had lost all evidence of ever being a truck to begin with. Gas was spilling out onto the grass, and a powdery substance emitted by the ejected air bags, burned my nose as it wafted from the windows.

Ethan tried to pull the driver's side door open, but it wouldn't budge. I ran around to the passenger's side, and, after a brief struggle, Ethan and I were able to pry the door open. Pieces of glass and half of a CD fell to the grass.

Brant was lying across the floorboard, his head right beside the door. There was blood everywhere. Both air bags were out, and the steering wheel was facing downward. Brant's left shoe was sitting on the seat, and he was lying in a pile of broken glass. His light blond hair was highlighted in red, and his body glistened with glass slithers. I'll never forget the white Nike t-shirt or the khaki shorts he was wearing that day because, as hard as I've tried, I cannot shake that image of him lying there from my memory.

I didn't know if Brant was dead or alive. I called his name as he lay motionless.

I turned to Ethan, and he read my mind. "It's okay," he told me as he tried to remain strong, "he's just unconscious…"

Brant's neck was a bloody mess, and Ethan couldn't find a pulse.

We both began to panic, then, by some miracle, Brant opened his eyes. I couldn't believe it. I gently brushed a piece of glass away from Brant's eye with the tip of my finger.

"Brant," I gulped.

"Jordan," he said softly, and my heart jumped.

"Where are you hurt, Brant?" I asked.

"Everywhere," Brant groaned.

I turned to Ethan. "What do we do?" I sighed.

"Keep him talking," Ethan nodded. "I've got to think."

Brant's eyes were full of tears. "It hurts, Jordan… help me," he cried painfully. My heart broke because I knew that his tears didn't come easily.

Brant closed his eyes.

"Hang with us, Brant," Ethan said. "Open your eyes."

"Please, Brantley," I begged.

When Brant didn't open his eyes, Ethan reached for Brant's wrist to feel for a pulse. "Ugh," he sighed, the pain transferring into his voice.

"What?" I exclaimed.

Ethan reached for Brant's right wrist. "His left wrist is broken… I can see the bone," he told me, not looking back.

"What are you doing?" I fidgeted.

"His pulse is weak," Ethan shook his head. "He's losing too much blood… we gotta get him out of there, but I don't think we should move him. What do you think?"

I thought back on everything that I had ever heard about neck injuries and spinal injuries. I remembered all of the episodes of *Rescue 911* that I had watched growing up, and suddenly I wished that I had paid a little bit more attention to the details.

Reluctantly, I asked, "does your neck or your back hurt, Brant?" It was a dumb question that I guess I just felt compelled to ask because, over the years, I had heard so many emergency personnel ask the same question to football players who were knocked out by a fierce hit.

Brant answered with a weak, agonizing cry, and I wanted to punch myself.

"I know, man," I sighed, still angry with myself for asking such a stupid question.

"Christian is getting help, Brant," Ethan assured him. Brant faded in and out of consciousness as Ethan and I prayed for help to arrive.

"He's gonna bleed to death if we don't do something," Ethan insisted.

"I don't think that we should move him," I broke down, scared to death of doing the wrong thing, "but I don't know… I just don't know…"

Ethan grabbed my shoulders. "He'll die before the ambulance gets here if we don't," he insisted. Ethan knew much more about that sort of thing than I did, so I agreed.

Getting my 5'11" little brother out of that smashed pile of metal was the hardest thing that I had ever done. Brant was bloody and bruised. I couldn't find a spot on his body to hold him where it wouldn't hurt him. I was smeared in his blood as I labored to get him out of the truck.

After we pulled him from the wreckage, I held Brant across my arms, unsure what to do and unwilling to let go.

"Come-on, Jordan," Ethan gulped as he ripped his own shirt from over his head.

"Will that work?" I gasped as I watched Ethan apply pressure to Brant's bleeding neck.

"I hope so," he replied with a considerable amount of uncertainty.

I looked at my brother, and, fearing that it would be the last time I saw him alive, I sighed, "I love you, Brant."

Brant looked up at me as his body trembled.

"He's going into shock," Ethan sighed, and he squeezed my shoulder, trying to shake me into action. "Use your body heat… keep him warm…"

Ethan felt for a pulse. "We're losing him, Jordan," he shook his head.

Seventeen years hit me in one instant. Brant opened his eyes. "Help me," he begged as his voice faded, and he fell unconscious again. With those words I lost every ounce of composure that I had mustered. I vividly remembered being his age and having him run into my arms screaming with a grin I never learned to turn down, "help me, help me!" Back then all I had to do was lift him up on my shoulders and smile as he harassed whoever or whatever had been chasing him. I was so accustomed to being the shield that surrounded his little world; for the first time there was nothing I could do for him, and I felt helpless. My whole life had been about being a superhero in Brant's eyes, and the obvious reality that I wasn't was devastating to me. My tears poured as I watched his tears stream down his cheeks.

I stood and paced as my brother lay motionless in the grass. Sweat pouring down my face, I knelt down and slipped Brant's one remaining shoe off of his foot. Then, in some attempt to relieve my anger and frustration, slung it at the truck.

It seemed like an eternity before I heard the siren and saw the lights of an ambulance speeding toward the hill. For a second I felt a tiny sense of relief; then I saw the way that the emergency workers looked at my brother, and the relief was gone.

"No way," I heard a familiar voice sigh. I looked up at Rick Jackson, one of our family's oldest and dearest friends. "Mr. Rick's gonna take care of you, Brant. Can you hear me? Watch his neck, fellas. We're gonna give you something for pain, kiddo. Hang on for us, buddy," he rattled as he and his crew prepared to load Brant into the back of the ambulance. Leaning against the back of the ambulance, Rick ran his fingers through his hair. "Please, God," he prayed as he rested his hands on his knees. "Please… he's like a son to me… don't do this to me again."

I had never seen my dad look the way that he did when he and Christian made it to the bottom of that hill. There was a group of men behind them, all of whom I knew had been in the Country Mart when Christian bolted inside and announced that their quarterback's truck had just flipped down the hill on North River Pass.

"Dad," Brant cried as he was pulled into the ambulance.

"I'm here, Brant. I'm right here, and I'm not going anywhere," Dad assured him as he climbed into the ambulance behind him. "Daddy's here, Brantley," he sighed to himself. Brant was such a tough kid, and hearing him scream for my father was the saddest thing I'd ever heard.

As Dad endured what can only be described as a terrifying ride to the hospital, his mind drifted back to happier times… back to a night when he had been coaching a particularly intense game. His adrenaline flowed, and his temper flared when, all of a sudden, a curly-headed two-year-old, adorned in a t-shirt bearing North River's logo, toddled to the rescue. He reached down and picked up his giggling baby boy, and, as Brant grabbed at Dad's headset, he bubbled, "I love you, Daddy."

As Dad, who had softened considerably since becoming the father of triplets, cooed, "Daddy loves you too," he lost track of the performance on the field that, only moments earlier, had provoked him into a tantrum.

Mom hurried down the fence line holding Christian in one arm and Ethan in the other. "I'm sorry… I'm sorry," she mouthed.

Dad only winked. "He's okay," he smiled, waving her off. "Were you too fast for your mama?" he laughed as he jostled Brant in his arms and imagined the look of sheer panic that must have crossed his wife's face when Brant had managed to escape her grasp and dart onto the field.

Brant, his eyes full of mischief, nodded proudly before he added in that irresistible baby talk, "play ball, Daddy?"

Dad looked up at the clock. "Two minutes and ten seconds, and I am all yours, buddy," he promised.

Brant's eyes sparkled as he grinned, "quarterback when I big?"

Dad nodded confidently. "Yes you are, son. Someday you are gonna be the best quarterback that this town has ever seen."

As Dad stared at Brant fighting for his life in the back of that ambulance, he saw that quarterback that he had dreamed of molding so many years before. He looked at the quarterback that he had drilled and trained, and for the first time in almost eighteen years, he didn't care if Brant never played another game of football again.

When we got to the hospital, Brant was unconscious. As they rushed him through the emergency room doors, I stood outside, my eyes wide with fear, my heart racing. I didn't think that Brant could survive the wreck that I had witnessed. I had done all that I could for my brother, and my emotions ran wild.

My father put his arm around my shoulders. "What happened?" he asked in a soft, solemn voice.

I cleared my throat before reluctantly answering, "a dog ran out in front of him… it came out of the brush…"

Dad shook his head in disbelief. "How fast was he going?"

I couldn't bear to tell him the truth. "Too fast," I muttered.

"Come-on, boys," Dad said sternly, "let's go find Mama."

Dad put his arm around Ethan, and we walked inside. My mother was standing at the desk with a clipboard in her hand. When she saw us, she tossed the file down and rushed over.

"Ethan…" she exclaimed. "David, what happened to him?"

I stared at my brother, shirtless and smeared in blood. My eyes moved to my own shirt, and the sight of my brother's blood made me shiver.

"I'm fine, Mom," Ethan's voice trembled.

"Where are you cut… what happened?" Mom examined Ethan.

"It's not my blood, Mom," Ethan shook his head. "It's Brant's."

Mom turned and saw the blood on my shirt and concern filled her eyes.

My father grabbed her hands. "I should have called ahead, Becky… I just wanted to be with you when you heard…"

"Heard what?" Mom insisted. "David… where's Brantley?"

"He wrecked his truck, Becky," Dad gulped.

"He flipped eight, maybe nine times, Mama," Christian cried. "It was awful."

My mom pulled Christian into her embrace. "Baby, it's gonna be okay," she promised, trying, for our sakes, to sound like a confident doctor and not a frightened mother.

Doctors are trained not to get emotional over patients, but her training wasn't enough to keep the tears from streaming from her eyes that day. An average day of work had suddenly turned into the day that every mother fears.

Mom took Dad's arm and pulled him aside. "How bad is it?" she asked.

"It's bad, Becky," Dad answered instantly. "You've gotta do something. You've gotta save our son," he begged.

Mom tried to control her tears. She hugged my father quickly. "Stay with the boys. I'll let you know something as soon as I can." She turned and began to walk, then to jog down the hall.

Dad hung his head. He unbuttoned his shirt and stripped down to his undershirt. "Here," he said as he extended his shirt to Ethan, "put this on."

"Thanks," Ethan said softly.

For what seemed like forever, my father, my brothers and I waited fearfully for word on Brant's condition.

Shock had faded into disbelief; I wanted to prepare myself for the worst, but I knew that I could never be prepared for that. No one said a word as we sat there, all lost in our own thoughts… our own memories. The waiting room chairs were uncomfortable, and the whole hospital scene seemed different than it did on days when I stopped by to see Mom or to bring her lunch. Growing up, that hospital, my mom's office, the elevators, had been my stomping ground, but that day it wasn't the same place at all. The chairs were hard; the clock ticked loudly, and death seemed to linger just behind the nearest, long, green curtain.

A beautiful summer day had suddenly turned into the most terrifying day of my life. At any time someone could come and tell us that Brant was dead, and that would be it. There would be nothing that we could do. We would all go home and try to imagine life without Brantley. Over and over again, the wreck played in my head like a bad song.

"Mr. McLachlan," a nurse smiled politely. At her words my father sprung to his feet. "Becky would like you to come with me," she said without a noticeable change in expression. My father nodded to us and quickly turned to follow her.

I looked at my brothers and smiled a sort of grimace.

"Do you think it's bad?" Christian swallowed.

I patted his back. "I don't know," I sighed.

"I'm so scared," he cried. His tears came so fast that I was sure he was going to hyperventilate. Of the four of us, Christian was, without a doubt, the most emotional. When he was a kid, he cried when he messed up a play during a football game; he cried when he made a bad grade at school. We all laughed at him when, as a teenager, he shed tears during a

TBS presentation of *Where the Red Fern Grows.* Today, he cried openly, but no one laughed.

"I know, Chris," I whispered. I looked at him and then at Ethan. I knew how scared they were. Everyone in our town knew the McLachlan triplets. They were the three musketeers. When they were little, we had three of everything… three walkers, three swings, three birthday cakes. They were brothers, friends; they were a team composed of three intricate parts. We were all sitting there wondering what it would be like to look around and not see Brant's smile or his sun-kissed blond hair. They sat there, and to look at each other was to know that one of the three was in trouble.

Rick Jackson walked into the waiting room, and it was obvious that he was holding back tears. I stood to meet him, hoping he had news on Brant's condition. He hugged me first, then both of my brothers. He sat down across from us and sighed, "I've seen him hurt so many times, you know." He exhaled loudly, "but I have never once seen him cry." We nodded in agreement. No one said anything for a moment; then Rick added, "I called Tommy. He's on his way."

"Good," I replied. "He needs to be here."

Tommy Jackson was a big guy, six-three, maybe three hundred pounds. He was the center on the football team and Brant's partner in crime. Best friends since childhood, they loved one another like brothers; Tommy would lie down in traffic for Brant and vice versa. Tommy was spending the summer at his mother's house near Jackson, Mississippi, but less than two hours after receiving the news of the accident, he would arrive at the hospital to sit and wait with the rest of us.

"Somebody's got to call Jen," Christian said when Rick Jackson left us alone in the waiting room.

"I can't do it," Ethan sighed.

"Me neither… not yet," Christian shook his head.

"Let's just wait," I suggested.

"Yeah," Christian nodded. "We'll call her when we know more… when we can start off by telling her that he's okay."

With those words, we were left to contemplate the obvious. In fact, we were so consumed by the thought of how Jennifer would react to the news of Brant's accident that we didn't notice Dad return to the waiting room.

"How is he?" I gasped when I saw my father standing before me.

"He's still critical," Dad replied.

"Can we see him?" I asked.

"No..." my dad shook his head. "No... not yet."

"He lost a lot of blood," Ethan sighed.

"Yeah," Dad nodded. He looked proudly at Ethan. "Whatever you did to stop his neck from bleeding... your mother says it may have saved his life."

I looked at Ethan, and we stared at each other knowing that if he hadn't been there that day, Brant would have died in the floorboard of his truck.

Dad nodded as he spoke. "Right now the main concern is the amount of blood he lost, but long term they are worried about head and spinal injuries."

"When will we know?" Christian asked.

Dad squeezed Christian's shoulder. "Well... they won't be able to do any further tests until they can stabilize him. Once he's out of the woods, then they'll run tests and worry about dealing with broken bones and such as that. They've stitched up his major injuries, but I'm sure he has less critical injuries that will eventually need some attention as well."

"Dad," Christian sighed, "you can't imagine what it was like to watch him flip down that hill."

Dad's face turned a little angry. "No," he shook his head. He paused. "You are probably right, but I can imagine how fast someone would have to be going in order for it to happen." None of us said anything in reply, and I could tell that Dad was battling the same guilt that had been eating at me. "He didn't have on a seatbelt either, did he?" Dad asked quietly. He didn't need us to answer. "How many times have I preached it to you boys," he scolded, "I don't care how short your trip is or on how rural of a road you're driving... my gosh, wear your seatbelts, boys!"

We all nodded obediently. We all wore our seatbelts. Dad was preaching to the choir and he knew it, so he let it go.

When the hospital door slid open, and I saw Tommy, I stood up. "How is he?" he asked, catching his breath after his dash through the parking garage.

"He's still critical, but he's hanging in there," I nodded as we shook hands, then hugged.

"I came as fast as I could," Tommy said, hugging my brothers before he took a seat next to Dad. He looked around, "where's Jen?"

"We haven't called her," Ethan sighed.

"We wanted to wait until we could give her good news," I added. "But," I shrugged, "I guess someone should call."

"Someone's got to call her," Tommy nodded, and I could tell that, like the rest of us, he didn't want to be the one to do it.

Christian stood up. "Word is going to spread all over town … we don't want her or her parents to hear it from anybody else… I'll call her," he offered.

Dad patted Christian's back knowingly. "You can call her from Mom's office," he gulped.

After a multi-year struggle, including several heart-breaking failed attempts at carrying a baby to full term, my mother's best friend, Kathy Smith, gave birth to her slightly premature but perfectly healthy daughter, Jennifer Leigh, two days before my mom went into labor with the triplets. We all joke that it was in the hospital nursery where Jennifer and Brant began their life-long love affair. Two babies so eager to see the world that they arrived before anyone expected them, Jennifer and Brant continued to write their own rules.

As toddlers Brantley and Jennifer shared toys and held hands. Back then their bond was innocent, cute, sweet, something for two moms who had always dreamed of raising their children together to laugh about and snap pictures of. But, even then, there was something inside all of us that was certain that these pint-sized companions were destined to become so much more. In fact, when Jennifer's mom caught Brant on video as he stole his first kiss in a playpen in our front yard, she vowed that very day to include it in a video she envisioned playing at Brant and Jennifer's wedding.

In kindergarten when all the boys sat at one table and all the girls at another, Brant and Jennifer broke the mold.

In elementary school Jennifer learned to catch a football better than any other girl in town, and, though he probably wouldn't have admitted it, Brant did his fair share of playing house… he rocked Cabbage Patch dolls; he sipped imaginary tea from a Strawberry Shortcake tea set. Once, his two front teeth missing, he even asked me if it was okay for a guy to have a girl for a best friend; with a smile he couldn't have understood back then, I assured him that I thought it was probably okay.

As they grew up, Brant began to see Jennifer as more than just a best friend. About the time he started middle school, Brant discovered that Jennifer's eyes were brown, her lips were full, her skin was smooth, and her hair was soft to the touch. He realized that he liked it when Jennifer smiled, and, more than that, he loved being the one to make her smile.

As they matured so did their feelings. Because of their long-standing friendship, they could talk about anything. Their attraction was natural and never awkward. They fell in love the way I always knew they would, and they began wanting to spend time alone, away from the rest of the group. For years, they were the perfect couple, and that is why when, at the end of their junior year, Jennifer had decided that she wanted to go back to being *just friends,* everyone, except Brant, who had always been able to read her mind, was shocked by the announcement. Even after their so-called breakup, Cummins' favorite super couple remained an inseparable twosome, very much in love.

When Christian got in touch with Jennifer from the phone in Mom's office, she was pulling into her driveway.

"Hey, Jen… it's Christian," he gulped when she answered her cell phone.

"Chris, what's up?" Jennifer said as she stopped her Tahoe and turned off the engine. "You sound strange. Did y'all get Jordan moved? Is everything okay?"

"No," Christian replied. He paused, considering what he should say. "Where are you?" he asked softly.

"I just got back from having some old film developed," Jennifer replied. "I put two rolls in the one hour at the Walmart in Meridian… wait until you see…"

"Jennifer," Christian cut her off, "are your parents home?"

"My mom is… why?" Jennifer could hear the fear in Christian's voice.

"I don't want you to be alone when I tell you this," Christian said. "Go inside… sit down."

"When you tell me what?" Jennifer replied quickly. "Christian… tell me."

"Jennifer… " Christian started slowly.

"What?" Jennifer exclaimed.

"Jen…"

"Christian McLachlan, you're scaring me to death," Jennifer gasped. "What's going on? Are you alright? Are you in some sort of trouble?"

Christian took a deep breath. "Brant had a wreck," he blurted before he could stop himself.

"What?" Jennifer exclaimed. Unwilling to consider the possibilities of what Christian was telling her, Jennifer forced herself to remain calm. "Well, he's okay, right?"

"No, Jen… he's not," Christian cried as he stared at the picture of Brant, Ethan and himself that sat in a silver frame on Mom's desk. "He's in critical condition. He's unconscious and right now… things don't look really good." He paused to regain his composure. "I think you should come to the hospital."

The phone dropped, and Christian was left calling Jennifer's name into the receiver.

Jennifer's entire family immediately rushed to wait with the rest of us. Because her mother and mine are best friends, Mrs. Smith has always been like a second mother to the triplets and me. She worked to hide her own emotion as her motherly instinct kicked into high gear. She comforted Christian and Ethan the way only a mother can, the way our mom would have had she been able to.

Jennifer's parents prayed with my father; they squeezed each other's hands tightly as they asked God to watch over Brantley.

"He'll be okay, David," Kathy Smith said as she and my father embraced. My dad could only nod hopefully.

Jennifer has always been like the little sister I never had, and, the way any big brother would, I held her as she cried. For a moment I was able to forget about my own pain and focus solely on hers. She reached into her purse and pulled out a single snapshot. I stared at my brother's grin, and I got misty eyed as Jennifer pulled the photograph to her heart. It was a picture that someone had taken of Brant and Jennifer after a football game the previous season… two all-American kids… the captain of the cheerleading squad and her quarterback boyfriend.

Ben Smith was small, even for a seven-year-old, and I smiled at his childlike composure as he climbed into the chair next to his big sister. Jennifer reached out and took his hand, kissed it and went back to staring at the snapshot.

I motioned Ben over and lifted him into my lap. He hugged me, then, with the innocence of a child, he whispered loudly, "Brant was gonna teach me how to beat my Rad Racer Nintendo game today. He promised."

My dad, sitting across from us, overheard him and said with a shake of his head, "maybe you should teach him, Ben… because the practice round didn't go so hot."

Jennifer swallowed. She looked at me all too knowingly. "He was going really fast, wasn't he? That's why he couldn't stop when that dog ran out in the road."

I nodded.

Dad's face turned angry again. He was mad at himself… at Brant. He wanted to yell at Brant, scold him for being so reckless, but he couldn't… not now… now he couldn't even find it in himself to be angry with him… it was too late for that.

By that evening Brant's condition had stabilized, and, only because Mom had the authority to permit it, we were allowed to go back to see him in pairs of two.

When their turn came, Christian and Jennifer walked back together, grasping hands as they went. When Jennifer laid eyes on Brant for the first time, her knees buckled, and her body went limp with grief.

"I've got you," Christian whispered as he held her to his side. "Come-on, let's get you out of here."

"He looks awful," Jennifer sobbed as she brought her hand to her mouth.

"Jennifer… maybe you shouldn't…" Christian started to say.

"No," Jennifer cried. "No… I want to see him." She put her arm around Christian's waist as she gently touched Brant's cheek with the back of her hand. "Hi, sweetheart," she cried, "I love you so much…" Her eyes welled up with tears as she turned her face into Christian's chest.

Christian rubbed her back. "Come-on, let's go."

"I talked to him on the phone this morning," Jennifer bawled. "He called me this morning while you guys were helping Jordan move; he told me he loved me…" She began to choke on her tears. "What if that was goodbye? What if that was goodbye, and I didn't even know it?"

"No," Christian gulped. "No, Jen… he's gonna tell you he loves you a million more times…"

"What if he can't?" Jennifer shook her head as she cried loudly. "Christian, what if he never tells me he loves me again? What if we never get to hear him sing again… or laugh…"

Christian wiped his eyes. "I don't know, Jen," he shrugged. "I don't know what to say."

"He has to be okay." Jennifer closed her eyes.

"Yeah," Christian sighed as he pulled Jennifer into his arms, "he has to be okay."

Jennifer turned back to Brant. She bent over and very gently kissed his cheek. "You hang in there… do you hear me?" she whispered insistently. "I can't lose you… I don't know what I would do…"

Christian pulled Jennifer back into his arms, and she allowed him to lead her back to the waiting room.

"Please," Ben cried, his arms folded, as he begged to be allowed to see Brant. "Please, Mom…"

"Ben…" Jennifer knelt down to Ben's level. "Sweetie… maybe you should wait and see Brant when he gets a little better. I don't think that you…"

"I want to see him now," Ben shrugged softly. "I just want to tell him that I hope he gets better real soon."

"I know you do," Jennifer nodded, "but, Ben… Brant hurt himself pretty bad…" Jennifer's voice cracked as she worked unsuccessfully to fight back her tears. "It's pretty scary back there…"

Ben persisted, however, and eventually his mother accompanied him to see Brant.

Ben stared at Brant for a moment and then tugged at his mother's arm. "I don't like it when Brant isn't being loud," he sighed.

"I know," Kathy Smith nodded as she wiped a tear from her eye. "That's why your sister didn't think you should see Brant yet. Do you want to go?"

"When will he be able to talk to me?" Ben asked.

"Soon," Kathy Smith nodded hopefully.

She watched as Ben curiously eyed the machines that surrounded Brant. Brant had been a permanent fixture in Ben's life since the day he was born. In Ben's eyes Brant did no wrong. He was the world's greatest athlete, the funniest guy on the planet, the definition of cool, and the only man in the world good enough for his big sister.

"He's the toughest guy I know," Ben teared up. "He'll be okay… I know it."

"Let's go, Ben," Kathy Smith said softly as she forced a weak smile. She kissed the side of her little boy's face. "Brant needs his rest."

"How long is he gonna sleep for?" Ben asked.

"I can't answer that," his mother sighed.

"Does he know we're here?" Ben asked.

"I think he probably does," Kathy Smith nodded. She leaned down close to Brant. "If you can hear me Brantley… I love you, baby. You hang on, okay… Mama's doing everything she can to get you well… you just hang tough for us, darlin'." She turned back to Ben, her eyes glistening with tears.

"Mom," Ben smiled, as she saw the wheels in his head turning, "I have a great idea. Can we go to the store and buy Brant some M&M's… when he wakes up… I know they'll make him feel better."

Kathy Smith wiped another tear, touched by the simplicity of her little boy's suggestion. M&M's were Brant's favorite candy… plain, peanut, peanut butter, crunchy… he wasn't picky. Every year after Christmas, when Walmart marked their Christmas candy down to half-price, Kathy Smith went to Meridian and bought several bags of red and green holiday M&M's, so that Brant would have them to munch on while he watched football at her house on New Year's Day.

"Of course," she smiled at Ben. "Of course we can buy him some M&M's… that's a good idea."

Ben smiled triumphantly, as though he had discovered a miracle cure that no one else had taken the time to consider.

When Ben ran back into the waiting room with a flicker of a smile on his face, I lifted him into my arms. "He'll be okay," he said confidently.

I smiled back at him, longing to have his faith.

I enjoyed Brant and Ben's relationship. It was special to me because watching Ben, I knew that he looked at Brant the same way that Brant looked at me when he was Ben's age.

Once upon a time, when Brant looked at me he saw his hero, the one person in the world that he wanted to be just like. In me he found security, trust, and never ending love. He took everything that I told him or taught him to heart. In *his* eyes *I* did no wrong. Now he was almost eighteen, and he didn't lift his hands up for me to pick him up any more, nor did he repeat my words with that priceless grin on his face. The way that he looked at me had changed over the years, but, as I stood watching him lie there in that hospital bed, I knew that the way I looked at him would never change.

When my mom joined us in the waiting room after everyone had seen Brant, she and my father embraced.

"How is he?" Dad asked quickly.

"No change," Mom shook her head.

Our pastor and his wife each took a moment to console my mother, offering her words of encouragement and promises of prayer.

"What's the next step?" Dad asked after a moment. "What do we do for him now?"

Mom shrugged. "We pray that he wakes up." No one said anything for a moment, then Mom sighed, "it doesn't look good, David." She walked into my dad's arms, and he rubbed her back more lovingly than I had ever seen him do before.

"Don't give up on him, Becky," Dad whispered tenderly. He shook his head vigorously, "we have to believe that he will come out of this just fine. He needs the best care that we can give him. He deserves the best doctor we can give him, and, honey… that's you."

Mom looked up at him. "I'm not giving up," she assured him. "I could never give up on one of our boys. I just don't know if I can handle this," she sighed, breaking down. "I love all of my patients, David; I really do. I strive to help and feel compassion for every person that gets brought in this place… it's what being a doctor is all about… I help people; I save people, but, occasionally, I can't… and those people die. It's hard… it's always hard, but I can't deal with this one… David, I cannot lose Brantley." She covered her mouth as the words came out.

We all formed sort of a group hug.

Jennifer's mom and my mom clung to each other as they cried. Two women who had giggled about boys at slumber parties as thirteen-year-olds had grown up to marry their high school sweethearts and gone on to live out their dream of raising their children together. All of the time they had spent imagining sharing in their children's joys… Brant and Jennifer's wedding, the birth of their first grandchild… they had never imagined having to see them go through anything like this.

Bro. Waterford placed a strong hand on my shoulder, and I tried to do the same for my father.

Tommy clasped Jennifer's right hand as Ethan held her left. Standing behind her, Christian wrapped his arms securely around her shoulders and gently rocked her back and forth as she rested the back of her head against his chest.

The waiting room was more crowded than it had been earlier. Word of Brant's accident had spread across town, and friends, old and young alike, had come to show support for our family during our greatest hour of need.

Amidst the growing crowd, Mom and Jennifer locked eyes and both, each sensing the other's uncertainty, began to weep. They gravitated toward one another and fell into each other's embrace. Neither said anything; there was nothing left to say that their tears hadn't already said. Each whispered a silent prayer as, all around them, each of us clung helplessly to a loved one while offering a prayer of our own.

CHAPTER THREE

My father, my brothers and I were standing by Brant's bed side as a day that had seemed as though it might never end had quietly, without our knowing it, faded into another. Dad's eyes were tired as he stared at Brant.

"You're scaring your old man, Brantley," he said with a painful smile, tears streaming down his face.

Standing there and seeing my father cry, I felt like the little boy of yesteryear sitting on his knee, placing my tiny hand up to his gigantic hand so full of strength and care. Not much had changed since then; I still looked up to my dad, and to see him cry was to see the strongest man I knew realizing that he was in jeopardy of losing his world.

"Talk to him." Mom's voice broke the silence that had fallen over the room. We all turned to her as she entered the cubical where we were gathered. "It's good for him to know that he's not in this alone… that we're all here helping him fight," she said with a confident nod.

None of us spoke. Mom patted Ethan's back. "Go on, sweetheart," she urged, "it's okay."

Ethan slid past Christian and me as he moved from the foot of the bed to Brant's side. He swallowed hard. "Hi," he gulped, "Brant, it's Ethan. I just wanted you to know I am here… we all are, and we just really want you to wake up. You gotta wake up because I've never told you how proud I am of you. You have a dream, and you've fought for it. I've been so impressed by the dedication you've put into challenging the NFL's minimum age rule. I don't know what will happen; you may have to wait three years to be eligible for the draft, but something tells me that you won't stop until you convince the court that a talent like yours can't be denied.

You were born to be a star. There are little kids out there that want to be you. They want to play football like you do. When they play football on the playground at school they pretend to be Troy Aikman, Joe Montana, Steve Young, Brett Favre and, in our town… they all want to be *Brant McLachlan*. That is big time company, but somehow saying your name with theirs only seems right.

One day you are gonna have that Super Bowl ring that you have been dreaming about, and we're all gonna be there to watch you earn it. In fact, that's probably what you're doing right now isn't it? You're probably dreaming that you're off playing in the Super Bowl."

Ethan shook his head. He paused and his speech became strained. "I love to watch you play ball, Brant… but more than that I love to go to the movies and be totally embarrassed when you talk too loud in the theatre. I love to laugh at you for practicing your autograph. I even love getting mad at you for wearing my clothes without asking. I guess what I'm trying to say is that if you wake up from this, and, for some reason, you can't play football again, it won't matter because, as much as I love Brant the superstar athlete, I don't know what I'd do without you… my obnoxious *little* brother."

Christian put his hand on Ethan's shoulder. "Let me," he said softly, and he forced a smile.

Ethan stepped back to compose himself as Christian took his place next to Brant. "Remember when we were little, how we used to stay with Dad at football practice and watch Jordan and his team play?" he began softly. "Those were some of the best times of my life. Those guys really made me love football. We wanted to be like them; we wanted to play on that field and hear the crowd shouting *our* names."

Christian smiled. "I remember one particular time when Dad let us ride on the team bus to a game. He sat all three of us on the same seat and made us promise to be still and quiet because his team had to focus on the big game. I don't know what he was thinking asking you to be *still* or *quiet*, but, needless to say, you didn't make it out of town in that seat. You snuck to the back of the bus… back to Jordan and his friends, and Ethan and I didn't see you for the rest of the trip."

Christian chuckled, "you were never bound by the rules that everyone else lived by, Brant, because you could grin your way out of anything. You always break the rules and stretch the limits, but any trouble you ever get into, you figure a way out of it." Christian hung his head. "I think that I'm just standing here rambling, Brant… trying to say that I don't know how you're gonna do it, but something makes me believe that you'll find a way out of this too."

Christian stepped back, and I patted his shoulder before stepping toward Brant's bed. For a long time I couldn't bring myself to speak; I stared at all the machines my brother was hooked up to, and I drifted into a daze. I could see Brant playing football, and I could see the million dollar smile that he flashed me each time he scored a touchdown.

I worked as my father's assistant coach; I loved working with him and with his team, but my favorite part about coaching was watching my little brother show off on the football field.

In our family we were born loving football. Dad claims that it is a gene we inherited from him, that and our good looks!

The triplets were raised playing football. I remember being fifteen or sixteen and playing football with them in the middle of the living room floor. Brant was never scared of anything. A couple of times he nearly gave me a heart attack, bumping his head on the coffee table or diving off the sofa, but he never once shed a tear. Rarely did he ever stop long enough to acknowledge that anything had happened. He always just jumped up and kept right on going.

He was so tough, always little but loud. As the old cliché goes, if I had a dollar for every time that someone told me that Brant was too small to play professional football, I would be a very wealthy man, but Brant never let what anyone said bother him. He had way too much confidence in himself and his abilities… and more than anything else in my life, I wanted to see him play professional football.

Many people believed that Brant would have to play somewhere else besides Cummins, Mississippi, for anyone to look twice at him, and Dad was determined to make sure that he did whatever it took to make that happen. The summer before their sophomore year, Brant and Christian spent two weeks at a football camp just outside Dallas, Texas. Brant had the time of his life at that camp because, for the first time, he could put on a show for the people that mattered, the scouts. He got to hobnob with high school coaches, college coaches and collegiate players. He could talk the talk as they say, and they were all eager to find out if this country boy from Nowhere, Mississippi, had the skills to back up his confident swagger.

After every drill and every scrimmage, everyone on the field was left amazed. When word got out that when school started Brant would quarterback his Cummins Eagles as a *sophomore*, people were flabbergasted to learn this gifted quarterback still had three years of high school left. There was one man who took particular interest in Brant. He wasn't a college scout; he wasn't even a coach, he was a scout for the Dallas Cowboys. He just so happened to be there watching his son, a high school senior who was looking for an opportunity to play wide receiver for any team that would have him. He watched his son as he worked with a quarterback who never failed to put the ball right in his hands. He watched Brant the next day, and Brant's energy, speed and accuracy awed him. After a particularly impressive scrimmage the following day, he introduced himself to Brant and, after only a brief conversation, immediately knew that Brant McLachlan was one in a million.

Before the following evening's scrimmage game, the scout was joined by a close friend of his who just so happened to be the Cowboys' offensive coordinator. Understandably, he had scoffed at his friend's absurd insistence that a five foot eleven, high school sophomore was about to become a top NFL prospect… then the game started.

It didn't take long before universities across the nation found themselves engaging in a bidding war over a quarterback they were sure was about to dominate college football. When the time came, Brant would have the luxury of choosing which scholarship he wished to accept… whose quarterback he wanted to be. Brant's ambitions were big ones though; he wanted to be a Cowboy, plain and simple, and he would settle for nothing less. Brant was barely sixteen years old when Dad began petitioning the courts to change the National Football League's long-standing policy against drafting underclassmen. According to the rule, Brant would not be eligible for the draft until he had been out of high school for at least three years.

Dad's initial argument was accepted by the trial court, only to be denied by the U.S. Supreme Court. Mom insisted that Dad should encourage Brant to go to college, get an education and then worry about making a career out of football. Dad had a talk with Brant about the perks of having a college education and the benefits of playing at the collegiate level where he would become bigger, faster and stronger, but Brant quickly convinced Dad to appeal the court's decision.

"Jordan," my father gulped as he put a hand on my shoulder, "why don't you take your mom and your brothers down to get some coffee? I'll be out in a second."

I nodded. I looked down at Brant. "I love you, Brant," I sighed.

Understanding that Dad wished to have a moment alone with Brant, Mom shuffled my brothers toward the exit. I followed them, then my father's voice caused me to stop in my tracks. I watched my mom and my brothers leave as I tucked myself behind a curtain. Unable to make myself go, I listened as Dad began to pour his heart out.

"Son," he began, and his voice sounded aged and worn, "I've got the four best kids in this world." He paused as he gathered his thoughts. "And you, kid," his voice faded, and his tone changed, "you're cocky, over confident, reckless, irresponsible, strong-willed, hard-headed, you've got a smart mouth; you could use a bit of an attitude adjustment at times," he was crying now, "and I love you more than anything else in this world." He cried harder. "There isn't a thing in this world I would change about you, Brant…" He paused, possibly recalling times he had failed to tell Brantley just how much he loved him. "But there is one thing I *would* change," he added, "I've been hard on you. I've tried to make you tough, and, as a coach, I have always told you that if you couldn't crawl off the field by yourself, only *then* would I come and get you. That sounds harsh to a lot of people, but we always had our common understanding, our shared goals."

Dad paused for a long moment as he choked back his tears, then he cried, "I just want to tell you that you don't have to do it by yourself this time, Brant. Daddy's here, Brantley. Forget the tough stuff, just please wake up and give your old man a hug."

I don't know what possessed me to linger behind that night, but what I heard I will never forget as long as I live.

***

The next day Tommy and I were sitting with Brant, talking to him and to each other the way my mother said we should do. Tommy looked at me with watery eyes. "You know," he sighed, "I try to tell myself that he's dead… like to prepare myself, you know? It's like if I pretend that I'll never see him again, thinking about the possibility that he might wake up actually seems pretty optimistic."

I had to say that I had been doing the same thing.

Tommy chatted casually with Brant. "Remember when you couldn't stop laughing right in the middle of our kindergarten graduation?" he laughed at one point, as though he was certain Brant could hear him. "You got the rest of us laughing, and your mom was *so* mad."

Later, as time ticked by, quietly stealing bits of optimism with each passing second, Tommy turned to me. "Sarah Ann loved *him* best," he said softly.

"Everyone loves Brant best," I nodded with a smile.

"She'd find him," Tommy said confidently, "in Heaven I mean… I know she would… she'd find him and neither one of them would be lonely."

I swallowed. It was the first time in years that I had heard Tommy mention his sister's name, yet it didn't surprise me to discover that she had been on his mind since he first received news of Brant's accident.

Sarah Ann Jackson, or Half-pint as she was affectionately known by all who knew her, was the sweetest little girl I have ever met. She enjoyed life to the fullest every day for the short time that she was here with us. When Sarah Ann was just four years old, she died after tragically falling from her father's tractor.

Tommy parents' marriage never recovered after the accident, and the divorce that followed devastated Tommy. His mother changed drastically after losing her only daughter. She blamed her husband for Sarah Ann's accident. She briefly battled an addiction to anti-depressants before skipping town, leaving twelve-year-old Tommy behind with his father. Tommy had a hard time dealing with his sister's death and his parents' subsequent split, but his friends rallied around him then the way they were all rallying around Brantley now.

I know that if we had lost Brant, Sarah Ann, his beloved, freckle-faced, little Half-pint would have been waiting for him in Heaven. For all selfish reasons, I thank the Lord that it wasn't Brant's time to go.

***

Nearly a week after the crash that had put all our lives on hold, Mom and Jennifer were sitting on Brant's bed, one on each side of him. Jennifer was holding Brant's right hand, and when he moved his fingers in hers, she gasped.

Slowly Brant opened his eye, and the room inhaled at once.

Brant stared at us for a second like he was shocked to see us all hovering over him. He smiled at Jennifer. "Jen?" he said with a hint of surprise, his voice sounding gruff. His eyes moved curiously to the bed, then he lifted his arm ever so slightly and examined the IV. Suddenly, concern filled his eyes. "What happened to me?" he gulped, seeming somewhat embarrassed that he had to ask.

For a moment no one spoke.

"You were in a car wreck," Jennifer explained calmly, as Brant's eyes fixed on her.

"Were you with me?" he asked weakly, and fear filled Brant's face as he seemed to be examining her for any sign of injury.

"No," Jennifer cried, shaking her head and wiping her tears, "you were by yourself. No one else was hurt… it was a one car accident."

"Really?" Brant seemed surprised, as though he could not fathom the possibility that he had managed to crash his truck without the help of someone else who desperately needed to learn how to drive.

He looked around the room and his eyes met mine. "Jordan," he said as if the sight of my face triggered a memory. He thought for a moment. "This morning… this morning we helped you move back home…"

"That was *last week*," Christian blurted with little tact.

Dad elbowed Christian. "Brant… buddy," he said, "you've been in the hospital for a week. You banged yourself up pretty good in the wreck."

Brant turned back to Jennifer. "How'd I wreck?" he asked.

"You, um… " Jennifer began explaining, leaving out the details, "well, you swerved to miss a dog that ran out in the road. Knowing you, I guess you didn't want to tear up your brush guard, but you were going too fast, and your truck flipped over."

"I flipped my truck?" Brant gasped.

"Yeah… nine times," Christian retorted.

"Christian," Dad shook his head.

"Nine times! Well, can my truck be fixed, is she okay?" Brant asked quickly.

Jennifer looked back at us.

"No, the truck's not okay," I replied quickly as I remembered watching the wreck.

"Well, we can fix her, right, Dad?" Brant nodded.

"Son," Dad smiled, "I don't think..."

"Your truck looks like an accordion, bro," Christian told Brant.

Dad popped Christian in the back of the head. "Do you mind?"

"What? You mean my truck is totaled?" Brant huffed as he became visibly upset.

"Calm down, Brantley," Mom intervened. "The truck is not important..."

Brant looked at her as if she had lost her mind.

"You really don't remember the wreck do you?" I shook my head in awe of the fact that someone could go through something like flipping a truck down a hill, survive it, yet have no recollection of it.

"No, I guess I don't," Brant sighed.

Jennifer gently stroked his cheek. "That's okay, it's probably better that way."

"Well, am I okay?" Brant asked, and a few of us laughed at the inquiry. Brant stared at his left wrist. "When will I be able to play football again?"

"Brantley," Dad replied, shaking his head. "Football is a game, son." Brant looked at him as though surely he was the one who had hit his head, and Dad smiled. "I know that it was never a game to me and that it isn't to you, but one week ago I had no idea if you would ever wake up. I wasn't sure if I would ever hear your voice again. The fact that you are alive means more to me than any football game you will ever play."

That was my brother for you. He had just survived a life-threatening crash that probably should have killed him, yet he was concerned about the condition of his Z-71 and the future of his football career.

Brant closed his eyes, and it was obvious that he was exhausted.

Jennifer held his hand. "I love you, Brant," she said, softly rubbing her thumb across his fingers. "We all do."

Mom looked at a couple of the machines next to Brant's bed and scribbled a couple numbers down on her clipboard. She put her hand on

Jennifer's shoulder. "Why don't you take a second with him while the rest of us clear out of here," she said softly. "But not long… he needs his rest…"

Jennifer nodded. "Thank you, Mrs. Becky."

The room cleared. "I'm gonna go call in a couple specialists to look at him," my mother said as she disappeared down the hall.

Jennifer touched Brant's face again.

Brant's eyes flickered, and he slowly moved his hand to his neck without opening his eyes.

"I see," Jennifer nodded as she eased Brant's arm back to his bed. "It doesn't hurt does it?" she asked, knowing that Brant was on too much pain medication to feel anything yet. "Don't you try to move too much… your Mom says you need your rest. Besides… I think it's gonna be a cute scar," Jennifer smiled as she read Brant's mind.

Brant grinned, and Jennifer kissed his forehead.

"Brant, I'm gonna go," Jennifer said softly. "You need your sleep, and you're not gonna rest as long as I'm here."

Brant opened his eyes. "To hear all of you tell it… I've been sleeping for a week. It sounds like rest is the last thing I need," he replied groggily.

Jennifer smiled. "Well, I guess you have a point."

Brant looked down at the hospital gown he was wearing. "I'm gonna have to talk to my mom about the look they're going for here," he sighed. "One look at one of these things and suddenly death doesn't seem so unappealing. I mean a guy with a heart condition wakes up, sees himself in one of these babies, and boom, they've got a code blue on their hands for reasons they don't understand."

"Brant," Jennifer rolled her eyes, "only you would comment on the hospital wardrobe at a time like this."

"Oh come-on," Brant said as he fingered the thin material, "not even I can make one of these things look good, and that's sayin' something."

Jennifer laughed. "Gosh, I've missed you."

"See what you can do about getting me some shorts and a t-shirt, huh?" Brant smiled.

Jennifer nodded. "I'll see if I can pull a few strings."

Brant smiled. "That'd be great."

"And what would you like for dinner tonight… steak and a baked potato?" Jennifer grinned.

Brant laughed softly. "I'll take my steak medium rare and my potato loaded... thanks for asking." He closed his eyes.

"Get some rest," Jennifer chuckled.

Brant fought sleep to inquire, "will you be here when I wake up?"

"I'm not going anywhere," Jennifer promised.

Brant weakly lifted his hand off the bed, and Jennifer took it in hers.

"I love you, Rocky," Brant said before drifting to sleep.

Jennifer's eyes filled with tears at the sound of Brant's pet name for her. "I love you too, Cowboy," she mouthed.

CHAPTER FOUR

In the days following the wreck, Brant's story was front page news in Cummins. Brant's recovery was on everyone's minds and in their prayers, and they made sure that he knew it. Brant was visited by family, friends, his teammates past and present, and even football coaches of rival teams from surrounding areas.

There was one visitor, however, that made Brant's recovery her personal mission. Every morning when Jennifer walked in Brant's room, he thanked God for making her a part of his life. Jennifer and Brant had a connection that I don't think any of us truly understood. The best way I know how to sum up Brant and Jennifer's relationship is to say that they were two teenage kids who had spent their entire lives acting like an old married couple. They were two pieces of a puzzle, each completing the other.

One particular day I walked in on the two of them playing *Checkers* on the rolling lunch tray. "Oh please, what kind of move was that, Jen?" Brant laughed. "She's letting me win," he announced as I entered.

"No, I am not," Jennifer grinned.

"Yes you are," Brant said seriously.

"Tell you what," Jennifer smiled, "when you feel better we'll play again, and I'll beat you like I usually do."

"You've never beat me at *Checkers*," Brant retorted quickly.

"Oh... you really did hit your head," Jennifer frowned playfully.

Brant puckered his lips, and Jennifer offered a quick peck.

"Out of all of us... why him?" Ethan pondered out loud as though the thought had been dancing around in his head for years.

We all stared at him as he sat in the chair by the window with his arms crossed.

Brant laughed. "Easy, E… because I'm cuter than you are," he shrugged as he poured the remainder of his bag of M&M's into his mouth. He nodded, his mouth full, "yep… you may be the brains… but I got the looks… and the girl."

"What I mean is," Ethan explained, ignoring Brant, "growing up it was always the four of us boys, and you were the only girl. You could have had any of us, but you never gave any of the rest of us a chance."

"Oh, Ethan, I never knew you felt that way," Jennifer giggled playfully.

Ethan rolled his eyes. "Yeah right… I could never see us together. You're like a sister to me… it would be incestuous!"

Brant shook his head, "there he goes again, using those big words… trying to seduce you with his superior intellect."

Jennifer slid off the bed and sat in Ethan's lap. "I think it was the time that you cut my hair when we were in the first grade," she grinned. "Up until then you might have had a shot, but that just really turned me off of you."

"I remember that," Ethan laughed.

"What about me?" Christian shrugged. "I never tried to give you a Mohawk, so what made me so unappealing? What did I ever do to turn you off?"

"What *is* this?" Brant exclaimed. "Newsflash, I didn't die, people!"

Jennifer exploded with laughter. "I was just never turned on to you to begin with, sweetie," she chucked.

Christian hung his head, and, as he began wiping at imaginary tears, we all laughed.

"Let's make a pact… right here, right now," Tommy nodded. "No matter what happens this next year… no matter what direction life takes each one of us after graduation… let's always remember what we have right here."

"Well, wasn't that just sweet and sentimental," Brant rolled his eyes with a smile. "Have you been watching *Lifetime: Television for Women* again? I'm unconscious for what… *a week*? And you're back to your old habits."

"I mean it," Tommy shrugged.

"Yeah," Christian nodded in agreement. "Brant… we almost lost you…"

"Yes..." Brant mused in a British accent that came out of nowhere, "I can see where that would have been tragic."

Ethan shook his head. "I think he really did hit his head harder than we thought."

Brant snickered. "Too bad for you that I didn't knock it a little harder, eh, bro? Glad to know you wouldn't have wasted any time moving in on my woman."

Jennifer slapped Brant's arm. "Not funny."

Brant smiled. "All kidding aside... Tommy's right... what we have here is really special. I know that no matter what happens in the future, I can count on each and every person in this room... that's a good feeling... and I hope that you all know that you can always count on me too."

Jennifer stuck her hand out. "Everybody in," she called. We all threw our hands on the pile.

Brant placed his hand on top.

"All for one... one for all," Tommy nodded.

"All for one... one for all," Brant concurred.

We all threw our arms into the air.

There was a knock at the door, and our pastor, Bro. Waterford, poked his head inside. "Are we interrupting something?" he laughed.

"Come in," I said motioning him inside.

Bro. Waterford and his young daughter Kristen walked inside. Kristen was holding a balloon tied to a family-size bag of M&M's.

"This is for you," she said shyly as she extended the gift to Brant.

"Thanks, Kristen," Brant smiled. "You're right on time... I just ran out."

Jennifer took the balloon and the candy and placed it with Brant's collection of flowers, balloons, cards and candy. "That was so sweet of you, Kristen," she smiled. "Thank you, Bro. Waterford."

"Where are you going with my M&M's, Jenny?" Brant huffed as Jennifer made room among the other gifts.

"We're gonna save those for later... you've had enough right now," Jennifer told him in a motherly tone.

"Oh, go easy on the poor fella, Jennifer," Bro. Waterford chuckled. "He's been through a lot."

"Yes," Jennifer smiled, "and I'll tell you what… if he eats another piece of candy today I'm gonna have to call one of his nurses in to give him an insulin shot, Bro. Waterford. He's got enough problems without going into sugar shock." She leaned down and kissed the side of Brant's head. "Not to mention, if you eat much more, you're gonna be Tommy's size before you leave here."

"See how she treats me," Brant shrugged. Brant shook the preacher's hand.

"It sounds to me like she's taking good care of you," Bro. Waterford replied.

"Always," Brant nodded.

"How are you feeling?" Bro. Waterford inquired. "You look good."

"They tell me I'm doing great," Brant nodded.

"I talked to your mom on the phone last night, and she tells me you are making an impressive recovery," Bro. Waterford agreed.

"Well… gotta be ready for football season," Brant smiled. He glanced at Kristen and winked. "Run over there and grab me those M&M's, Miss Cutie Pie," he whispered.

Kristen grinned as her cheeks turned bright pink, then she looked to Jennifer for approval, and we all laughed.

"If he wants them," Jennifer chuckled. She helped Kristen untie the bag of M&M's before sitting another box of candy on the end of the string to keep the balloon from floating around the room.

Mom opened the door. "Well… don't you have quite a crowd," she said as she moved to hug Bro. Waterford.

Mrs. Smith and Ben filed in behind her. "Got room for two more?" Kathy Smith laughed.

"Hey, Ben," Kristen smiled excitedly.

"Kristen!" Ben exclaimed at the sight of his friend.

"Do you want to come over to my house and play later?" Kristen asked.

"I don't know… maybe," Ben shrugged.

"Oh… Ben… no… we've got to work on that, pal," Brant shook his head with a groan. "A little hottie like that asks you over to her house, and you say YES, my friend… no thought required, no checking the calendar… just a little sly smile and a big, fat YES…"

Jennifer turned to Brant. "And how many little *hotties*' houses have you ever been to, pray tell?"

"She's got a point there, Ben," Brant nodded. "Don't get tied down when you're young… play the field a little…"

"Eat your candy," Jennifer said as she popped Brant's shoulder.

"I brought you something," Ben announced as he rushed over to Brant's bed. He reached into his pocket. "I got this in a pack from Walmart," Ben said as he produced a single, slightly bent, football card. "It's your favorite quarterback of all time!"

"Ben," Tommy chuckled, "you're talking to Brant McLachlan… *he's* his favorite quarterback of all time!"

"Troy Aikman," Brant smiled as he held the football card Ben handed him. "Thanks, Ben."

Ben crawled up into Brant's bed and dug into Brant's bag of M&M's.

Brant stared at the football card in his hand, and he frowned. "Mom… when do I get to go home?" he asked.

"I'm gonna get you out of here as soon as I can, Brant," Mom replied.

Brant turned the card to us as he held it up for us to see. "I can do this," he said confidently. "I can play with guys like him." He rolled his eyes. "At least I *could…*"

"Don't worry, Brant," Ben shook his head. He shoved a handful of candy into his mouth. "You're gonna be a Cowboy one day… I know it."

"I don't know, Ben," Brant sighed, "there are a lot of doctors around here that don't sound so sure."

"Why not?" Ben inquired curiously.

"Because of my back," Brant shrugged. "They think I need surgery."

"Why?" Ben's eyes grew big.

"Something about my spine…" Brant grumbled. "I don't know… they spent almost an hour trying to explain it to me, and I didn't understand a word of it."

"That's because you weren't listening," Mom interjected.

"I *was* listening, Mom," Brant huffed. "It's just that the guy you brought in here… Doctor… what's his name… wouldn't answer any of my questions."

"Brant," Mom shook her head, "baby, the only questions you asked were *When? When? How Long? When will I be able to play football?* And the fact is that we don't know... the recovery time for this type surgery is different for everyone... that's all we can tell you..."

"But... I may not have to have surgery... I mean they haven't decided yet... right?" Brant stared at Mom.

"Brant, I was going to wait and tell you this later," Mom sighed, "but we all talked, and we want to do the surgery."

The room fell silent.

"What?" Brant gulped. "Who talked? I didn't talk... don't I have any say?"

Mom swallowed. "Do you want to play football again?"

Brant's eyes moved to Jennifer, and he found her on the verge of tears.

"Brant," Mom said sternly, "we are doctors, and we are only doing what we feel has to be done."

"When?" Brant snapped.

"In the morning," Mom nodded. "I just talked to the surgeon, and he thinks..."

"No!" Brant exclaimed.

"Is it gonna hurt?" Ben swallowed.

"No," Mom said as she helped Ben off of Brant's bed. "No, Ben... he won't feel a thing."

"It just might end my season before it begins... that's all," Brant rolled his eyes.

"Why don't we all clear out of here for a while," Mom suggested.

We all agreed and began filing out into the hall to give Brant some time to process the new information.

"Rocky," Brant called, "you stay."

Jennifer looked toward my mom. "That's a good idea," Mom nodded. "You stay with him until I get back." She patted Brant's hand lovingly. "I'm sorry, sweetheart," she frowned.

When the room was empty and Mom had pulled the door closed, Jennifer smiled. "He's right," she nodded.

Brant looked at her, perplexed.

"Ben," Jennifer smiled. "He's right... you will be a Cowboy one day."

Tears filled Brant's eyes, and he tried to blink them away.

"Oh... Brantley," Jennifer said tenderly as she put her arms around him, "please don't cry... it's gonna be alright."

"What if it's not?" Brant sighed. "What if I can't play football any more?"

"Then we'll deal with it," Jennifer said confidently.

"I can't deal with it, Jen," Brant shook his head. "How am I gonna deal with spending the rest of my life sitting on the sidelines knowing that I could have run circles around the quarterback on the field if only I hadn't been so stupid and wrecked my truck… and my career?"

Jennifer sat on Brant's bed and took a deep breath as she rubbed his knee reassuringly. "Brant… when Christian called me and told me about the wreck, I thought to myself… *What if I never see him alive again?* Then you began to recover; I knew you were gonna pull through, but I looked at the gash on your neck, and I asked myself… *what if he can never sing to me again?* But you did. Now, I'm listening to all this talk of back surgery, and I keep asking myself… *what if he misses his senior season… or what if he never plays football again?* Time answered my other fears, and only time will answer this one."

Jennifer and Brant both rested their heads against Brant's pillow. "Jen?" Brant said after a moment.

"Yeah?" Jennifer replied.

"I'm scared," Brant said.

"I know," Jennifer whispered as she kissed his cheek, "but you don't have to be. Because we're all gonna be here every step of the way. No matter how long your recovery takes… none of us are going to let you give up… and none of us are going to give up on you. It's part of the pact we all made… good or bad… fun or frightening… we're all gonna go through it together. You will play football again, Brantley. I believe that. Do you know why?"

"Why?" Brant asked a few seconds later.

Jennifer smiled. "Because I believe in you. When we were kids and you told me that you were going to play professional football one day, I thought… *cool.* When you told me that all you wanted in the world was a Super Bowl ring, I thought… *he'll have it someday.* When you told me that you dreamed of playing for the Cowboys, I thought… *I wonder how I'll like living in Dallas?* Do you get the point I'm trying to make, Brant? When you set your mind to something, I know you're gonna make it happen.

This is a setback, but it's not the end of the world unless you give in to it, and I've never known you to let anything get the best of you."

"You really believe in me don't you... a hundred percent, I mean?" Brant smiled.

"I always have, and I always will," Jennifer said as she snuggled next to him.

Brant kissed the top of Jennifer's head. "Ethan had a point earlier," he grinned. "You could have any guy you wanted. Why me?"

Jennifer rolled her eyes. "Oh I don't know, Brant... I've asked myself the same thing for years."

Brant laughed as Jennifer rested her head against his shoulder.

***

On the day of the surgery, I woke up early.

Whether it was the way that Brant had always talked about famous quarterbacks or the way that he called the pass and run as we watched college football on TV, I knew that if Brant never played football again that the world would never see one of the greatest to ever play the game. They hadn't made a level of football where Brant McLachlan wouldn't be the star.

Watching Brant play, however, was not a lesson for youngsters on the fundamentals of the game. He was always a hyper quarterback with the confidence of a giant. He made dangerous passes and refused to take the sack. My dad always says that it is not the size of the dog in the fight that matters but the size of the fight in the dog, and Brant believed that. He was considered a little man in a big man's world, but he simply dominated. He was cool in the most pressure packed situations, and, more than anything else, he believed in himself and convinced others to believe in him as well.

His freshman year, while his fellow freshmen were standing on the sidelines, carrying equipment and fetching water bottles for upperclassmen, he was the star quarterback of a State Championship team and became the season's Most Valuable Player. He became an All-State quarterback as a freshman, and, as a sophomore, he was named Mississippi's High School Player of the Year.

Back in those days, Brant was a trash talker and a notorious showboat. He had it all, and he didn't mind shoving it in others' faces. Following in the footsteps of his famous former coach, my father was determined to keep his star humble. He worked Brant harder, ran him longer, and frequently sent him to the showers in the middle of practice. Brant learned a lot his freshman year. He learned that if you're really good, you don't have to tell anybody… they know. As Mom always says, don't toot your own horn; if it needs tooting, there will be plenty of people willing to toot it for you. Brant quickly acclimated to his role as a team leader and matured into a team player.

While Dad's constant scolding had something to do with the transformation in my brother's style of play, I honestly think that it was the season opener of his sophomore year that provided Brant with an entirely new outlook on his role as North River's quarterback.

With seconds left in the fourth quarter of the closest game that Brant had ever played, he threw an interception that almost cost his team the game. The interception was a mistake, but the decision to disregard the play Dad had called from the sidelines and run a play of his own design can only be described as one hundred percent intentional and classic Brant McLachlan. I thought Dad was going to come unglued in front of my eyes. To make a long story short… Brant ran the guy down himself and made the tackle to end the game. At midfield, the opposing coach shook my dad's hand and smiled, "how on Earth did your quarterback catch him? I know Brant's fast, but my guy was off to the races."

Dad replied, "I'm sure you have heard the expression, 'your guy was running for six points; mine was running for his life.' Well, believe me… he was."

Brant learned the hard way that he made mistakes just like everyone else, but, like me, Dad is convinced that it was that interception that made Brant the player that he became. He believes with all his heart that at the rate Brant's head was swelling, a potentially bright career was headed for self-destruction. Everyone else has long forgotten that interception, and its faded memory has been replaced by memories of unreal fakes, unexpected quarterback sneaks and on-the-money passes.

With his quick wit, confident grin and undeniable talent, my little brother was always marked to become not only a football star but, also, a media darling.

We were all gathered in Brant's room early that morning when the surgeon came in.

"Hi," Brant smiled, extending his hand.

Dr. Ash shook Brant's hand and said with a wink, "I'm new around these parts, but they tell me that I should get an autograph from you."

"You tell me," Brant shrugged, "should you?"

"I'm not gonna lie to you, Brant," the doctor replied confidently. "You may not play football this year… in fact you may not ever play football the way you once did."

He put his hand on Brant's shoulder. "Basically, Brant… even with the surgery, you may not be the player you were, but, without the surgery, you'll never play ball again."

Brant nodded. "Well then… it sounds like I better take my chances."

Dr. Ash shook Brant's hand again before he and Mom walked out into the hall.

When Brant and I were alone, I sat on the end of his bed. "It's gonna be alright," I nodded.

Brant groaned.

"What is it?" I asked him.

"To tell you the truth," Brant shrugged, "I'm sick of hearing all of you telling me that it's going to be okay when none of you really know."

"It's okay to feel that way," I replied. "Let me tell you this though… none of us do know. What we are all trying to say when we tell you that everything is going to be fine is just that we love you. That is all any of us is trying to tell you… we love you… whatever happens."

Dad walked in, his face stern. "It's going to be okay, Brant," he said as he popped Brant's leg with a folded newspaper. "You're gonna be my quarterback again in no time."

Brant looked at me before turning back to Dad. "I love you too, Dad," he grinned.

Brant reached for the newspaper my dad was holding. He held it up, and I saw the awful headline: "MCLACHLAN SHOWING SIGNS OF MORTALITY."

Dad snatched the paper back as Christian and Ethan strolled back in. "You don't need to read that," Dad shook his head.

"I want to," Brant insisted.

Dad handed the paper to Christian. "Get this out of here," he sighed.

"Read it to me, Chris," Brant said loudly.

Christian looked to Dad for approval.

"Christian, just read it!" Brant persisted.

"Brant, no," Dad groaned.

"Just read it," Brant shrugged.

Christian cleared his throat and began reading. "Seventeen-year-old Brant McLachlan is the product of a town rich in football spirit. He, only a short while ago, possessed what most can only dream of… an arm built like a cannon and legs as quick as an Olympic sprinter's.

He is Cummins, Mississippi's golden child. He grew up as everyone's favorite coach's superstar son; he matured into a local celebrity, but, in a split second, an automobile accident left Brant's future hanging in the balance.

Today, the boy with the famous grin that has so often adorned the pages of this paper will undergo back surgery that will ultimately decide his future in a game he holds dear to his heart. Feelings around town are mixed regarding the possibility of a full recovery.

'I just can't imagine a Friday night without #13 on the field,' one man said. 'I've gotta believe he's gonna come through this.'

The majority, however, seems to believe that Brant's once bright future suddenly appears hazy. 'It's just unreal. He's such a talented kid. For something like this to happen… it's just really sad. Even if he's able to play this season, and I hope he can, he's never gonna be the player he was. Athletes having back surgery at his age just don't play professional ball.'

North River High School looks for another State Championship this coming season, but as the early morning hours fade, we can only hope that we will not be left to do battle this season without our key to victory. It's a sad day in Cummins when one whose power to thrill us seems nothing less than superhuman must face the light of mortality."

"That's the most ridiculous thing I have ever heard," I exclaimed. I knew the man responsible for the article, and I made a mental note that he and I needed to have a little talk.

"Hand that to me, Christian," Dad grimaced. He popped Brant with the paper again and smiled, "you hang in there."

"I never thought of myself as *immortal*," Brant rolled his eyes. "I'm just a kid who wants to play football. But what if they're right? What if my career ends today?"

"Brant, let me tell you something," Dad sighed. "This is only the beginning of a program, a media... a world of critics, misquotes, sound off columns and Monday morning quarterbacks. They can talk all they want, but... ultimately it's all up to you. How bad do *you* want it? Let this motivate you. Prove them wrong, son. They're probably right... the odds *aren't* in your favor... so, you know what I say... beat the odds, Brant, and make believers out of this town again."

Later that morning we all bid our final well wishes as Brant was rolled into surgery.

"Our switchboards are full, Becky," Betsy Harper said as my mother paced back and forth in front of her. "Everyone wants to check on Brant; what should I tell them?"

Mother stopped pacing, pushed her hair back, looked down at her watch, and sighed, "I don't know... tell them that as soon as we know anything that Channel Nine is here with a camera. We'll give an official statement to them. That's the best we can do... we really won't know much today."

Betsy patted Mom's hand. "I'll tell them, honey."

Mom nodded and resumed pacing. She paused abruptly. "And," she said boldly, "you can tell them that Brant is not the golden child; he's just a kid that, like my other three sons, has a specific talent. Believe it or not, Cummins could survive without football, and football can survive without Brantley at the helm."

Betsy smiled. "Good luck convincing them of that, honey."

"Yeah," Mom sighed.

***

Five days later, Mom was at the desk at the end of Brant's hall signing hospital papers when she and Betsy heard a racket blaring from the opposite end of the corridor.

Mom glanced up, straining her ears only slightly. "Garth Brooks," she nodded knowingly. "*Friends in Low Places*."

"Well, somebody must be feeling better," Betsy smiled.

Mom shook her head. "That," she gestured, "is his way of saying *if you aren't going to let me out of this place, I am going to make you wish you had.* Luckily for all of you… I'm taking him home today!"

"Oh, Becky, that's wonderful news!" Betsy exclaimed as she hugged my mom.

"It's gonna be a long road to recovery," Mom nodded as she squeezed her friend's hands, "but if anybody can do it… it's Brant."

Tommy raced Brant's wheelchair down the hall as the boys laughed and screamed over the steady rhythm of the music that poured from the CD player clasped in Brant's hands.

"Is it my imagination, or have those two taken over this place?" Dad smiled as he approached.

Mom turned at the sound of his voice, nodding, "yes they have." She put her arm around Dad's waist and thought for a moment about the day that Brant had been rushed into the emergency room. "Isn't it great?" she nodded resolutely.

***

As the summer progressed, so did Brant's recovery. He walked, slowly at first, then a little faster. He used a treadmill and a stationary bicycle to build up his endurance. Slowly, he started lifting weights again, and, quickly, he progressed to doing things that Dr. Ash had specifically insisted could jeopardize his recovery. He threw a football with one of us daily. Though not on his throwing hand, I was surprised and thankful at how remarkably well his wrist healed, and, with the help of a couple tools from Dad's shed, he disposed of his final cast before he was told he could. He was a workaholic with one goal in mind. I was so proud of Brant's dedication to the sport he loved and even prouder of his determination that, if it was up to him, he wasn't going to miss a single game of his senior season.

CHAPTER FIVE

Just as it did each year, official football practice began at the end of July. Being forced to sit on the sidelines while all of his friends took the field in the glorious heat of summer to prepare for the upcoming season infuriated Brant. When two-a-days began in August, Brant insisted that he was ready to practice with the team.

I was looking forward to my brothers' senior year, but I was afraid that Brant was moving too fast when he suited up for the first time on the hottest day of August. He wanted to play, and, when he said that he was ready, I knew he was thinking with his heart and not with his head.

On Brant's first day back near the end of August, Dad and I watched as the boys ran laps around the field. Brant appeared sluggish to us, yet he was still hanging with the middle of the pack.

During each drill Brant pushed himself to the limit.

After a particularly grueling drill intended to enhance one's agility, Brant rested in the grass, looking up to the sky, his knees bent, his chest rising and falling.

"Dad," I grumbled, "you've got to do something… you've got to stop him before he gets hurt because he's way too stubborn to tell himself it's time to quit."

"Brant, buddy," Dad sighed, "I can't run a practice with you lying in the middle of my field. Go on… take five."

Brant got up, sweat pouring from his face. "I'm sorry… I'm fine… let's go…"

"Brant," Dad said, tossing me the ball and motioning for me to resume the drill, "why don't you take a break? We're about to start hitting and…"

"And what?" Brant shrugged.

Dad called for the boys to line it up.

"No sir, #13," Dad said with a stern shake his head as he watched Brant jog into line. "You get over here with me."

Brant fastened his chinstrap. "I came out here to practice, not to watch," he shook his head.

"Son," Dad grumbled.

"Dad," Brant snapped, "you're the one who told me to beat the odds, break the rules… now you're not even going to give me a chance to prove to everyone that I'm okay… because you're too scared. I'm not scared, Dad… you can't be either."

"I really shouldn't let you do this," Dad sighed.

Brant's anger faded into a smile. "But you're going to, right?"

"Dad… no," I moaned. "Dad, what if he gets hurt before the season even starts? Why chance that?" I begged, trying to appeal to my father's better judgment.

"Shut up, Jordan," Brant huffed.

"Dad," I shrugged, "why are you letting him talk you into this?"

Dad ignored me as he looked at Brant. "Your mother would kill me," he shook his head.

"Well, Mom's not here is she?" Brant shrugged. "Besides, she knew I was coming to practice. What did she expect me to do… play *Hopscotch* on the sidelines while the other guys had the real fun?"

Dad ran his fingers through his hair, considering the statement, and my jaw dropped. It was written all over his face… he was about to give in.

"Alright, Brantley," he sighed, "if you think you're up to it then go for it… just please… be careful…"

"Dad!" I exclaimed.

Because he knew I was right, Dad chose to continue ignoring me.

Brant jumped, sprung even, to his feet the first two times he was hit. After the third lick, I noticed that he got up a little more slowly than he had before.

"That's enough, Brant," I called, a sentiment I would repeat to deaf ears for the remainder of the summer.

There were days I watched Brant peel himself off the field in the August heat and pick the grass out of his helmet while trying to hide the pain in his face, his eyes full of a fierce focus and an overwhelming determination to continue.

***

Summer ended; school began, and, on a Friday night in September, to the delight of a crowd of screaming fans, the North River Eagles took the field led by their team captain and star quarterback, Cummins, Mississippi's golden boy with that familiar 13 plastered across his jersey. Brant was back, and people shouted his name, but, somewhere behind their triumphant smiles, doubt still lingered. Throughout the stands the concern wasn't a question of whether Brant was ready to play football or not, but, rather, looming large over the night was a general consensus that he wasn't ready to go out and be the Brant McLachlan that everyone expected to see.

For the herd of alumni and former players gathered along the fence with their gray hair and their bellies protruding over their belt buckles, an average performance would mean failure. Some wearing letterman jackets from the Class of 1962, stood with their arms crossed. Eagles football was their life. They had stood in the same spot there along the thirty yard line when I played for North River, my then three, four, five-year-old little brother playing at their feet, destined to become their hero. I knew each man there. They were good men at heart, but there were times when I hated them for the pressure they put on the boys of Cummins. I remembered their jeers, their harsh words after a botched play. Nothing had changed, only now it was my brothers' names they were yelling. For three years they had hailed Brantley as the greatest to step on North River's field. I knew that if they had even one discouraging thing to say about Brant that night, my entire outlook on the sanctity of football in Cummins, Mississippi, would change forever.

Kathy Smith and my mom stood side by side along the fence in front of the North River cheerleaders.

"It sure is good to see him out there," Jennifer's mother smiled.

"I'm just ready to get this first game under our belt," Mom sighed. "I think I'll be okay then."

Kathy Smith looked around at the restless crowd. "Yeah… Brant's under a lot of pressure to perform tonight."

"Yeah..." Mom shrugged with a drawn out sigh, "the support Brant has gotten from everyone has been phenomenal; I just wish that they wouldn't act like the very survival of this town depends on whether or not my son can shine on the football field tonight. The hopes of an entire town are on his shoulders, and that just isn't fair."

Kathy Smith took a bite of her popcorn and hollered for Ben not to wander too far from his father before adding, "Jennifer tells me that Brant says he's ready."

"He's too hardheaded for his own good," Mom laughed. "You know that."

When the boys took the field that night under the bright lights that illuminated the hundred and twenty yard focal point of our little town, the summer seemed like nothing but a distant memory.

Christian started off the game with a sixty yard return, and Brant took over from there. Football season was upon us, and my little brother was about to take Cummins, Mississippi, for a ride that none of us will ever forget.

The morning after the season opener, the front page of the *Cummins Daily News* read in big, bold print, "HE'S BACK!" Under the headline was a giant, color photograph of Brant preparing to throw what the caption identified as his third touchdown pass of the night.

Sitting at the kitchen table with a bowl of cereal in front of me, I opened the paper. In Cummins there was no need for a sports section on Saturday mornings during football season because unless half the town burned down or there was an event more news worthy than the usual bulletin about the lady's Saturday night quilting bee at the church, high school football got the entire front page.

I smiled as I began to read. "*Can he make a comeback?* That was the question on all our minds last night as we gathered at North River High School to watch our Eagles face off against the Wildcats of West Harrison County..."

Brant ran down the stairs, pulling a t-shirt over his head and entering the kitchen at full speed, sliding across the kitchen floor in his sock feet. "What does the paper say about me?" he asked as he reached into the refrigerator and gulped orange juice straight from the jug.

I turned the paper around for him to see. "It's got your ugly mug on the front page," I smiled.

Brant snatched the paper. "McLachlan may even be better than before!" he read the caption with animated enthusiasm.

Christian strolled into the kitchen wearing only his boxer shorts. He too walked over to the refrigerator and turned up the jug of orange juice.

"Do we not have any glasses?" I blurted, my brow wrinkled in amazement.

Christian glanced over Brant's shoulder at the paper. "Does it say anything in there about me?"

"No," Brant grinned, not looking up from the paper. "No one cares about you."

Christian snatched the paper. "Let me see that."

Dad walked inside from the front porch. "Nice article, huh?" he said walking past the boys as they tugged at the paper, each trying to read it at once.

Dad opened the refrigerator door.

"Brant, stop it," Christian insisted, "let me see it."

"I had it first," Brant said with a shove.

"You're hogging it," Christian retorted.

Dad rolled his eyes.

"Dad, what time does Alabama play today?" Christian asked, giving in and letting Brant keep the newspaper.

"Two o'clock," Dad replied. "Did you ever fill out those forms I gave you and return them to the registrar's office?"

"Mom mailed them this morning on her way to the hospital," Christian replied.

Brant softly hummed the tune of *Sweet Home Alabama* as he continued to look at the paper.

Dad slapped Christian's back. "ROLL TIDE ROLL!" he grinned proudly.

Playing for the University of Alabama had been Christian's dream since he was a kid. Tuscaloosa is only about an hour and a half drive from Meridian, and, as kids, Dad took the triplets and me to watch Alabama football games on a fairly regular basis.

Almost every weekend during football season, Dad and I had the triplets in Tuscaloosa watching Dad's Crimson Tide or in Starkville watching the Mississippi State Bulldogs.

We traveled to games in Tennessee and in Texas, but there was something about going to Tuscaloosa, Alabama, that made my dad's face light up and his step quicken. As kids, the boys picked up on that. Tuscaloosa was a special town for Dad, so it became a special place for them… especially for Christian. Though he was a huge fan, Brant was always too busy talking Super Bowls to spend much time dreaming of National Championships, but, for Christian, the University of Alabama was the place, the only place, he wanted to be.

"And what about you?" Dad asked Brant. "Have you given college any thought?"

"Yeah," Brant said as he looked away from the paper, "I thought about it just long enough to decide I'm not going."

"Is that so?" Dad raised his eyebrow.

"Well, yeah," Brant shrugged, "I mean I thought about college when I thought my senior season might not happen… but now… I mean…" Brant turned the paper around to us. "Didn't you get the memo?" he grinned. "I'M BACK!"

Dad rolled his eyes but couldn't resist a chuckle. "The second appeal goes before the court in two weeks," he said seriously. Then he reached into the open refrigerator, unscrewed the cap on the orange juice and turned it up to his mouth.

"Note to self," I grumbled, "if you want something to drink around here… have milk."

"Dad," Brant frowned, "do you think the accident will have any impact on the court's decision?"

"No," Dad shook his head, but we could all hear the uncertainty in his voice, "if anything it only proved that you're strong and determined. And, as far as anyone needs to know, you were driving the speed limit like any responsible adult when the accident happened. It could have happened to anyone."

I rolled my eyes. It had always been my belief that the NFL knew that there were some young athletes who were strong enough, fast enough and talented enough to compete on the professional level. I viewed their ban on underage players to deal more with the pressures players face and privileges they are given off the field more than their ability to perform on the field. For the same reasons, I wasn't entirely convinced that my brother was ready for everything that came along with being a professional athlete.

Brant sank down into a chair at the kitchen table, the morning paper still in hand.

"Are you done admiring your picture yet?" Christian laughed as he reached for the paper. "Let me read it."

"Wait your turn," Brant grumbled.

"Come-on, Brant," Christian said as he snatched at the paper again.

Brant elbowed Christian away. "Hold up!"

"Don't hit me, Brantley," Christian retorted.

Brant shrugged. "Then get away from me while I'm reading."

"Dad… tell him to stop hoggin' the paper," Christian insisted

"Brant," Dad called behind him as he walked into the living room, "stop hoggin' the paper."

"I'm not done reading it, Dad," Brant huffed.

"Christian, he's not done reading it," Dad mocked as he sat down in his recliner and reached for his remote control.

Brant and Christian looked at each other and rolled their eyes.

"Now both of you hush," Dad said seriously as he flipped on the television. "Southern Miss is on… and it's time for the kick off."

Brant handed the paper to Christian, and Christian dropped it on the table as both boys scurried into the living room to watch the game.

As I picked up the paper and resumed reading, I couldn't help but smile because, for the first time in months, life at the McLachlan house was finally back to normal.

***

The week leading up to the Eagles' second game of the season was full of high expectations. The focus had shifted from Brant's health. He had proven that he was ready to play football again, and everyone's fears seemed to have vanished. I, however, couldn't shake the feeling that Brant was moving too fast. On nearly every play, I found myself almost expecting Brant to get hurt. I couldn't shake the feeling that the season would not be all smooth sailing.

On Friday night, Brant and Christian went to midfield to call the toss, and we received the kickoff. Christian ran a beautiful return, and then Brant took the field. Tommy snapped the ball, and Brant dropped back. His options were under perfect coverage. He scrambled as Christian broke deep. He fired a beauty down field, and Christian took it in for the touchdown. Christian ran well; he was seeing his holes and pushing for extra yardage, and Brant, as always, was putting on a show.

Sometimes it seemed that football was like a novel that Brant wrote as he went and, therefore, possessed the power to say who would do what and what the outcome would be. At other times it looked as though Brant was simply dreaming the impossible and making it come true.

On our next drive, Dad and I watched from the sideline as Brant broke tackles here and there until he only had one man left to beat. He turned on the jets, kicked into high gear and won the footrace with ease.

"I hope they got that on tape," Dad smiled as he glanced over at the camera crew.

I couldn't help but laugh. For a second Dad wasn't an overbearing coach, he was a proud father.

We had scored on our first two possessions, and, though our third would be no different, it would not be without a little added drama.

Brant dropped back; his protection was nowhere to be found. He scrambled for a few yards gain, then got flattened. It was a vicious hit, one of those hits where even the people loitering out in the parking lot can hear pads colliding. Brant's body slammed to the ground. Slowly, he rolled over on his side, where he lay motionless for a long moment.

"Get up, Brant… come-on, kid," Dad whispered to himself.

I watched as Christian knelt down next to Brant. He turned to the sideline and waved for the trainer. A lump formed in my throat. I turned toward the bleachers. Everyone was standing… watching and waiting.

Dad put his headset around his neck and stepped on the field. He began walking slowly at first, then faster until he broke into a jog.

"What are you doing out here?" Brant snapped when Dad knelt next to the trainer.

"Are you alright?" Dad asked, ignoring Brant's frustration.

"I will be if you'll just get off the field," Brant insisted. "Newsflash… this is football… you can't run out here every time I get knocked down."

"Brant… where are you hurt? Is it your back?" our trainer inquired.

"My back is fine," Brant insisted as he extended his hand to Tommy, and Tommy slowly and carefully pulled him to his feet.

"Are you sure?" Dad persisted.

"Get off the field," Brant huffed as he stared at Dad. "Gosh, can't I take a decent hit without everyone jumping to the conclusion that my season is over?"

Dad nodded an unspoken and, I feel, unnecessary apology.

The crowd cheered as Dad and our trainer jogged off the field.

"I shouldn't have gone out there," Dad sighed as he got ready to call the next play.

"After what he's been through, you wouldn't be much of a coach or a father if you hadn't," I shrugged. "How is he?"

"Stubborn," Dad replied as, through a series of hand signals, he relayed the next play to Brant.

In the huddle, Brant, eager to prove to everyone that he was unfazed by the blow, called Dad's play off and called his own number for a quarterback sneak instead. He broke tackles and made moves all the way to the two yard line. The crowd loved the fluid way in which Brant moved, the artistry behind a spin move that had allowed him to evade capture by mere inches, but Dad was not impressed at all.

"That's not the play I called. What does he think he's doing?" he screamed.

"He's paying you back for going out on the field," I nodded as I crossed my arms.

Dad emphatically called the goal line play, and I crossed my fingers, hoping that my brother wasn't about to do what I was absolutely certain he was about to do.

I could only nod knowingly as Brant ran to the outside and reached the ball across the goal line for a touchdown. Dad's veins in his forehead began to show as he slammed his clipboard to the ground.

The crowd was excited, but my dad was far from impressed.

The boys came off of the field celebrating, but the celebration didn't last long. Dad grabbed Brant's jersey and ripped him from the center of the pack. Dad had the entire #13 on the front of Brant's jersey in his grasp as he shook him violently. Taking hold of Brant's facemask, he screamed, "I have never seen such selfish, unorganized football in my life. You blatantly disobeyed me, and I won't stand for it. You just try that with me again, I dare you."

Brant glared back at him with a stare that said he thought he was too tough for Dad and too good for this lecture. Dad slung him toward the bench. "You may think you're the boss on that field, but you're looking at *the boss*. You got that, hotshot?"

"Loud and clear," Brant said sarcastically.

Dad crossed his arms. "Nobody likes a showoff, Brantley."

Brant looked back at his host of adoring fans. "They don't seem bothered…"

"One more word… and you and that bench are going to become very aquatinted," Dad swallowed, "and if you think I'm bluffing, you just test me."

"Okay," Brant insisted, "but if you run out on the field to check on me after I get hit by some high school kid, that doesn't say much for the prospect of guys like me being eligible for the draft, so just try not to ruin my career because you're afraid I might get hurt."

Dad pointed at Brant. "No… you shut your smart mouth, Brant… there is nothing left to say. The day you think you are too good for this team, too good for my plays… then you're done playing for me. Are we perfectly clear?"

Brant nodded. "Yes, sir," he said softly.

After the game, a reporter from Meridian pulled Brant aside. "That was an amazing performance," he said as he stuck a tape recorder in Brant's face.

"Well, it was fun. I just go out there every week and play my game and hope that I please all of my fans," Brant grinned. "I am so lucky to be able to play with such a talented group of guys. I'm not the only reason that we are able to dominate. We win because we have the best receiver in the country and a defense that gets the other team off the field quickly, so that I can do what I do."

"What have you decided about college, Brant?" the reporter fired back.

Brant laughed. "Only that I don't want to go!"

The reporter was relentless. "So you're moving ahead with your appeal? Do you really think you'll be eligible for the draft?" he asked.

Brant shrugged. "Yeah... probably," he smiled. "Don't get me wrong... I'd love to win the Heisman and a National Championship... but I think I'm gonna leave that to my brother. He was amazing tonight, huh?" Brant shook the reporter's hand. "I have a team meeting to get to," he told him.

"That's the second time you've mentioned your brother," the reporter smiled. "Has Christian committed to Alabama yet?"

"He was awesome tonight. Don't you think?" Brant grinned.

"He was alright," the reporter shrugged.

"What does that mean?" Brant frowned. "I don't know what game you were watching..."

"He's a great athlete... for a high school kid," the reporter chuckled. "But, Brant... nobody wants to talk about your brother... he's not gonna sell any of my papers... everyone wants to talk about you."

"Well, that's too bad," Brant frowned, "because this interview is over." Had he stopped there, tempers probably would have cooled, but he went on to call the reporter a few choice names that I won't mention here.

"Can I quote you on that?" the reporter snickered.

"Do you want a quote?" Brant fired back. "Here's a quote for you. You can take your little tape recorder and..."

"Brantley!" came my father's stern warning, and Brant swallowed the rest of his sentence. Moments later, Dad led Brant by the arm, through the crowd, back to the locker room as cameras flashed around them."

***

On Saturday morning Mom walked into our den that Dad had transformed into his office. She was waving the morning paper in her hand. "Honey," she asked with a grimace, "have you seen this?"

"Seen what?" Dad shrugged as he glanced up at her.

Mom opened the paper and began reading, "McLachlan admitted that his brother Christian McLachlan quite possibly does not have the talent it takes to play for a program like the University of Alabama, the boys' father's alma mater."

"Is that our paper?" Dad inquired. "I thought I read..."

"No," Mom said, tossing him the paper, "I bought a Meridian paper this morning... for the sales... but I found this."

"Brantley!" Dad called sternly.

"Brantley, now!" Mom hollered up the stairs.

Brant trotted down the stairs proclaiming his innocence. "I didn't do it," he said holding his hands up in surrender. "I did *not* say that."

"Sit down," Dad pointed.

"Dad," Brant insisted as he eyed the portrait of Bear Bryant that hung over Dad's desk, "Jen just called. She told me to go get a copy of the Meridian paper. She told me what it says, but it's not true."

"Did she read you the article?" Dad asked.

"No," Brant sighed.

"Read it," Dad insisted as he handed Brant the newspaper.

"Start here," Mom pointed.

Brant glanced up at her. His eyes moved back to the newspaper as he began reading out loud: "Following the game in which he managed to make a respectable high school basketball score look like a weekly occurrence on the football field, Brant McLachlan was eager to share about the success of his team…"

"Blah… blah… blah," Mom huffed. "Skip to here," she said, plastering her finger in the middle of the next paragraph.

"However," Brant continued reading, "McLachlan admitted that his brother Christian McLachlan quite possibly does not have the talent it takes to play for a program like the University of Alabama, the boys' father's alma mater. It is rumored that Brant himself will most likely sign with Alabama if he is not drafted."

Brant sat the paper down. "I didn't say that. I swear," he insisted. "And… *not drafted*… what is that?"

"Brant," Mom shook her head.

"I'm kidding," Brant smiled.

"Focus, son," Dad grumbled.

Brant's expression turned angry. "I didn't say that about Christian!"

"Nothing like that? Nothing that would imply that?" Dad interrogated.

"No," Brant said loudly, "I said that he played good… because he did. He played great. Dad, you heard that reporter… he hated me."

Dad scoffed, "Brantley, you called him a…"

Christian walked into Dad's office, and everyone turned to stare at him.

"Chris," Brant gulped as he jumped up, "we need to talk."

"About what?" Christian shrugged as he reached for the morning paper.

"Wait," Brant rolled his eyes, "Christian, before you see that…"

Christian seemed confused. He lowered his head and began reading to himself. When he was done, he looked up at Brant.

"Christian…" Brant sighed.

"I see," Christian nodded.

"No… Christian… you don't," Brant shook his head.

"I can see why you wouldn't want me to see this," Christian chuckled, and Brant could hear the hurt in his voice.

"You don't understand," Brant replied.

"I don't believe this," Christian said as he stared hatefully at Brant.

Brant's face turned angry. "You shouldn't believe it… it's not true."

"That's what you think of me, huh?" Christian screamed, ignoring Brant's words as he slung the paper at him.

"Whoa… hold up," Brant shot back. "You actually believe I said that? Didn't you hear what I just said? It's not true… it's a load of bull, but… no questions asked… you're just gonna take this guy's word for it? You really think I said that about you?"

"Obviously you did," Christian shrugged.

"No," Brant shook his head, "I didn't… but at least now I know what *you* think of *me*."

Brant started to storm out, but Mom stopped him. "I don't think so," she sighed, grabbing his arm. "The two of you need to straighten this out."

Brant and Christian stared at each other.

"I would never say anything like that about you," Brant said softly. "Even if I thought it, which I don't, I still wouldn't tell it to some reporter. And, honestly, it hurts a lot that, without any hesitation whatsoever, you assumed that I did."

"Well, it was right there in black and white," Christian replied.

"So who are you gonna believe, some reporter with an ax to grind or your own brother?" Brant shrugged.

"You really didn't say that you don't think I can play at Alabama?" Christian sighed.

"No," Brant shook his head. "Why would I say that? Christian… you're my brother, my teammate, my best friend. I'm excited that you're going to Alabama. I'm proud of you. I don't just *think* you can play for a program like that… I *know* you can."

Christian swallowed, "I just…"

"You just jumped to a really quick and hurtful conclusion about me," Brant sighed.

"Brant, I'm sorry," Christian nodded. "You're right. I should have known that you wouldn't say that about me."

"And I'm sorry that some idiot wrote that for you and everyone else to read," Brant said sincerely. "Christian, listen, I think you are a terrific football player. Not only do I know that you can play Division I college football, but I think the University of Alabama will be lucky to get you."

Mom walked to the phone.

"Becky, what are you doing?" Dad asked.

"I'm calling that newspaper and giving them a little piece of my mind," she replied.

Brant and Christian looked at each other and smiled.

"Brant," Christian said as the boys walked into the living room, "I want to apologize again."

"I'm sorry too," Brant nodded.

"You don't have anything to be sorry about," Christian shook his head. "You didn't say that… I know that now."

"No, I didn't say those things," Brant replied, "but I am sorry that people don't seem to appreciate your talent like they should."

"It's okay," Christian nodded.

"It's not okay," Brant shook his head.

"Brant," Christian said, putting his hand on Brant's shoulder, "you don't have to be sorry for all the attention that people give you. You deserve it."

"But you could go to any other high school in the country and be the star," Brant sighed. "I just think…"

"But I *don't* go to any other high school, nor do I *want* to," Christian blurted.

"Not even if it meant that people would give your talent the respect it deserves?" Brant asked.

"No, not even then," Christian shook his head.

"Why not?" Brant asked curiously.

"Because," Christian smiled, "you and I won't have forever to play on the same team, and going out there on Friday nights and having you and Ethan out there with me... well, that means a whole heck of a lot more to me than which one of us gets to be the star."

The boys hit fists.

***

The absence of any signs of a sibling rivalry between my brothers always seemed to surprise people. At times they were mean and cruel to each other, the way that all brothers are. They argued; they pushed and shoved, of course. But when it came down to it... if you messed with one of them, you messed with all three of them.

At times when sibling rivalry could have reared its ugly head, my brothers always seemed to find a way around it. At times they avoided it consciously, knowing that jealousy could destroy so much that was worth treasuring. At other times, conflicts between them simply seemed to resolve themselves in the most unsuspected ways before they had time to develop into anything serious.

Several days after Mom was done sending stern e-mails to the sports editor of the Meridian paper, Christian sat in his room staring at the bulletin board above the triplets' desk. He was lost in his thoughts and didn't hear me walk in.

I stared at the picture that I was pretty sure had caught his attention. The boys couldn't have been more than four years old in that picture. Dad had them all dressed alike in matching Alabama t-shirts that swallowed them whole. Brant was sitting on Dad's shoulders, flanked by Christian and Ethan, one on each side of him in Dad's arms.

"I remember that," I said after a moment.

"Yeah," Christian said, sounding a little startled, "so do I."

"What's wrong?" I asked.

"Oh, nothing," Christian shrugged as he picked up his pen. "I was just about to finish this take home test for my literature class."

I took the pen out of his hand. "Really... what's up?" I insisted.

"I can't explain it," Christian said softly.

"Try me," I said, sitting down on the edge of his bed.

"It's just Dad," Christian began. "I don't know."

"He's proud that you're going to Alabama," I replied.

"Yeah," Christian sighed, "I don't really know what it is."

"Christian, talk to me," I urged.

Christian thought for a moment. Then, frowning, he said, "maybe just once I want Dad to grab my jersey and slam me against a locker, you know, and tell me how out of control I am… how terrible… how cocky… how doomed for failure…"

"Why?" I scoffed, but I knew.

"Because," Christian sighed, "it's what he does to Brant. He holds him to a completely different standard than any of the rest of us. Nothing Brant does is quite good enough."

I raised an eyebrow, and Christian elaborated.

"There are guys on our team that pretty much anything that they do is fine with Dad because he knows that he got their best, and that's all that he wants.

Then there are guys like me who he knows have a real shot at playing at a good football college. He yells and lectures us and tells us that if we work hard we'll go far.

Then there's Brant. He can do something that is so enviable… so seemingly perfect… yet, Dad points out the flaws. So many people think that Dad is unfairly hard on him, but they're missing the bigger picture. Coaching Brant, Dad knows he is responsible for molding the future of the NFL.

Mr. Football comes out there to practice, sings out the plays and makes unbelievable passes between hollering at the cheerleaders and attempting to play *Hacky Sack* with the football… not saying that he doesn't work hard… no one works harder… but I go out there and give it my all… and…" He paused.

I knew exactly what he was saying, but I didn't know how to respond. "Trust me," I smiled, "Dad won't be able to contain himself when you put on that crimson and white. He's proud of you, Christian."

"I'm just glad that I got that off my chest," Christian replied. "Don't get me wrong… Brant works harder than any guy that I know. He deserves all the attention that he gets. This isn't about Brant… it's about Dad."

"Dad does what he thinks is best," I said as I stood. I turned back as I got to the doorway and said softly, "just between you and me… there is nothing left that Dad can teach Brant about football, and the way that he goes about coaching him is a reflection of his unwillingness to admit that. Every guy has to be coached differently. Some guys need to be pumped up while others need to be calmed down. Dad is a good coach. In fact, truth be known, he probably stays off your back because he trusts you to make good decisions on your own… while he might feel like Brant still needs his guidance. He's proud of you, Chris. Your football career is every bit as important to him as Brant's."

"You're good to talk to, Jordan," Christian nodded.

"That's what big brothers are for," I said proudly.

Christian took the pin out of the picture on the bulletin board, removed it from its spot above his desk and held it close as he examined it.

Just then, Brant came jumping down the hall like a Mexican jumping bean in a pair of oversized, gray sweatpants, singing the lyrics of *American Pie* at the top of his lungs.

"What's going on?" he asked as he scooted past me and into his bedroom.

"We were just talking," I shrugged.

"About?" Brant asked as he flopped on his bed. He noticed the photograph in Christian's hand. "Do you remember that day?" he smiled as he tossed a football into the air and fell back onto the bed as he caught it.

"Yeah…" Christian nodded.

Brant stood and peered over Christian's shoulder. "Look at us… do you think those shirts were big enough? And look at Dad… he's having a blast." Brant reached for the picture, and Christian handed it to him. "Man," Brant grinned, "those were the days. Back then Dad was determined that all three of us would play for Alabama." He handed the picture back to Christian, and Christian pinned it back on the bulletin board. "I'm so jealous that you're actually gonna get to play there… just like Dad did."

"What?" Christian seemed surprised. "You… jealous of me? Brant… they would kill to get their hands on you."

"But I'm not going," Brant shook his head. "You know how badly you want to play for Alabama?" he shrugged.

"Yeah," Christian nodded.

"That's how bad I want to play for the Cowboys," Brant nodded back.

"So let me get this straight," Christian smiled as he turned to Brant. "I'm gonna play college ball… you're gonna get paid to play pro ball, perhaps even as soon as next season… and *you're* jealous?"

"A little I guess," Brant nodded sincerely. "I mean… I can't imagine how proud Dad is gonna be to see one of his sons playing for the Crimson Tide. It was his dream for all of us, and you're making it come true. Sometimes, I wish I was going with you."

"You do?" Christian smiled.

"Sure," Brant nodded.

"So," Christian inquired, "if you aren't eligible for the draft, is it safe to say that you've made your decision?"

Brant grinned. "Our secret," he nodded.

I smiled to myself.

Christian glanced at me, and I winked at him.

Brant didn't notice. He was much too busy marching around the room playing an air trombone and humming the Alabama fight song for his own amusement.

"Brant, don't you have a literature take home test to do?" I asked with a chuckle.

"Brant's idea of doing a take home test is waiting until Ethan completes his," Christian grinned.

Brant shrugged as if to say, *duh,* then continued his march around the room.

***

Brant's name received national attention when a three-judge panel of the U.S. Supreme Court of Appeals agreed with he and Dad's argument that the National Football League should consider underclass men on an individual basis rather than generalizing that all men under a certain age are not strong enough or mature enough for the life of a professional athlete.

"Football doesn't warrant an age restriction," Brant told an ESPN anchorman during a telephone interview. "I understand why the NFL established the rule, but there are exceptions to every rule, and I'm glad that the courts have agreed that I shouldn't be prevented from working just because of my age. I'm not a liability to the NFL. I'm not interested in the money or the fame. I just want to play football. I'm not afraid of getting hurt. I know I can play with the older guys. I'm ready for both the physical and mental challenges that will come my way."

I listened to Brant's words, and I wanted to believe that he was right. I knew that he could handle the physical aspects of professional football. Certainly I knew it wouldn't hurt him to spend a few years in college, lifting weights and playing with bigger guys, but, all in all, I didn't worry about his ability to compete physically. Yet, I still had my doubts that, at eighteen years old, Brant was mature enough to face the responsibility that came along with the job. Little did any of us know that, in the coming months, Brant's ability to make mature decisions would be put to the test right there at home in Cummins, Mississippi.

***

I was up drinking a glass of milk one morning when Mom walked into the living room in her gray, flannel pajamas. "Triplets still asleep?" she asked, continuing into the kitchen to pour herself a cup of coffee.

"I guess so," I nodded.

"Well, I guess they're just gonna sleep the day away," she shook her head.

"The boys' report cards came in the mail this morning," Dad announced as he walked in the front door.

Mom sat down on the couch to open the envelopes. Opening the first envelope, she smiled. "Christian got all *A's* and a *B-* in chemistry," she told us.

"That chemistry teacher is tough," Dad replied. "He's that new, young guy from Starkville."

"I guarantee you that Ethan got an *A* in there," I said confidently.

"*A+*," Mom laughed as she opened Ethan's report card.

She peered at the remaining envelope. "Do I even want to open this?" she sighed. She tore it open, and, though her jaw dropped, she couldn't resist a chuckle. "He leaves for school at the same time as Christian and Ethan every morning, drives faster than anyone, but, miraculously, Brant has managed to be late for homeroom nine times this quarter."

"How about his grades, Becky?" Dad smiled.

"David, we a have a list of checkmarks to discuss before we get to that," Mom groaned. "Eliminate unnecessary talking… complete assignments on time," she rambled.

I glanced over her shoulder. "Two *A*'s, four *C*'s and a *D*," I read.

"*D*?" Dad huffed. "In what?"

"History," Mom fretted. "David… he told me that he was keeping his grades up. Maybe we need to get him a tutor."

"He doesn't need a tutor, Becky, he needs a swift kick in the rear end," Dad laughed.

"Somebody should at least tell him that the person he's cheating off of in that history class isn't getting the job done," I shrugged.

"Sit him behind Ethan," Dad kidded back.

"This isn't the least bit funny," Mother scolded.

I heard the stairs creak, and I turned to see my three sleepy-eyed brothers filing down.

"Report cards!" Ethan exclaimed, suddenly wide awake.

Brant made a quick turn back up the stairs, but he was halted by my father's stern cry. "Brantley, freeze!"

"Busted," Ethan grinned as he shoved Brant.

Mom handed Ethan his report card. "All *A's* as usual," she smiled proudly.

"How did you get an *A* in Mr. Roberts' history class?" Brant huffed.

"I did too," Christian smiled.

Brant rolled his eyes. "Chris, I didn't ask, and I don't care."

"Well, I care," Mom blurted. "I want to know how Christian and Ethan both got *A*'s, yet you managed to bring home a *D*."

"It doesn't matter, Mom," Brant argued. "I mean… it could have been worse."

"Yes, I guess an *F* would have been slightly worse, Brant," Mom rolled her eyes.

"Not to mention," Brant pointed out, "I knew that my report card was coming in the mail this morning, so, technically, I could have gotten up early and easily changed that *D* to a *B* before you ever saw it… that would have been worse, right?"

"Are you asking?" Mom smiled.

"For future reference," Brant shrugged.

"Yes, Brantley, lying would have been worse," Mom nodded in disbelief.

Dad seemed unconvinced. "On the other hand," he shook his head, "it would have shown a little concern on your part, whereas you slept past noon and couldn't have cared less… I don't know… it's a toss up for me…"

"Brant," Mom groaned, "what is the problem with history? Why is it so hard for you?"

"I can't remember those stupid dates or those people whose names I can't even pronounce," Brant snapped. "I guess I just don't get it. When you have three at a time, one is liable to end up stupid, Mom!"

"You're not stupid," I said, crossing my arms.

"Well, that's debatable," Dad shrugged as he did the same.

"David, this is not funny," Mom scolded.

She stared at Brant. "You better start remembering," she said as she wagged her pointer finger at him. "Remembering those *stupid dates,* as you say, better become more important than who quarterbacked what *stupid* Super Bowl and what kind of *stupid* offence he ran or what his *stupid* passing accuracy was."

Brant moved his hand to his heart, and even Mom couldn't resist a smile.

"Maybe you're doing some of your *excessive talking* during your teachers' explanations," Dad added.

"I never talk in class," Brant insisted. "Did Mr. Roberts say I talk in his class? I never talk in his class."

Christian chuckled.

"Brant, you don't honestly expect us to believe that, now do you?" Mom rolled her eyes.

"Hey, I believe him," Christian smiled sarcastically, "it's hard to do a lot of talkin' while you're sleepin'."

Brant shoved Christian, and Christian shoved him back.

"Boys," Mom sighed.

Brant frowned as he looked down at his report card. "At least I got *A's* in public speaking and varsity athletics," he shrugged.

"Oh, you can run your mouth and throw a football… no doubt about that," Mom moaned.

"You've got to bring your grades up, Brantley," Dad said matter-of-factly.

"I will," Brant promised quickly, adding, practically in the same breath, "do you want to throw the football with me?"

"Sure… I'll get the ball," Dad smiled. He felt Mom's eyes burning a hole through him. He turned to her and grinned. "I'm mean… I'll get the ball, so that we can play later… after you study, of course."

"David," Mom scolded, "you can't just let him get away with grades like this."

"What am I supposed to do?" Dad shrugged. "Becky, *he* doesn't want to be a doctor!"

"Oh, that is a weak argument if I have ever heard one," Mom scoffed.

"Is it?" Dad fired back. "Because I think it makes a lot of sense. You don't see me getting all upset that Ethan doesn't run the hundred meter dash like Brant does, so why are you getting all upset that Brant doesn't have a perfect report card like Ethan's? The boys have different talents, Becky. And, frankly, as long as he passes… I don't care what kind of grades Brant makes. His future is set."

"I don't believe this, David. I thought that we all learned this past summer that football could be over for him in a second," Mom said angrily. "I pray to God that he stays healthy, but come-on, David. If he hurts that machine he's got for a right arm or his back gives out on him, it's over."

"Your mom's right, Brant," Dad agreed. "Football is a tedious profession… but you know that."

"Brant," Mom interjected, "Sweetie, I hope that one day you have a Super Bowl ring on every finger, but I want you to make sure that you have something to fall back on if you need it."

"I know… you want me to go to college," Brant rolled his eyes.

"Yes," Mom nodded, "Brantley, I think that you should go to college. There will be plenty of time later to play professional ball once you have a degree under your belt. But with grades like this you aren't even going to get in any good college. My goodness… you're walking a fine line between graduating in May and spending next summer finishing up high school while your brothers, Jennifer and all your friends get ready to head off to college."

"College isn't for me, Mom," Brant insisted.

Mom nodded. "I know that you don't want to go to college; believe it or not, I have even accepted the fact that you probably won't go, but this isn't about college... it's about you thinking that it is okay to fail a couple tests a week as long as you win the ultimate test on Friday night. That is not okay with me, and I'm not going to tolerate it. This town has made you think that you can get away with anything because of who you are, and I'm scared to death that you're going to start believing that." She looked to my father for support.

"Brant," he sighed, "you're grounded."

"Dad," Brant grumbled.

"Until you bring your grades up, you can't..."

"Brant," Mom interrupted, "just bring your grades up, okay?"

"I will, Mom. Can I go throw the football now?" he begged.

"Yes," Mom shook her head, "yes... go... get out of here!"

"What about me, honey? Can I go throw the football too?" Dad joked with Mom.

Mom turned her nose up at him, and he knew better than to say another word.

"Come-on, guys," Dad grinned as he shuffled the boys toward the door.

Brant, carefree as ever, began singing an old Tim McGraw song as he scurried outside ahead of the others.

"He's so crazy!" Mom exclaimed as the screen door closed, only slightly muffling Brant's voice. "What in the world am I going to do with him?"

I stood to go join the others in the yard. "It'll be alright, Mom," I smiled. "I don't know how he does it... but he always lands on his feet," I reminded her.

CHAPTER SIX

When a national magazine called *North and South* contacted Brant about posing for the cover of their November issue, which was to spotlight outstanding, high school athletes, he was thrilled.

As soon as the magazine hit stores in October, people began asking Brant to autograph their copies. Between Jennifer and my mother, I don't know how anyone else was able to obtain a copy to purchase, but somehow they managed. Brant relished the attention.

Going into a grocery store and seeing my brother's face on the cover of a magazine was overwhelming for all of us… especially Mom. To see Brant posing, shirtless no less, on the cover of a magazine as she stood in the checkout line at Walmart was something that she was sure she would never get used to.

To us, Brant was the rough and tumble, happy-go-lucky, blond-haired kid he'd always been. To the rest of the world, Brant McLachlan was a funny talking Southerner, a good ole boy from Dixie who had challenged the National Football League and was now on the verge of national stardom.

***

The Friday after Brant's magazine hit stands, the Eagles had a big game, and I mean that in the most literal sense. By five o'clock Friday evening, the bleachers were packed, and people were standing two and three rows deep all around the fence.

Ethan was sitting on top of the lockers in the locker room, looking out a window that ran around the top of the room and keeping everyone up-to-date on how rapidly the crowd continued to grow.

Jennifer motioned her mother and mine toward the fence.

"What is going on?" my mother asked after she and Kathy Smith made their way through the crowd. "The parking lot is full… people are parking all down the street."

"All these people are here to see the show promised to them in *North and South*," Jennifer replied excitedly. "*Cover boy* just sent me after Sharpies… everyone wants an autograph."

"All these people are here to see Brant?" Mom gulped as she watched a family of four walk past them… the father with his video camera and the youngest daughter gripping her copy of the magazine and smiling nervously as if she was about to meet her favorite pop star. The older daughter looked as though she might just break into a high pitched scream at any minute. "Where did they all come from?" Mom asked.

"Who knows," Jennifer replied. "Isn't this amazing?"

The boys had come out onto the field, and people were pointing at Brant.

"There he is!" a small boy said as he looked up at his father.

Brant walked over to the fence, and people swarmed around him, all asking at once for an autograph.

Kathy Smith smiled. "Brant's loving every minute of that," she laughed.

"Yeah," Jennifer grinned as she watched as many girls as guys vying for autographs in the distance. "I better hurry up and marry him before some lovesick fan steals him away."

Mom rolled her eyes as she and Jennifer laughed. "He thinks he's famous!" she exclaimed.

Jennifer glanced around. She smiled as the three of them stood examining the scene. "Guys… I've got news for y'all," she nodded, "I think he is!"

"I think you're right," Mom concurred.

"We always knew it would happen someday," Jennifer shrugged. "Now it's time to sit back and enjoy it."

Brant looked down the fence toward Jennifer. Jennifer waved, and, with a wide smile, Brant turned back to his impromptu autograph session.

That night it was unreal to look out at the mass of people that had gathered at North River High School to watch Brant run around on the ragged patch of grass that we called North River's football field.

It was a cold night, and Jennifer was wrapped in Brant's blue and white letterman jacket as she cheered.

The bleachers were full of blue and white pom poms, shakers, horns, and homemade signs. I had never seen anything like it.

All of the unexpected hoopla raised the intensity level of the game for both teams, and, early on, I could tell that it was going to be a game to remember. Nothing quite angers a defensive line like a blond, curly-headed, high school quarterback who spends his pregame warm-up signing autographs for their fans and taking pictures with their little sisters.

Early in the first quarter, Brant got slammed to the ground long after he released the ball. "I believe that'll cost you fifteen yards, pal," he laughed as he jumped up.

Christian stepped in. "That was real cheap," he said, knocking shoulder pads with the guilty party as he walked back to the huddle.

"Hit my quarterback like that again," Tommy added, "and you can dance with somebody your own size."

On the next play, Brant fired a bullet into the end zone for a touchdown. The crowd went wild. "Don't feel bad," Brant smiled at his aggressive counterpart, "I could have thrown it another fifteen yards, easy."

The crowd roared as Brant ripped off his helmet and turned to jog off the field. He took only a few steps before he was knocked flat from behind. It was like slow motion as Brant's body contorted from the unexpected jolt, and his helmet bounced down the field. Brant rolled in the grass, clutching his back, desperate to stop the pain. He was hurt, hurt badly, and everyone there knew it. Secretly, I had been expecting it to happen all along, but I had never imagined it happening like that.

Christian immediately went after the guy who had hit Brant. He was furious, and he didn't need any help wrestling the three-hundred-pound lineman to the ground and manhandling him on his own. The opposing team acted as surprised as we were that their player had hit Brant from behind, and Christian fought uncontested for nearly a minute.

Dad immediately ran onto the field in an angry rage, yelling at the officials about how an action like that should keep someone off of a football field forever.

Tommy was kneeled down beside Brant frantically motioning for help.

As the boys began pushing and shoving on the field, Dad and I screamed at our players, demanding them to get back to the sideline, away from the other team.

Rick Jackson and his crew on the ambulance hurried onto the field.

Brant was thrashing and screaming in pain when they got to him.

Jennifer stood watching from the sideline, her hands over her mouth, as her friends tried to comfort her.

"Get Christian off of that punk before he gets himself suspended," Dad snapped as he rushed over to check on Brant.

Tommy helped me pull Christian to the sideline, though he and Christian continued to shout threats at the other team.

The opposing coach was informed that his player was done for the year, and his reaction was surprising to me. "You can't end his senior season," he argued with the head referee.

"Oh I can… and I did," the head referee said angrily. "And if I could, I'd ban him from football for good."

"Then you've got to end #16's season too!" the coach hollered as he jumped up and down. "It's only fair. He did more hitting than anyone."

That sent Dad flying off the handle. "You can't be serious," he screamed as he got in the other coach's face.

The referees pulled the two coaches apart.

"#16 will sit this game out," the presiding referee announced.

"Why?" Dad yelled. He threw his arms open. "You're going to punish him because he stood up for his teammate… his brother? What was he supposed to do?"

"He attacked one of my players; he was out of control," the coach argued lamely.

Dad snarled his upper lip and said sternly, "well, Coach, I taught my boys that when you have a problem with someone you deal with it face-to-face… if you catch my drift."

"Two wrongs don't make a right," the coach protested. "He should have to sit out for what he did to my player… that sort of behavior is uncalled for."

"What he did to your player?" Dad exploded. He turned and pointed to Brant on the ground. "Do you see that? Huh? *That* is *uncalled for*!"

"Gentlemen, I've heard enough from both of you," the referee interrupted. "#16 has got a warning; he looks at anybody else wrong the rest of this game, and he's out for the night."

"I can't believe it," the outraged coach shook his head, "not after what he did. He deserves to be punished as well."

"Heck, he probably saved my job," Dad shrugged. "In fact, you still might want to get the jerk that did this away from this field before I have a chance to get *my* hands on him." Dad turned and jogged back to where the medical team was tending to Brant.

"Brant… stay still for me, okay, buddy?" Rick Jackson pled with Brant as Brant tried to sit up.

"No… I want to play," Brant winced. He shoved a paramedic away from him.

"Not tonight, you're not," Rick Jackson sighed. "We're gonna get the backboard out here and take you to the hospital to get you checked out."

"No," Brant insisted as he sat up, "I'm fine." He insisted on standing, so Dad and I helped him to his feet. When Brant stood, the crowd erupted in cheers. One hand clinched to his back, he walked gingerly toward the sideline.

"How bad is it?" Dad asked Rick Jackson.

"I really can't say without an MRI," Rick replied.

Brant sat down on the bench, and Jennifer hurried over to check on him. "Are you okay?" she exclaimed as she reached for his hand.

"I don't know, Jen," Brant panted. "Tell me this isn't happening."

"You aren't going to try and play are you?" she replied quickly.

"Look at all those people," Brant sighed. "They are all here to see *me*."

"They would understand if you couldn't play," I blurted. "Everyone saw what just happened."

"Yes, Brant," Jennifer agreed, "Sweetie… nobody wants you to play hurt. You could do serious damage to your back… if you haven't already."

"It's football, Rocky... playing hurt is part of the game," Brant said as a sharp pain shot through his back.

"There is a big difference between playing in pain and playing injured," Jennifer argued.

"Brant," Mom said as she made her way to the bench, "come to the locker room with me. I want to take a look at you."

"No," Brant insisted.

Mom lifted the back of Brant's jersey and felt along his back. "Your back is swelling, son," she sighed. "I think you might have done some serious damage."

"Should I go get him some ice?" Jennifer asked.

"No!" Brant exclaimed before Mom could answer. "I don't need any ice or an MRI or anything else. I'm fine, and, if you would both excuse me, I have a football game to win."

Moments later, the pain still evident, though he was doing all that he could to hide it, Brant went back into the game. His gutsy effort was lost on no one, and the fans who had come to see if the kid pictured on the cover of *North and South* was the real deal, left knowing just how truly driven my little brother was.

CHAPTER SEVEN

Homecoming week is a big part of every kid's high school experience, but North River is notorious for its homecoming spirit. Jennifer and all the cheerleaders worked hard decorating the campus and planning activities that everyone could participate in.

Before sunrise on Monday morning, there was a big bonfire to kick off the week. At six o'clock a.m. the telephone rang at home. Mom and I had already left for work, and Dad had been at the school for over an hour. The answering machine picked up, and Jennifer was horrified. "Guys, why am I getting the machine?" she called into the telephone. "I have called cell phones, and I know y'all aren't on your way! Brant, Christian, Ethan, wake up *now* and get to school! I'm not hanging up until one of you picks up the phone!" She waited. "I can't believe this!" she went on. "I am in charge of hosting this big ordeal, and I can't even get *you guys* out of bed. I'm dying here, Brantley!"

Brant rolled over and picked up the phone. "What time is it?" he moaned.

"After six o'clock," Jennifer huffed. "Five o'clock, Brant… you were supposed to be here by *five* o'clock this morning! I have a third of the town here celebrating, but my keynote speaker is in bed. I thought I could contain them, but I was wrong! I am going down the tubes fast here, and it's your fault, Brantley."

"Is my dad there?" Brant asked.

"Yes," Jennifer snapped, "*he* managed to be on time, but he's already given his speech, now I need *you*."

"Stall 'em, we're on our way," Brant promised as he jumped out of bed. "Get Tommy to give a pep talk to tide them over until I get there."

"They are throwing things at him *and* me," Jennifer exaggerated. "They want *you*. Get here! Bye!"

"Christian, Ethan, get up!" Brant screamed, as he scrambled to get his clothes on.

Christian's arm hung off of his bed, and Brant kicked him with his sock feet. "Get up! We're late!" Christian was unfazed.

As Brant reached for the hat hanging on his bedpost, he yanked a pillow off of his bed and slung it at Ethan who buried himself farther under the covers.

Fifteen minutes later the triplets raced into the school parking lot, and Jennifer breathed a sigh of relief. Brant ran toward Jennifer as Christian and Ethan dragged behind.

Jennifer kissed Brant's lips. "Get up there, Cowboy," she smiled as Brant hurried up onto the makeshift platform where Tommy was busy entertaining the masses. The crowd applauded.

Jennifer laughed at Ethan's wrinkled clothes as he took her hand. "What are you doing?" she grinned as Ethan inspected her pinkie finger.

"Just looking for Brant wrapped around your little finger," he said sleepily.

Jennifer leaned her head over on Ethan's arm. "I am so tired," she grinned, "I have been going out of my mind all week getting ready for this."

"Poor baby," Ethan mocked as he wrapped her in his arms.

"It's all okay now, Jen," Christian said smiling. "Primetime has arrived to provide crowd control… look at this… they love him…"

The three of them looked at each other and laughed. Jennifer grinned, "I think he's just campaigning for Homecoming King! What do you guys think?"

"I'd say it's in the bag," Christian nodded.

Ethan nudged Jennifer with his elbow. "And I wonder who will be crowned queen at week's end?"

Jennifer rolled her eyes. "We'll see!"

***

Tuesday of that week was designated as costume day. Everyone was supposed to wear a silly costume to show school spirit; costumes would be voted on, and the best costume would win a prize from the cheerleaders.

Tuesday morning Brant walked out of the upstairs bathroom to find Ethan decked out in Superman attire. He examined the bulging, blue, padded muscles and the red and yellow insignia. "It's a bird, it's a plane... no, it's Ethan in tights," he smiled.

Ethan rolled his eyes.

"Well, at least he's in the spirit," Christian added. "Jen worked hard on this. The least you could do is wear a costume."

"I'm sorry, Ms. Lane, did I ask your opinion?" Brant chuckled.

Christian and Ethan glanced at each other. "Get him!" they said in sync.

Brant grinned. "Oh, you guys wouldn't!"

"Oh, we would," Ethan nodded as Brant took off down the hall.

He slung my bedroom door open screaming, "quick, Jordan, get the kryptonite!"

I looked at his pursuers and laughed as they tackled Brant onto my bed.

Christian punched Brant in the chest as Brant clutched a chunk of Ethan's hair, screaming, "whatcha gonna do about it, huh, Superman?"

As the boys wrestled, Jennifer, dressed in a beautiful gown and a rhinestone tiara, peeked her head inside the door. "Hey... your dad let me in," she smiled at me. "What's going on in here?"

"Help me, Rocky!" Brant hollered as he laughed from the bottom of the pile.

"Come-on, guys," Jennifer said over the noise. "Let him go... we'll be late, Brantley."

"We won't be late," Brant said as the boys quit their tussling. "I'm ready to go."

"No..." Jennifer smiled, "you're not ready. You promised you'd be my Prince Charming." She held up Brant's costume.

"And I am," Brant said kissing Jennifer's cheek, "but I ain't wearing that."

"Go put it on," Jennifer urged. "We have to go."

"You look beautiful, Jen," Brant smiled. "Take a twirl for me."

"Give it up… I'm not changing my mind, Brant," Jennifer shook her head.

"Jen… do I gotta?" Brant whined.

"Yeah," Jennifer nodded as she poked her lip out at him, "you gotta."

Brant jerked the costume from her. "I'll be back," he grumbled as he walked toward his room.

"It'll be cute," Jennifer called after him.

"Precious… I'm sure!" Brant scoffed.

"The baby blue will bring out your eyes," Ethan called.

We all laughed.

"Jennifer, let's go," Brant called moments later.

"Come in here. We want to see what you look like, Prince Charming," Christian laughed.

"Shove it, Lois," Brant huffed.

Jennifer patted Christian's arm. "He thinks that if he whines enough I'll let him take it off before we get there."

Christian rubbed his hands together. "Oh, whatever you do… please make him keep it on long enough for me to find a camera and get a picture for the yearbook."

"He'll kill you," Jennifer nodded, "so… sure… it's a deal."

Christian smiled, then his smile faded into a look of recognition. "Hey!" he exclaimed.

Jennifer stuck her tongue out at him as she hurried out to the hall, and we all heard her giggle.

"What is so funny?" Brant grumbled.

"Brant, Prince Charming doesn't wear his hat backwards!" Jennifer exclaimed as she chased Brant down the stairs.

"Careful, she'll be done turned you back into a frog," Ethan yelled as he and Christian high-fived.

"Come-on," Christian smiled, "I wouldn't miss this for the world."

***

That evening Mom was cooking supper when the gang piled in our front door, each trying to talk over the other. "Hey crew," she called with motherly enthusiasm.

Tommy sniffed the air. "I'm staying for supper," he announced.

"There is plenty for everyone," Mom smiled.

Brant opened the oven. "It's not quite ready yet," Mom shook her head as she shooed him away. "If you're hungry there are chips and snack cakes in the pantry… offer some to everybody."

As Brant disappeared into the pantry, the kids gathered around the counter and immediately began disclosing their secrets to winning the big talent show on Wednesday.

"It's got to be something upbeat," Ethan said, "something fun and energetic."

"I say we just pick something that Brant can wail on," Tommy added. "They love to hear him sing. Let's use that to our advantage."

"*Surfin' USA*," Jennifer smiled. "He's so cute doing that one."

"Yeah," Mom agreed, "that would be cute… I like the part about the blond hair… it's perfect."

"No… I got it," Christian said victoriously. "There are five of us, right?"

"I like where you're going with this," Brant nodded as he returned with a can of Pringles in hand and half a Fudge Round hanging from his mouth.

Brant and Christian high-fived.

"What are they talking about?" Ethan shrugged.

Tommy shrugged. "I don't know? Aren't triplets supposed to have that sort of *reading each other's mind* thing happening… know each other's thoughts… finish each other's sentences?"

Ethan shook his head, "maybe some triplets… not so much with us though… no…"

"We're dressing up," Christian announced, "like the Jackson 5."

"No," Brant shook his head. "I'm the one that's got to sing, so that makes me Michael, and that just ain't happening … though my moonwalking is pretty stellar."

"So let's just think of another boy band," Christian suggested.

"I know who I want to spoof!" Jennifer exclaimed.

Brant nodded knowingly. "I'm only doing it if I get to be *Justin*," he blurted playfully.

"Then I'm the dude with the funky braids," Christian added. "What's his name?"

"Chris," Jennifer replied.

"What?" Christian shrugged.

"No," Jennifer laughed, "*Chris*... that's his name."

"Oh... perfect," Christian smiled.

"We're gonna win!" Jennifer celebrated as she hugged Christian.

"Now you're really losing me," Ethan groaned. "First off... who the heck is *Chris*? Who's *Justin*?" Ethan asked as he threw his hands in the air. "I've never heard of these people... is this New Kids on the Block?"

"Jen says Justin is... what were your words, Jen... *a total hottie*?" Brant picked as he raised his eyebrow at Jennifer.

"That's correct," Jennifer smiled, "or I might have said *total, total hottie*."

"Ouch," Brant exhaled as he brought his hand to his chest. He puckered his lips, and Jennifer kissed him.

"Somebody!" Ethan demanded. "Who is this guy?"

"The white boy with the Afro that Jennifer's in love with," Tommy replied.

"Afro?" Ethan shrugged. "I thought Brant nixed the Jackson 5."

"Hey, you... *the smart one*... get on the same page as everyone else," Brant scoffed, "we're not talking about the Jackson 5, we're talking about Justin Timberlake from 'NSYNC."

Ethan stared at Brant. "Thank you... now that wasn't so hard... was it?" he shrugged. "I remember now," he nodded, "yeah... Jen's been in love with him for years."

"She is not *in love* with him," Brant smiled as he shoved Ethan playfully.

"Oh, I don't know, Brantley," Jennifer mused as she leaned against the counter. She brought her finger to her mouth as stars filled her eyes. "If he showed up on my doorstep..."

"Yeah... yeah," Brant rolled his eyes.

"What... you don't believe me?" Jennifer grinned as she winked at Mom.

"Well," Brant shrugged, "that's alright... 'cause I got news for you, baby... Britney Spears shows up at my doorstep in that little school girl's uniform, and you're out of luck yourself."

"Ooooh!" the boys all cheered as they shared high-fives all around.

Jennifer laughed. "I'm *really* worried," she grinned.

"Me too," Brant nodded. He threw his arm around Jennifer's shoulders as he burst into the chorus of a popular 'NSYNC song.

"Come-on," Jennifer smiled. "You boys are about to take the Jennifer Smith crash course on 'NSYNC choreography."

"Just move the coffee table," Mom chuckled. "This I have to see."

The next day Mom and I couldn't help ourselves. We both took our lunch breaks at eleven o'clock, so that we could see the gang win first prize at the North River Homecoming Talent Show. They had their moves down just right, and Jennifer had dressed them all according to character. They won easily and entertained the judges and the crowd way beyond the call of duty.

Dad stood shaking his head as Brant captivated his audience. "My quarterback is a pretty boy," he sighed. Mom and I cackled as we examined the utterly horrified look on his face.

As Brant sang and danced, he enticed the girls in the front row, and the female audience shrilled. There were also plenty of catcalls coming from his teammates, which had me rolling. Brant was shameless as he worked the song.

"Oh thank God that no major media outlets got wind of this," Dad blurted as he turned and walked away. "He's killin' me!"

***

Every year on game day of homecoming week, North River Elementary, which is located right next door to North River High School, gets to have football players and cheerleaders come to all the classrooms to answer questions and encourage the kids to come out to the game.

On Friday morning Brant and Jennifer walked into Mrs. Harper's second grade classroom to the delight of Ben and his fellow classmates. Ben ran to Brant. "Benji!" Brant exclaimed as he lifted Ben into the air.

As all the kids gathered around Brant, tugging at him, hugging him, and all talking to him at once, he handled it with humility and class.

"How many touchdowns are you gonna make tonight?" one little boy asked as he tugged excitedly at Brant's jersey.

"How many would *you* like me to score?" Brant smiled back.

"How many is the most you *can* make?" one little girl asked in awe.

"Duh, he can make as many as he wants," Ben shrugged, rolling his eyes at the little girl's silly inquiry. "Why do you think he's gonna play for the Cowboys?"

Jennifer smiled as Brant laughed at Ben's pronouncement. He ruffled Ben's hair, lifted him into his arms and smiled as Ben stared down at his envious classmates.

After leaving the second graders and making his way back to the high school, Brant ran into Tommy in the hall. "You will not believe this," Tommy huffed. "I had some snot-nosed kindergartner boohoo because *you* didn't get to come to his classroom. *Where's Brant? This isn't fair. Where's Brant?*"

"Who was it?" Brant smiled, obviously pleased.

"Hunter Haines," Tommy snarled. "I said 'listen here… Brant couldn't do much with the football if I didn't snap it to him. You see, I'm the man behind *the man.* I'm the key to the whole operation. I'm the real star!'" Tommy recalled. He frowned, "then he kicked me in the shin… darn kid."

Brant laughed. He glanced down at his watch. "Tell Dad I'll be at the team meeting in a minute."

Tommy walked into the gym where Dad had called a special team meeting and hurried to take his seat. "Everybody here?" Dad asked as he scanned the team, all sitting in the gym bleachers. "I don't hear Brant anywhere." Again, he scanned the group.

"The Brant McLachlan Fan Club called," Tommy said sarcastically.

"Me and T.J. had a class actually start chanting, '*We want Brant! We want Brant*!'" someone mimicked.

T.J. Haines laughed. "Made us feel really good, you know?"

Tommy looked back at T.J. and his older brother Nathan. "Your bratty, little brother *cried*," he chuckled.

"No way!" T.J. laughed as he shook his head. "But, it figures… he thinks Brant is Brett Favre or something."

"Some fifth grade girl asked me if I have ever seen Brant without his shirt on," Nathan smiled.

"What did you say to that, Nate?" Dad chuckled.

Nathan raised his eyebrow. "I said, 'Yeah, girlfriend, he looks good!'" Nathan said in a voice that made everyone explode in laughter. "I mean, come-on, it's not like everyone didn't see Brant without a shirt on the cover of that magazine. I know I have it hanging on my bedroom wall," he joked.

"It's hangin' on mine," Christian rolled his eyes.

"I don't think we'll wait for Brant," Dad smiled. "Let's get this meeting going. I'll fill our quarterback in when he isn't too busy shaking hands and kissing babies."

After the team meeting came the pep rally. Before the actual pep rally began, Brant had to put on a tuxedo for an assembly, so that he could escort Jennifer, who had been voted by her classmates to represent their class as one of the three, senior homecoming maids, one of which would be crowned queen at that night's game.

That night the fans came out to the game in droves. While the defense was on the field, Brant danced playfully with the cheerleaders while Jennifer watched in her beautiful, emerald green gown.

There were a lot of my old friends at the game. I was excited to get to see so many people from my graduating class that had moved away after we graduated.

Those who had not been back in years could not believe how much my then *baby* brothers had grown up.

A guy named Sean Kirk was North River's quarterback my senior year. He had gone to Auburn University and gotten married right after he graduated college. It was the first time that he had been back to Cummins since his senior year at Auburn when he came back often to antagonize Dad about his having gone to Auburn rather than Dad's beloved University of Alabama. Sean had two little girls, and both seemed to be enjoying the game. One was three and the other, her hair in braided pigtails, was five. Watching Brant play was a big thrill for Sean because when Brant was younger he had watched Sean religiously every afternoon at practice. I stood by the fence talking to my former quarterback as he shook his head in disbelief. "The last time that I saw Brantley," he said, pointing at his oldest daughter, "he was a little older than her." He laughed. "Look at him now."

All of a sudden, I heard a familiar voice in the distance. The crowd was loud, but his voice rose above the roar as I heard him holler, "whatcha say, Hollywood?" I looked down the fence and I saw Brant shaking hands with a guy I hadn't seen in years.

"Carter?" I muttered to myself as I stared at my best buddy.

Carter Jenkins had always enjoyed teaching Brant to act like the superstar that he was sure that Brant would become, and he hadn't been able to resist coming back home to catch a glimpse of McLachlan mania for himself.

Brant pointed toward me as I stood staring. I made my way down the fence, and Carter and I shook hands.

"Long time, no see," he said after a moment.

"Way too long," I replied. "Where have you been?"

"Here and there," Carter smiled. "I just had to come see if my little pal was half as good as I hear that he is."

"He is," I nodded.

"I don't doubt it," Carter grinned.

"He's all grown up," I added, a little hurt that Carter had missed the years in between.

We watched Brant as he wandered down the fence line.

"Wow! Who's his main squeeze?" Carter asked when Brant leaned across the fence to steal a quick kiss from Jennifer.

"You wouldn't believe me if I told you," I shook my head.

Carter stared harder. "That's not... oh my gosh... that's little Jenny?"

"Some things never change," I shrugged.

As Carter and I stood watching the game, old times came flooding back to us. Our senior year, Carter and I regrettably, at least on my part, enjoyed teaching my mischievous, little brother how to be a kindergarten teacher's worst nightmare. He was five growing on eighteen, and we thought that he was ours to raise. He was tough as nails, and we loved that about him.

As we watched him play, we couldn't believe that the little boy who we had taught to be tough beyond his years had turned out to be the phenomenon that we somehow always knew he would.

Mom and Dad both worked and that made life with triplets hard. Carter and I took Brant everywhere with us that year. He was our little buddy, our favorite toy, and we would have done anything for him. We were parental figures without parental authority or responsibility, and it was fun.

Even as a five-year-old, I taught Brant to be his own person and to never be afraid to dream big. Carter taught him how to spike a football, how to drive a car, hence the ferocious speeding habits, and how to kiss the way that the girls liked it, though I don't know what made Carter think he was the expert in that area by any means.

As a young kid, and even more so as a teenager, Carter was always getting in trouble. He didn't have a solid family life like I had growing up, but we were always pals. I didn't think that Carter would ever change, but I loved the guy anyway.

Our senior year, Carter fell in love with my five-year-old little brother, and, in one year, Brant unknowingly changed my best friend into the man that I always knew he could be. I always trusted Carter with Brant, but I begged him to remember that my brother was only five years old, despite the fact that he hung around eighteen-year-olds all the time. I always reminded him that little, impressionable eyes were watching him, and little ears were listening to and, often, little lips repeating, every word that he said. The day that Brant got in trouble for a word that he said on the playground, Dad knew just where to go to find out where he heard it.

"It's not a bad word," Brant insisted innocently, "Carter says it all the time." Carter felt awful, and, though it took him a while to find replacement words for all his favorites, I can't ever remember hearing him curse again, at least not around my brothers anyway.

It may sound too good to be true, but the day that Brant put a cigarette between his fingers and mimicked taking a puff, Carter gave up smoking. By the time we graduated, Carter was a different person.

He got hurt playing football in the last game of our senior year, and it destroyed his college plans. We went off to Southern Mississippi together. I went to get an education and to play football; he went to get away.

Sophomore year Carter got a decent job driving trucks for some company based near campus. Eventually, he quit school, and I got used to him being around very little. By the time I graduated with a degree in journalism, Carter had stopped coming around at all.

Standing there on the sideline watching Brant play, Carter and I saw the same little boy that had won our hearts so many years before, and it was as if Carter had never been gone.

"You're right," Carter mused. He smiled broadly as he glanced around at his hometown, his eyes fixing on the huddle of former players that had been a permanent fixture on the thirty yard line every Friday night for decades. "Some things never change."

At halftime the homecoming court was announced, and Dad allowed the team to stand on the sideline and watch the girls be escorted onto the field by their fathers. Each year the tradition was for the senior football players to vote on which of the three senior maids should be crowned queen, and, though she most likely would have won anyway, Brant's influence over his teammates resulted in Jennifer being crowned queen by a unanimous vote. The gang all hollered, cheered, whistled and made a big scene for her when her name was announced. Her mom and mine came out on the field with cameras, and the boys gathered around her in their sweaty football uniforms for pictures.

***

It was late when Brant and Jennifer left the school that Friday night. Brant navigated Jennifer's black Chevy Tahoe down a path in the woods on the outskirts of town.

"Brant," Jennifer smiled, "where are we going?"

"We've been here before... several times," Brant replied.

"Not at night," Jennifer grinned as she stared out the window.

"Listen," Brant whispered as he punched off the radio.

Jennifer strained her ears. "I don't hear anything," she gulped.

"Exactly," Brant smiled, "it's the only place I could think of to come where I could have you all to myself." He stopped the car and turned off the engine. He turned to Jennifer. "You looked really pretty tonight," he said as he took her hand.

"Are you flirting with me?" Jennifer smiled back.

"Maybe," Brant shrugged as he leaned in for a kiss.

Jennifer leaned in so that her lips met his.

Brant ran his hands up Jennifer's back as Jennifer did the same to him. Jennifer ran her fingers through Brant's hair as he kissed her neck.

Jennifer lifted Brant's chin. "I love you," she said, leaning in to kiss his lips.

After another round of passionate kissing, Jennifer pulled Brant's shirt over his head and placed her hands on his strong chest. "I can feel your heart beating," she gulped.

"My heart beats this way every time I'm with you," Brant whispered. "You have no idea what you do to me."

"Kiss me," Jennifer said softly.

"I love you, Jennifer," Brant replied as he maneuvered himself into the passenger's seat. Straddling Jennifer, he moved his lips from her earlobes down her neck and then to her chest. As he kissed her, he reached down and pulled the lever that reclined the seat, making Jennifer squeal with excitement as she fell back, and Brant's body fell gently on top of hers.

Jennifer wrapped her arms around Brant as his kisses moved down her neck toward her chest. He unbuttoned the top button of Jennifer's shirt and kissed her again; he quickly moved to the second button.

"Brant, stop," Jennifer sighed, as she reached for his hands.

"You don't want me to stop," Brant whispered. He moved back to Jennifer's lips, and they kissed passionately.

"Brant," Jennifer sighed as she turned her face away, "we've gotta stop this."

"We will," Brant nodded. He kissed Jennifer's bare shoulder. "We're just kissing."

"No… we've gotta stop this now," Jennifer insisted.

Brant nodded as he continued to kiss Jennifer's neck. "We'll stop, Jen… just…"

"No!" Jennifer pushed on Brant's shoulder.

"You really want me to stop?" Brant sighed.

"No," Jennifer shook her head. She was nearly in tears. "No, I don't want you to stop. Why did you have to bring me out here? Do you have any idea how difficult it is for me to tell you *no*?"

"Then don't," Brant shrugged as he took Jennifer's hand in his. "Jen, I love you. I always have, and I always will."

"I love you too," Jennifer shook her head.

"Jen, listen," Brant gulped.

"No," Jennifer said boldly. "Brant, put your shirt on, okay?"

"Fine," Brant groaned as he moved back to the driver's side. "I'm not the one who took it off in the first place; that was all you."

"Brant, this is why we broke up in the first place," Jennifer said as she adjusted her seat and quickly buttoned her shirt.

"Which was stupid, by the way," Brant nodded, "because as you see, whether we are *calling* ourselves a *couple* or not doesn't change the way we feel about each other."

"Brant, we just need to go home," Jennifer sighed. "When we're alone like this, you know things start moving too fast."

"Oh yeah, you're right," Brant rolled his eyes as he slumped down on the wheel, "things are moving way too fast. I mean… we've only been together… what… eighteen years now?"

"Brant," Jennifer huffed.

"Jen, we are in a committed relationship," Brant sighed. "I am one hundred percent devoted to you."

"I know that, Brant," Jennifer nodded. "I feel the same way about you. I love you. I've always loved you. I know that you are the one… the only one, but I have always been raised, and you have too if you would stop long enough to think about it, to know that being in a committed relationship with someone is not reason enough to have sex with them. Marriage is sacred, and on my wedding night I want to be able to…"

"Well, then marry me already," Brant snapped.

"Well, wasn't that a romantic proposal," Jennifer gulped as she crossed her arms.

Brant crossed his in response.

"I can't believe you just said that," Jennifer said coldly.

Brant frowned. "I didn't mean it that way, Jen. Come-on now, don't get upset… I'm sorry…"

"You should be," Jennifer nodded. "I'm trying to do us both a big favor… and all you can do is make fun of me?"

"No," Brant said matter-of-factly, "no, Jen… I'm not making fun of you. I would never make fun of you for anything. I love you and *respect* you; you're right; I'm wrong, and I'm sorry."

"It's okay," Jennifer frowned.

Brant reached for Jennifer's hand. "I'm sorry… that was insensitive and uncalled for." He paused and there was a long silence before he offered, "Jen… I wasn't serious before… and one day I am gonna propose to you for real… down on one knee… and all that good stuff, but why don't we get married? What's stopping us? And before you say anything… this isn't about me wanting to have sex with you… it's about me loving you and wanting to spend the rest of my life loving you."

"We can't get married, Brant," Jennifer shook her head.

"Why not?" Brant replied.

"Brant," Jennifer insisted, "right now we don't even know what the immediate future holds. We aren't even sure where I'll go to college. We're eighteen… neither of us has a job…"

"Jennifer, I'm gonna be making plenty of money to take care of us. Do you have any idea how much money they paid me just to take my shirt off for the cover of that magazine? And that was nothing, pocket change, pennies compared to what I will be making… there will be more magazines and endorsement deals… not to mention the signing bonus we're looking at when I sign my contract."

"Brant, I'm sorry," Jennifer shook her head, "I know it must seem like you've been waiting forever."

"Jen… it's not that," Brant smiled. "I believe that we should wait too. It's not that I don't respect the decision that you've made… that *we've* made. It's just that I'm a guy… and, Rocky, I don't know if I've ever told you this… but I find you *incredibly* hard to resist."

"I promise you," Jennifer said softly, "our wedding night will be worth the wait. I'll make it all up to you."

"It's really important to you to wait… isn't it?" Brant smiled back.

"Yes," Jennifer nodded, "I think that every girl should wait until her wedding night to have sex. Trust me, I know that a lot of girls would tell me I'm crazy or a prude or whatever, but on our wedding night I want to be able to give you a gift like no other."

Brant touched Jennifer's face. "How did I get so lucky?" he whispered.

"We're both lucky," Jennifer gulped. "There are a lot of girls that don't think they can talk to their boyfriends the way that I feel comfortable talking to you. It's good that we can talk about these things. It's what makes our relationship so solid and so special."

"I've got an idea," Brant said, turning the key so that the headlights came on. He turned on the radio as he opened the car door. "Let's go for a little walk… cool off and forget about some of the stupid things I said tonight."

Jennifer opened the passenger's side door. "You know what I think our problem is?" she called across the hood of the car.

"I didn't know we had one," Brant replied as he rolled his window down, so that the lyrics of a Garth Brooks' love song filled the night. As they met at the front of the car, Brant took Jennifer's hand. "I've never danced with the homecoming queen before," he grinned.

"Well, it looks like tonight's your lucky night after all," Jennifer smiled as she rested her head against Brant's chest, and they swayed back and forth in each other's arms.

"Brant," Jennifer asked after a moment, "do you ever feel like we got gypped?"

"What do you mean?" Brant chuckled as he raised a curious eyebrow.

"Well," Jennifer sighed, "it seems like everyone else I know had or will have that one moment… that special moment when they got to fall in love. We never really had that moment… we always just sorta *were*…"

"No," Brant shook his head, "I don't feel like we got gypped. Do you know why?"

"Why?" Jennifer asked as she looked up at him.

"Because," Brant said as he looked down at Jennifer, his eyes fixing on hers, "I've had eighteen years to fall in love with you a little more every single day… and that makes me the luckiest guy in the world."

"Brant, that is the sweetest thing I think you've ever said to me," Jennifer gulped, and her eyes filled with tears.

"Why are you crying?" Brant sighed, and he couldn't help but smile.

"Because I'm happy," Jennifer nodded. "Because you're right… we are so lucky."

"Yeah," Brant smiled as he pulled Jennifer close and held her tightly, "we may not have that one moment that we can recall as the second it all happened, but we have so many moments that very few people will ever get to have. I've spent a lifetime loving you, Jennifer."

"Isn't it strange when you think about it?" Jennifer mused. "I never wondered who would take me to my prom… I never had to imagine what the man I was going to marry looked like or what he would like to do for fun."

"Well, we've always been a little strange… you and me," Brant grinned.

"You're right," Jennifer agreed. "We're really *not* normal, are we?"

"Being normal is overrated," Brant shrugged. "Take my brothers for instance… they're dating different girls every other weekend. That just doesn't sound like any fun to me."

"I don't know," Jennifer smiled. "The mystery... the nervousness of the first date... will he call, won't he call... the anticipation, finding the right outfit, getting to know someone... it's all part of dating..."

"How would you know?" Brant laughed.

"I've heard," Jennifer rolled her eyes.

"*I've got it,*" Brant said evenly, as he raised his arms.

"What?" Jennifer laughed, unsure what epiphany Brant had come to.

"Our moment," Brant nodded.

"You remember the moment you fell in love with me?" Jennifer smiled, and excitement filled her face.

"Yes," Brant nodded. He smiled. "We were two years old, and you were running around on those short, flabby, little legs I loved so much..."

"Brant!" Jennifer exclaimed as she slapped his arm.

"Hey, I'm not complaining," Brant laughed as he held his hands up. "Kudos on how the legs turned out, by the way."

Jennifer smiled, and Brant's expression turned serious again. "You were running, and you tripped and fell down," he recalled. "You cried, and that absolutely broke my heart... that's when I knew."

A tear ran down Jennifer's face.

"Oh, come-on," Brant whispered, "I didn't mean to make you cry."

Jennifer spoke through her tears. "I remember sitting in my playhouse that my daddy built for me," she smiled. "We were six years old. I talked about my dreams; you talked about yours. We talked about getting married and about how many kids we wanted to have."

"And you know what's even stranger than two first graders planning the next twenty years of their lives?" Brant nodded.

"The fact that they've stuck to the plan," Jennifer smiled back. She turned to stare up at the moon.

Brant wrapped his arms around her shoulders, and she rested the back of her head against his chest as she stared up at the sky.

Thunder rumbled in the distance. "Sounds like it might rain," Brant said.

Jennifer didn't seem to hear him as she stared at the cloudy, sparsely lit, night sky.

"What are you thinking?" Brant asked as he kissed the side of her cheek.

"I'm wishing on that star," Jennifer smiled as she pointed skyward.

"What are you wishing for?" Brant asked.

"If I tell you… it might not come true," Jennifer grinned as she shook her head.

"I wished that you and I could stay as happy as we are right now… forever," Brant said softly.

Jennifer turned to face Brant. "So did I," she smiled.

Brant kissed Jennifer's forehead, and his eyes moved upward. "It looks like the weather could get bad out here," he nodded.

Suddenly, thunder clapped, and rain began to fall.

Jennifer screamed as she scurried back to the car. Brant stood for a moment in the storm watching her as she ran and laughing out loud as she rushed to roll her driver's side window up, all the while screaming for him to have the sense to get in out of the rain.

CHAPTER EIGHT

On Monday morning, Brant was sitting in history class shooting rubber bands at Tommy and dodging the ones that Tommy was firing back when Mr. Roberts walked into the classroom with an announcement. "Class," he said, clapping his hands together to get everyone's attention, "as some of you may have learned during your first period class... we have a new student joining us here at North River. Her name is Brianna Clarke, and I know that it isn't often that we get new students, so I want each of you to make sure Brianna feels welcome here in Cummins."

"Where's she from?" someone asked.

"Texas," came a voice from the doorway.

The class turned at once to see an extraordinarily beautiful girl in a tight, short, black, mini skirt smiling back at them. She was wearing knee high boots, and her white blouse was low-cut and very revealing on her voluptuous figure.

"Wow," Brant whispered.

"No kidding," Christian sighed.

"I didn't believe in love at first sight until she walked in this room," Tommy added, his eyes fixed on the mysterious stranger.

"How come girls from Cummins don't look like that?" Christian gulped.

Brant scanned the room. "Christian, move up a seat," he laughed with a little shove, "and close your mouth. You look like a moron, and I'm not about to claim to be related to you!"

"Well," Mr. Roberts pointed, "Brianna, it suddenly seems that the only empty desk in the room is right there between the McLachlan boys." His eyes moved to Brant and Christian. "Imagine that," he snickered.

"Hi," Christian said as he extended his hand to Brianna, "my name's Christian McLachlan."

"Hi, Christian," Brianna said as she leaned down and kissed Christian's cheek, "nice to meet you." Christian swallowed hard as he looked away to keep from staring straight down her shirt.

"You okay, Chris?" Brianna asked.

"Fine," Christian nodded, silently reprimanding himself for being such a gentleman.

"I can call you *Chris*... you don't mind, right?" Brianna inquired.

"You can call me anything you want," Christian gulped.

"Oh, brother," Brant groaned.

Brianna winked at Brant as she took her seat, her skirt creeping up a good two inches as she crossed her legs underneath her desk.

"I'm Brant," Brant smiled back, "and you can call me... well... Brant."

"And you're even cuter in person, *Brant*," Brianna quipped.

"What?" Brant laughed.

"You're famous... didn't you know that?" Brianna said as she opened the cover of her binder to reveal Brant's magazine cover.

Brant shook his head. "Oh, that. Well, I'm *not* famous... *not yet*."

"*Not yet*," Tommy mocked, hoping Brianna would request an introduction.

"So, Brianna," Brant shrugged, "what part of Texas are you from?"

"I got about a million questions floatin' around in my head right now, and that's the best you can come up with?" Tommy grumbled.

"Married life'll do that to you, Tom," Christian nodded.

"Married life?" Brianna inquired.

"Oh yeah... lover boy there is taken," Tommy nodded confidently. "I, however, happen to be very much available at the moment. Tommy Jackson... nice to meet you." When Brianna failed to greet him with the same kiss she had offered Christian, Tommy frowned.

"Coincidentally... my calendar seems to be free as well," Christian added.

"Why did they say you were married?" Brianna asked Brant. "You aren't married, are you? You aren't wearing a ring."

"Listen, *sweetheart*," Tommy groaned, "he'll be sure to send you an invitation to the golden anniversary party. What do you say to dinner and a movie?"

"No," Brant rolled his eyes, "I'm not married. They're just joking around." He nodded toward Tommy, "he, however, is every bit as desperate as he seems."

"Funny too," Brianna smiled. "They told me you were the total package."

"I thought *I* was pretty funny," Tommy sighed. "Where did I miss? Was it my timing? My delivery? The material was good..."

Christian reached over and patted Tommy's back.

"I was funny... right, Chris?" Tommy nodded.

"You were funny," Christian shrugged.

"She's not listening to me is she?" Tommy shook his head.

"Nope," Christian replied quickly.

"She's talking to Brant isn't she?" Tommy nodded.

"Afraid so," Christian groaned.

"At least you got a kiss on the cheek," Tommy grumbled, "I got nothin'."

Christian shook his head. "She *used* me... she *used* me to get to my brother. If I had it to do over again, I would *so* look down her blouse."

"I'd settle for being used," Tommy sighed. His face contorted. "You really didn't look?"

"I think I gave myself whiplash I turned away so fast," Christian said as he rubbed his neck.

"I don't know that we can even be friends any more," Tommy frowned.

"It's understandable," Christian shrugged.

"Do you think they're real?" Tommy asked as he tilted his head to get a better view.

Brianna turned her head. "What are you looking at?" she asked.

"I like your shirt," Tommy gulped.

Brianna leaned toward Tommy. "They're real," she whispered.

"Good to know," Tommy nodded.

Mr. Roberts called the class to order, and Tommy sat up straight in his desk.

"I hate the first day at a new school. I can never find any of my classes," Brianna whispered over her shoulder as Mr. Roberts began his lecture.

"Let me see your schedule," Brant replied.

Brianna's face radiated as she placed the small piece of paper in Brant's hand, making sure that her hand brushed his.

"You can just follow me," Brant smiled, "we have the same schedule."

"That's great," Brianna said happily. "Are you sure that your girlfriend won't mind me tagging along?"

"No," Brant shook his head. "She… well… actually… you know what… *technically* I guess I don't have a girlfriend."

Tommy gasped, and, as a result, began coughing wildly.

"What is the problem, Mr. Jackson?" Mr. Roberts asked as he looked up from his podium.

"I'm sorry… I'm sorry… nothing… nothing, sir," Tommy coughed as he waved his hand. "Sorry to interrupt. Go ahead with whatever y'all were talking about."

"Do you even know what we're discussing?" Mr. Roberts inquired as he removed his glasses. "Open your text book, Tommy. We're on page 113, and we're talking about the Battle of Bull Run…"

"Oh, well that's appropriate," Tommy nodded. "*Bull* seems to be the order of the day, and I'm afraid that, in more than the one instance, it could end in an ugly battle."

"As usual, I have no idea what you're talking about," Mr. Roberts sighed.

Christian snickered, and Brant shot a rubber band at him.

"Ouch!" Christian yelped as it nicked his ear.

"That's it," Mr. Roberts conceded as he tossed his hands up, "I'm done… do whatever you want for the remainder of the class… just stay in your seats and keep the noise down… and whatever you do… please… none of you speak to me. I need a moment to contemplate early retirement."

Brianna ran her fingers along Brant's arm. "How often do you work out?" she asked.

"Brianna," Brant grimaced, "there is something that I think I need to make clear to you."

"Uh-huh," Christian whispered.

"Okay," Brianna smiled widely, "what is it?"

"I'm very much in love with someone… so you're wasting your time flirting with me," Brant shrugged.

"Oh you think so, huh?" Brianna smiled.

"I know so," Brant said as he removed Brianna's hand from his arm.

"Well," Brianna frowned, "you sure know how to make a girl feel mighty uncomfortable."

"I'm sorry," Brant shook his head. "I didn't mean to make you feel uncomfortable. It's just that you made me a little uncomfortable... you were coming on a little strong..."

"Would it make you uncomfortable if I told you that I knew the second I saw your picture on the cover of that magazine that I had to meet you?" Brianna interrupted. "I won't beat around the bush, Brant... that's not my style. I envy the lucky Mississippi gal... whoever she is..."

Brant swallowed. "Jennifer... her name's Jennifer."

"*Jennifer*," Brianna nodded. "Well, I hope Jennifer knows how lucky she is." Brianna gently touched Brant's face. "That smile." She moved her hand down Brant's chest. "Those muscles." She winked at him. "And abs to die for."

Brant smiled. He loved flattery, and Brianna was full of it.

"You just don't quit, do you?" Brant grinned.

"I've been known to be pretty persistent," Brianna agreed.

"Abs to die for, huh?" Brant smiled as he lifted his shirttail to tease Brianna.

"Will you flex and let me feel?" Brianna asked, gently biting her bottom lip, so that Brant stared at her mouth for a long moment before pulling his eyes away.

Brant took Brianna's hand and poked his abs with her fingertips.

"Mr. McLachlan!" Mr. Roberts laughed, as he glanced up from his desk. "I don't know what you call yourself doing, but STOP IT... right now!"

"I'm just trying to make our new student feel welcome, sir," Brant grinned innocently.

"Really?" Mr. Roberts pondered as the class laughed. "Well, Miss Clarke, I apologize. I should have shown you my six pack when we met... I didn't realize that is the way you young people introduce yourselves these days," he rolled his eyes.

Brant leaned back in his chair.

"So," Brianna smiled, "how much money do you think you'll make playing professional football?"

"A lot," Brant grinned.

"How much?" Brianna inquired.

"Why are you so interested?" Brant smiled.

"Oh, I don't know," Brianna shrugged. "I'm a woman… and women like guys with cash… the more the better."

Brant scoffed. "That sounds pretty… I don't know…"

"Shallow," Brianna rolled her eyes.

"I wasn't going to say that," Brant shook his head.

"It's okay, you just don't know what it's like to be poor," Brianna sighed. "Ever since my mom split with her last husband, she and I have had close to nothing."

"So, may I ask how you ended up here?" Brant asked curiously. "I mean Cummins, Mississippi, isn't exactly on the map."

"And perhaps it wasn't the best choice," Brianna shrugged.

"You don't like it here?" Brant replied.

"I don't know yet… I like you," Brianna smiled.

"There you go," Brant shrugged, "so just stick with me and my friends, and we'll make sure you feel right at home."

Brianna nodded. "I was hoping you would say that."

***

When the bell rang for lunch, Brant led Brianna to the cafeteria. He stopped by his truck and took out a family-size bag of Doritos. "My friends and I like to have *community lunch*," he explained. "We take turns bringing different things, so that someone who brings the main course today might only have to bring a bag of chips tomorrow."

"Brant," Christian called across the parking lot, "what kind of milkshakes do you and Brianna want?"

Brant looked at Brianna. "Chocolate, vanilla, strawberry or banana?" he smiled. "He's making a run."

"Strawberry," Brianna smiled, amused.

Christian jogged over. "Have you seen Jen?" he asked.

"She made a hamburger run," Brant replied. "Get chocolate for her, and I'll have the same."

"Make that three chocolate shakes," Brianna smiled.

"Can do… be back in a sec," Christian called mischievously as he hurried back to his truck.

Brianna followed Brant into the cafeteria. Brant tossed the bag of chips in the middle of the table as he pulled up an extra chair for Brianna.

"That's what I'm talkin' about!" Tommy exclaimed when Jennifer followed through the door close behind them with a bag of Whoppers.

"Did you get me extra mayo?" Brant inquired as Jennifer began passing out the burgers.

"Oh no… did you want mayonnaise on that?" Jennifer grinned as she handed him his burger.

"What?" Brant gasped.

Jennifer laughed. "Extra mayo… easy on the lettuce, hold the pickles… just like you like it."

"You're good," Brant nodded.

Jennifer's eyes moved to Brianna for the first time. "Hi," she said, sounding almost startled, as she smiled at Brianna, "I'm Jennifer… I'm sorry… who…"

"Brianna Clarke," Brianna replied almost shyly. "I just moved to town. Brant said I could tag along; I hope you don't mind."

"No," Jennifer smiled, "no… of course not… it's nice to meet you, Brianna."

"Today is Brianna's first day," Tommy said. "She moved here from *Dallas*."

"Oh," Jennifer smiled as she gathered her thoughts. "Well… Brant," she said in an almost motherly tone, "you should have called my cell phone and let me know to bring her a sandwich."

"That's okay," Brianna shook her head, "I packed a lunch. I wasn't sure what to expect on the first day."

Jennifer took her seat to Brant's right, and Brant put his arm around her and kissed her cheek.

"Chris is coming with milkshakes," Ethan said as he tore into a bag of Sprinkled Chips Ahoy cookies.

"He got busted last time he tried to leave campus," Jennifer snickered. "Whose idea was it to let him go after the shakes?" She opened the bag of Doritos. "Brianna... just help yourself to anything," she said, leaning across Brant.

"So Brianna," Tommy asked, his mouth full of chips, "do you play any sports?"

"Sports... *no*," Brianna shook her head. She smiled at Brant, "but I do like *watching* football."

"Jennifer's a cheerleader, *and* she's on the dance team," Brant said, nodding toward Jennifer. "She can catch a mean football too."

"She's pretty tough," Ethan added.

"Yeah," Brant grinned, "I'm telling you... Rocky could take Ethan in a fight, easy. Ain't that right, Rock?"

"Growing up playing tackle football in the back yard with four boys, you better learn to be pretty tough," Jennifer smiled, "but I'm like you Brianna... I like *watching* football too."

"What did you call her?" Brianna pondered as she stared curiously at Brant.

"Oh," Brant laughed. "*Rocky*... that's my nickname for her."

"Why?" Brianna blurted.

"It's a secret only she and I know," Brant said nonchalantly, and he shoved a cookie in his mouth.

"It's an old inside joke," Jennifer smiled. "You know how that goes!"

"Sure," Brianna shrugged, rolling her eyes, "so do you like being called *Rocky*?"

"Should I not?" Jennifer replied defensively, with a look that let Brianna know she didn't appreciate her tone and that Brant was only half joking when he suggested that she could take Ethan in a fight.

Tommy snickered, amused by Jennifer's feistiness.

Christian walked inside carrying an armload of drinks, and the tension was broken. "Milkshakes all around," he announced. He kissed the top of Jennifer's head. "Where's my food, sweets? I'm starving!"

Smiling, Jennifer reached into the Burger King bag and produced the only remaining burger. "Extra mayo, no tomato."

"Ooh... you're good," Christian nodded. "So Brianna," he asked as he sat down next to her, "I've been curious all day. How is it that you ended up in Cummins, Mississippi anyway?"

"My mom and I move around," Brianna explained. "I've lived in Dallas for the past two years. Before that, I lived out in California. My mother was married for about two months to some actor who never made it past being an extra in low budget movies. They divorced; we went to Dallas to live with my mom's friend. He was a jerk who always pestered Mom about paying rent, so we left, and now here I am… right out here in the middle of nowhere with you guys."

"Well," Christian said with a little grin, "we have a lot of fun out here in the middle of nowhere."

"It *will* be kind of nice to have a girl around for a change," Jennifer added. "I mean, I have a lot of girlfriends, but, basically, it's always just been me and *my* guys."

Brianna nodded. "Yeah, I can already see that you and I are going to have a lot in common."

"So where do you plan on going to college, Brianna?" Ethan asked.

"Back in Texas," Brianna said confidently. "I definitely want to be back in Dallas."

"Thinking about college is so scary… so, let's not do it," Tommy groaned.

"You aren't even going to college," Ethan chuckled.

"I know," Tommy replied seriously, "but y'all are all leaving me."

"We're going to graduate before we know it," Jennifer sighed.

"Isn't it going to be so weird all living in different states?" Christian said with a questioning glance. "Not seeing everyone every day?"

Everyone nodded.

"I don't want to graduate," Jennifer blurted. "Really, I mean it… this is all too sad!"

"We have had so many unforgettable times at this place," Ethan sighed.

"We can't stay in high school forever," Christian laughed.

"I wish that we could," Jennifer smiled. "I wish that things could stay just like they are right now, forever."

"Before you all start rehashing old memories," Brianna chirped, "I'm going to take a tour of this place." She snatched Brant's hand. "Show me around?" she asked in a flirtatious tone.

Brant turned to Jennifer.

"Y'all go ahead," Jennifer smiled. "I'm not done chowing down on these cookies."

Brant leaned down to kiss Jennifer, and she fed him a bite of her cookie instead.

As Brant and Brianna walked out of the cafeteria, the boys all stared.

"Excuse me!" Jennifer huffed. She waved her hand in front of the boys' faces, but they didn't seem to notice. "Oh great," she sighed, rolling her eyes.

"Have mercy," Tommy laughed as he, Christian and Ethan looked at each other in awe.

"Oh, she is not *that* pretty," Jennifer insisted.

"Oh, but she is," Tommy nodded.

"And, as usual," Christian shrugged, "she looked right past all of us and went straight for Blondie."

"He always gets the girl," Ethan agreed.

"He did not *get* the girl," Jennifer laughed.

"I don't think I've ever seen a chick like that in real life before," Tommy shook his head. "I thought bodies like that only existed in the movies."

"No," Jennifer rolled her eyes, "you can find surgically enhanced breasts almost anywhere."

"They're real," Tommy insisted.

"Really expensive, maybe," Jennifer fired back. "And," she added, "last time I checked we had a dress code around here. What pervert in the office approved that fashion statement?" She stared at the boys. "Besides, her body isn't *that* great." She glanced at the cookie in her hand, then, with a curl of her lip, tossed it on the table.

"Is it just me or does it sounds like somebody is a tad bit jealous?" Ethan smiled.

Christian shrugged. "You would be too if your significant other just left holding hands with a goddess."

Jennifer slapped Christian's arm. "He is just showing her around campus," she insisted.

"He's holding her hand," Christian picked at Jennifer.

"*She* grabbed *his* hand! As if that means anything," Jennifer groaned.

"Doesn't it?" Christian pondered.

"No," Jennifer rolled her eyes, "it doesn't mean anything. Do you know how I know that?"

"How?" Christian smiled.

"Because, I hold your hand all the time," Jennifer grinned, and she stuck her tongue out at Christian.

Christian tossed his chip at her.

"I can't wait to find out if they made a trip behind the bleachers," Tommy added. He nudged Christian. "If you know what I mean…"

"We all know what you mean," Jennifer mocked in a deep, condescending voice.

"I'll bet you five bucks he doesn't," Christian said as he and Tommy shook hands, giant grins spreading across their faces.

"Thirteen years old, I got my first kiss behind those bleachers," Tommy recalled. "My parents kissed for the first time behind those bleachers."

"I still say he won't do it," Christian said confidently.

"Yeah, you're right," Tommy sighed, "bet's off… it's *Brant*… bless his heart… you should be ashamed of the things you've done to that boy, Jen."

There was a long pause before Jennifer groaned, "she's a lot prettier than me, isn't she?"

"No, nobody is prettier than you, Jenny," Christian said as he pulled her into a headlock.

"She's just the sort of girl that you'd never dream of putting in a *headlock*, right?" Jennifer sighed as she shoved Christian away.

"No," Christian laughed as he playfully jabbed Jennifer back, "she is the type of girl that I *constantly* dream about putting in a headlock."

"And dream and dream," Ethan added.

"Exactly," Chris laughed.

"*Headlock*, maybe," Tommy shook his head, "*handcuffs*… oh yeah."

"You're sick," Jennifer barked.

The boys all laughed.

"Come-on," Jennifer demanded as she stood up, "I think that we should all help show her around."

"Jenny… Jennifer," Christian said, catching her arm, "we are just messing with you… sit down."

"But she's beautiful and interesting," Jennifer whined. "She's lived in California. I've only seen California in pictures, and I own underwear that cover as much as that skirt she's wearing."

"Maybe so," Christian shrugged sincerely, "but you've got one thing she'll never have... *Brant's love.*"

"Yeah, you're the girl who is going to be married to a professional athlete," Ethan weighed in. "You'll go to California; you'll go all over the country and have money to burn on manicures and pedicures and all the clothes you want."

"Even so," Jennifer smiled, "I'll always just be Jenny from the sticks."

The boys all laughed.

"You have to trust him, Jen," Christian smiled.

"I trust *him* completely," Jennifer replied, "it's her I'm not so sure about." She plopped down in Christian's lap. "I don't think I like that girl," she shook her head.

"Well, if you don't like her, I don't like her," Christian said as he wrapped his arms around Jennifer.

Ethan and Tommy both chuckled, and Jennifer scolded them with a frown.

"Oh, *right*," Tommy nodded, "I don't like her a bit... you, Ethan?"

"Nothin' special 'bout her if you ask me," Ethan shrugged.

Jennifer snarled, and Christian handed her a cookie.

***

On Thursday of the same week, football practice ended early.

"Brianna, you didn't have to stay and watch practice," Jennifer smiled. "We would have been happy to swing by and pick you up before the movie."

"That's okay," Brianna shrugged, "I wanted to stay and watch Brant."

Before Jennifer could reply, a red truck, its bed loaded with guys armed with what, at first glance, looked like heavy artillery, came speeding by, screaming and cheering as they pelted the NORTH RIVER HIGH SCHOOL sign with red paintballs.

"Oh my goodness!" Jennifer exclaimed as she brought her hand to her mouth.

Tommy jumped off the tailgate of Christian's truck. "Let's ride, Chris!" he called without a moment's hesitation.

"Who do you think that is?" Ethan asked as he tossed his gym bag into the back of his own truck.

"Well, bro, we're gonna find out," Christian said, twirling his keys around his finger. "You in or you out?"

"I'm in," Ethan nodded confidently as he climbed into the back end of Christian's truck.

Brianna seemed confused. "It's just a little paint… I'm sure it'll wash off. It's really not a big deal. Right?"

"Maybe not where you're from," Tommy laughed. He put his arm around Brianna's shoulders and smiled proudly. "Welcome to Cummins, Mississippi, sweetheart!" he exclaimed.

"Guys… you're all gonna make Brianna think that we're nothin' but a bunch of rednecks around here," Jennifer grinned.

Christian slapped Jennifer hard on the rear end. "So you drivin' or what?" He tossed her the keys.

"Come-on," Jennifer motioned to Brianna, "you can ride shotgun."

"Am I to assume you've done this before?" Brianna gulped as she opened the passenger's side door of Christian's truck.

"Where's Brant?" Jennifer called out the window.

"I don't know… come-on, they're getting away," Christian hollered back.

As Jennifer was about to pull away, Brant strolled from the locker room. "Brant!" Tommy screamed. "Let's go… we got trouble!"

Brant grinned as he jumped into the back end of the truck with the rest of the guys. "What's going on?" he asked as Jennifer peeled out of the parking lot.

"Look at our sign," Ethan pointed as the boys' hair blew in the wind.

"Who was it?" Brant hollered into the wind.

"We don't know," Christian screamed back.

"Did you get a good look at them?" Brant barked.

"Look!" Ethan pointed as he spotted the truckload of guys up ahead.

"Faster, Jen!" Tommy yelled as he beat on the cab window.

"They're stopping!" Christian shouted.

"Hang on, guys!" Jennifer hollered as she leaned out the window.

The boys braced themselves as Jennifer slammed on brakes, stirring up dust along the old dirt road.

"Go… go," Brant said urging Christian with a shove. Both boys swung themselves over the side of the truck.

"Be careful!" Jennifer called.

Brant chuckled as he eyed the driver of the beat up, red truck. He looked up at Tommy and smiled cockily, "you didn't tell me we were chasing this loser."

"You have such a smart mouth, McLachlan," the boy, who outweighed Brant by eighty pounds or more, replied angrily.

Oh," Brant smiled, turning his back on the Starkville lineman whose cheap shot had re-aggravated his back injury, "here we go… those sound like fightin' words, and I know face-to-face isn't your style. So, take your best shot."

The boy took a step toward Brant, and Christian shoved him away.

Brant spun around and grabbed Christian's arm. "You've already had your turn," he smiled, spreading his arms wide. "This time he's all mine."

"There are a lot more of us than there are of you, McLachlan," the guy chuckled as he glanced behind him.

"Well, that's good… because you're gonna need every one of them," Brant shrugged.

The guy took a swing at Brant, and Brant ducked.

"Quick, ain't he?" Ethan laughed.

"Honestly," Brant nodded, "you're gonna have to do better than that to make it a fair fight… else I'll feel bad for what I'm about to do to you."

"Shall we show them how it's done?" Christian smiled.

Brant nodded slowly. "Yeah, let's do," he smiled as he threw a strong right hook and connected hard with the side of the former lineman's jaw.

The brawl that ensued made Jennifer and Brianna wince.

Tommy slung one of the guys forcefully into the side of Christian's truck.

"Hey," Christian hollered as he took a swing at another guy, "put a dent in him… not in my truck, please."

"Ethan… watch out!" Jennifer screamed as a guy in a red bandanna charged up behind him.

Ethan turned quickly, and he was blindsided by a fierce punch.

Brant rushed to Ethan's rescue, and, together, he and Ethan pounded the overweight, freckle-faced, and much older, attacker to the ground.

Brant was laughing the entire time, screaming things such as, "I'll beat those freckles right off of your face, punk," as his fists flew.

Suddenly, two boys in blue jeans came to their friend's aid, and Brant was knocked to the ground. Jennifer and Brianna both squealed in perfect unison as his shoulder slammed into the ground. After a moment of rolling around in the dirt, Brant came out on top of one of the boys. He delivered blow after blow before being jumped by the other guy and finding himself face down in the street.

"Christian!" Jennifer screamed. "Help!"

"What do we do?" Brianna panicked.

"Ethan!" Jennifer yelled.

"Here comes a car," Brianna pointed.

"Cops!" Jennifer shouted.

The fighting stopped abruptly, and the boys in the old, red truck hurriedly piled back into their ride and took off down the road.

"Cops?" Brant groaned as he peeled himself off the dirt road.

"No… not really… worse," Jennifer pointed.

The boys turned. "Dad!" they exclaimed.

Brant jumped up and began dusting himself off.

Dad helped Tommy off the ground. "What's the matter with you?" he asked angrily.

"It's my wrist," Tommy groaned as he cradled one hand in the other. "I think it's broken, Coach."

"Then a lot of good you're gonna do us tomorrow," Dad snapped.

"Our house is the opposite way, Dad," Brant blurted. "What are you doing coming this way? Who ratted us out?" he insisted.

"That's not important," Dad snapped.

"Oh, they'll think it's important when I find 'em," Brant said, rolling his eyes.

"Dad," Christian pled, "they shot our sign just for kicks. What did you expect us to do?"

Dad popped Christian in the back of the head. "This ain't Hazzard County, son," he scolded. "You don't just jump in the General Lee and take off after them."

Brant put one hand on his back as he leaned up against Christian's truck.

"What's the matter with you?" Dad stared at him.

"I'm fine," Brant rolled his eyes.

"Did you hurt your back?" Dad crossed his arms. "That's just great…"

"I said I'm fine," Brant snapped.

Dad groaned. "Jennifer," he said as he eyed Tommy, "will you take this big baby to the hospital and ask my wife to X-ray his hand and then maybe his head?"

"Sure," Jennifer nodded with a frown.

Dad looked at Brant. "And you should have your mother get someone to look at your back," he sighed.

"I'm fine," Brant shrugged.

Dad shook his head as he walked back to his truck. "Come with me, and I'll drive you to the hospital," he offered.

The gang stood looking at each other.

"Brant," Jennifer said, gently stroking Brant's arm, "be honest with me… are you hurt?"

"No," Brant shook his head confidently, "I'll be fine."

"Are you sure?" Ethan inquired. "Maybe you should…"

"Maybe you should shut up," Brant groaned. "I'm fine."

"I'm not," Tommy blurted, "just in case anyone cares."

"I'll drive him to the hospital, Jen," Christian offered.

"I'll go with you," Ethan nodded.

"So much for the movies," Brianna sighed.

Jennifer's cell phone rang. "It's my mom," she said as she stared at the caller ID.

"Brant," Brianna said as Jennifer walked away to take the call, "you wouldn't mind giving me a ride home would you?"

"Nah," Brant smiled, "I'll run you home."

Jennifer hung up the phone. "My mom needs me to come home and watch Ben for her. Christian, will you drop me off at school, so I can get my car?"

"Drop us off too," Brant added. "Jen, I'm gonna take Brianna home, okay?"

"Boys!" Dad called sternly. The triplets turned to him, all three avoiding eye contact. "I expect to see you all at home shortly," he snarled.

The boys nodded.

"Hey, Brant," Dad called.

Brant glanced back at Dad.

"Eighteen year old, *high school kids* pick silly fights with a truck load of hoodlums," Dad sighed.

Brant rolled his eyes.

"Just think about it," Dad shrugged.

***

Brant grimaced as he pulled his truck into Brianna's driveway.

"Your back *is* hurting isn't it?" Brianna sighed.

"Maybe a little," Brant replied.

"Why don't you come in?" Brianna offered.

"I can't," Brant shook his head. "You heard my dad… I need to get home."

"At least come in long enough to take a pain pill for your back," Brianna said as she opened the passenger's side door. "It will have time to start working on your way home."

"That's okay…"

"Don't be so stubborn, Brant," Brianna rolled her eyes. "What? Are you afraid that Jennifer would be upset that I invited you in? Come-on… I promise to be on my best behavior."

"I *could* use a pain pill," Brant replied.

"Well, then get out of the car, silly," Brianna motioned as she strapped her backpack on her back, making sure to draw attention to her voluptuous chest in the process.

Brant opened his door as he curiously eyed her, anything but subtle, attempts to gain his attention.

"My mom has some really good stuff," Brianna said as she fumbled with the key at the front door.

"Can I help you with that?" Brant offered as he reached for the key, and his hand brushed Brianna's.

"Thanks," Brianna smiled.

"Not a problem," Brant said, opening the door. He walked inside. "What did you mean when you said your mom has some really good stuff?" he asked.

"You know," Brianna shrugged, "pills… painkillers."

Brianna walked into the kitchen. "Make yourself comfortable," she called. "I'll find you something guaranteed to make you feel better."

"Don't you just have some Aleve or something?" Brant asked as he followed Brianna.

Brianna reached into a cabinet above her microwave. "Take one of these," she smiled as she extended a medicine bottle to Brant.

"What *is* this?" Brant shrugged as he stared at the label. "This is a prescription…" A sharp pain shot through his back.

"It's for pain," Brianna replied. "What else do you need to know?"

"Maybe I shouldn't…" Brant winced as he grabbed his back. He swallowed hard as he stared at the label on the bottle.

"It's not going to kill you," Brianna laughed.

"You know what… whatever," Brant sighed as he opened the bottle. "I don't like the idea of doing this, but the pain has got to stop."

Brianna handed him a bottle of water.

"Thanks," Brant said as he tossed a pill into his mouth and swallowed it.

"There you go," Brianna smiled, "that should make you feel better in no time, but you should probably go ahead and take two."

"Are you sure?" Brant asked, and he started to consult the label.

"Yes," Brianna nodded as she reached for the pills, "you want to feel better don't you?"

Brant laughed as he swallowed the second pill. "My mom's a doctor; she'd have a stroke if she knew I just did that."

"It's okay," Brianna smiled, "my mom takes them all the time, and they haven't killed her yet."

"Well, that's good to know," Brant nodded with a smile. He looked around the house. "This is a pretty nice place you've got here."

"I don't like it," Brianna shook her head.

"Why not?" Brant inquired.

"Let's just say I've lived in nicer," Brianna rolled her eyes as she reached into the refrigerator and took out a bottle of water for herself. "So are you hungry?" she asked. "There's leftover pizza in here."

"Yeah, sure," Brant nodded, "I'll take some."

"Coming right up," Brianna smiled.

Brant and Brianna talked over pizza. "My mom made a chocolate cake last night," Brianna said as she cleared their dishes. "It's really good."

"Sounds tempting," Brant nodded.

"I'll cut you a slice," Brianna said as she reached into the cabinet for a plate. "My mom is really a good cook. She knows that the way to a man's heart is through his stomach."

"Right," Brant laughed.

"You are gonna love this cake," Brianna smiled.

"If you don't mind me asking," Brant said, taking the fork that Brianna handed him, "what does your mom do for a living?"

"She's out of work right now," Brianna replied quickly.

"Oh," Brant raised his eyebrow, "so where is she right now? I figured she was at work. What's she on painkillers for anyway?"

"She's out looking for husband number five, I assume," Brianna replied smugly.

Brant nodded, sorry that he had asked. He looked down at his plate. "So what does your mom takes pain pills for?"

"Bri!" a woman shouted as the front door swung open. "Whose truck is that in my driveway?"

"It's okay, Mom," Brianna called, "it belongs to a friend of mine. He gave me a ride home from school."

"Oh," Brianna's mother said as she stepped into view and eyed Brant, "well, hi there."

"Hi," Brant said, sticking out his hand. "Brant McLachlan… nice to meet you, ma'am."

"Nice to meet you, Brant," Ms. Clarke smiled as she squeezed his hand much longer than necessary. "Any friend of my daughter's is a friend of mine. Just make yourself right at home." She turned to Brianna. "He's gorgeous!" she said, making no attempt to lower her voice.

Brant nodded toward the kitchen table. "You make a mean chocolate cake," he said, trying to be polite.

"Well, thank you, Brant," Ms. Clarke smiled. "You'll have to try my pecan pie some other time. It's my specialty, and you country boys… you all love pecan pie… right? That's what I've heard."

"I can't speak for everyone, but this country boy'll eat most anything you're willing to put in front of him," Brant grinned.

"How's your back?" Brianna asked as she took Brant's hand.

"Much better," Brant nodded, subtly pulling his hand away. "Thank you... for everything, but I better be going." Then, as an afterthought, he asked, "do you mind if I use your bathroom before I go?"

"First door on the right," Brianna pointed toward the hall.

"Thanks," Brant nodded.

As Brant got ready to leave the bathroom, the medicine cabinet over the sink caught his eye. It was slightly open, and he saw what looked like a collection of pill bottles inside. Suddenly, he noticed how much better his back was feeling. He stretched his shoulders in the mirror before sliding the medicine cabinet open. "Whoa," he sighed as he stared at the assortment of prescription drugs, "looks like somebody might have a problem."

He took a bottle from the shelf and read the label. Sliding it back into place, he reached for another bottle. He noticed that the bottle in his hand contained the same label as the bottle Brianna had shown him in the kitchen. It even had the same stranger's name on it. Brant looked around as if looking for some sort of hidden camera. He slid the bottle back on the shelf and started to close the cabinet. Then he stopped; he stretched his shoulders and smiled. He bent down and touched his toes... no pain. He dropped back and threw a mock pass... he felt great. He reached for the bottle again but pulled his hand back. He reached for the bottle yet again and, this time, removed it from the shelf. He thought for a moment... tomorrow was game day. Sliding the bottle into his jacket pocket, he eased the cabinet door closed, remembering to leave it slightly cracked.

***

Friday, a week later, Brant and Brianna were sitting in history class when Brianna asked to borrow a pen.

"Front pocket," Brant groaned in response. Without opening his eyes to look up from his desktop, he slid his backpack toward her with his foot.

Brianna unzipped the front pocket of Brant's backpack and curiously examined the bottle of painkillers that he had stashed alongside a pen, a broken calculator and an assortment of loose change. "Brant?" she sighed.

Brant lifted his head and frowned. He jerked his backpack from Brianna, looking to make sure that Christian nor Tommy had seen the bottle of painkillers. "Is *this* what you were looking for?" he huffed as he tossed a pen at Brianna.

"You took those from my house?" Brianna gulped.

"I was gonna tell you…" Brant began.

"Whatever, I don't care… you can have them. Brant, how many of those have you taken?" Brianna asked.

"Just a few," Brant replied.

"A few!" Brianna exclaimed in a whisper. "The bottle is nearly empty. Brant, are you crazy?"

"It was almost empty when I found it," Brant lied.

"You can't take that many painkillers, Brant," Brianna insisted. "Look at you. I should have known. You look like my mother when she's passed out on the couch."

"My back hurts, okay," Brant sighed. "The pills make it feel better… just like you said."

"Football players and painkillers have a well-documented history," Brianna whispered.

"Bri," Brant shook his head, "I don't have a problem with painkillers. The only problem I have is that I wrecked my truck, screwed up my back, and now it hurts."

"I think that's what that quarterback for the Packers said," Brianna nodded. "I remember reading about him in the newspaper, years ago. He didn't think he had a problem either."

"Brianna," Brant assured her, "Brett Favre was on some *serious* stuff, and he was taking *way* more of it than I am. Besides, I'm *not* addicted. I can stop any time that I want."

"I think that's what he told himself for a long time too," Brianna huffed.

"It's only been a week," Brant snapped, "I had to have them to make the pain go away, but, I'm done with them. I can't play while I'm on them. The way that I have been practicing lately, Dad is probably out looking for a new quarterback as we speak."

"Do you swear that you won't take them any more?" Brianna persisted.

"I promise," Brant nodded, "so let's just keep this between us. Okay?"

"Why should I?" Brianna shrugged.

"Please, Brianna," Brant begged, "Jennifer already suspects something is up with me. I don't want to lie to her, but I can't tell her the truth. Something like this would really upset her."

"Well, we wouldn't want that," Brianna rolled her eyes.

"What?" Brant grumbled. "Come-on… don't be like that. I thought you guys were friends?"

"We are, I guess," Brianna shrugged.

"Alright then, Brianna… please," Brant pled, "don't tell her. This is no big deal."

"Alright then," Brianna nodded. "This can be our little secret." Brant knew that Brianna liked the idea of keeping a secret from Jennifer, and he frowned.

Brant lay his head back down on his desktop as Mr. Roberts began to lecture about great leaders in the history of our nation. "Who can name a renowned, national leader of this century for me?" he asked, pointing to a girl in the front row.

"Ronald Reagan," she replied quietly.

"Good… wonderful example, Darla," Mr. Roberts nodded as he scanned the classroom. "How about you there in the back, sleepyhead?" he called. When there was no reply, Mr. Roberts' face turned angry. "Brant!" he shouted as he slammed his hand on the podium.

Brant lifted his head. "Tom Landry," he replied seriously.

"We don't have time for your jokes today," Mr. Roberts snapped.

"I'm dead serious," Brant fired back.

"Wake up and listen to the question. I asked you to name an influential American leader," Mr. Roberts said sternly. "I don't know who Tom Landry is, and neither does anybody else in this classroom who actually read their assignment last night."

"That's not my fault," Brant shrugged. "You asked for an influential American. Tom Landry definitely qualifies… I'm an American… he influenced me."

"He was a great football coach for the Dallas Cowboys," Christian announced.

"See, someone else *does* know," Brant smiled. "Come-on, Mr. Roberts… haven't you ever heard of *America's Team*?"

"Get outside, Brant," Mr. Roberts said, as he pointed at the door.

"Bad day?" Brant rolled his eyes.

"He's serious, Mr. Roberts," Christian interjected. "It may not have been the answer you were looking for, but he…"

"Christian, would you like to join him in the hall?" Mr. Roberts shrugged.

"Franklin Roosevelt," Christian shook his head.

"Very good," Mr. Roberts nodded. "Brant… I mean it… get outside."

"I won't say another word," Brant grumbled as he sank down in his chair. "In fact, I'll go back to sleep if you don't mind. You won't hear another word out of me."

"Get out before I write you up," Mr. Roberts said loudly. "You have slept through this class all week, and, quarterback or not, I'm sick of it."

"Fine," Brant smiled, "just tell me why you're kicking me out. I mean, sleeping or not, I answered your rather general question."

"Out! Now!" Mr. Roberts said, slamming his fist on his podium. "You are out of control. One more word, and I'll see to it that you don't play tonight."

A few people in the room giggled under their breath.

"Right," Brant snickered.

"Brant, come-on, man, just be quiet," Tommy sighed.

Brant laughed. "This town would fire you before they sat me out of tonight's game," he said confidently.

"Brant, that's enough," Christian rolled his eyes.

Mr. Roberts hit the switch on the intercom mounted to the wall. "Put me through to Coach McLachlan's office, please," he said evenly.

"Fine," Brant huffed, "I'm leaving. I'll be in the front office eating Tootsie Roll Pops with the secretaries if you need me."

"Stay right outside that door," Mr. Roberts pointed.

"Yeah, okay," Brant nodded sarcastically as he walked outside, slamming the door behind him.

"Brantley!" Christian scolded.

Christian and Tommy stared at Brianna. "Don't look at me; I don't know what's wrong with him," she shrugged.

***

"Jordan, does Brant seem okay to you?" Jennifer asked me as I headed toward the locker room prior to our final home game of the season.

"Yeah, I think so," I shrugged. "Why?"

"I can't shake the feeling that something just isn't right," Jennifer frowned.

"I think he's just in a bad mood," I laughed her off. "He didn't have the best week of practice, and Dad's been on his case."

"Maybe," Jennifer nodded.

"You don't buy that do you?" I said as I crossed my arms and stopped walking. "You seem like you're really worried about him."

"Yeah," Jennifer gulped, "I am."

"You don't think his back is bothering him worse than he admits, do you?" I inquired.

"I don't know," Jennifer sighed. "When I ask him about it, he swears he's never felt better."

"That's what he keeps telling me too," I nodded, "and I sure don't buy that. He's been sluggish, lethargic even."

"And moody," Jennifer added.

"Maybe he's just exhausted," I suggested.

"Yeah, it's been a long season," Jennifer agreed.

The conversation was soon shrugged off, forgotten, and the game started without so much as another thought about it. Once the lights came on and both teams took the field, the Brant I had watched all week in practice seemed to have morphed back into his energetic, hard-charging, overly competitive self just in time for kickoff. With Tommy still out and two of our starting offensive lineman also out with injuries, the defense seemed to have an easier time getting to Brant, and he was forced to put on a one-man show all night long.

He played smart; he was strong and fast. Judging by his play, the pain in his back was not apparent. It seemed as if, with one quick glance, he could see everything that was going on on the field, read it and instantly know how to divide and conquer. I was amazed as I watched him make running a football look like an art form.

By the end of the game, our team was tired, and they were executing half-heartedly. It was a type of play that Brant didn't know, and it infuriated him.

"All of you just go sit down!" he screamed during a timeout. "You're getting in my way out there."

"I'm out of steam, man," someone sighed.

"Well, if you don't have the guts to suck it up and lay it on the line for the next eight minutes, then take off that jersey because you don't deserve to wear it," Brant hollered, as he shoved the large lineman.

"You tell 'em, Brant," Fred Thornton hollered as he kicked the fence. "You boys get with it… let's go!"

"I don't have anything to say to you boys," Dad said exasperatedly. "I have never seen a bigger bunch of sissies in my life. The North River Eagles *can* be beat, and those boys over there are about to prove it!"

"This is our field," Brant screamed. "I've never lost here! I've never lost wearing a North River uniform, and I am going to do anything it takes to keep from seeing those guys over there run around on my field thinking that they're something special when this game is over."

"That's not gonna happen," someone insisted.

"That is exactly what is going to happen if we don't wake up!" Brant yelled. "Anybody who doesn't want this game bad enough to go out there and take it… stay over here! I don't need you!"

"Brant, calm down," Christian hollered.

"I won't calm down!" Brant screamed. "I don't need to calm down… the rest of you just need to wake up. And *you*… go find some super glue and smear it on your hands. What is your problem? You're gonna cost us this game!"

"I dropped *one* pass," Christian yelled.

"It was right in your hands," Brant snapped. "We can't win like that."

"Brant, that's enough," Dad huffed. "If they don't want it by now, nothing you say is gonna change their minds."

Christian rolled his eyes.

Fathers leaned over the fence hollering at their sons. Some yelled at other's sons and bickering broke out amongst the crowd.

"Christian, you gotta catch the ball, son," Lonnie Harper ranted.

"Nathan, you gotta block, boy. You look like you're scared of breaking a nail out there," Fred Thornton hollered.

"Brant, you can do this… don't let us down," Tom Massey clapped.

"We're counting on you, Brant," someone behind him shouted.

I stared at my brother, bruises on his arms, a nasty gash across his chin, grass in his helmet, and I couldn't fathom what more they could possibly have wanted out of him.

Brant ran the ball himself every chance he got for the rest of the game. People were dropping passes and fumbling the ball, and he simply didn't trust the game in anyone else's hands that night.

After each down, he got up off the field more slowly than the time before. Just when I thought surely he must have had enough, he would make a move that made me believe that his back felt every bit as good as he said it did.

It was the worst game that North River had played in four years, but it was a memorable one. Everyone there that night got to see heart overcome performance. With fifty-nine seconds left on the clock, the Eagles were down by a field goal, and Brant boldly announced that he was taking the kickoff.

"Alright," Dad agreed, slapping Brant's helmet, "if you want it... you got it."

Christian slung his helmet down, and he and Brant began exchanging words.

"Chris, it's just not your night, buddy," Dad said as he patted Christian's back. He turned to Brant, his face stern. "Make it happen," he said boldly. As Brant ran onto the field, the crowd was rejuvenated, and hope was reborn. Dad turned to me. "It's over," he sighed, "they'll never be stupid enough to kick it to him."

The other team was confident that they had beaten the three-time consecutive State Champion North River Eagles, and they dreamed of ending the game by stopping the biggest name in high school football. I understood their excitement; this was shaping up to be the biggest upset in the history of North River football, custom made with the dramatic ending every player dreams of. Every boy on that other team wanted to be able to say that he was the one who laid out Brant McLachlan and ended North River High School's streak of four undefeated seasons. It would be something they could tell their children about. By then, Brant would have surpassed them, moved on to bigger and better games, but tonight they could leave their mark on his unblemished career. Despite the heroics of the ending they might have envisioned, I *never* would have dreamed that they would actually kick him the ball.

As Dad saw the ball sailing toward Brant, he grasped my shoulder, and we stood watching in open-mouthed astonishment. An eighteen wheeler couldn't have brought that boy down. The opposing team saw their dream crumble as Brant ran the ball seventy-seven yards for the game-winning touchdown.

When the final horn sounded, the Eagles were victorious on the scoreboard, but, by North River standards, they had failed miserably. An ugly black eye had nearly marred what would become known as the McLachlan Era of North River football, and the emotional backlash that ensued threatened to destroy the team and the town's unity.

Brant shook his head in disgust as he walked off the field. Dad grabbed him and kissed the top of his helmet. "Thank you! Thank you! Thank you!" he exclaimed.

The team, their heads hanging, filed silently into the locker room where they, minus their captain, would stay listening to my dad preach about North River football and the importance of never giving up. How you play football is a mirror image of how you'll live your life, he told them. He told them that if you give in during a close game, then you'll give in when the chips are down in life.

Brant had played his heart out, and Dad didn't want him in the locker room to say things that, however true they might have been, could undermine the team as a unit. I thought he should have been there. He was the leader of our team on and off the field, and he owed it to those boys to demonstrate his confidence in them. The decision wasn't Brant's; it was Dad's, but I think it was a bad one.

Brant stood on the field reflecting on how something that meant so much to him could mean seemingly so little to his teammates that night.

Jennifer ran into Brant's arms. "I'm so proud of you," she smiled.

"Thanks, baby," Brant replied as he forced a smile.

"Are you alright?" Jennifer frowned.

"Yeah," Brant nodded, "just do me a huge favor and go find me something to take for pain, will you?"

"Here," Jennifer said, "I have some Extra Strength Tylenol in my bag."

"Wonderful," Brant smiled.

Brant grabbed a water bottle as Jennifer dug the medicine from her bag.

Brant quickly dumped a small pile of pills in his hand. "Brant, those are pain pills, not M&M's," Jennifer exclaimed as she grabbed his hand. "Slow down!"

"It's just Tylenol," Brant shook his head as he swallowed the pills.

"Extra strength," Jennifer shot back.

"Rock, I feel like somebody is stabbing me in the back with a knife over and over again. It has got to stop," Brant explained.

"I knew it," Jennifer nodded. "Brant, when do you see the doctor again about your back?"

"Why... so they can say that they need to do surgery again... no way," Brant rolled his eyes. "Do you have any idea what an eighteen-year-old with two back surgeries on his résumé has going for him? Nothing... that's what! No one wants a *liability* on their team, Jen."

"I know," Jennifer said sympathetically, "I just don't want you to be in pain if there is something that a doctor can do for you."

"It'll get better; I just took a *beating* tonight," Brant insisted.

"That *was* horrible," Jennifer agreed. "You hit the ground like a million times... no wonder you're in pain."

"Tell me about it," Brant frowned. "Do you want to play next week?"

"I think you may need me to," Jennifer smiled.

"We need something," Brant smiled back. "A healthy O-line would be a start."

"What was wrong with Christian tonight?" Jennifer asked quietly. "He dropped one pass and fumbled twice!"

Brant shrugged. "I don't know," he rolled his eyes, "and he probably hates me for taking the kickoff, but I wanted to win."

"Don't worry about it," Jennifer said with a long hug. "You were awesome!"

"Thanks," Brant groaned, "the only problem is football's not a ME thing, it's a WE thing." He winced in pain. "I should be in the team meeting right now encouraging my guys. I should have trusted my brother to bring the game home. I shouldn't have acted like I could have won this game without their help. I was just upset... it looked like we were gonna lose, and I couldn't take it."

"And you hurt yourself in the process, didn't you?" Jennifer frowned.

"I'm in pain every time I step on the field," Brant sighed. "Listen, Jen, just between us… something is really wrong with my back."

"I'm scared that you do way too good of a job hiding it," Jennifer replied. "If you're hurt, someone needs to know."

"A great football player never shows weakness to his opponents, his teammates, his fans, and most of all to himself," Brant said as if quoting from some Ten Commandments of the game.

Jennifer shrugged. "That sounds really good and all. I suppose that we all have our philosophies. *Here's mine…* weakness means having a problem but being too stubborn to admit it. You're hurt, Brantley, and you could be doing long-term damage to your back. What good is a State Championship ring if you hurt your back and never get to pursue your Super Bowl ring? Those old men from the class of '62 have State Championship rings, Brant. Is that what you want? Do you want to be an old man standing by that fence, wearing all four of your State Championship rings and remembering your glory days back in high school? If you keep doing what you're doing, you could jeopardize everything that you've worked for. It's time to be smart; it's not time to lay it all on the line… not yet."

"You're always looking out for me, aren't you?" Brant smiled as he put his arm around Jennifer.

"It's in the job description," Jennifer smiled up at him.

"I couldn't live without you, Jen," Brant said sincerely. "I mean that."

"Right back at ya, Cowboy," Jennifer winked.

Brianna waltzed toward them.

"Do you think that skirt is short enough?" Jennifer sighed. "Who wears *that* to a football game?"

Brant shrugged, "I don't know… I was sorta thinking you should get yourself one."

"In your dreams!" Jennifer elbowed him in the ribs, and they both laughed.

"Good game," Brianna smiled at Brant.

"Thanks," Brant smiled back.

"Tommy says he wants all of us to go out for milkshakes," Brianna relayed.

"That sounds great," Jennifer nodded. She glanced up at Brant. "You up to it?"

"Sure, why not," Brant smiled. "But first, I'm due in the training room for an ice bath and a massage."

"Alright then... I'm just gonna run go find my mom and let her know that I'll be late getting in tonight," Jennifer said before kissing Brant's cheek. "I'm sure they're together, so I'll tell your mom too." Jennifer smiled. "*And*... I'll talk to Christian for you," she nodded.

"Love you," Brant smiled.

Brant watched as Jennifer walked away. When she was out of earshot, he put his arm around Brianna. "I need a big favor," he sighed.

"Anything," Brianna smiled.

"Get me some more of your mom's pills," Brant gulped.

For a moment Brianna stared at him with questioning eyes.

"Please," Brant sighed.

"Have you lost your mind?" Brianna exclaimed.

"Keep your voice down," Brant huffed.

"Can you say *addict*?" Brianna blurted.

"Can you say *blowing things way out of proportion*?" Brant snapped back defensively. "Brianna, please. I just need the pills until football season is over."

"What am I to you... *your dealer*?" Brianna sighed.

"No," Brant frowned, "but you are my friend... aren't you?"

"Of course, I'm your friend," Brianna insisted. "Brant, I care a great deal about you..."

"Alright then," Brant nodded, "so will you get me some more pills?"

"What happened to the rest of the bottle you had earlier?" Brianna asked as she looked around to make sure that no one was listening in on them.

"I threw them out," Brant shrugged.

"Don't lie to me," Brianna snapped. "You took them."

"Fine... I took them," Brant rolled his eyes. "Are you happy now?"

"How many did you take? Do you even know?" Brianna gasped.

"Brianna... I don't have time to play *Twenty Questions*," Brant groaned. "Will you get me the pills or not?" He grabbed her hands. "Listen... if you'll just do this one thing for me... I'll owe you big time."

Brianna stared down at her hands clasped tightly in Brant's as she began slowly nodding her head, "sure... sure... I'll do it... for you."

"Great!" Brant smiled with a wink. He planted a kiss on Brianna's cheek. "I knew I could depend on you."

Brianna smiled as she gently touched her cheek. "I'd do anything for you, Brantley… don't you know that?"

"Brianna…" Brant sighed, opening his mouth to say more.

"Brant, you gonna get ready to go?" Jennifer called from the fence.

Brant turned back to Brianna. "Thanks again," he nodded before he hurried off to catch up with Jennifer.

CHAPTER NINE

After two weeks of playoff victories on the road, the North River Eagles were staring another State Championship game in the face. State Championship week was always exciting in Cummins. For an entire week, our town turned into a football paradise where players walked on air as the community, with their painted store windows, banners, balloons and parades, made it a week of the boys' lives that they would never forget.

During the week leading up to the State Championship game, North River's quarterback couldn't buy a hamburger from any joint in town; he couldn't even buy a coke from the Country Mart. His money was no good in any store in town. The people of Cummins wanted to make sure that Brant had fond memories of his high school glory days to look back on when he fled Cummins in search or stardom. They wanted to make it a week he would always remember, but, for Brant, it would be a week that he would always wish he could forget.

***

"Brianna," Jennifer smiled as she helped Brianna clear the dishes from the kitchen table, "it was really sweet of you to have us over for dinner tonight."

"I wanted to do something special with the big game coming up," Brianna replied.

"Well, it was delicious," Ethan said as he hugged Brianna appreciatively. "I hate to eat and run, but Jennifer and I have a big chemistry project due tomorrow…"

"Yeah, we're gonna have to go," Jennifer said as she picked up her purse and kissed Brant's lips. "Dinner was great. Thanks again." She hugged Brianna, then, smiling up at Ethan, said, "the poster board is waiting at my house, bud… you ready?"

"Let's do it," Ethan nodded as he followed Jennifer out the door.

Christian hugged Brianna tightly. "Thanks for everything," he smiled.

"Are you leaving too?" Brianna asked.

"Yeah, I think so. I'm pretty tired," Christian replied. "We had a rough practice today… I'm gonna have to call it an early night."

"And I'm parked behind him, so I guess I'll head out too," Tommy added. "Thank you for the food. It was all really good."

"I'm glad you enjoyed it," Brianna smiled as Tommy kissed her cheek.

Brant turned toward the kitchen as he sat relaxing on the living room sofa. "I'm just gonna stay and help Brianna clean up," he told Christian. "I'll be home in a second."

"See you at home," Christian nodded.

"See ya," Brant smiled.

Brianna walked Christian and Tommy to the door before walking back to the couch.

"It looks like it's just me and you," she smiled as she squeezed Brant's shoulders.

"Bri… I need a favor," Brant sighed.

"Let me guess," Brianna rolled her eyes, "you want more painkillers?"

"Come-on, Brianna," Brant gulped, "you're the only reason I made it through the playoffs. The State Championship game is in four days… there are a lot of people counting on me. Don't bail out on me now."

"What happened to all the pills I gave you two weeks ago?" Brianna shrugged. "There is no way that…"

"Yes… I finished them off," Brant nodded.

"Brant!" Brianna exclaimed.

"I know," Brant sighed, "but I swear to you… once football season is over, I will never take another one. Please, Bri…"

Brianna frowned. "Okay," she agreed quickly.

She placed her hands back on Brant's shoulders. "You're tense," she sighed.

"Yeah, no kidding," Brant grumbled. "It's just that if anyone else knew that I was taking all these painkillers…"

Brianna began massaging his shoulders. "How does that feel?"

"Good… better," Brant smiled.

"Is your back hurting right now?" Brianna inquired.

"Yeah," Brant sighed, "I ran out of pills yesterday. That's why I had to stay and talk to you. I need something to help me get through this week…"

"How about a cure-all?" Brianna asked.

"If you think you've got one, I'd be glad to try it," Brant snickered.

"Wait here," Brianna smiled.

"I was kidding," Brant called after her.

Moments later Brianna returned with a glass in her hand. "Try this," she said as she extended it to Brant.

"What is it?" Brant asked as he glanced up at Brianna, then down at his glass.

"Orange juice," Brianna smiled.

"Orange juice… that's your cure-all?" Brant laughed. He took a big sip. "Bri!" he exclaimed as he jumped up, his face contorted. "This is not orange juice!" He grabbed his back and groaned in pain.

"Sure it is," Brianna rolled her eyes.

"What's in it?" Brant insisted.

"Don't tell me you've never tasted Vodka," Brianna grinned as she stared at Brant. "Not even at one of those wild post-game parties?"

"Brianna," Brant groaned as he shoved the glass back at her, "you know I don't go to the parties, and I don't drink."

"Brant," Brianna said, refusing to take the glass back, "don't be such a goody two-shoes! A little good liquor never killed anybody!"

"I don't drink," Brant shook his head.

"Don't tell me that a big, strong football player like yourself has never had a drink?" Brianna laughed.

"I told you… I don't drink," Brant huffed, still reeling from the burn lingering in his mouth. "Lose the flattery."

"Suit yourself," Brianna shrugged. "You were the one who said you'd do anything to make your back stop hurting. I was just trying to help."

Brant sniffed at the glass.

"You're cracking me up," Brianna smiled.

"Why?" Brant stared back at her.

"One sip… one glass isn't going to make you an alcoholic," she laughed.

"I didn't say it would," Brant rolled his eyes. "Another bottle of painkillers isn't going to make me a drug addict either."

"So what are you so afraid of?" Brianna shrugged. "Take another drink…"

Brant stared down at the glass, sloshing the orange juice with a slight, suspicious movement of his wrist.

"It'll make your back feel better," Brianna repeated. "Besides, it has got to be better for you than all those painkillers."

"Don't remind me," Brant rolled his eyes. He took a small sip of his drink. "This is sick!" he groaned. "Why do people like this?"

"You have to acquire a taste for it," Brianna smiled. "Sit down. Relax. Get comfortable."

Brant sat down on the sofa and took another sip. He shook his head. "This guy you know… the guy that steals painkillers and drinks alcohol… that's *not* me. This isn't who I am." He moved his glass back to his lips.

"Well, that's too bad," Brianna gulped as she sat on the edge of the coffee table in front of Brant, "because I like the guy I see."

"You don't know me," Brant shook his head before taking another big sip of orange juice.

"Maybe *you* don't know you," Brianna whispered as she touched Brant's knee.

"Brianna, what are you doing?" Brant smiled as he moved away.

Brianna shrugged innocently. "I'm out of painkillers," she lied, "so how about some more Vodka?"

Brant looked at his empty glass. "Why not?"

Brianna walked back into the kitchen and returned holding a bottle.

She filled Brant's glass. "No orange juice this time, champ," she smiled.

"Where did you get that?" Brant laughed as he stared at her. He took a sip of his drink, and Brianna laughed at the face he made.

"Out of my mom's cabinet," Brianna shrugged. "Don't your parents have…"

"No," Brant shook his head, "my parents don't drink. My parents would absolutely flip out if…"

Brianna turned the bottle up and took a big swig as Brant stared at her in disbelief.

"Won't your mom be upset when she discovers it's missing?" he asked, sitting his drink aside. "I've been worried to death she was going to catch us taking her pills."

"My mom knows I drink," Brianna replied casually.

Brant picked up his glass and finished off his drink.

"It's growing on you, huh?" Brianna smiled as she refilled it.

Brant rested his head against the back of the sofa as Brianna began massaging his knee... then his thigh.

"I should go," Brant sighed. He tried to stand but stumbled back onto the couch.

Brianna laughed.

"You think it's funny do you?" Brant laughed. He rested his head against the back of the sofa. "I guess I'm stuck here for awhile, huh?"

"I think that sounds like a good idea," Brianna smiled.

Brant laughed loudly. "What if I lied, and I took some painkillers today before practice... would this make for a lethal mixture?"

Brianna straddled Brant on the couch. "No... I think that sounds just about perfect," she smiled.

"What are you doing?" Brant laughed as he picked up his drink and took another long sip.

"Whoa," Brianna said as she took the glass and placed it back on the table, "slow down there, Cowboy... I want you drunk... not unconscious." She began unbuttoning Brant's shirt.

"I think I'm drunk," Brant blurted.

"I think you are too," Brianna smiled.

"What are you doing?" Brant protested when he noticed that Brianna was undressing him.

"Relax," Brianna whispered as she handed him the drink. "Here, have another sip."

"I don't want it," Brant shook his head as he moved Brianna aside. He shook his head again, harder, in an attempt to clear his mind. "I've got to go."

"You can't even walk; how are you gonna drive?" Brianna rolled her eyes.

"I can walk… I just tried to get up too fast before," Brant insisted, his head spinning.

"Well, at least do me a favor before you go," Brianna said as she reached for his hand. "I can't reach my zipper. Unzip me, so I can slip into something a little more comfortable."

Brant unzipped Brianna's dress with one quick motion. "There you go," he said as he searched for his truck keys. He turned back to Brianna. "Have you seen my keys?"

Brianna pushed the straps of her dress away from her shoulders and let her red dress fall to the floor.

Brant stared.

Brianna stepped out of her dress. "What's the matter," she winked as she shoved Brant back onto the sofa, "you never seen a strapless bra before either?"

Brianna reassumed her position on top of Brant, and Brant reached for the bottle on the table. "Here, try this instead," Brianna whispered in his ear before planting a kiss on his lips.

"Bri… come-on, stop it," Brant said with what little conviction he could muster.

Brianna kissed him again, more passionately, and this time he kissed her back. She kissed his neck as she finished unbuttoning his shirt. She kissed his chest and then his lips.

Brant pulled Brianna toward him, and he caressed her bare back as he kissed her.

As Brianna unbuckled Brant's belt, she glanced at the front door and smiled, then she and Brant stretched across the sofa, her body pressed against his.

***

North River won the right to host the State Championship game on our field, a big honor for any team, and the boys were ready. For some, it was the last football game that they would ever play. For others, it was the last game that they would play on their hometown field. For those who would return the following year, it was a game when they would have to say goodbye to a class that had never lost a game in their high school careers. For some, it would be the game that defined their athletic careers.

For others, it was merely a stepping stone along a road leading to bigger games and better trophies. It was inevitable that tears would be shed that night, no matter the game's final outcome... it was just that sort of night.

Brant took two painkillers at first, knowing that he could overcome the effects of those with pure adrenaline. Two soon became four. Brant looked at his watch; it was only one hour before the boys were supposed to take the field to begin warm-ups.

"Hey, #13!" Christian called as he sat atop the lockers, "come check out this crowd."

Brant climbed up next to Christian, and they looked out the locker room window side-by-side.

"This is the last game we'll ever play together," Christian said after a moment.

The boys hit fists. "Me and you, brother," Brant grinned, "let's go win this thing."

Ethan joined Christian and Brantley atop the lockers as I stood watching them from afar with all the pride in the world. Ethan looked at Christian and then at Brant. "Teammates, tonight," he said sincerely, "brothers, forever."

"One for all... all for one," Christian nodded.

"I love you guys," Brant added.

The triplets jumped down in unison, and I smiled broadly.

"Guys!" I called.

My three brothers stood before me, and, as I looked into their faces, there was so much I wanted to say, yet I had trouble finding the right words. "I remember the night I played my last high school football game," I recalled. "I can't believe that tonight you guys will play yours. I'm so proud of each of you," I smiled as I pulled all three of them into a hug at once.

***

Tommy was standing in front of his locker when Brant waltzed over. They shook hands. "It has been a pleasure, brother," Tommy smiled.

Brant nodded. "It's hard to believe that this team will never play together again. We have something special here, man."

"I don't want it to end," Tommy sighed. "Some of the best memories of my life happened right here in this locker room and out there on our field."

Brant thought about everything that the game that was about to be played represented, and he knew that he needed to give the performance of a lifetime. He wanted to walk off that field at game's end knowing that he had given every person filling the stands the show that they had come to see. He walked over to his locker, and, looking around to make sure that no one was watching, he popped another pill into his mouth.

He walked over to the water fountain and shook his head in disbelief. He glanced into the mirror in front of him. "Brant McLachlan, what's happening to you?" he sighed.

***

Moments before the boys were supposed to take the field, Dad walked up to me, his arms crossed. "Where's Brantley?" he asked.

"I don't know," I shrugged.

"I'm ready for him to lead the guys out on the field, and I can't find him," Dad said as he scanned the room.

"I'll find him," I smiled.

"Thanks," Dad nodded, "I'm gonna go grab our headsets out of my office."

Dad opened the door to his office. "Brant?" he gulped as he stared at the floor.

I turned toward Dad's office, and that's when I saw Brant lying motionless on the carpet.

Dad dropped to his knees beside Brant.

Christian, Tommy and a host of others heard Dad calling Brant's name, and they hurried over to see what was going on.

"What happened?" Christian exclaimed as he stared at Brant, unconscious on the floor.

"Chris, go find Mom," Dad pointed.

"My dad's here on the ambulance tonight… I'll go get him," Tommy said as he hurried to catch up with Christian.

I knelt down next to Dad's desk, and something on the floor caught my eye.

"He's breathing," Dad sighed. "Brant… can you hear me?" he yelled.

I reached under the edge of the desk and picked up an empty bottle.

"What's this?" I asked, holding it up for Dad to see.

Dad snatched the bottle. He read the label, and his eyes grew wide with disbelief. He glanced down at Brant. "I don't believe it," he sighed.

Brant opened his eyes just as Mom rushed into Dad's office. Rick Jackson wasn't far behind.

"Brantley," Mom exclaimed, slowly helping Brant sit up, "baby... what happened?"

Dad cleared his throat. He took Mom's arm and pulled her aside. "Becky, I think you need to see something." He handed her the empty bottle of painkillers. "We found this under the desk right after we found him on the floor."

Mom stared at Brant, and Brant, suddenly nervous, stared at the bottle, his groggy eyes growing wide with panic.

Mom examined the bottle's label. "Where did you get these?" she barked at Brant.

"That's not important," Brant shook his head.

"Brantley... I won't ask you again," Mom said sternly.

"They belong to Brianna Clarke's mom," Brant gulped.

"What?" Mom shuttered. "Whose name is this on the bottle?"

"I don't know," Brant shrugged nervously.

"Why do *you* have them?" Dad interjected.

"I mean... well," Brant stammered, "I'm not sure what she takes them for really, but I... I... they just... you know... make my back... my back... feel a little better."

Mom handed the bottle to Rick Jackson. "Why would you do this, Brant?" she sighed.

"Mom, I'm fine," Brant insisted as he started to stand.

Mom pushed his shoulder back down, disappointed. "You are not fine... you *passed out.* How many of these did you take?"

"Mom... I didn't want my back to hurt tonight... I guess I just got carried away," Brant pled.

"How many did you take?" Mom insisted.

"I don't know," Brant shrugged, "I mean... I'm not really sure..."

"Brant, these could have killed you," Rick Jackson said angrily.

"Well, they didn't," Brant gulped, "I'm fine."

"Praise God!" Dad snapped as he crossed his arms.

"If your back was hurting, why didn't you just tell me?" Mom shook her head as she stared at Brant.

Brant frowned. "Mom, I'm sorry. This wasn't a smart move…"

"Yeah," Mom nodded, "taking medicine that isn't prescribed to you is pretty irresponsible… pretty stupid."

"And overdosing on them… that's even stupider," Rick added, ripping the blood pressure cuff off of Brant's arm. "Brantley… you passed out, son."

Dad threw the empty bottle at Brant. "Unreal," he groaned.

"I know… I'm sorry," Brant sighed, his mind flashing back to the collection of empty bottles that had preceded the one he was holding now.

Mom turned to Dad, crossing her arms the way she did when she was demanding an answer.

"Becky, I had no idea," Dad shook his head.

"How long have you been taking these things, Brant?" Rick inquired.

"A few weeks," Brant replied softly.

"What?" Mom gasped.

"I had to be able to play. Everyone was counting on me," Brant insisted. "Nobody wanted to know how bad my back was hurting… everyone just wanted to know that I could go out there and win them the game."

Mom bubbled with anger. She shook her head in a way that told me she didn't know if she was more angry at the town for the pressure that they put on young, high school boys or more angry at Brant for buying into it.

"Have you lost your mind, son?" Dad hollered.

"Dad… I'm sorry," Brant insisted as he stood.

"Me too," Dad nodded as he stared back at Brant, "because you're not playing tonight."

"What!" Brant exclaimed. "What do you mean I'm not playing? Dad, it's my last game! It's the State Championship!"

Dad shrugged angrily.

"You can't do this to me!" Brant argued.

"Brant," Dad said as he closed his office door, shooing his disbelieving players out, "when one of my boys is in so much pain that he feels the need to sneak around taking pills that aren't even his to take in the first place… I'm sorry… but he doesn't play football."

"You're benching me?" Brant stared at Dad in disbelief.

"Yes, Brant… I am," Dad said confidently.

"Dad, please," Brant begged, "this is an important game… it's no time to be teaching me a lesson."

"Brant, this is the dumbest thing you've ever done," Dad hollered.

Brant hung his head. "I wish," he mumbled under his breath.

"What?" Dad huffed.

"Nothing," Brant rolled his eyes.

"Brant… this isn't debatable," Dad sighed. "You're not playing… that's final."

Brant pounded his hand on the desk. "But, Dad…"

Dad shook his head. "You know, Brantley," he said softly, "I believe it was Eddie Robinson who once said, 'Coaches should build men first and football players second.' Well, that goes double for dads. Right now… winning this football game is not my first priority."

Brant nodded, "Dad… I understand." He put his hand on Dad's shoulder. "But," he smiled, "it was *Bear Bryant* who said, 'when you make a mistake, admit it; learn from it, and don't repeat it.' I know I messed up, Dad. I've learned my lesson… it'll never happen again. Please don't bench me."

"I know what you're doing, Brant," Dad shook his head. "You think that if you start quoting Coach Bryant I'll give in…"

"Am I right?" Brant gulped. "I've learned from my mistake, Dad. Don't punish the entire team because I screwed up."

Dad glanced over at Mom.

"No, David! He's not playing this game," Mom insisted.

"Dad…" Brant pled.

"Brant," Mom said sternly, "I am making you an appointment to have another MRI done on your back. Until then… no football."

"Just one more game," Brant begged.

"No," Mom frowned. She pointed to the clock as she walked from Dad's office. "David, your boys need to take the field."

Dad frowned as the office cleared.

"Dad," Brant sighed as he put his arm around Dad's shoulders, "she's not a football player… she doesn't understand. Come-on, I know how important this game is to you, and you know how much it means to me. Don't make me watch from the sidelines…"

"Here's one for you," Dad shook his head. "'Never try to make friends with your head coach.' Terry Bradshaw."

"Dad…" Brant grumbled.

"Sorry, son," Dad shook his head as he walked toward the door.

"You're willing to lose this game just to teach me a lesson?" Brant huffed.

Dad turned around. "If you get the message… then yeah… I am. Tonight I'm not your friend or even your coach… I'm your father… and I am very disappointed in you."

"The team is depending on me," Brant argued. "Dad… if I don't play, there's no way we'll win!"

Dad shrugged, as he quoted, "'defeat is a bitter pill, but if you take it as a lesson, defeat may not be as bad as it seems.'"

"Homer Norton," Brant nodded.

"Very good," Dad replied.

"Dad… I'm sorry," Brant gulped.

"Me too," Dad nodded, and he walked from the office.

Brant turned to me. "I don't believe this. Jordan, you've got to do something," he begged, nearly in tears. "You've got to talk to him. My team needs me out there. It's my senior year. This is the State Championship. Everyone is counting on me."

"*Yeah…* and you let us *all* down… *big time*," I shrugged as I followed Dad out.

Brant groaned loudly as he kicked Dad's desk.

***

Dad emphatically delivered the signs as he relayed the next play to Jimmy Hayes, our struggling rookie quarterback who had been unexpectedly thrust into a fire that was now consuming him. Watching him play that night was like watching a passenger of a jet who had previously tinkered with planes as a hobby being forced into desperately trying to land a crashing commuter plane after the pilot went down… and, given the importance placed on high school football in Cummins, Jimmy was likely just as terrified.

Our fans didn't know what was going on, and many of them were demanding answers.

Jennifer ran over to the bench, pom poms in hand. "What is going on?" she exclaimed in Brant's ear.

"It's a long story," Brant gulped.

"Well, are you okay?" Jennifer asked, unable to fathom why Brant wasn't on the field.

"I would be if I hadn't been benched for the State Championship," Brant huffed. "Look at this... we're getting killed out there. Can you believe this circus?" He slammed his hands on the bench. "Come-on, Jimmy," he hollered, "Chris was wide open!" He rolled his eyes. "He's gonna throw into double coverage just because that's the number Dad called," he said angrily. "He's lucky that ball wasn't picked again."

"Everyone, including me, wants to know why you aren't out there. People are getting very upset," Jennifer sighed as she glanced back at the bustling crowd.

Brant looked back at Jennifer. "Maybe if they start protesting louder, they can wake my dad up," he said sarcastically. "Get one of your megaphone thingies and encourage 'em to storm the field and stop this riot."

"Brant, I don't understand," Jennifer shook her head. "Has your dad lost his mind?"

"It's not my dad's fault," Brant frowned, "it's mine. I'll explain it all to you later."

"Tell me now," Jennifer insisted.

"It's not the time," Brant shook his head.

"But you're okay?" Jennifer swallowed.

"Yeah," Brant nodded, "I'm fine, Jen."

As the second quarter began, all of Cummins was in an uproar. No one understood why our star quarterback was yet to see the field, and pandemonium ensued. Most just hollered; some threw things, and a few others actually began making their way onto the field to have a talk with Coach McLachlan.

Ron Sanders from the Country Mart and Leroy Williams, star linebacker of the 1962 State Championship team, led a mob of men who hurled insults at Jimmy while begging for an explanation from Brant.

"Brant, what kind of bad joke is this?" Leroy barked.

Brant shrugged, refusing to comment.

"This is the State Championship, Coach," Ron hollered.

Behind them a chant of "WE WANT BRANT!" broke out, and the men, their voices gruff and off beat, joined in.

Brant smiled as the chant spread and the words became a booming demand. The people had spoken loud and clear.

"Becky," Kathy Smith whispered to her best friend. "I understand what you and David are doing, but…"

"I know," Mom nodded. "We're punishing more than one person. What do you think I should do?"

Jennifer's mom glanced at the scoreboard. "Tell David to put him in the game," she sighed. "I don't think I can take much more of this myself, and the rest of the town looks to be forming a lynch mob with intentions of going after your husband."

"You're right," Mom nodded. "He has to put Brant in the game."

Jimmy Hayes tossed another interception, the final straw before the crowd went ballistic. They were screaming, demanding answers and booing loudly before, but now things were getting out of hand.

Jennifer jogged down the sideline and over to Brant. "Poor Jimmy. He's having a rough night," she said in Brant's ear. "We're getting slaughtered!"

"They shouldn't boo him… this isn't his fault," Brant sighed. "Or Dad's. It's *my* fault. If they want to boo someone, they should boo me."

Mom hurried down to the fence as we got ready to head to the locker room for halftime. "David!" she shouted.

"Knock some sense into him, Doc!" I heard someone holler, and I rolled my eyes.

"David!" Mom shouted again, but so many people were shouting at once that Dad couldn't hear her.

I nudged Dad, pointed, and he turned to look at Mom. She smiled and gave us a big thumbs-up.

Dad's face lit up. He hurried over to the fence. "What changed your mind?" he exclaimed.

Mom looked behind her as angry fathers and fans shouted at Dad. "You heard the people… we've got a State Championship to win," she smiled as she kissed Dad.

"I love you," Dad smiled.

"I love you too," Mom smiled back. "Go on… give him the news!"

"Coach?" Principal Simmons said sternly as he pushed his way through the crowd. "I know you must have your reasons, but I just don't understand what…"

Dad cut him off. "It's okay, John," he smiled. "Spread the word… the Eagles are coming out for the second half with a vengeance." Then we hurried to the locker room to deliver the good news to Brant and the rest of our dejected team.

After Dad announced that Brant was back in the lineup, Brant did something that left me and every player on that team a little misty-eyed. I said before that it was an emotional night, and it reached its pentacle when my little brother climbed up on a locker room bench and, standing amongst a sea of teammates, called, "listen up, Eagles!"

The room fell silent.

"My whole life," Brant began, "I dreamed about playing for the North River Eagles. It was my dad's team. It was my big brother's team." Gone was the cocky attitude; gone was the swagger. "I know it was the same way for most of you… your dads played here, your grandfathers, your uncles, your brothers," he said. "When I was a kid I watched my brother play on this field, and I couldn't wait for the day that I would get my chance.

My freshman year when I played my first game on this field, I knew that the years I had spent waiting had been worth it. That team… we had something special. Through the years, we have lost guys who we didn't think that we could survive without, but we have always found new faces, fresh talents who were more than ready to fill their shoes. Four years ago when many of us here tonight put on this uniform for the very first time, we began to hear all the talk. They all said… *this is the class… this is the group of guys that is going to turn North River football into a force to be reckoned with.* Year in and year out we've proven all those people right. We have continued to get stronger as a unit. Together, we have been through so much during the past four years, but we have always come out on top… and come out stronger. We have survived the loss of people we loved dearly. We played football on the Friday night after we buried Chris Sanders that Friday morning three years ago, and we dedicated that victory to him. This past summer there were a lot of people who believed that our winning streak would end after doctors questioned whether or not I would play this season. During practice in August, each one of you guys told me how much you believed in me; you pushed me to get stronger, and I did… we all did. We have survived because, no matter what happened, we knew that we could depend on the guy standing next to us. And to me… that's what football is all about…"

He paused for a moment before continuing. You could have heard a pin drop in that locker room as we all listened to what Brant had to say. "Tonight… tonight was the night that was supposed to be the crowning moment of these past four years. We were supposed to go out and win our fourth championship in dominating fashion… and then stick around for the rest of the night taking pictures with the trophy and being praised as the class that never lost a single game at North River.

It's what we all wanted; it's what we all dreamed about, and it is the way it should have been. But tonight, I let every single one of you down. You were all depending on me tonight, and I failed you in a way that I never thought possible. I live for football; you all know that. I have devoted eighteen years preparing to quarterback this team, and I've spent the last four years tying to do it just a little better every Friday night.

I've quarterbacked every North River game that's been played over the past four years, until tonight when I was supposed to lead you in the most important game of the year… of our high school careers.

I messed up, and I want all of you to know that I'm sorry. This night hasn't turned out like any of us had hoped, and I'll understand if all of you are mad at me and want to finish this game without me. But this game is far from over. There're two quarters of football left out there, and, if it's okay with all of you, I would love a second chance."

Brant looked at his very inexperienced backup. "Jimmy," he said with a gentlemanly handshake, "this is your game if you want it. Just say the words, and I'm behind you a hundred and fifty percent. I mean that."

Jimmy smiled through his tears.

Tommy laughed, "yeah… and say you want to stay in the game, Jimbo, and I'll be on *top* of you… all two hundred and fifty percent of me. And I mean *that*."

Everyone laughed.

"Two-fifty?" Brant raised an eyebrow.

Tommy shoved Brant off the bench as he shrugged, "two-fifty… two-ninety… three hundred… I was working with a pattern there, Brantley… it went with what I was doing…"

Brant grinned playfully as he slapped Tommy's gut with the back of his hand.

Jimmy smiled broadly. "Brant, all night I've been out there getting pounded into the ground, asking myself why I ever dreamed of quarterbacking this team to begin with. You just reminded me, so thanks."

Brant smiled.

"I dug you a pretty big hole out there," Jimmy frowned.

Brant threw his arm around Jimmy. "Yeah, you did," he smiled, "but lucky for us… I'm pretty good at damage control."

"Well, the second half is all yours, Mr. McLachlan," Jimmy nodded.

"Thanks, Jimmy," Brant smiled.

"Hey, Brant," Jimmy grinned, "do you think this town will ever love me as much as they love you?"

"When you become their quarterback, they'll get behind you," Brant nodded with a smile. "Win, and they'll love you."

"It must be pretty cool, huh?" Jimmy shrugged.

"Yeah," Brant smiled, "it's a lot of fun… you'll enjoy it."

"I don't know," Jimmy laughed, "I'm pretty sure that, in the eyes of this town, I'll always be the guy who could never measure up to Brant McLachlan. You're a pretty tough act to follow."

Brant frowned as he put his arm around Jimmy. "Enjoy their praise," Brant said with a voice of experience. "They'll love you when you win, but they'll kick you when you're down. You'll never please everyone all the time. Accept their compliments; always do your best, so you feel comfortable ignoring their criticism. Know that their love is fun while it lasts, but it's false in the end. Real love is the support you get from your family and friends… the dad who has *your* best interest at heart, that brother who stands beside you when you don't deserve it, and that girl who loves you with all her heart, though you're not really sure how you got so lucky. Don't ever get caught up in all the hype. The second you do, you'll start believing what people say about you. And, whether it's negative or positive, you'll find yourself wondering when your reality became so confused."

Jimmy smiled. "They'll never love me like they love you, will they?"

Brant laughed. "No way," he shook his head. "Are you kidding me? I'm *Brant McLachlan*."

Jimmy laughed as he walked away, and I could hear the relief in his voice. The pressure was off, and he was ready to go out and watch Brant do what Brant did best.

Brant pulled his helmet on. "Hang on there, #13," Dad said as he grabbed Brant's jersey. Dad smiled as he pulled Brant into a hug. "I'm proud of you, son," he said sincerely.

Brant smiled. "Well, you know what Bear said, 'when we have a good team, I know it's because we have boys that come from good mamas and papas.' He was right… and I've got the best."

When Brant finally took the field that night the crowd roared, but, as I watched him take the football into his hands, it became obvious to me that the rumble of the crowd, the chanting of the cheerleaders and the crackle of the loudspeakers all merely provided a backdrop to his passion. When Brant stepped on that field, he owned it. He was born to play football and destined to become a champion.

***

After the game and the hoopla that followed, our family went to Jennifer's house to celebrate the victory.

Brant sat on the kitchen counter sticking his finger in the icing as Mrs. Smith cut the cake. She laughed as she jokingly poked her knife toward his hand.

"What do you want to drink, Brant?" Brianna asked as she and Jennifer filled paper cups with ice from the freezer.

"Dr. Pepper," Jennifer answered for him.

"Yep," Brant nodded as he licked the icing from his fingers.

"He's predictable," Kathy Smith chuckled.

Jennifer leaned on the counter beside Brant. "So let's hear it," she whispered. "Are you gonna tell me what happened tonight or what?"

Brant wiped the icing from his fingers, and put his hands on Jennifer's shoulders. "I took some painkillers," he said.

"Yeah," Jennifer nodded.

"Prescription painkillers," Brant said softly.

"Okay," Jennifer gulped.

"I took too many of them because I didn't listen to you in the first place and have my back taken care of before it got to the point where I couldn't take the pain," Brant told her. "I took some before the game… quite a few of them, and I passed out."

"Sweetie," Jennifer sighed sympathetically. She hugged him. "Thank goodness you're okay."

Brianna walked over. "I should have known it, Brant," she scolded. "What have I been telling you all along?"

"Have you been telling him to have his back examined too?" Jennifer asked innocently.

"I've been telling him that taking serious painkillers in unreal dosages isn't the best way to deal with the pain," Brianna rattled off.

Brant exhaled loudly.

Jennifer's face immediately turned angry. "You knew?" she exclaimed. "You knew that he was overdosing on prescription painkillers?"

Everyone turned to look at Brianna. I stopped tussling with Ben as the room grew quiet, and we, like everyone else, awaited Brianna's explanation.

"Wow… like calm down," Brianna smiled.

"I will not calm down," Jennifer said, raising her voice. "You knew that Brant was taking pills that could hurt him, and you didn't tell anyone?"

"It's okay, Jennifer," Brant said as he rubbed her back, "it was all my fault, not hers. I begged her for the pills..."

"Wait. What?" Jennifer huffed. She turned quickly to Brianna. "Not only did you know he was taking them, but you were getting them for him?" she screamed. "Where? How? Why? I don't understand!"

"Oh, step down off your *Little Miss Perfect* pedestal, Jennifer," Brianna laughed.

"You don't have to reply to that, Rocky," Brant frowned, grabbing Jennifer's shoulders and pulling her toward him.

Jennifer snatched her shoulders away from Brant's hands. "She knew that your health was in serious jeopardy, and she didn't tell anyone," Jennifer argued. "I don't care if you begged her for the pills or not. She should have seen that you needed help."

"I know; I see your point," Brant nodded, "but this is on me…"

"I should have known you'd always take *her* side," Brianna scoffed.

"Brianna," Jennifer exclaimed, suddenly fed up, "you know what… *leave*! Get out of my house! I have put up with your attitude long enough. I have tried so hard to be nice to you, but this is a special night for me and my friends, so you should just go before you ruin it for everybody."

Brianna rolled her eyes. "Let's go, Brant," she chirped.

"Why in the world would he leave with you?" Jennifer laughed as astonishment shone on her face.

Brianna smiled at Brant. "Oh, I don't know," she batted her eyelashes.

"You should leave, Brianna," Brant said sternly.

"This party is lame anyway," Brianna grumbled.

"Feel free to leave," Brant pointed at the door.

"Last chance," Brianna smiled at Brant. "Come with me, and we'll go celebrate right."

"Jennifer asked you to leave," Brant snapped. "Now get on out of here before I escort you out myself."

Brianna put her hands on her hips. "You jerk!" she exclaimed as she raised her hand to slap Brant's face, but he caught her arm in mid-swing.

"Somebody ought to slap *you*!" Jennifer exclaimed as she charged at Brianna.

Brant dropped Brianna's arm and held Jennifer off as Brianna stood her ground. Brant stepped in front of Jennifer, and Jennifer wrapped her arms around his waist, her face hidden behind his back.

"So, that's gonna be how it is? You're choosing her?" Brianna sighed.

"There was never a choice to be made," Brant shrugged as he stared hard at Brianna.

"Well," Brianna rolled her eyes, "I guess there is just no accounting for some people's taste. You'll regret this, but I guess we all make mistakes because thinking I saw something in you was a big one."

"You know, Brianna… you have some nerve!" Jennifer's mother exclaimed as she rushed over.

"Oh great," Brianna rolled her eyes, "here comes Mommy to the rescue."

"You heard my daughter," Kathy Smith pointed, "get out of our home."

Brianna walked toward the door, but, before leaving, she turned back to Brant. "You have no idea what you're passing up," she shook her head.

Brant rolled his eyes before slamming the door in her face.

"Brant," Brianna called, "I need a ride home!"

"Call a cab!" Brant yelled.

"In Cummins?" Christian laughed.

"Walk!" Brant barked toward the door.

"I'll take her home," I offered.

"Thank you," Mom smiled as I reached for my keys, "hurry back."

Kathy Smith pointed at the front door as I exited. "That girl is nothing but trouble!" she declared.

"Wait until I have a chance to talk to her mother," Mom added. "Her stash of painkillers could have… *oh*, I don't even want to *think* about it."

"Well, you can tell from the daughter's actions that the mother must be a real piece of work," Kathy Smith added as she put a comforting arm around her friend.

"That's right," Mom nodded in agreement, "that child wouldn't act the way she does if she had a role model at home."

"Absolutely not," Jennifer's mom agreed as she went back to cutting the cake.

"Well," Jennifer smiled as she put one arm around Brant's back, "at least we got rid of her before she could cause us more heartache than she already has."

Brant frowned.

"You okay?" Jennifer asked.

Brant forced a smile. "I am now," he said as he kissed Jennifer's forehead. "I love you."

CHAPTER TEN

Mrs. Edna Massey put her hand on my shoulder as we walked from the church sanctuary. She was eighty-seven years old, had thin, gray hair and walked with a cane, but Mrs. Edna always had a smile and a kind word for everyone.

"Hey there, Mrs. E," I said, leaning down to kiss her cheek, "I hope you're hungry… it looks like we've got plenty of food around here."

"Yes," she nodded in her feeble voice, "if there is one thing this church is good at, it's eatin' and fellowshipping." Then she smiled broadly. "I made my good ole, mashed potatoes especially for you."

"Oh… Mrs. E," I said, my mouth watering, "I thought about your mashed potatoes throughout most of the service."

"Oooh! Shame on you, Jordan McLachlan!" she scolded. We both laughed.

Ms. Harriet Brewer strolled by in one of her infamous large-brimmed hats. "Where is that brother of yours?" she asked me.

"They're all around here somewhere," I replied.

Harriet Brewer hugged Mrs. Edna as she said, "I made bad ole Brantley my chicken casserole that he likes so much… so he won't have to get on to me like he did at our last dinner on the ground when I made something else instead."

Fred Thornton chuckled as he approached in his good pair of Sunday overalls. He and I shook hands. "Y'all spoil that boy, ladies," he said gruffly.

Stan Huffman, a jolly, former North River defensive lineman, joined our conversation. "After that performance at the State Championship a few weeks ago… my lands… I think any of us would buy the kid whatever he wanted," he declared.

Mr. Thornton shook his head. "Wanda cooked all day yesterday; last night I went in the kitchen for a snack, and I'll have you know she was still up cookin'. I told her she had done made enough to feed the entire church, and she said that she'd be done as soon as she got Brant's cookies out of the oven... wouldn't even let me have a dang one when they was done either."

Wanda Thornton, a once beautiful North River cheerleader, turned from her own conversation to interject, "oh, hush-up, Fred. Brantley's been eating Mrs. Wanda's chocolate chip and M&M's cookies since he was a baby."

Ben Smith and Kristen Waterford raced past us. Kristen laughed as she ran, the bow on the back of her pink dress untied and blowing behind her as Ben gave chase.

Jennifer trailed them with the Susie Carpenter's eleven-month-old on her hip, calling, "Ben! Come change into your play clothes before you ruin your dress pants!"

Ethan walked by holding a pie in one hand and a basket of cornbread in the other. "I see they put you to work already," I smiled.

"Brantley!" I heard my mom's voice call. "Baby... will you run out to the car and see if you can find my purse?"

Brant turned his nose up, but headed toward the car. His cell phone rang. He answered it, talked for a moment, then, forgetting the purse, he changed directions. He glanced over at Jennifer, and, seeing that she was busy lassoing kids, he headed toward his truck. He placed his *Bible* on the dash and started the engine. I rolled my eyes and excused myself to go to the car and find Mom's purse.

In the community where my brothers and I grew up, dinner on the ground after church was common. People who went out of their way making special dishes to show their love for the kids they had watched grow from infants into men and women were even more common. In a town where everybody knew everybody, perhaps no one was more beloved than Brant. He was the All-American boy... blond hair, blue eyes, the star quarterback of a town obsessed with football... what wasn't to love? He was a good kid... a small town, country boy with big dreams and a bright future. In the eyes of the people of Cummins, Brant had it all. That is why, over the next couple days, his fall from grace would shock not only our family, but our entire community. For the people of Cummins, the news would give them something to gossip about. For our family, the news would be devastating. For Brant, it would change his life forever and threaten to destroy the life he had always known.

***

When Brant arrived at Brianna's house, she was standing outside waiting for him.

"This better be important," he huffed as he got out of his truck. "I left a lot of good food to come over here, and I need to get back... I'm starvin'."

"I need to talk to you," Brianna gulped.

"What in the world could be so important that it couldn't wait until later?" Brant shrugged.

Brianna turned from him as she began to cry.

Brant followed her inside. "What is your problem?" he huffed.

"Maybe you should sit down," Brianna said pointing at the sofa.

Brant glanced over at the sofa and rolled his eyes. "No thank you," he cringed as he sat down at the kitchen table instead. "Why are you crying? You cried on the phone... that's the only reason I agreed to come over here. I thought something might actually be wrong? What is it?" he insisted.

"I'm scared," Brianna whimpered.

"Okay," Brant shook his head with a confused shrug, "so are you going to tell me *why* you're scared, or do I have to guess?"

"Something is wrong," Brianna shook her head.

"What is it, Brianna?" Brant asked harshly as he became frustrated with her game. "Are you sick? Are you hurt? Is it your mother? What?"

Brianna glanced over at the sofa. "Do you remember what we..."

"Oh my gosh," Brant yelled angrily, as he stood up, "why are you bringing that up? I want to forget that night ever happened, and I would appreciate if you would do the same."

"We can't," Brianna shook her head.

"I already have," Brant fired back.

"Brant, I'm pregnant," Brianna trembled.

Brant's shoulders slumped, and he fell back into his chair. "What did you say?" he gulped.

"I'm pregnant," Brianna repeated.

"No," Brant shook his head.

"Yes," Brianna sighed.

"This can't be happening," Brant said as the color left his face. He stood again. "Are you sure?" he snapped.

Brianna nodded.

Brant paced quickly back and forth. "So how can you be so sure that this baby is even mine?" he blurted. "Huh? Tell me that."

"Brant," Brianna sighed, "how could you ask me that?"

"Oh I don't know, Brianna," Brant shrugged emphatically. "How am I supposed to know how many guys you've trapped into having sex with you? I'm not the only big, strong football player in this town, you know."

"That's not very nice," Brianna snapped. She crossed her arms. "No one forced you to... gosh... this is hard enough without..." Brianna began to cry.

Brant ran his fingers through his hair. "This can't be happening to me," he told himself as he dropped into the chair again.

"I'm sorry," Brianna sobbed, "but listen, Brant... just get me some money, and we'll take care of this."

Brant looked up quickly. "What?" he sighed.

"Don't look so shocked, Brant. You didn't think I was planning on *having* the baby... did you?" Brianna replied quietly. "Is that why you were freaking out... did you think that I would want to keep the baby?"

"What do you mean?" Brant asked as he stared at her.

"I mean... get me some cash, and I'll have an abortion," Brianna explained with a shrug.

"An abortion?" Brant repeated slowly. "You can't do that. That's murder."

"Oh, don't be so dramatic," Brianna rolled her eyes. "Abortion isn't murder... it's a woman's right."

"I don't believe I'm hearing this," Brant sighed as he leaned back in his chair.

"Brant, what would you like me to say?" Brianna raised her voice. "I can't have a baby. You don't want a baby and neither do I."

Brant buried his face in his hands. "How could I be so stupid?" he yelled. He jumped from his chair and kicked the back of the sofa. "I don't believe this is happening," he cried as he kicked the sofa again.

"No one has to know that I had an abortion, Brant," Brianna insisted. "No one... not your parents... not Jennifer... no one ever has to know that I was pregnant... or even that we had sex for that matter."

"Jen..." Brant sighed as he sat down again.

"Would you calm down, please?" Brianna rolled her eyes. "I just told you that Jennifer never has to know about this. Jennifer is not the one who has to deal with this... I am... so would it kill you to show a little sympathy for *me*?"

Brant took a deep breath. "Yeah... okay... you're right... I'm sorry. It's just that we can't hide this from Jennifer, and I don't know..."

"What?" Brianna laughed. "Do you just *want* to tell her that you and I slept together? Is it weighing on your conscience so much that you are going to destroy your relationship with her because the thought of keeping a secret from her is too much for you to handle?"

"Brianna, you're pregnant," Brant snapped.

"Open your ears, Brant... I'm going to have an abortion," Brianna smiled. "I'm giving you a way out. You have no problem. I just need cash!"

Brant shook his head. "You can't have an abortion," he sighed. "You might think it sounds good now, but you'll hate yourself later."

"I've done it before, Brantley. You get over it," Brianna confessed.

"I am an idiot," Brant said softly, and he wiped the sweat from his forehead.

"It's the only way out," Brianna shrugged.

For half a second, Brant allowed himself to wonder if she was right. *Nobody would ever have to know...* and he was horrified that the thought could even cross his mind as a consideration. "There is no way out," Brant stomped, "it's too late. Don't you see that?"

"Listen to me," Brianna said, taking Brant's hand.

Brant jerked his hand away.

"This is the only answer," Brianna insisted. "A simple abortion will solve all of this. I won't be pregnant, and you won't have to tell your precious, virgin girlfriend that you and I had really great sex..."

"*Drunken sex* ..." Brant argued, "which I don't even know why I bothered to preface, since it does nothing to make me feel any better about myself."

"You would feel better about all of it if you just came up with some cash," Brianna persisted.

"Killing your baby… that's your idea of a solution?" Brant snapped.

Brianna frowned. "*Our* baby, Brant," she nodded.

"Our baby," Brant repeated slowly.

"Brant, we made a mistake," Brianna sighed.

"Yeah," Brant nodded, "and in the process… we made a baby. Brianna, *we* deserve to be punished for what we did… but that baby… he… or she… is innocent."

Brianna crossed her arms. "You're acting like we deserve a life sentence for sleeping together?" she rolled her eyes. "That's what having a baby would be like, Brant…"

Brant put his hands over his face and muttered, "I was always taught that if you do the crime, you do the time."

"Since when was having sex a crime?" Brianna laughed.

Brant paced around the room. "Brianna, you and I were raised differently," he sighed. "In my world, having sex before you're married is a sin… and *abortion*… well…"

"Well," Brianna groaned, "you're right, I guess. I don't know much about any of that stuff, but isn't God like famous for forgiving sins? So what's the big deal?"

"Unreal," Brant exhaled as he closed his eyes.

There was a long silence.

Then Brianna spoke first. "So, if God will forgive you, since that seems to be so important to you, why don't we just get the abortion, and then you can beg for forgiveness later?" she suggested.

"Brianna, it doesn't work quite like that," Brant replied, "and even if it did, my Earthly father is not nearly as kind, understanding or patient as my Heavenly Father."

"Your dad never has to know," Brianna protested.

Brant ignored her. "More importantly," he sighed, "how am I supposed to explain this to Jennifer?"

"There you go again," Brianna rolled her eyes. "Jennifer! Jennifer! Jennifer!"

"I love her, okay?" Brant snapped. "I don't want to hurt her!"

"You don't have to… don't you see that?" Brianna begged.

For another split second, Brant considered what Brianna was telling him. Then, hating himself for the cowardly thought, he shook his head. "No, Brianna," he said as he continued to pace the floor, "the way that I see this... there is a human life growing inside of you, and it is not up to you or me when that life ends. We don't have that sort of authority."

"Don't think that I'm a horrible person, Brant," Brianna sighed. "I was sixteen the first time, and my boyfriend was all for the abortion. He had rich parents, and they paid more than willingly. I know that your career means everything to you... that Jennifer means everything to you... so I figured that you'd want the same thing that he did."

"No," Brant shook his head.

"Okay," Brianna said after a moment, "if it's really what you want... we'll keep the baby and raise it together."

Brant closed his eyes, and he pictured Jennifer's face. "Now I know why everyone says wait," he gulped as he opened his eyes to look at Brianna. "This should be a happy time shared by two people who are in love and ready to start a family. Jennifer has dreamed of this moment since she was a little girl. I was supposed to hold her in my arms... we were supposed to be so excited, so happy... ready to provide for and raise our family. Instead, I'm eighteen years old, and I'm gonna be somebody's daddy. And, in the meantime, I am gonna break the heart of the only woman I'm ever gonna love."

No one said anything for a moment. "I can't go through this by myself, Brant," Brianna cried.

"You don't have to," Brant shook his head. "I'm gonna be here for you every step of the way... I'm gonna help you through this. Just promise me..."

"If you don't want me to have an abortion, I won't," Brianna nodded, "but you have to swear to be here for me... throughout the pregnancy and especially after the baby is born. This is not something *I'm* going to do... it has to be something we do together."

"I promise," Brant gulped.

Brianna wrapped her arms around Brant. "I love you, Brant," she smiled.

Brant moved away; he sat down at the kitchen table and buried his face in his hands. He looked up at Brianna. "I've got to go," he gulped. "People are gonna start missing me."

"Yeah, you better go," Brianna agreed. "I guess you and Jennifer have a lot to talk about."

Brant stared at the door.

"Brant, this baby is going to bond us for life," Brianna said as she touched Brant's arm.

Brant looked at Brianna's hand. He knew that she was right, and he stood, wondering how he would ever tell Jennifer what Brianna had just told him.

***

When Brant pulled back into the church parking lot, he watched as everyone sat eating and talking in the distance. The kids ran and played; the adults lounged and laughed.

Brant reached for his *Bible* on the dash and tossed it onto his passenger's seat. When he did, the *Bible* fell open. Brant stared at the open page. Slowly, he picked the *Bible* up, and, as he began to read the inscription, his eyes filled with tears.

"Brantley Tyler McLachlan,

On this occasion, the day of your kindergarten graduation, I give you this *Bible*. I realize that, as you grow, there will come a day when you don't hold my hand as you cross the street. There will come a day when you will have to make a life decision, and I won't be there to offer advice. As you grow up, you will face challenges and hardships that won't be mine to solve, and you will have questions that I can't answer. The one piece of advice that I can offer you today, Brantley, is that, as you grow, there are three things in your life that will never change. One, God loves you. Two, Mom and I love you. And three, the answer to any question you may have can be found in this book. So, on this special day, as you graduate from kindergarten, 'I'm giving you the ball, son, and naming you quarterback for your team in the game of life. It is a long game with no timeouts and no substitutions. You'll have a great backfield with great reputations. They are named Faith, Hope and Love. You'll work behind a truly powerful line. End to end, it consists of Honesty, Loyalty, Devotion to duty, Self-respect, Study, Cleanliness and Good behavior. The goalposts are the Gates of Heaven. God is the referee and sole official. There are ten rules. You know them as the Ten Commandments. The ball, it is your immortal soul. Hold on to it. Now, son, get in there and see what you can do with it!'

Love, Daddy"

Brant lay his head on his steering wheel as he wept for the first time.

When Tommy knocked on Brant's truck window, it startled him. He quickly wiped his tears.

"What are you doing out here?" Tommy asked as he opened Brant's truck door.

"I had to go somewhere," Brant said.

"Where?" Tommy replied nonchalantly. He studied Brant's face. "Have you been… *crying*?"

"No… and I don't want to talk about it," Brant shook his head.

Tommy stared curiously at Brant as he climbed into the passenger's seat. "Alright… but… you've got to come eat… Mrs. Kathy made her famous barbecued chicken," he nodded.

"Yeah, I know," Brant smiled, "you've got a little there on your shirt that you must be savin' for later."

Tommy laughed. "Well, come-on," he shrugged, "let's eat."

"I'm not too hungry," Brant shook his head.

"What do you mean you aren't hungry?" Tommy frowned.

"I'm just… not hungry," Brant shrugged.

"Brant, is everything okay? You're acting a little strange," Tommy sighed.

Brant turned to look out the window, away from Tommy. "I'm fine… just… Tommy, I need to be alone for awhile. Okay?"

"Okay," Tommy nodded after a moment, "well… I guess I'll be over there finishing off your mom's banana pudding if you decide you want to talk."

"Thanks," Brant replied softly.

"Alright, Brant! That's it!" Tommy insisted. "What's going on? Where did you go, and why are you acting like you just lost your best friend in the world?"

Brant glanced over at Tommy but said nothing.

"Brant talk to me," Tommy frowned. "You aren't taking those stupid pills again are you? You could have killed yourself…"

"No," Brant groaned, "I'm done with the painkillers. Scared straight I guess you could say."

"Good," Tommy nodded, "so if it's not about the pills… what then?"

Brant took a deep breath. "If I got into trouble, you'd have my back… no matter what… right?"

"How big is this guy?" Tommy moaned.

"There's no fight," Brant rolled his eyes.

"Something's going on… and I'm not leaving until you tell me what it is," Tommy insisted as he crossed his arms.

"Tommy," Brant sighed, "I messed up, man. I messed up bad."

"It sounds serious," Tommy gulped.

"It's Brianna," Brant nodded.

"Is that where you were? With Brianna?" Tommy barked.

"Yeah… she called me and insisted that I had to come over to her house."

"And what could possibly have you so rattled?" Tommy shrugged.

"Brianna's pregnant," Brant replied softly.

Tommy stared at Brant in disbelief. "How's that *your* problem?" he laughed.

"Tommy, I never meant for this to happen," Brant sighed. "It only happened once… I didn't…"

"No," Tommy gasped, "you mean… *you and Brianna*… no way…"

"Do I have to spell it out for you?" Brant snapped. "Once… one time…"

"How could you do this, Brant?" Tommy asked as he stared at his best friend.

"I don't know," Brant shook his head as the tears returned.

Jennifer walked by in front of the truck, a baby on her hip and a little girl by the hand. She glanced over at the boys, smiled, and continued on her way.

"How could you do this to *her*?" Tommy yelled at Brant. "How in the world are you going to tell Jen that you not only slept with Brianna, but you got her pregnant?"

"I can't tell her," Brant shook his head. "She is going to be devastated, and Jennifer is everything to me, Tommy."

"Was she everything to you when you and Brianna were busy losing your clothes?" Tommy shrugged angrily.

"Tommy," Brant begged.

"No," Tommy shook his head, "listen to me, Brant. You've done some pretty stupid things in your life, but you really outdid yourself this time. Are you crazy? What were you thinking?"

"I don't need a lecture," Brant huffed, "not from you of all people. It's not like I meant for this to happen. It's not like I went over there that night hoping that I would end up in bed with the girl. That's not how it happened. I had a little to drink…"

"I don't care whether you meant for it to happen or not," Tommy snapped. "I don't care what your intentions were. Brant, you had *sex* with her! How could you let that happen? And since when do you drink?"

"Lay off, okay," Brant barked back. "Don't you pretend for a second that if Brianna Clarke had been all over *you* that night that you would have said *no*."

"You're absolutely right," Tommy gulped, "I probably wouldn't have. Who am I kidding… of course, I wouldn't have." He looked out the window and stared at Jennifer in the distance. "But, then again, the greatest girl that God put on this Earth isn't madly in love with *me*."

"I can't tell her," Brant shook his head.

Tommy exhaled loudly. "You had it all, Brant," he shook his head. "You had the looks, the talent, the career, the charisma, and, most notably, you had the girl that any of us would have killed for, and you blew it, man."

"I know," Brant nodded tearfully.

"She loves you," Tommy shrugged, "and I *thought* you loved her."

"I do love her," Brant insisted. "Tommy, I love her more than anything in this world. I just messed up."

"Yeah," Tommy sighed. "Yeah, Brant, you sure did." He opened the door, slid from the truck and slammed the door behind him.

Brant pounded the steering wheel with his fist before draping himself over it as he began to cry.

***

The following night Brant called us all together to deliver the news that would turn all our lives upside down.

Mom and Dad were sitting on the couch, and my brothers and I were all gathered around the living room eager to hear what Brant swore was more important than Monday night football. Dad was already miffed about missing his Saints game, which made Brant even more apprehensive about what he had to say.

Mom patted the sofa. "Come sit," she said almost gleefully.

"I'd prefer to be out of Dad's reach when I say this," Brant sighed.

"You aren't out of my range all the way over there, buddy," Dad smiled, wondering what silly mischief Brant had gotten himself into this time.

"Well," Brant nodded, "what I need to say… I mean… what I need to tell you is… that… okay, how should I put this…"

"Oh, come-on! You've got to be kidding me. The entire game will be over, boy," Dad groaned.

"Let him finish, David," Mom interjected.

"There's something I need to tell you," Brant said.

"Yes… we've established that," Dad nodded, "so how about spitting it out before halftime?"

"Brianna," Brant began, "well, she's *uhhh…*" His voice faded.

"She's what?" Ethan shrugged.

"Yeah… is what?" Christian added.

"Um…" was all Brant said as he rubbed his hands together nervously.

"What is his problem, Becky?" Dad groaned.

"Just say it, Brantley," Mom urged.

"She's pregnant," Brant blurted.

Dad's face was instantly drained of color. "What do you mean she's pregnant?" he asked slowly. "You aren't saying that…"

Brant took a step back. "Yeah… that's what I'm saying… Brianna is pregnant," he swallowed before adding, "with my baby."

Dad's face went from ghost white to steam engine red. I will never forget the way he stood up and walked straight into the kitchen. I don't think that he had ever helped with any housework in his life until that night. He didn't say a word to Brant or anyone else; he just strode into the kitchen and started washing dishes.

"You slept with Brianna?" Christian sighed.

Brant stared at the carpet.

"I don't believe this," Ethan shook his head.

"Not even you can talk your way out of this one, Brant," Christian said angrily.

"Just shut up, okay?" Brant snapped.

"No… I won't shut up," Christian fired back. He stood up and took two steps toward Brant. Brant shoved him away, and Christian shoved Brant back hard enough to knock him into the table. A picture frame crashed to the floor, and both boys stared down at the picture of Brant and Jennifer in a sandbox as kids, their arms wrapped so tightly around one another that it looked as though nothing could ever separate them.

"Boys!" Mom intervened. She looked at my brothers and me. "Jordan, Christian, Ethan, go upstairs," she sighed.

Christian, Ethan and I walked slowly up the stairs.

Mom stared at Brant. "I don't know what to say," she said exasperatedly. "I am so disappointed in you."

"I know," Brant nodded. "I'm so sorry, Mom… I don't know what else to say."

A dish shattered, and Dad burst back into the living room so suddenly that it startled my brothers and me as we watched from the stairs. "Come here!" Dad's voice echoed throughout the house. He grabbed the sleeve of Brant's shirt. "Outside… now!" he demanded.

"David… what are you doing?" Mom gulped.

Dad shoved Brant out the front door. "If we aren't back in five minutes, you might want to call him an ambulance," he hollered back.

"David," Mom insisted as she followed Dad out the door, "let go of him. That is not helping the situation."

"Your irresponsibility has gotten out of hand, Brantley," Dad yelled as he backed Brant against a column on the porch. "You wrecked your truck, and I bought you a brand new one. You and Brianna stole hundreds of dollars worth of painkillers, and I didn't have you locked up like a common criminal. But, I am through putting up with you…"

Dad jerked Brant away from the column just so he could shove him back into it.

"David," Mom screamed, "stop it, right now! You're going to hurt his back."

Dad turned to Mom. "Becky, I raised four sons to be mature, responsible, Godly men," he said angrily, "but, through no fault of ours, this one turned out to be some sort of reckless heathen, and I won't stand for it."

"Whatever you want to say to him about this situation obviously should have been said way before now, David," Mom replied. "Now, it is your job as a mature, responsible, Godly man yourself to let him know that, though what he did was very wrong and it went against everything that he's ever been taught, he could never mess up to the extent that you wouldn't love him and stand behind him."

Dad crossed his arms. "How can you be so rational about this?" he sighed.

"Somebody has to," Mom shrugged.

Dad stared at Brant. "Do you have anything to say for yourself?" he asked.

Brant shook his head. "Just that I'm sorry," he sighed.

"You've turned into somebody I don't know, Brantley," Dad frowned. Brant started to reply, but Dad added, "yet, I think I still know you well enough to know that you didn't cheat on Jennifer without some extenuating circumstances that you're leaving out. What happened? Were you drinking? Were you drunk… is that how this happened?"

"Yes, sir," Brant said after a moment, "I was drinking and taking the pills… it was all really stupid."

"Right," Dad scoffed. "Are you hearing this, Becky? Our son does drugs, drinks alcohol and has sex with girls he hardly knows. Aren't you just full of motherly pride right now?"

"Calm down, David," Mom sighed.

"Go to your room, Brant," Dad pointed. "Go now… I can't look at you right now, and, while you're up there, go ahead and decide where you're going to college."

"Dad," Brant rolled his eyes.

"What?" Dad shrugged. "You have proven to me over and over again these past few months that you are not mature enough or responsible enough to live on your own in Dallas. You aren't ready for that sort of freedom, and you sure aren't ready to face the temptations that you'll be faced with while playing professional football. The NFL was right to begin with; you might have the skills to play, but you're far from ready."

"That is ridiculous," Brant protested.

"What are you getting so defensive about?" Dad huffed. "You have proven that your judgment… well, frankly, son… it sucks. Playing pro ball, there will be drugs and women available to you… you'll be traveling from city to city… and your mother and I don't need to have to worry about having grandchildren spread all across the country…"

"Oh my gosh, Dad," Brant rolled his eyes.

Dad shrugged. "Brant," he sighed, "you have proven that you act before you stop to consider the consequences of your actions. That tells me that you still have a good deal of growing up to do."

"I won't go to college," Brant insisted.

Dad grabbed Brant's shirtsleeve and jerked him toward him.

"David," Mom shook her head as she tapped Dad's arm. "Let go of him. If he doesn't straighten his life out, he'll end up in just as much trouble at any college as he would in Dallas. That really isn't the issue at hand."

Dad let Brant go, and, frustrated, he exhaled loudly. He turned to Mom. "How do I even punish him for something like this?" he shrugged. "This isn't something that I can send him to his room for, and, short of killing him, I just don't know what to do."

Mom stared at Brant. "Does Jennifer know yet?" she asked softly.

"No," Brant shook his head, "I don't know how to tell her. What do I say? How do I make her understand?"

Mom crossed her arms. "I think figuring that one out is all the punishment he can stand," she nodded, tears streaming down her face.

Dad nodded. "She is the best thing that ever happened to you, Brant," Dad shook his head.

"How could you do this to her?" Mom asked as her eyes filled with sympathetic tears for the young woman she had always loved like a daughter. "Bless her heart… she is going to be devastated, Brantley," she cried.

Brant stared at the ground. As hard as it had been for him to tell Mom and Dad that Brianna was pregnant, he knew that he was yet to tell the person that the news was going to hurt the most, and a sick feeling consumed him.

***

The next morning Brant got up early and drove to Jennifer's house before school. She was just about to leave when Brant walked into her bedroom.

"Hey there, Cowboy," she smiled as she finished tying her shoelace.

"Hey, Jen," Brant replied, unable to force a smile.

Jennifer stopped what she was doing. "Is something wrong?" she asked.

"Yes," Brant nodded.

"Well, what is it?" Jennifer asked as concern registered on her face.

"Rocky, I have to tell you something," Brant said softly. "I'd give anything to change it, but I can't..."

"You're scaring me, Brantley," Jennifer gulped.

Brant stared at a picture sitting in a frame on Jennifer's nightstand. He had his arms around her, and the smiles on both their faces told of their love for one another.

Brant sat down next to Jennifer and took her hand. "For the past couple days I have been trying to come up with the best way to say this to you," Brant began, "but any way that I say it, it's gonna break your heart, and that kills me."

Jennifer stared back at Brant, unsure of how to respond.

"I used some really bad judgment one night," Brant continued, "and..."

"And what? Why is this so hard for you?" Jennifer sighed. "Brant, you tell me everything."

Brant stared at the floor.

"You can tell me anything," Jennifer gulped.

"You're gonna hate me," Brant sighed.

"Never," Jennifer shook her head slowly. "Just tell me."

"I'm so sorry," Brant insisted.

"Okay," Jennifer smiled sympathetically, "I'm sure that everything will be fine as soon as you tell me."

"Jennifer, I got Brianna pregnant," Brant cried.

Jennifer shook her head in disbelief. "No," she gulped, "I must have misunderstood what you..."

"No," Brant cried, "Jennifer, you heard right..."

Jennifer eased her hand away from Brant as she remained frozen in a state of shock. "You slept with her?" she struggled to get out.

"It wasn't like that," Brant shook his head. "My back was hurting… she gave me a drink… I wasn't thinking clearly…"

Jennifer moved away from Brant as she began to cry. "How could you?" she quivered.

"I'm so sorry, Jen," Brant turned away, unable to bear the heartbreak that was written all over Jennifer's face.

"I think I'm gonna faint," Jennifer said softly as she eased herself onto her bed.

Brant made an attempt to help her, but she resisted his touch.

Jennifer curled up on her bed and pulled her teddy bear close to her as she cried.

Brant put his hand on Jennifer's shoulder. "I'm so sorry," he said through his tears.

Jennifer shook her head. "I thought you loved me," she wailed.

"I do, Jen. I do love you. Brianna means nothing to me… she never has and never will…" Brant pled.

Jennifer sat up and pulled her knees to her chest. "When did it happen?" she asked.

"Right before the State Championship," Brant sighed.

"Where?" Jennifer replied quickly.

"At her house," Brant told her.

"Why?" Jennifer insisted.

Brant closed his eyes. "That one I can't answer, Jen," he shrugged. "All I can tell you is that I'm sorry, and that I love you with all my heart."

"No," Jennifer shook her head, "not if you could do this to me… not if you could hurt me like this… you don't love me."

"I do love you, Jennifer," Brant nodded tearfully. "That's the only thing in my life that I'm sure about right now… I love you, and I'm certain about that."

"You had *sex* with her," Jennifer whimpered.

"I'm sorry," Brant gulped. "I know that must sound pretty lame right now, but it's all that I can say. What do you want me to do? Just tell me what to do… I'll do anything…"

"I want you to go away, and I don't want you to come back… not today… not ever," Jennifer cried as she buried herself under her pillow.

"Jen," Brant sighed as he reached for her.

Again, Jennifer shied away from his touch.

"Jennifer, I've got to make you understand. Please, just give me a chance to explain," Brant begged.

Jennifer only pointed toward the door.

"Jen, let's not leave it like this," Brant pled.

Jennifer ripped the pillow off of her face. "Get out, Brant! I mean it!" She hit him with the pillow. "Get out!" she shouted as she began pounding his chest with her fists. Brant grabbed her arms and restrained her as he swore his love for her. "Get out," Jennifer said softly. Brant let go of her arms, and, exhausted, she dropped gently back onto her bed.

Brant nodded slowly as he turned toward the door. He stopped in the doorway, and his eyes filled with tears at the sound of Jennifer's muffled cry. "I'm sorry, Jennifer," he said before easing her bedroom door closed and leaving her to grieve on her on.

***

Months passed; April 21st was NFL Draft Day. It was supposed to be the day that all of Brant's dreams came true. Though half the town, it seemed like, gathered at our house to anxiously await the phone call that we had all thought about, dreamt about and prayed about for years, Brant's day was not the special day he had envisioned ever since he started playing pee-wee football at North River Community Park.

The problem wasn't all of the people who were gathered, with their noisemakers, painted t-shirts and balloons, to share in Brant's day; Brant didn't seem to notice how many people were there standing behind him and supporting him. Instead, his attention was focused on the one who wasn't there, and her absence made the day difficult for him to get through. When the phone rang, the people cheered. Brant answered, but, as his dream came true, he didn't even sound excited.

***

Brant walked up to Jennifer as she stood at her locker. "Jen… I want to talk to you," he said.

"If you want to tell me that you were taken nineteenth overall by the Cowboys… I already know," Jennifer said, not looking at him. "Congratulations."

"I wish you had been there," Brant sighed, "I really…"

"Brant, I'm not having a very good day," Jennifer cut him off, "so please just leave me alone."

"I'm not having a very good day myself," Brant shook his head.

"Why not?" Jennifer shrugged. "You've got everything you've ever wanted…"

"That's not true, and you know it! I don't even know if I'm gonna go to Dallas," Brant said confidently.

"Of course you're going," Jennifer rolled her eyes at him.

"I haven't decided yet," Brant shook his head.

"Brant, you decided when you were like *five*!" Jennifer exclaimed. "You fought hard to make yourself eligible; you're going! If you think that hanging around here is going to fix things between us, you're mistaken. I've decided to go to the University of Alabama."

"Yeah," Brant nodded, "Christian told me."

"I might even go early and take some classes this summer," Jennifer added.

"You don't have to do that… you don't have to run away from me," Brant swallowed.

"I don't want to be here this summer," Jennifer insisted.

"When the baby comes," Brant nodded. Jennifer started to speak, but Brant cut her off. "You know… I shouldn't have to hear things like *where you decided to go to school* from my brother. That was a big decision, one that we…"

"Don't *even* go there, Brant," Jennifer sighed.

"I know," Brant nodded as he lowered his head.

There was a long pause.

"Hey," Brant shrugged suddenly, "maybe I'll sign with Alabama. I'll play football, you'll cheer… just like old times."

A small, single tear ran down Jennifer's cheek.

"Jen… please don't cry," Brant sighed.

"I cry a lot these days, Brant," Jennifer shrugged as she turned away.

"I know," Brant nodded, "and I'm sorry."

Jennifer turned to Brant, her face angry. "Do you have any idea how sick I am of hearing people tell me that they're sorry? I'm so sick and tired of everyone in this town asking me if I'm alright."

"I don't know what to say," Brant shook his head. "What do you want me to say? What can I say to make you understand how sorry I am?"

"What do I want you to say?" Jennifer cried, "I want you to wake me up from this nightmare and tell me that it was all a bad dream. Then we can have a good laugh about the past few months and go back to living our lives."

Brant put his hand on Jennifer's shoulder.

"Don't," Jennifer gulped.

"Rocky," Brant begged.

"Gosh!" Jennifer exclaimed as she jerked her shoulder away and slung her book at Brant. "Get away from me, Brant!"

Brant bent down and picked up the book, never taking his eyes off of Jennifer. He slid the book back into her locker. "Jennifer, I'll do anything if you'll just stop and listen to me," Brant sighed.

"You mean, like we're best friends?" Jennifer snapped. "Buddies? Pals? Chums? Soulmates? Should I ask you what it was like to get in Brianna Clarke's tight, little pants? Did you want us to run over to the locker room and sit around while you give me the hot details?"

"Jennifer, please don't talk like that. It doesn't even sound like you," Brant sighed.

"Oh! Well, excuse me for being cynical," Jennifer rolled her eyes.

"Listen," Brant lowered his voice, "I didn't just…" He looked around to make sure no one was listening.

"Just say it," Jennifer huffed. "It's not like everyone doesn't already know."

"Jennifer, I've told you a million times," Brant continued, "it wasn't like I just… Jen… I had…"

"I don't need to hear the details again, Brant," Jennifer groaned.

"I was drunk," Brant sighed.

"Yes, that has been duly documented," Jennifer grimaced. "It doesn't make me feel any better. It just reaffirms the fact that, after eighteen years together, I didn't know you as well as I thought I did."

"Jennifer… I messed up… I know that… but that's *all* that it was… a mistake," Brant pled.

Jennifer stared at Brant. "I hate you," she said boldly. She started to turn away, then she stopped. "No… *no*… I'm not stooping to that. You may say and do things in the heat of the moment that you live to regret. You may do something one moment and swear that it meant nothing the next, but that's not who I am. I don't hate you, Brant… no, I don't hate you at all… of course not… *I love you*." Tears filled Jennifer's eyes.

"I love you too, Jen. I do. I love you," Brant pled.

Jennifer took a tennis shoe from her locker and hit Brant with it. "Don't do this to me," she insisted, "not now… not here."

"Jen, we've got to stop this," Brant said, gesturing toward the shoe in her hand. "The communication between the two of us has completely broken down…"

"That's your fault," Jennifer snarled.

"You're the one throwing books and shoes," Brant huffed. "Stop hitting me, and *listen* to what I have to say."

Christian walked up, books in hand. "Is everything okay here?" he asked.

"Go away, Christian," Jennifer snapped. Jennifer couldn't ignore the fact that Christian looked hurt as he stared back at her. "I'm sorry," she frowned, "I didn't mean to snap at *you*. None of this is your fault."

Brant grabbed Jennifer's hand. "Jennifer, forget about going to class," he shrugged, "let's get out of here. We need time to talk."

"You can't skip any more classes," Jennifer shook her head. "You won't graduate."

Christian slipped off as Jennifer and Brant remained fixed on one another.

"Jen, we have to talk," Brant insisted.

"There is nothing to talk about," Jennifer shrugged.

"There is *everything* to talk about," Brant replied.

"No, Brant," Jennifer frowned. "Brianna is pregnant with your baby. Period. End of story. You and I are ancient history. Our immortal friendship… it's over. You chose to move on with your life and leave me behind. It's too late to change your mind now. So leave me alone, and let me move on with my life too."

"Jennifer, are you ever going to forgive me?" Brant sighed. "I know I messed up, but…"

"I have forgiven you," Jennifer nodded.

"No, you haven't," Brant shook his head.

"Yes, Brant," Jennifer nodded, "I have. I have forgiven you. Believe it or not I even feel sorry for you. I know you didn't really want to sleep with Brianna. I definitely know you didn't mean to get her pregnant. I'm sorry that you're having to go through all that you're going through these days, and I am even sorrier that such a troubled, manipulative woman is going to be part of your life… forever."

"Jennifer, I need you in my life," Brant sighed.

"You betrayed me, Brant," Jennifer shook her head. "You disrespected all that I stand for. You hurt me…"

"I know," Brant broke in.

"I'm not finished," Jennifer snapped. "You said you wanted us to communicate, so I'm going to be completely honest with you. I feel like you not only hurt and disappointed me, my family and yours… I feel like you turned your back on Morgan and Brandon as well. Do you remember them… huh? We have talked about the two kids that we were supposed to have together since I was a little girl toting around two Cabbage Patch dolls, Brantley. It was my goal in life to be a wonderful wife to you and a loving mother to our two children… *Morgan and Brandon*."

"Jen, I don't know how to go on without a future with you to look forward to," Brant shook his head. "I realize that I don't deserve you, Rocky; I know that, but I don't know what to do, how to act without you. I know that what I did was wrong… unforgivable even, but, Jen… it was a mistake…"

"A mistake that you can never take back," Jennifer shook her head.

Brant became visibly upset. "But… Jen… I… I… I just…"

"You're stuttering, Brant," Jennifer frowned. "Just say what you want to say."

"The truth is I don't know what to say," Brant sighed. "I did the same thing that the average guy would have done in my situation. She was all over me… she tricked me into getting drunk, and then…"

"And now that is the sort of woman who is going to be the mother of your child," Jennifer shrugged.

"Jennifer, what I'm trying to say…" Brant swallowed hard.

"You're trying to make excuses," Jennifer nodded.

"Jennifer," Brant begged.

"No," Jennifer said, taking a deep breath, "you're absolutely right."

"I am?" Brant gulped.

"Yes," Jennifer nodded confidently as her eyes filled with painful tears, "the average guy *would* have done the very same thing in your situation. I guess the reason that it's so hard for me to accept is that this is the very first time in my life that I have *ever* thought of *you* as *average*." Jennifer gently closed her locker as she turned and walked away.

Brant started to go after her, but he stopped himself. He leaned against Jennifer's locker as the bell rang and the hallway cleared. He turned and slammed his fist against the row of lockers as he fought back tears. He stood in the nearly empty hallway feeling hollow, abandoned and alone. Even there, in the surroundings he knew so well, he was lost.

Jennifer glanced back over her shoulder at the one man in the world she thought would never hurt her, and she stared coldly at the only man who had ever broken her heart.

***

On a stormy afternoon a week later, Brant drove to Jennifer's house, only to find Christian's truck parked in her driveway. He knocked on Jennifer's door as the rain beat down; she and Christian came to the door together.

"I thought that you were going over to Tommy's house to work out?" Brant said as he glared at Christian.

"I'm on my way," Christian shrugged, "I just stopped in to check on Jennifer."

"Well, she appreciates it. Bye now," Brant smiled sarcastically.

"Don't be rude to your brother, Brantley," Jennifer said, her arms crossed.

Christian slid past Brant. "I thought that you and Brianna were going shopping to buy some things for the baby?" he questioned.

"We got done early," Brant replied. "I'll catch you over at Tommy's later."

"Bye, Christian. Be careful in this weather!" Jennifer called as she closed the door behind him.

"Hi," Brant said as Jennifer turned to face him.

"So, she cleaned you out early, huh?" Jennifer snickered.

"Were you and Christian talking about me?" Brant replied.

Jennifer stared at Brant. "Some people have other things to talk about besides *you*, believe it or not," she said, rolling her eyes.

"That was a good one, Jen. It really put me in my place," Brant huffed.

"Get over yourself," Jennifer sighed.

Ben walked into the living room with his new toy airplane in hand. "Look at this, Brant!" he exclaimed.

Brant glanced at Ben. "I can't play today, buddy," he shook his head.

"Go to your room, Ben!" Jennifer snapped.

Ben hung his head. "I don't wanna," he whined.

"Now!" Jennifer said, pointing.

"Did Christian leave?" Ben inquired.

"Yes," Jennifer nodded, "he fixed your toy… it's on the kitchen table. Go to your room… I'll play with you when Brant leaves. It won't be long."

"I don't want Brant to leave," Ben sighed.

"Go, Ben!" Jennifer demanded.

"Don't be rude to your brother, Jennifer," Brant mocked.

"Why are you here, Brant?" Jennifer asked as Ben turned and walked back to his bedroom.

"Because for the past few months, you and I have avoided each other way too much," Brant shook his head. "We don't talk at school. We don't talk on the phone… you don't come over…"

"What am I supposed to say to you?" Jennifer exclaimed. "Tell me, Brant, what do I say?"

"I know you're hurt, Jen. I know you're angry. But you know… in all of this, I think it should be said that it's not like I cheated on you… not really. We broke up… we broke up because that's what *you* wanted. You came to me and said you wanted us to just be friends. I was fine with our decision to wait to have sex… that's not what the whole thing with Brianna was about, Jennifer. But regardless of all of that, I'm sorry that this happened, and that's all that I can say to you," Brant shrugged. "I'm very, very sorry."

"Shouldn't the fact that you feel the need to tell me that you're sorry tell you that *you* don't even buy your own weak argument?" Jennifer snapped.

"You broke up with me, remember?" Brant practically yelled.

"I know that," Jennifer yelled back, "and, for that, I'm sorry too, but… honestly… if I hadn't decided that we were going too fast too soon and decided to cool things down for awhile… would it have changed things… would it have changed the way you felt about me… would you have loved me enough then to say no to the walking Barbie doll?"

Brant shook his head. "No… no… you're right… it wouldn't have changed anything because I loved you as much after you broke up with me as I did when we were together… as much as I have all our lives."

"It's silly to say we *broke up*," Jennifer rolled her eyes, "we may not have been *calling* ourselves a *couple*, but nothing had changed between us… at least not for *me*…"

"Stop it!" Brant screamed. "Just stop it. Nothing has ever changed the way I feel about you. I love you, Jennifer! Get that through your thick skull, please… *I love you*… and only you."

"Stop saying that," Jennifer insisted. "It hurts me when you say that."

Ben peeked out his bedroom door, and tears gathered around his eyes as Brant and Jennifer exchanged angry words.

"I want you to leave," Jennifer insisted, "because what I have to tell you, you don't want to hear."

"Try me," Brant said as he jumped up on the kitchen counter to prove that he had no intention of leaving just yet. "Try talking this out with *me* instead of running to my brother all the time… tell *me* how you're feeling."

"Christian has been a loyal friend… he's been there when I needed him," Jennifer gulped.

"You called my house, and when I answered the phone, you asked to speak to him," Brant snapped.

"Hurt, didn't it?" Jennifer nodded. "Yet… you still have no idea the pain…"

Brant swallowed. "You said you had something to say… I want to hear it," he insisted.

Jennifer patted Brant's knee. "She's a manipulative gold digger," she shrugged confidently. "Brianna wanted you for one reason and one reason only, and I hate to burst your bubble, but it wasn't for the sex."

"Stop it," Brant rolled his eyes.

"That girl had a bullseye on your forehead before she ever gallivanted to Mississippi, Brant," Jennifer argued, her voice rising. "Can you not see that?"

"You've seen too many movies," Brant grimaced.

"You are being so naive," Jennifer sighed. "People don't just move to Cummins, Mississippi, on a whim, Brant. You've heard the stories about her mother the same as I have. She goes after men with money, gets what she can, and moves on."

Brant stared at the ceiling.

"You see the best in people, sweetie," Jennifer explained. "I love that about you, but I guess that it isn't always a good quality. Brant, what happened was no accident. We think it was a calculated act… she waited until the time was right; she got you drunk; she had sex with you… intending all along to get pregnant, so that she could do exactly what she's doing now…"

"*We*?" Brant groaned. "So, I was right… you and my brother were having a nice little chat about me behind my back."

"We both care about you, Brant. It's just that some of the things that she's said, we've noticed," Jennifer replied quickly. "Personally, I think that if you aren't careful, she's going to play you for every penny you'll ever make. She wanted you Brant, and she was willing to do whatever she had to do to get you."

"You don't know what you're talking about," Brant shook his head.

"Brant," Jennifer scoffed, "it doesn't take a genius to see that Brianna played you for a fool…"

"Are you calling me stupid?" Brant fired back.

Jennifer rolled her eyes.

"Answer me," Brant shrugged, "do you think I'm stupid?"

"Well, I didn't… not until you slept with her," Jennifer huffed.

Ben ran into the living room. "Stop it!" he cried out. "I can't stand it when you fight with Brant."

"Benjamin, this is not a conversation you need to hear. Go to your room and do not come out again until I come and get you," Jennifer scolded. "Brant and I are almost done here."

"I've never heard you and Brant yell at each other like this," Ben whined. "You never used to fight before."

"I don't guess that we have ever really argued," Jennifer frowned at Brant.

"No," Brant replied, "but you've never called me a fool before either."

"I didn't say it like that," Jennifer fired back, "but... *hey*... if the shoe fits!"

"I am an idiot... I know that," Brant yelled. "I messed up, and I'm sorry."

"Great," Jennifer shrugged, "it still doesn't change anything."

"Stop it!" Ben begged.

Brant and Jennifer squabbled back and forth and nothing that Ben did could distract them from name calling and bickering.

Tired of being ignored and fed up with all the screaming, Ben stomped his foot before running to the back porch and sliding the glass door closed behind him. He squatted down and covered his ears with his hands as rain splashed onto the porch.

"How should I put this?" Jennifer hollered. "Brianna wouldn't have *fallen in love*, and I say that in the *most* loose sense of the term, with the guy in the hospital last summer because he wouldn't have been any good to her. We didn't know if you'd ever play football again. There was no guarantee that the guy laid up in that bed all summer would make millions in the NFL one day, Brantley."

"Why did you have to go and bring that up?" Brant lashed back. "You know I don't like to talk about last summer."

"Just go," Jennifer said as she pointed to the front door in disgust.

"Fine," Brant rolled his eyes as he turned to leave.

"No!" Ben screamed as he watched Brant storm toward the front door. He sprung to his feet in a desperate attempt to run inside and beg Brant to stay. As he did, his shoe slipped in a puddle, and he skidded across the concrete porch on the side of his bare leg, knocking over his father's miniature grill in the process.

Jennifer heard the racket and turned to see Ben lying on the back porch, holding his leg. "Brant... wait!" she shrilled.

Brant was half way out the front door when he was halted by Jennifer's cry.

"It's Ben!" Jennifer panicked as she pointed to her little brother.

Brant ran through the living room and slung the sliding glass door open. He scooped Ben into his arms. "You're okay," he promised the little boy, "I've got you." He examined Ben's injury as he carried him inside. "He's okay, Rocky," Brant assured Jennifer. "Aren't you, buddy?"

Ben nodded as he sniffed back tears.

"Jen, grab me some peroxide and some Band-Aids, and I'll fix this little guy right up for you," Brant said as he carried Ben into the bathroom down the hall.

"Are you gonna make it, little man?" Brant smiled sweetly as he sat Ben on the counter top.

Ben grinned as he nodded.

"Well, that's good," Brant kidded, "I thought that I might have to take the leg off… you know… " Brant laughed as he tickled Ben, "amputate it… right about *here*… at the knee…"

Ben giggled.

Brant examined the bloody scrape. "Yeah," he nodded, "it looks like I'm gonna have to operate after all. Jennifer, get me a knife from the kitchen, so I can saw this thing off."

Ben giggled wildly.

"There's nothing funny about emergency surgery, son," Brant smiled.

"You're so funny," Ben laughed.

"Well, thank you… thank you…" Brant grinned as he took a bow. He rubbed his hands together playfully. "Now, let Dr. McLachlan see what he can do."

"Do you think you can save my leg, doc?" Ben sighed.

Brant shook his head. "I've already told you, lad," he said gruffly, "the leg is as good as gone, but don't you worry. I know the captain of this ship, and I'll see to it that you get one of those top-of-the-line wooden legs that they keep below deck, and your legs are so skinny, heck, you'll never know the difference!"

"ARRG!" Ben laughed in his best pirate imitation.

"Aye, Aye, matey," Brant smiled.

Brant took a towel and wrapped it around Ben as he shivered in his damp clothes. He placed Ben's injured leg over the sink and unscrewed the cap on the peroxide bottle. "This is gonna burn a little," he warned as Ben's chin quivered.

Ben let out an anxious whimper.

"Here's some advice," Brant smiled. "This is what I do. Just start screaming *before* I start cleaning the cut. Go ahead… try to scream as loud as you possibly can, and you will be concentrating so much on screaming that you won't ever feel a thing, and it'll be over before you know it."

"Promise?" Ben gulped.

"Doctor's orders," Brant winked. "Bet I can scream louder than you can!"

Jennifer couldn't resist a smile as both of the boys hollered at the top of their lungs while Brant cleaned Ben's scrapes. When he was done, Brant gently blew on Ben's leg. "That's what my dad always did," he told Ben. "I think it kinda helps."

"Me too," Ben agreed.

"Good deal," Brant smiled back.

Ben smiled proudly as Brant bandaged his leg. "I love you!" he frowned when Brant was done playing doctor.

"I love you too, Ben," Brant said as he lifted Ben off of the counter. He kissed Ben's forehead quickly. "Now, go get yourself into some dry clothes, and I'm sure that your sister will be more than willing to fix you a big bowl of chocolate ice cream coated in M&M's."

"Yeah!" Ben exclaimed as, seeming to forget about his injury, he scurried off to his room.

Brant looked over at Jennifer. She was leaning against the door casing with a tear running down her cheek. "You are gonna make a *wonderful* father… I always knew that about you," she said softly.

"Jen," Brant sighed.

"Shh," Jennifer shook her head.

"I'm sorry, Jen," Brant nodded.

"I know," Jennifer nodded back.

Brant started to speak again.

"Shh, Brant," Jennifer whispered as she placed her finger over his lips.

There was a long silence. Jennifer smiled at Brant, and he smiled back.

"Can you stay for ice cream?" Jennifer asked after a moment. "You know… since you did promise him *your* favorite… chocolate ice cream coated in M&M's."

"I was hoping that you would ask," Brant grinned.

"Thank you for that," Jennifer said, gesturing towards Ben's room. "I didn't even know that he was outside."

"I may not be a real doctor, but I'm fairly sure he's gonna live," Brant nodded.

"Yeah," Jennifer smiled, "you're probably right."

"He didn't want to see us fighting," Brant sighed.

"Me neither," Jennifer shook her head.

"That makes three of us," Brant added as he pulled Jennifer into his arms.

Jennifer rested her face against Brant's chest, then, looking into his eyes, she mouthed, "I love you."

"You may not believe me after all that's happened, and I don't blame you… but, I love you too," Brant echoed.

"I know that you do… that's why this hurts so bad," Jennifer said as she worked to contain her tears.

Brant held Jennifer close. "You are the only girl that I want," he promised. "You're my life, Rocky… not football, not anything else… you."

Ben waltzed out of his room, and his face lit up as he stared at his sister cradled in Brant's arms. "Are y'all gonna kiss?" he exclaimed.

"I don't know… are we?" Brant grinned at Jennifer.

"No, we aren't going to kiss," Jennifer sighed as she moved away from Brant.

"How about if Ben took a nosedive off the back of the couch… maybe then I could work my way up to a kiss?" Brant joked.

"Brant!" Jennifer rolled her eyes.

"Kiss me… just once," Brant smiled as he reached for Jennifer's hands.

"No… no, Brant… I can't," Jennifer shook her head as she kissed his hand, "I'm sorry."

"Well, if you aren't gonna kiss him, then I want that ice cream!" Ben blurted, his hands on his hips.

Brant and Jennifer cackled as they stared down at Ben.

"What?" Ben shrugged innocently.

Jennifer walked toward the kitchen. "I'm going to go by to see Brianna and see if there is anything that I can do for her," she offered. "I know her mother isn't being very supportive, and she could use a friend right now."

"Really," Brant gulped, "you would do that?"

Jennifer nodded.

"Thanks, Jen," Brant said as a little hint of a smile broke out on his face, "everybody ought to have a friend like you."

"Don't get me wrong. It won't be easy," Jennifer admitted.

"I know," Brant nodded solemnly.

"I'm doing this for you… not for her," Jennifer added.

"I know," Brant gulped as he leaned on the counter next to Jennifer.

Jennifer kissed her finger and gently touched Brant's lips. "What do you say we have that ice cream now?" she asked softly.

"I'll get the M&M's," Brant smiled.

CHAPTER ELEVEN

Every year my brothers and their friends went to Gulf Shores, Alabama, the first week of May, for their spring break. It was a tradition that they started as seventh graders, but with everything that was going on when spring break rolled around that year, no one was really up for a week of fun in the sun.

When Tommy's mom called and invited the gang to come spend the break with her in Jackson, everyone decided that it wouldn't hurt them to get away from Cummins for awhile. In a small town where everyone knows everyone else's business, sometimes a week away can be just what the doctor ordered.

***

"Are we ready to go yet?" Christian asked as he cracked the front door open and poked his head inside.

Mom and Jennifer were sitting on the couch pointing to something in a catalog.

Ethan walked in from the kitchen, turkey sandwich in hand. "We're all packed… we're just waiting for Brant and Brianna," he replied.

"They're upstairs having *another* huge fight," Jennifer nodded as Tommy and Christian came inside to wait.

"Brianna's in one of her strange moods this morning," Mom added.

"Great," Tommy groaned.

"Brant! Let's go!" Christian hollered up the stairs.

"Yes, *Brant*, let's go," Jennifer muttered under her breath.

Mom patted Jennifer's knee. "You remember what I told you," she insisted.

"I remember, Mrs. Becky," Jennifer nodded.

"I mean it," Mom smiled as she stood from the couch.

Jennifer smiled, then her eyes moved to the stairs.

Mom bumped Ethan with her hip. "Did you finish filling out that form for me to mail in?" she asked.

"It's on the kitchen table," Ethan gestured. "You and Dad still have to sign it."

"Okay," Mom nodded, "we'll sign it, and I'll mail it this morning on my way to the store." She kissed Ethan's cheek. "You guys have fun."

Mom hugged Christian. "Bye, baby," she smiled broadly.

"Bye, Mom," Christian smiled back.

"Y'all be good," Mom chuckled as she pointed at Tommy.

"Always, Mrs. B!" Tommy shrugged.

Mom laughed.

Christian started up the stairs. "I'm gonna go see what the holdup is," he grumbled. "We need to get on the road."

As he walked down the hallway toward the boys' bedroom, he could hear Brant yelling, but he couldn't make out his words. He pressed his ear against the door just in time to hear Brant's fist slam against the other side.

"I'm fat… I'm miserable… if you don't like the name I came up with for our baby, then you name him!" Brianna huffed.

Brant exhaled loudly. "It's not that I don't like the name you picked… I love it… it's just that…"

"What?" Brianna insisted. "What's wrong with the name *Brandon*? Brandon McLachlan… it sounds good to me."

Christian swallowed hard. He glanced toward the stairs to make sure Jennifer hadn't followed him up.

"Brianna, please," Brant begged, "anything… anything that you want to name the baby is fine with me… just not *Brandon*… okay?"

"Fine," Brianna snapped, "we won't call him Brandon, but since you're the one who wanted this baby in the first place… you worry about naming it."

"Keep your voice down," Brant yelled. He lowered his voice, "and stop saying that you don't want your baby."

"It's no big secret," Brianna shrugged.

"No one knows that you wanted to terminate your pregnancy," Brant sighed, "and I'd like to keep it that way."

"You mean to tell me that you haven't told your little princess, *Rocky* or whatever gosh awful name it is that you call her, that I'm a despicable excuse for a human being who wanted to get rid of her unborn child," Brianna snickered.

"Brianna," Brant grumbled, "I don't think of her as a princess and you as some sort of evil villain."

"No… but you love her and you hate me," Brianna replied quickly.

"I don't hate you," Brant huffed. "If you're asking me if I love Jennifer, then the answer is *yes*… I've loved Jennifer my entire life, but that doesn't mean I *hate* you."

"Could have fooled me," Brianna rolled her eyes.

"However, when you act like you have this morning, you make it very hard not to," Brant fired back.

Christian knocked on the door. "Hey, Brant! You guys ready to go?" he called.

Brant ripped the door open. "The sooner the better," he groaned.

He started down the stairs. "There you two are," Jennifer smiled. "We're all ready to go."

"Well, if she's ready then, by all means, let's hurry," Brianna chirped sarcastically as she hurried down the stairs, as fast as she could with her pregnant belly, and out the front door.

Jennifer glanced at Brant.

"I'm sorry," he shrugged.

"It's okay," Jennifer shook her head, "it's not your fault."

Brant exhaled loudly, and Jennifer squeezed his shoulders sympathetically.

Mom put her arm around Christian. "I wish she hadn't insisted on going," she sighed. "I really wanted Brantley and Jennifer to have a nice, relaxing trip."

Christian swallowed as he recalled the conversation he had overheard upstairs. "Somehow I don't think that's gonna happen," he said with a confident shake of his head.

Outside, Brianna crawled into Ethan's truck, and everyone stood around staring at her as if to ask why.

"Aren't you going to ride with me?" Brant asked her as he poked his head in the window. "They'd probably appreciate it!"

"No, I'm fine right here," Brianna snapped.

Brant turned to Ethan. "That okay with you and Chris?" he sighed.

"It's fine with me," Ethan nodded.

Brant glanced back at Christian.

"Yeah, whatever," he shrugged.

Brant put his arm around Jennifer. "Looks like it's me and you," he smiled.

The two of them got into Brant's truck, and Dad knocked on Jennifer's window. She rolled the window down, and Dad began rattling off, "seatbelts were not invented for decoration. Speed limits were set for a reason. No animal in the middle of the road is worth your life. Cell phones are a no-no while you're driving. And, Brant… meet Jammin' Jenny, the *only* DJ in this truck."

"Thank you, Reverend McLachlan," Brant grinned.

"So," Dad smiled as he looked curiously at Brant, "how did these little riding arrangements pan out?"

"Don't ask," Brant rolled his eyes.

Dad held his hands up. "Okay," he smiled, "be careful, and have some fun for me too."

Jennifer rolled the window up as Brant draped himself over the steering wheel. Jennifer frowned as she rubbed his back. "What you did was wrong," she said confidently, "but now you're trying to do right by Brianna and your baby… I'm proud of you, Brant."

Brant turned to her as if to ask if she could possibly mean what she said.

"Really," Jennifer nodded with a slight smile, "you've acted very admirably, and I'm sorry she's giving you such a hard time."

Brant sighed. "Sometimes I don't think I can make it another day… it's like she's draining the life right out of me."

Jennifer shook her head. "You'll make it," she assured him. "I'll make sure of that."

Brant smiled, and his love, respect and admiration for the woman sitting next to him shone in his eyes.

Jennifer put her favorite Garth Brooks album into the CD player, reached for her cell phone and quickly dialed Christian's number.

"Yeah?" Christian answered as Ethan pulled away behind Tommy.

"Are we going to stop to eat?" Jennifer asked.

"Up the road," Christian relayed. "We'll signal, but you and I both know that's not why you called."

"What has Brianna had to say about being so rude to everyone?" Jennifer continued.

"Hang up, Jennifer," Brant insisted.

Jennifer nodded, "Chris… just say *yes* or *no*… is she…"

"Jen… hang up the phone," Brant begged.

"Brant wants me to hang up, but I expect full details later," Jennifer grumbled as she hung up the phone.

"Let's just all try to get along this week," Brant sighed.

Jennifer nodded.

Brant put one hand on the wheel and turned up the volume on the CD player as he began singing along to a slow, romantic ballad. With his right hand, he squeezed Jennifer's shoulder affectionately.

Jennifer glanced at him and smiled. She took his hand and wove her fingers in his, letting their hands rest together on the seat between them.

***

That night after supper, Brianna and Ethan relaxed in the living room watching an episode of *Celebrity Jeopardy*.

"Hey, it's spring break!" Tommy barked. "*Jeopardy*? Really, E?"

Brant was sitting outside alone on the front porch when Tommy's mom's car pulled back into the driveway.

"Where have y'all been?" Brant asked as Jennifer danced up the stairs.

"Piggly Wiggly," she giggled as she pointed to the bags Christian was toting.

"Late night sweet tooth!" Tommy's mom laughed.

Jennifer jumped up on the banister next to Brant. "What are you doing out here by yourself?" she smiled.

"What's going on in there?" Christian asked as he slid the glass door open with his free hand.

"*What is geekfest?*" Brant grinned.

"Oh no way, we ain't watching *Jeopardy*!" Christian exclaimed as he slid the door closed behind him.

Peggy Jackson stared at Brant and Jennifer sitting side-by-side there on her porch. She pulled up a chair and sat down, something obviously weighing heavily on her mind. "Would you two be too upset if I offered you some advice?" she blurted.

"Of course not," Jennifer smiled.

"I love both of you," Peggy nodded. "I've known you both since you were born; I may not have always been there in Cummins, but I've watched you two grow up..."

"We love you too," Brant smiled. "You know that."

Peggy stood. She took Jennifer's hand and placed it in Brant's. "Don't let him go, Jennifer," she insisted.

Jennifer glanced at Brant and then back at Tommy's mother. "I don't want to," Jennifer said timidly.

Brant squeezed Jennifer's hand. "I messed up... *bad*, Ms. Peggy," he frowned, "I can't expect her to forgive me."

Peggy Jackson looked only at Jennifer. "I know what it's like to love a man and have something so awful happen between the two of you that you are sure you can never feel the same way about him again," she said sincerely.

Jennifer nodded.

"You still love him, don't you?" Peggy smiled.

"Yes," Jennifer gulped, "I'll always love him."

Peggy took Jennifer's free hand in hers. "Then don't make the same mistake I did, Jennifer," she said as she shook her head. "Get past what has happened and fight for the love that the two of you share."

Jennifer frowned. "Do you wish that you had done that?" she asked. "Do you wish that you hadn't left Mr. Rick after the accident?" Over the years the horrific images of that day had come to be referred to simply as... *the accident*.

Peggy Jackson's voice cracked as she nodded a confident, "yes."

"Well, why don't you tell him that?" Brant spoke up as his thoughts flashed back to Cummins and the family portrait that hung over Rick Jackson's fireplace. That house had always seemed so empty without Peggy and Sarah Ann, and, though nothing could change what had happened to Sarah, Brant couldn't help but think that Rick had always held on to the hope that his wife would come home.

"We waited too long to resolve our feelings… too much time has passed… the love that we had is a thing of the past. It's too late for us," Peggy shook her head.

Brant glanced at Jennifer. "Is it too late for us?" he asked softly.

Jennifer looked away to break Brant's gaze.

"Jennifer," Peggy smiled, "right now, forgiving and especially *forgetting* seems like the hardest thing you'll ever do, and it probably is; but, if you guys can't make love survive… then there's no hope for any of the rest of us."

Brant turned to Jennifer. "Rocky, will you come for a walk with me?" he asked.

Jennifer glanced inside the glass doors. "What about Brianna?" she sighed. "She'll just get upset if you and I leave together, and her getting upset isn't good for the baby."

Peggy Jackson shook her head. "You leave Brianna to me," she insisted. "I'll make sure she doesn't have time to miss you." She nodded to Jennifer, urging her with her eyes to say yes.

"I'd love to take a walk with you, Brant," Jennifer nodded after a moment.

Peggy winked at Brant. She kissed his cheek as she whispered, "don't let her get away, Brantley. She's the best thing that has ever happened to you."

Brant smiled as he turned to Jennifer. "Yeah… that seems to be the sentiment," he laughed.

Jennifer grinned back at him. "Well, it's true you know," she shrugged. Then she let out a little laugh.

"It *is* true," Brant nodded confidently as the two started down the stairs, hand-in-hand. "If you don't believe me… just ask my parents. They love you a whole heck of a lot more than they love me these days."

"That's not true," Jennifer rolled her eyes. "If I had been the one who hurt you, my parents would have stood up for you just like your parents have stood up for me. It's just because they all know how right we are for each other."

"I'm glad everyone has stood behind you through this," Brant agreed. "Especially Christian, he's been a really good friend to you these past few months."

"Yeah… everyone has been very supportive," Jennifer smiled, "and, believe it or not, Chris spends *a lot* of time defending you. We both know that Brianna wasn't going to give up until she had you."

"I guess I didn't put up a very good fight," Brant sighed.

"Agreed," Jennifer nodded, "but do we have to talk about that?"

"Sorry," Brant replied.

"Let's talk about something else… anything else," Jennifer suggested

Brant walked on a little ways, his hands buried in his pockets.

"Penny for your thoughts?" Jennifer sighed.

"I wish I could go back in time," Brant confessed. "I mean, when I look at Brianna it's like a slap in the face every time, and I know it must be a million times worse for you."

"It's not any fun, but I've accepted that it's just the way things are," Jennifer shrugged.

"She's nothing like you, Jen," Brant thought aloud. "She's so callus and…"

"Selfish," Jennifer offered.

"Yeah," Brant sighed.

Jennifer walked on.

"Alright… now it's your turn," Brant said as he caught up, "what are you thinking?"

Jennifer shook her head.

"Tell me," Brant insisted.

"Brant, I couldn't wait to be pregnant," Jennifer sighed. "Not now… I don't mean that I wish I was the one who is pregnant now, but *eventually*… I looked forward to carrying our baby inside of me."

"Do you think there's any chance that could still happen one day?" Brant asked as he looked deep into her eyes.

"It's hard to say right now, Brant," Jennifer shook her head slowly.

"I love you," Brant declared.

"I know," Jennifer smiled sweetly. She put her arm around Brant. "Your mom and I had a nice talk this morning."

"About what?" Brant asked.

"She just told me that she loves me, and she reminded me how much *you* love me; she promised me that one day this is all going to seem like a bad dream," Jennifer recalled.

"And do you believe that?" Brant asked softly.

"Yeah," Jennifer nodded reluctantly, "I do... but it may take a long time..."

"Brianna keeps talking like I'm gonna marry her after the baby gets here," Brant exhaled.

"Maybe that's the right thing to do," Jennifer replied quickly.

"Jen!" Brant gasped.

"For the baby I mean," Jennifer shrugged.

"I can't marry Brianna," Brant huffed.

"She's your son's mother," Jennifer sobbed as she turned away.

Brant grabbed Jennifer's shoulder. "Maybe it isn't what is considered respectable or the right thing to do," he sighed, "but I think that if I married Brianna it would only be more painful for my son to see his parents trapped in a loveless marriage and know that they only got married because they had to... because of him."

"Have you told Brianna that?" Jennifer asked curiously.

"Brianna and I don't communicate very well," Brant rolled his eyes. "I can't talk to her like I can talk to you. She still has this big illusion that I'm eventually going to fall in love with her."

"She just wants your money," Jennifer rolled her eyes.

"I don't have any money yet," Brant groaned. "Even my signing bonus is still in negotiations."

"Brant," Jennifer protested, "your parents have money. Your mom is a doctor. You guys live in a nice house. You and your brothers all drive nice trucks, and one day, in the not too distant future, you are going to make millions playing football. Trust me... the girl looks at you, and she sees the dollar signs."

"I'm willing to pay child support... that's not a question," Brant shrugged.

"Child support isn't going to buy her the house that she wants... it's not going to provide her with a car or the wardrobe she wants," Jennifer scoffed.

"Well, she won't be getting any of that from me," Brant said confidently, "so I hope she doesn't plan on holding her breath... on second thought... I wish she would."

"Brant, don't say that," Jennifer sighed. "She's your child's mother."

"He'd be better off without her," Brant rolled his eyes. "We all would."

"Well, I certainly won't argue that point with you," Jennifer shrugged, "but, Brant, you are going to have to maintain a civil relationship with Brianna for the baby's sake."

"Maybe she'll let me have custody," Brant said hopefully.

"No," Jennifer frowned, "Brant, that isn't what Brianna has in mind. She's going to want to keep the baby, so she can use your son as a pawn in her scheme to be close to you forever. You have to recognize that and always be careful to do what's in your son's best interest without letting her use him to manipulate you."

"Come here, Jen," Brant said, pulling Jennifer into a hug. "You are so amazing."

"What brought that on?" Jennifer smiled.

"*You* did... just the way you are being so mature about this," Brant nodded. "It amazes me."

"I've had my moments," Jennifer sighed.

"You are certainly entitled," Brant nodded, "but the way you have reached out to Brianna, you've really shown what a special person you are... of course, I already knew."

"Believe me... trying to be Brianna's friend isn't easy," Jennifer confessed. "I try to be nice to her, and she just looks at me with such..."

"Jealousy," Brant said confidently.

"I guess that's what it is," Jennifer shrugged.

"It is, Jennifer... she's so jealous of the fact that I love you that she doesn't know what to do," Brant nodded. Suddenly, he grew quiet, and he turned away.

"Brant, what's wrong?" Jennifer asked.

"Brianna said something this morning that I think you need to know," Brant confessed.

Jennifer raised a curious eyebrow. "Does it have anything to do with what the two of you were arguing about upstairs?"

"Yeah… listen, Jen," Brant nodded, "did you, by chance, ever tell Brianna what you planned on naming our kids?"

"Why?" Jennifer asked slowly.

"So you *did* tell her?" Brant groaned.

"Maybe… a long time ago… back when I thought she and I actually had a shot of becoming real friends," Jennifer recalled. "I took her to girls' night at the church. I wanted to introduce her to everyone and help her make new friends. You know how a bunch of girls are when we get together… it came up. Everyone thought that I'd be first to get married and have a baby, so they wanted to know if I had any names in mind… they were my friends, so I told them."

"I thought so," Brant nodded. "This morning Brianna informed me that she wants to name the baby… Brandon."

"What?" Jennifer gulped as her eyes watered.

"It's okay… I told her *no way*," Brant shook his head. "I should have figured out then that it wasn't a coincidence. Of course, she acted like she just couldn't possibly understand why I was opposed."

"She's determined to hurt me in every way she can, isn't she?" Jennifer sighed.

"I'm just sorry *I* hurt you," Brant gulped.

Jennifer started to walk away as she tried to gather her thoughts.

"Jen, wait," Brant begged, "I knew this would upset you."

Jennifer turned around, her eyes filled with tears. "I want you to name your baby Brandon," she said softly.

"Jennifer… I can't do that," Brant shook his head.

"I want you to," Jennifer said more confidently.

"Jen," Brant insisted, "you shouldn't feel like you have to give Brianna that name… it means so much to you."

"I'm not…" Jennifer gulped, "I'm giving it to you."

"You would do that?" Brant sighed. "I mean after everything that I've…"

"Brantley?" Jennifer blurted.

"Yeah?" Brant said as he stared down at her.

"Will you stop this?" Jennifer demanded, though her tone was soft and loving.

"What?" Brant shook his head.

"Brant," Jennifer sighed, "you asked God to forgive you for the mistake that you made. He has forgiven you, and so have I. Now, it's time for you to forgive yourself."

"I don't think I can ever do that," Brant said after a moment.

There was a long pause.

"Well, you have two choices," Jennifer began. "You can either spend the rest of your life regretting a decision you made when you were eighteen years old, or you can accept the fact that you made a very poor choice and decide that you are going to acknowledge it, own it and allow yourself to move on with your life."

"My life can't go on if you're not in it," Brant said softly.

"I'm not going anywhere," Jennifer smiled.

Brant turned to her, his eyes wide. "But, I thought you said..."

"Brant, you're my friend... my best friend," Jennifer explained, "and no matter what happens... that's never going to change."

Brant took Jennifer's hand in his.

Jennifer looked up at the star-filled sky. "It's a beautiful night," she commented.

Brant stared at Jennifer. "Yes it is," he nodded.

"You're not looking at the sky," Jennifer sighed as she watched Brant out of the corner of her eye.

"No," Brant shook his head.

"Why are you looking at me like that?" Jennifer grinned.

"I was just thinking," Brant smiled.

"About what?" Jennifer asked curiously.

"About what you'd do if I did this," Brant smiled. He pulled Jennifer close to him and pressed his lips against hers.

After a moment Jennifer pulled away. Brant pulled her back into his arms, and Jennifer gently pushed her hands against his chest. "Wait," she whispered.

"I'm sorry," Brant sighed as he slowly moved his hands away from Jennifer.

"I'm not," Jennifer shook her head. "Tommy's mom was right; our love *is* strong enough to survive even this."

"What are you saying?" Brant asked.

"Here, I'll show you," Jennifer smiled. She stood on her tiptoes and removed the blue and white baseball cap that Brant was wearing. Brant smiled as she pulled it, backwards, onto her own head. "I love you," Jennifer declared as she slid her arms around Brant's neck.

"I love you too. I'll never hurt you again... I mean it... I'll treat you like a princess, just like you deserve," Brant promised. "I want to earn back your trust. I want you to know just how much I love you and that I'll always be faithful to..."

"I've always wanted to say this," Jennifer interrupted. She grinned broadly, "Brant, shut up and kiss me."

***

When Brant and the gang got back to Mississippi, the school year was quickly coming to an end, as were Brant's chances of actually graduating on time with his class. He barely passed history, and most likely did because the thought of spending another semester with Brantley made Mr. Roberts have nightmares, yet literature looked as though it would force him into summer school.

Brant, as we had always expected, had decided to opt out of college for a chance to play in the National Football League. Christian was going to the University of Alabama on a combination athletic and academic scholarship, and Ethan had decided to accept a scholarship from Duke University in Durham, North Carolina. My brothers seemed set to move on with the next phases of their lives. The only hurdle that remained was that my mother insisted that Brant make certain that he was able to graduate on time and walk with the rest of his senior class. She had waited eighteen years for graduation day pictures of her triplets, and she would have graduation day no other way.

With each passing day, as graduation became more of a reality, so did the possibility that Mr. Football would not receive his cap and gown to walk with the rest of his class.

After the last day of final exam review in Mrs. Walker's literature class, she called Brant up to her desk. "You can do this, Brantley," she assured him, "but you're going to have to really study for the final."

"I'll study," Brant promised.

"You have to have an *A+*," Mrs. Walker said sternly. "An *A* won't do it, Brant… I'm sorry… I've pulled all the strings I can… now it's up to you."

When I got home from my job at the newspaper that evening, our driveway was full of automobiles. I walked inside expecting the living room to be bustling with teenagers, the television blaring, cokes on the coffee table with no coasters in sight and bags of Doritos being passed around the room. Instead, I was surprised to enter the room and find it empty. In fact, the whole house buzzed with an unsettling, uncommon silence. Suspecting mischief, I walked upstairs and peeked into the triplets' room.

Brant was listening to Ethan explain the plot of *Macbeth* as Jennifer and Tommy quietly prepared flashcards of vocabulary words. Christian was skimming the prologue of *The Canterbury Tales*, occasionally highlighting a line or two. No one gave me more than a glance.

"Let's talk *Macbeth*," Ethan announced.

"I hate Shakespeare," Brant grumbled.

Ethan groaned.

"Hey," Jennifer smiled, "he knows who wrote it… nobody's asking him to like it!"

"You have a point," Ethan nodded.

"She has a point," Christian concurred.

Everyone looked at Tommy. "Hey… don't look at me. I doth hateth Shakespeare myself," he shrugged.

"Remind me again *why* you're here?" Brant smiled. "If I'm not mistaken, your literature grade is all of like six points higher than mine."

"All for one, one for all, buddy," Tommy shrugged. "I'm strictly here for moral support."

"No date tonight?" Brant nodded.

Tommy shook his head. "I had to break a few hearts… told them all I had to help a fallen comrade…"

"Thanks, pal," Brant rolled his eyes. "I'm touched by your gesture of loyalty, and, might I add, impressed with your ability to come up with a bald-faced lie on the fly."

"You taught me well," Tommy nodded as he reached for a cookie from the plate in the middle of the circle.

Ethan glared at the boys. "If the two of you are finished…"

Tommy caught Ethan's eye. "Break's over, Brantley!" Tommy barked with his mouth full of chocolate chip cookie. "Back to the books! Chop! Chop!"

Everyone laughed.

"Okay," Ethan said, taking charge, "does everyone have their *Macbeth* questions ready?"

Everyone did, so Brant faced his firing squad.

"Alright, Brant," Jennifer said, speaking slowly and praying for a correct response as she enunciated, "what was the turning point of *Macbeth*?"

"Ooh… when that dude got away," Brant answered quickly, snapping his fingers.

"Judges?" Jennifer smiled.

"Judges say," Ethan huffed as he grabbed a pillow off of his bed and hit Brant in the head, "you have to have an *A+*, so I don't recommend answering *any* questions with *that dude*. Got it, genius?"

"I don't remember his name!" Brant smiled.

"Fleance!" Jennifer and my brothers exclaimed at once.

"Okay… okay… sorry… gosh," Brant held his hands up.

"Fleance… it was definitely *Fleance*," Tommy nodded confidently as he reached for the plate of cookies.

I laughed to myself as I pulled the door closed.

When Brant's makeshift tutors were done with him, he knew every answer to every question that could have possibly been on that test.

The next morning was exam day; the moment of truth had arrived. Ethan was on pins and needles as he worried about Brant's ability to put everything that he knew on paper without being completely distracted by one of a million other things going on that day.

When Brant came down to breakfast with headphones on, Ethan gasped. "Take those off, you have to concentrate!" he screeched.

"Thanks, E, but I'm pretty sure that I can listen to Garth and eat this here pop tart at the same time," Brant grinned.

"Dad?" Ethan stomped.

"What?" Dad replied, not so much as looking up from the morning paper. "Leave your brother alone."

Brant took a gulp of his orange juice as Ethan began to rant. "You've got my nerves in spasms, Brant! Are you trying to push me over the edge?"

If you have never seen orange juice spray uncontrollably onto an already high-strung victim, you have never seen anything half as funny as what I witnessed that morning.

As Ethan, orange juice dripping from his face, chased Brant around the living room and then up the stairs, Dad called, "Brant, Ethan, come clean this up, now!"

"Brant can clean it up," Mom interjected. "He made the mess." She raised her voice, "Brant! Get down here!"

"From where I was sitting Brant might have made it, but Ethan caused it," Dad mumbled. "Talkin' about his *nerves* and such."

Mom shook her head as she reached for a dishrag.

"Mom," Christian hollered down the stairs, "where is my green shirt? Will you iron it, please?"

"Okay," Mom called back, as she began cleaning the floor, "find it and throw it down."

"Mom," Brant shouted, "tell Ethan that if he touches me again I'm gonna punch him out."

"Ethan," Mom called.

"I mean it, Mom," Brant screamed.

"David," Mom snapped, "a little help here, please."

"Hit him and die, Brantley," Dad barked, his mouth full of toast.

Mom rolled her eyes.

"Mom," Christian grumbled, "one of my new tennis shoes is missing."

"Keep looking… it's got to be there somewhere," Mom called.

"Gosh, Brant," Ethan yelled, "what'd you do that for?"

"Brant, what did you do?" Mom hollered.

"Nothing… I didn't touch him," came Brant's all too innocent reply.

Mom took a deep breath. "Get down here… all three of you… now!"

I leaned back in my chair. "Yep… sometimes you think you should have stopped with one, huh?" I smiled.

Mom nodded playfully, then she smiled that loving, motherly smile we all knew so well. "Never," she shook her head.

***

When Brant finally got around to taking his literature exam that morning, he knew he aced it. "Just tell me where I can pick up my cap and gown," he smiled confidently as he tossed his paper onto the teacher's desk.

Ethan paced as Mrs. Walker graded Brant's paper.

She looked up from her desk. "100 A+," she nodded proudly. "Great job, Brantley!"

Ethan snatched the paper from her and stared at it in disbelief. "No way!"

Brant snatched the paper back and tossed it onto the desk. "Yes way!" he mocked.

***

Graduation day came, and, suddenly, it felt like the past eighteen years had flown by. Dad had the video camera focused on Ethan, North River High School's class valedictorian, as he delivered an inspiring speech about his class' years at North River and his visions for their futures.

We all sat wiggling in our chairs as the salutatorian babbled on and on, personally thanking every person that she had ever met in her entire life. Half way through her speech, Brant was slumped so far down in his chair that I thought Mom was going to strangle him when she got her hands on him, but she had to admit that she too had looked at her watch once or twice.

After the graduates received their diplomas, we were all dismissed to a reception where Brant's #13 would be officially retired.

It only seemed right that no one else would ever wear Brant's #13 in Cummins, but his acceptance speech truly reminded all of us that North River High School football would never be the same without him.

Brant stood up at the podium and adjusted the microphone. "I'm not gonna bore y'all," he said with a smirk. "Listening to Ethan was punishment enough!" He got the rise that he wanted out of everyone. "I'm kidding," he clapped, "everyone give him a big round of applause… he deserves it. He taught me last week what it means to really study, and, all I can say is, I sure am thankful that he always enjoyed it so much, so that I could be irresponsible and undependable without totally destroying my parents' hopes of raising a contribution to society." The crowd chuckled.

"I know that I am supposed to be up here talking about my football career… so here you go," Brant smiled. "First, I would like to thank God for blessing me with the ability and the opportunity to do what I love.

Next, I would like to thank my dad for always seeing to it that my God-given talent was used to its full potential. Dad, you are my father, my coach, my friend, and the motivation behind everything that led me to this stage today.

Mom, thanks for deciding to become a doctor when you fell in love with a football fanatic. It was a smart move; you must have seen me in your future! Thank you for bandaging me up but always being brave enough to let me go right back out. I know a lot of big, tough football players, but you are the strongest person I know."

"Jordan," Brant smiled. Then he paused. "I just want to tell all of you a little story," he nodded. "Y'all know that this past summer I flipped my truck about eight times over by what *was* the old bridge until I got done with it! I can honestly say that I remember two things about that entire day. One, pain like I had never felt before, and, two, lying in my big brother's arms, scared that I was about to die, and hearing Jordan say, 'Brant, I love you.'" He looked out into the audience, right at me and said, "I didn't say it then because it seemed way too much like 'goodbye,' but I love you too. Thank you for being the best big brother that anyone could ever ask for. You've always been there for me. When I was wrong, you told me; when I was right, you defended me, and, no matter what I did, I knew I could always count on you to love me."

"Christian, Ethan, Tommy," Brant grinned, "you guys made my football career fun. When they told me that they wanted to retire my number, I thought to myself… *well… #13 isn't really all that special without #16, #2, and #67 right beside it.* But, they insisted that they wanted to hang my jersey on the wall in the gym, so I gave in! You know… what do you do? But you all know that #13 was who he was because of all of you.

Christian, I love you, bro. You're an amazing athlete and an even better brother. Good luck and Roll Tide, man! For any hard of hearing reporters who might be in the room, the quote was *amazing*... A-M-A-Z-I-N-G." Chuckles spread across the auditorium.

"Ethan," Brant grinned, "the class might have voted me *Most Likely to Succeed*, but we all know that I could screw up at any moment. You, however, are destined for success. I'm proud of you, and I wish you only the best...always.

Tommy, they called me the *Class Clown*, but, throughout the years, no one has made me laugh quite as much as you have. They named me *Most Handsome*... oh, wait, sorry... that was right... my bad." Laughter erupted.

"Rocky," Brant winked, "you are my *everything*... the reason I play ball... the reason I believe in myself... the reason I smile each day... the reason that I'm standing here now. It's hard for me to find the words to describe how much you mean to me, so I'm gonna try to say it in a song." He wiggled the microphone out of its stand, and the crowd began to cheer. "Jennifer, this is to you from me. Everyone else, this is Garth Brooks' *Cowboys and Angels*."

Jennifer smiled as she watched Brant serenade her in front of the entire town, and, by the end of the song, she was wiping tears from her eyes.

When Brant was done singing, he blew Jennifer a kiss. "It's true that only Heaven knows why you love me," he smiled. "You will always be my angel, and it certainly has been a heck of a ride these past eighteen years, but it's not over yet. The best is yet to come. I love you."

"I love you too," Jennifer mouthed.

Brant looked out over his audience. "There are so many people that I wish I had time to thank, but *I* won't name them all," he snickered. The crowd exploded in laughter. "I don't know what y'all are laughing at," Brant chuckled. Tommy and Christian were bent over double laughing, and they continued to laugh when everyone else stopped, which was mildly embarrassing considering that the salutatorian and her family, all of whom are close friends of my parents', were sitting directly behind us. It seemed as though they were simultaneously struck with that uncontrollable laughter that only breaks out at the most inappropriate moments... in church, at a wedding, or worse, at a funeral. Still, I think that if Mom could have crawled under her chair, she would have.

"It's been an amazing journey," Brant said seriously. "Thank you to everyone out there for all the love and support that any guy could ever ask for out of a school and a community. This town has stood by me through so much, and I can't tell all of you how much your love, support and prayers have meant to me. And, of course, thank you for this incredible honor. I hope that I make you all very proud in Dallas. Go Cowboys!"

We all stood to our feet as we cheered, and Brant egged on his standing ovation.

When Brant walked off stage, Jennifer was waiting for him. "So how'd you like my speech?" he smiled.

"Bravo! Bravo!" Jennifer grinned. She looked around. "Have you seen Brianna?"

"She wasn't feeling well earlier," Brant frowned. "She headed home before my speech, which was just as well, but I promised her that I'd be by to check on her as soon as I could get away. I guess I should go."

"Do you want me to go with you?" Jennifer offered.

"Nah… you stay here," Brant urged. "Have fun and save some cake for me."

Jennifer kissed Brant's cheek. "Hurry back!"

"Brant!" Tommy called from across the auditorium. "Come check out this cake, man! It's huge!"

Brant and Jennifer laughed. "Don't worry," Jennifer smiled, "I'll make him save you a piece."

"Yeah… good luck with that," Brant scoffed playfully.

Jennifer smiled, but her smile quickly faded into a frown. "You too," she nodded seriously.

***

"Brianna!" Brant called as he knocked on her front door. There was no answer. He knocked again. "Brianna open up! Are you home? It's me."

Still, there was no answer.

Brant looked at his watch. He knocked on the door again, this time pounding on it with his fist.

Finally, Brianna cracked the door open. "Sorry it took me so long… I was in the kitchen," she laughed pleasantly.

Brant stared at the less than appetizing concoction in the bowl in Brianna's hand. "What is that?" he inquired curiously.

"Pickles and ice cream. Want some?" Brianna asked as she extended the dish toward him.

"No," Brant exclaimed as he turned away, "Brianna, that's sick!"

"You try being pregnant," Brianna nodded, "it makes you crave strange things."

Brant stared at the dish. "I'll take your word for it, but I hope you don't expect me to hang around and watch you eat that."

Brianna sat the dish aside. "It can wait… come in."

Brant walked inside. "How are you feeling?" he asked quickly.

"Okay," Brianna nodded, "most of the time."

"Well, why don't you sit down and get off your feet for awhile?" Brant suggested as he led Brianna to the sofa.

Suddenly, Brianna doubled over in pain.

"What? What's wrong?" Brant panicked. "I thought you said you were okay. You don't look okay to me."

Brianna gripped Brant hand. "I said I felt okay *most of the time*," she snapped, "but every now and then I have these sharp pains."

"Maybe we should take you to the doctor," Brant gulped.

"No," Brianna said as she sat, "it's okay. I'm only seven months along, so my mom says that what I'm experiencing are called Braxton Hicks contractions…"

"What's that?" Brant shrugged.

"Just a false alarm," Brianna said as the pain eased.

Brant nodded. "Well, she's probably right. Obviously she's had a baby before, but maybe we should call my mom just in case… I mean, she *is* a doctor."

"I'm fine," Brianna smiled, "but it's very sweet of you to worry about me."

"Are you sure you don't want me to call my mom?" Brant offered again.

"No… I'm okay now," Brianna shook her head.

"Well, can I get you anything?" Brant offered. "A pillow? A magazine? How about some ice cream… maybe minus the pickles… or, if you insist on the pickles, I guess I might could stand it."

Brianna laughed.

"You want the pickles and ice cream don't you?" Brant nodded with a smile.

"No," Brianna laughed, "that's the funny thing… the cravings usually pass before I get a chance to eat whatever it was I was craving in the first place."

Brant sat down next to Brianna. "Yeah," he smiled, "that's because the baby gets a good whiff of what you're about to feed him, and he's like *'No, Mommy! Please no! Pickles and ice cream? That's gross! Are you out of your mind?'*"

Brianna slapped Brant's arm playfully. "Are you making fun of me?"

"Yes," Brant nodded, "yes I am."

Brianna laughed.

Brant rubbed Brianna's stomach. "It's okay, Brandon! I won't let her eat it, buddy!"

"Would you stop it," Brianna laughed. "I can't stand when you start talking to my stomach."

"I'm not talking to your stomach," Brant rolled his eyes. "I'm talking to the baby. You get that, right? I mean you get that there is a baby growing inside of you… a real, live, little baby boy?"

"Our baby," Brianna smiled.

"Well, if you're alright," Brant said as he stood, "I should really be getting back to the school."

"You just got here," Brianna sighed.

"I know," Brant nodded, "but it's graduation day, and I need to…"

"To be with your friends," Brianna sighed. "I understand."

Brant frowned. "It's just that my mom wanted to take some more pictures, and Jennifer's saving me some cake from the retirement ceremony. Hey, I could come back by and bring you some cake if you want, and, if you prefer, I could even cover it in mustard, barbecue sauce or anything you might like."

Brianna looked up at Brant. "Can I tell you something?" she gulped.

"Sure," Brant nodded.

"I think you're a great guy," Brianna said sincerely.

Brant was a little taken aback. "Well, thank you, Brianna. I'm glad you think so," he smiled.

"I love you," Brianna declared.

Brant put his hands in his pockets. "Brianna, is there anything I can get you before I leave?" he grimaced.

"You can't say it can you?" Brianna huffed.

"Can't say what?" Brant shrugged, trying to play it off.

"I love you," Brianna rolled her eyes.

"Bri," Brant shook his head.

"You and Jennifer toss it around like it's some sort of common, meaningless phrase, and you can't even *say it* to *me*, the mother of your child… not even once."

"It's not meaningless, Brianna," Brant shook his head, "that's why I didn't say it back."

"Oh, well that makes me feel a whole lot better," Brianna rolled her eyes as she propped her feet up on the coffee table.

"Brianna, when are you going to get it?" Brant snapped. "I don't love you, and I'm never going to. I'm sorry if that sounds harsh, but you don't seem to get the message when it's put any other way. I don't love you. I will never love you. I love Jennifer."

"You were being so sweet to me," Brianna frowned. "Why would you…"

"Because I'm a nice guy, Brianna," Brant sighed, "not because I'm in love with you."

"Why can't you love me?" Brianna cried.

"Brianna," Brant groaned, "you need to understand that…"

"I'm prettier than Jennifer," Brianna interrupted. "I'm not nearly the prude she is… we both know that."

"Hold it right there," Brant insisted. "If you think you're going to get anywhere with me by insulting Jennifer…"

"I didn't mean to insult her," Brianna grumbled. "I just don't understand…"

Brant cut her off. "Brianna, love is about more than looks… more than physical attraction…"

"So you do think I'm pretty?" Brianna blurted.

Brant crossed his arms. "Why are you doing this? Getting upset isn't good for the baby."

"Answer the question," Brianna insisted. "Do you think I'm pretty?"

"Brianna, it's no secret that every guy you come in contact with thinks you're drop dead gorgeous," Brant shrugged. "Why is it so important that you hear me say it?"

"Do you think I'm prettier than Jennifer?" Brianna continued.

Brant shook his head. "I don't believe this. You really are as shallow as everyone says you are. It's all about outward appearance to you. Brianna, that's not *love.* Because you find me attractive, because you like my muscles or the money I'm gonna make… that doesn't mean you're in love with me… none of those things have anything to do with who I really am on the inside. I love Jennifer, not because of the way she looks on the outside, but for who she is on the inside. That's *love.* But, for the record, I think Jennifer is the most beautiful girl I have ever seen."

"Well, isn't that sickeningly sweet," Brianna rolled her eyes, "but I saw you the day I arrived in town… you nearly fell out of your desk when I walked through that door."

"There you go," Brant pointed. "See… Brianna, you just don't get it. You may be a knock out now, but that's gonna fade one day, and then what are you going to be left with?"

Brianna doubled over in pain. "Would you stop yelling at me!" she shouted.

Brant stared at Brianna. "What's going on? Do you think it's one of those false alarms… what did you call those things?"

"No!" Brianna cried. "I don't know! Brant, do something!"

"I'll call my mom," Brant gasped as he reached in his pocket for his cell phone. He instantly began to pace.

"Oh no!" Brianna cried.

"What? What is it?" Brant called as he rushed to Brianna's side.

"It's the baby," Brianna panicked. "Brant, I think the baby is coming!"

"No… it's too soon… he's not due for several weeks," Brant said as he struggled to hold on to the phone as Brianna latched on to his arm.

"Brant, I'm scared!" Brianna bellowed. "Do something!"

"Mom… come-on… pick up," Brant sighed.

Brant hung up the phone.

"We have to get to the hospital," Brianna cried.

Brant slipped his phone in his pocket and put his arm around Brianna. "Let's get you to my truck… I'll call again on the way."

Brant sped down the road, one hand on the wheel and the other holding the phone. He glanced over at Brianna. "Mom, where are you?" he screamed into the phone.

"Brant," Brianna squealed.

Brant hung up the phone and quickly began to dial another number.

"Who are you calling now?" Brianna yelled.

"Jen!" Brant exclaimed into the phone. "Thank God! Listen, Brianna's having the baby… I don't know what to do…"

"Okay," Jennifer nodded as she took a deep breath, "Brantley, calm down. Where are you?"

"We're on our way to the hospital," Brant panicked.

"I don't think we're gonna make it," Brianna cried.

"We have to make it," Brant barked back. "I can't deliver a baby!"

Brianna screamed in pain, and Jennifer had to move the phone away from her ear.

"How far apart are the contractions?" Jennifer asked as she began frantically searching for someone to help her talk Brant through this.

"I don't know," Brant sighed, "maybe a couple minutes."

"How far from the hospital are you?" Jennifer gulped.

"Brant! Slow down!" Brianna yelled. "What are you doing?" She slapped his arm. "Slow down!"

"How about *you* concentrate on not having that baby until I get you to a doctor, and let *me* worry about the driving," Brant snapped.

"Brant, don't be short with her," Jennifer coached. "She's scared, and she needs you to be strong for her."

"I'm trying," Brant barked back. "Where's my mom?"

"I'm looking for her as we speak," Jennifer assured him.

"Hurry!" Brant yelled.

"Calm down, Brant," Jennifer said softly. "Remind her to breathe."

"What?" Brant yelled into the phone. "Jennifer, I'm losing you… what did you say… can you hear me?"

The phone went dead.

"Dang it!" Brant huffed as he slung the phone onto the seat.

Brianna let out an anguished cry.

"Hang on… we're almost there," Brant said reassuringly.

"How fast are you going?" Brianna exclaimed.

"Who cares!" Brant snapped. "Right now I'd *pay* a cop to pull me over."

"How much further?" Brianna sighed.

"We're almost there," Brant replied. "Stay green... stay green!" he yelled as he sailed underneath a red light.

"Are you color blind?" Brianna screamed.

"Shut up and breathe," Brant yelled back. He hung a sharp right. "Everything is going to be fine," he nodded as he saw the hospital in the distance.

***

Brandon Tyler McLachlan entered the world nearly two months before we were expecting him. Weighing in at only two pounds and two ounces, he would make sure that he got all the nurses' attention. I guess the art of making an entrance was in his blood!

Brant stood for hours staring at Brandon through a tiny glass window. He wouldn't take his eyes off of him. He wouldn't talk to any of us. We all tried comforting him, but he had so much on his mind. As often was the case when something important was happening in Brant's life, the only person he wanted to talk to was Jennifer. She stood beside him, peering in the window at baby Brandon.

Brant plastered his hands on the glass as tears formed in his eyes.

"Come sit down," Jennifer sighed as she rubbed his back consolingly.

"I'm not leaving him," Brant shook his head.

Jennifer wrapped her arms around Brant's waist. "He's gonna be okay, Brant," she said softly. "He's just going to have to stay in the hospital a little longer than most babies."

"Look how tiny he is," Brant sighed as he turned to her. "He's so little... so helpless... what if he's not strong enough to fight?"

Jennifer glanced up at Brant. "Something tells me that Brandon is tough, just like someone else I know," she nodded.

"I don't feel very tough right now," Brant shook his head. "I feel pretty helpless myself to tell you the truth. I just want to hold him. I want to tell him that I'm here for him."

"He'll know that soon enough," Jennifer nodded.

"Yeah, he will," Brant gulped, "because I'm not going to Texas. I'm staying right here. I guess that it took me eighteen years to learn that some things are more important than football, but one look at that little guy... and football's just a game."

"Playing football for the Cowboys has always been your dream," Jennifer gulped.

"Dreams are for kids, Rocky," Brant shook his head. He stared into the window and fought back tears as he watched Brandon fighting for his life. "I stopped being a kid today."

Jennifer rested her head against Brant's chest.

"He's really sick, and I don't know how to help him," Brant cried. "The doctors don't think he's gonna make it, do they?" he sighed.

A tear rolled down Jennifer's cheek. "Last summer there were a lot of doctors who didn't think *you* were gonna make it. You proved them wrong, and so will Brandon."

"You're right," Brant nodded. "He's a fighter..."

"And, just like his daddy, I'm sure he thrives on beating the odds," Jennifer smiled. "There were a lot of people that thought you'd never play football again after your wreck... but they were all wrong."

"Yeah, I guess they were," Brant agreed.

"Look at that little boy in there," Jennifer pointed. "Look past all the machines, and I see a little boy with light blond hair and perfect blue eyes, and, if I look close enough, I think I even see a hint of a little smirk on his tiny face. Remind you of anyone you know?"

"He looks just like me doesn't he?" Brant smiled.

"He got the hair, the eyes, the smile, the dimples I'm guessing," Jennifer smiled as she glanced up at Brant, "and I'd be willing to bet you he has the willpower too."

Brant kissed the top of Jennifer's head. "I know he does."

The two of them stood holding each other as they stared in the window at Brandon.

"Brant?" Jennifer said after a moment.

"Yeah?" Brant replied.

"I think you got it backwards," she smiled sincerely. "Trix are for kids; dreams are what make the world go round."

Brant took his eyes away from the window and stared down at Jennifer. "No," he gulped, "love... *love* makes the world go round. That I'm sure of."

Jennifer smiled.

Brant kissed her lips before wrapping his arms around her and squeezing her tight.

With Brant's arms draped over her, Jennifer stared in the window at Brandon. "Come-on, tiny man," she whispered.

Brant kissed the side of Jennifer's head. "He's gonna be okay. It won't be long before we're buying him his first football."

Jennifer smiled. "He looks like a quarterback if you ask me."

"Why, Rock… I think you're right," Brant grinned.

Jennifer put her hand on the glass and leaned close to the window. "We love you, Brandon," she whispered, and, as she stared at that baby lying there in that nursery, she saw Brant's baby boy and loved him effortlessly.

CHAPTER TWELVE

When the time came for the gang to go their separate ways, it was an emotional time for all of us. For as long as Christian, Ethan, Brant, Tommy and Jennifer could remember, they had always had each other to lean on. Now, as they each prepared to leave the town that had nurtured them since birth, they each promised to carry with them the assurance of one another's friendship as they ventured into their separate lives.

For Brant, leaving Brandon behind was almost unbearably difficult. He and Brianna agreed that Brandon would stay behind in Cummins with Brianna until Brant could get settled in Dallas. My brother loved his son, and, for that reason, he chose to pursue a career that, while it would take him away from Brandon, would allow him to provide not only for Brandon's needs, but would create a sense of financial stability that would allow him to give Brandon everything that his little heart desired. As Brant was in the process of learning, the things Brandon needed most from him, no amount of money could buy.

After graduation, Tommy decided that he wasn't staying in Mississippi while Brant was having all the fun out in Texas, and, though Mom was uncertain about the prospect of Brant and Tommy living on their own, miles away from home, she gave in. Dad installed a stern *one strike and you're out* policy, and when Brant suggested that it should be *three strikes and you're out,* Dad reminded him that he had never been much of a baseball man, and, as far as he was concerned, it was just one!

For the first time in months, Brant seemed truly happy. He couldn't wait to see Texas Stadium again. He remembered being there as a little boy and dreaming about the day he would play on the same field as his heroes. The time had finally come... Brant was going to be a Cowboy at last.

Christian and Jennifer set off for Tuscaloosa with a U-Haul packed to the hilt. He was going to Alabama to play football, and she was going to dance… both of them were thankful to have the other along for the ride.

When Ethan left for North Carolina in August, suddenly our house felt very empty.

That September, the problem-plagued construction on my house was finally completed, and I too moved out.

Mom took it hard, all of us being gone. She planned a big, three-state, round trip not long after the boys left, but Dad very bluntly informed her that none of the boys had been given time to miss her yet.

Mom and Jennifer talked on the phone at least once every couple of days, so that Mom could get the scoop on everyone without having to nag. The boys all told Jennifer everything, and Mom loved hearing the gossip about the boys' love lives, their successes, their failures, their most embarrassing moments, their doubts, their fears, their fun and especially how much they each loved and missed their mama.

Christian said that he loved Alabama football so much that he was never coming home, which was devastating to Mom but thrilled Dad.

Ethan didn't care much for his roommate because he was too loud while Ethan was trying to study. Mom was ready to go to North Carolina and demand a move; Dad assured Ethan that if he could have a perfect GPA through four years of high school while sharing a room with Brantley, he'd be just fine.

As Brant went on and on about his teammates and the friends he had made in Dallas, all obviously a good bit older than he was, Mom swore that Brant was going to end up in trouble. Dad only joked that a little jail time might just be the best thing that could ever happen to Brant.

Being a young, attractive, blond-headed kid determined to make a name for himself in professional football made Brant an immediate commercial success. The fact that he possessed a natural gift for gab was an added bonus that made him a hot commodity amongst the media. He was cute, cocky and confident; he was charming and charismatic. The public loved him; Dallas loved him, and, heck, a day in Cummins, and you'd be convinced that Brant McLachlan hung the moon. But, it didn't take Brant long to discover that if people were going to respect him as a quarterback and not just as a good looking teenager who could talk the talk, he had lots of learning to do.

I think it's safe to say that Dallas overwhelmed Brant at first. He was adjusting to life away from Cummins, life away from his friends and family, and trying to acclimate himself to life in a place where people didn't bow down at the mention of his name.

For Brant, the goal of playing in Dallas stemmed from understanding and respecting the heritage of Cowboys football. When Brant set foot on the gridiron in Texas Stadium, he was not merely standing on a football field, instead, he was walking in the very footsteps of those who had gone before.

Love them or hate them, the Cowboys will always be America's Team, and, for Brant, walking in the shadows of his football heroes was what putting on a Cowboys jersey was all about. When Brant stepped on the field where greats like Don Meredith and Troy Aikman had carved their legacies, he was no longer just Brant McLachlan… he was the next Roger Staubach. Staubach, a Navy quarterback and Heisman Trophy winner, was dubbed *Captain America* for leading America's Team to four Super Bowl Championships in the 1970's. When Brant was a little boy playing football on the school playground, he dreamed of being like Roger Staubach. Now, standing on the very field where Staubach had played, Brant dreamt of victories, of Super Bowls, and of emerging as the next Captain America.

As Brant adjusted to life in Dallas, late night phone calls home became common. At first, Dad tried to explain to Brant that he was being too hard on himself.

"Rome wasn't built in a day, son," he told him over and over again.

Yet, Brant was frustrated. For him, the learning curve was lasting much longer than he had expected.

Eventually, Dad learned that the best thing to do was just to listen as Brant vented.

Dad would hold the phone away from his ear as Brant shouted about how he hated the offence or how he had never even read a book as thick as his new playbook.

Brant's confidence level had always been so high that Dad and I were actually a little relieved to know that at least the NFL could make him do a double take at his arsenal of talents.

"'If things don't start going my way, I'm going to be remembered forever as the big mouthed, laughing stock who thought that he could play professional football but had to run off and join a boy band just to pay the bills,'" Jennifer quoted through her laugher as she relayed to Mom one of the many messages Brant had left on her answering machine. "He said he doesn't want to be the Anna Kournikova of football," Jennifer cackled.

Brant may not have been ready to go to Dallas and be the star… no one expected him to be… no one even expected him to set foot on the field during his first year, but, as Brant began to settle into his new role as a rookie with a lot to learn, his natural ability began to shine through the inexperience. Brant was a quick study on the football field, a perfectionist by nature and determined to prove that he belonged on the same field with quarterbacks like John Elway and, fellow Mississippi native, Brett Favre. Brant found himself working harder than he ever had in his life. The demand on his time would have been overwhelming for someone less inclined to thrive on the attention, but Brant relished the spotlight. He loved meeting people and rubbing elbows with the big names. Though he was determined to handle himself like a man out to do his job, Brant couldn't help but feel like a fan as he stood amongst his childhood heroes… men he now called teammates.

Brant may not have been ready to take the NFL by storm just yet, but one analyst put it best when he said, "some day… *some day*!"

***

One Saturday morning, Jennifer surprised Brant and Tommy by showing up on their doorstep unannounced at six o'clock in the morning. She got to see firsthand what happens when two guys have a place of their own for a couple months without anyone to tell them what to do or when to do it.

There were pizza boxes lying around, dirty clothes draped over recliners or thrown carelessly on the floor, and there were two gallons of ice cream sitting on the coffee table with the spoons still in them from the night before.

"Tommy, get the door!" Brant hollered from his bedroom when Jennifer knocked.

"Who is it?" Tommy shouted as he hurried down the hallway. He flung the door open. "Jen!" he exclaimed.

"I hope I didn't catch you at a bad time," Jennifer smiled. "I should have called, but I wanted to surprise you guys. Is Brant here?"

Brant strolled down the hall as he finished buttoning his shirt. "Who was it?" he called as he walked into the living room. He looked toward the door, and, when he saw Jennifer, his face lit up. "Rocky? What are you doing here?" he exclaimed.

"Surprise!" Jennifer smiled with a shrug.

"Well, don't stand out there, come in," Brant said quickly. He began gathering laundry off of the furniture. "Do you ever do laundry any more?" he huffed as he tossed the pile to Tommy.

"I'm your roommate… not your maid," Tommy chucked. He dropped the laundry on the floor. "Besides… I wasn't expecting company."

"Don't worry about cleaning up for me," Jennifer smiled. She took the pizza box from Brant's hand and tossed it back onto the counter. "I didn't come to see the apartment… I came to see you."

Brant threw his arms around Jennifer. "I'm glad you're here," he said.

"Is it a bad time?" Jennifer asked. She glanced at Brant's attire. "Were you headed out… because I don't mind hanging around here until you get back. Don't let me keep you from…"

"I'm off today," Brant shrugged.

"Brant," Tommy interjected, "you have to…"

"I said I'm taking the day off," Brant insisted as he gestured toward the sofa. "Sit… can I get you anything?"

"I would love something to drink," Jennifer nodded.

Tommy smiled as he walked toward the refrigerator. "We have Dr. Pepper, bottled water and sweet tea."

"I drank the last Dr. Pepper last night," Brant shook his head. "You need to go to the store."

"In that case," Tommy nodded, "I recommend the bottled water because Brant made the sweet tea, and let's just say, *it ain't like Mama makes it…* if you know what I mean."

"Then water it is," Jennifer grinned.

"The tea ain't that bad," Brant smiled.

"No… not if you prefer a little tea in your sugar," Tommy rolled his eyes.

Tommy tossed a bottled water across the living room. Brant caught it and handed it to Jennifer.

"Thank you," she smiled. "Did you get the pictures I sent of Brandon?"

"Tommy, did you check my e-mail?" Brant inquired.

Tommy laughed as he opened a trash bag and began clearing the coffee table. "No, master… I was too busy doing the rest of my chores to check your e-mail."

"I understand," Brant nodded, "I mean, you did the laundry… oh wait, no. You went to the store… no, no, my bad, you didn't do that either, but you took the trash out… oh look, that hasn't been done in weeks. What did you do yesterday, pray tell?"

Jennifer laughed, and then so did Tommy.

"I should go download those pictures," Brant smiled as he stood.

"Oh, don't worry about it," Jennifer said as she reached into her purse, "I brought more."

Brant sat on the arm of Tommy's recliner as he held the stack of pictures.

The boys laughed and pointed as they flipped through the large stack of photographs. The last picture was of Jennifer and Brandon on a swing set; he was laughing, and she was smiling down at him.

"He looks like he's having a blast," Brant smiled.

"He did," Jennifer nodded with a laugh. "Last weekend I went home, and your mom and I took Brandon and Ben to the park for the day."

"That was nice… I'm sure Brianna appreciated the break," Brant said as he flipped back through the pictures.

"I've been meaning to mention that to you," Jennifer eased into her statement. "Your mom says that she'll go by to check on Brandon, and he'll need his diaper changed, or Brianna won't have fed him yet."

"Mom mentioned it to me," Brant sighed.

"Several times," Tommy added.

"Yeah," Brant sighed.

"Brant," Jennifer said in a concerned tone, "Brianna has everyone else keeping Brandon just so she won't have to. Luckily, Brandon is a very bubbly, good-natured baby despite the way Brianna treats him, so people actually don't mind keeping him. He really is a pleasure, but lately I've heard he's been spending more time with Janet Waterford and Susie Carpenter than he has with Brianna. I feel much more comfortable when he's with them, but he's not their responsibility, and I don't want to see Brianna wear out his welcome."

"My mom said that she'd take him in fulltime if it wasn't for her work schedule," Brant nodded, "but I wouldn't want her to have to do that anyway. Brandon is Brianna's and my responsibility. I want to prove to myself, and especially to Brandon, that I can take care of him without having to involve his grandparents in raising him."

"Don't be so stubborn," Jennifer shook her head. "You have to do what's best for Brandon, and, right now, you need the help."

"I don't know," Brant shrugged.

Jennifer exhaled. "Christian and I drove home one night a few weeks ago for one of Ben's football games. We decided to give Brianna a call and see if she wanted to go with us, or, if not, if she'd mind us picking up Brandon and taking him along. Her phone was busy, so Christian swung by her house. She was sitting out on the front porch talking on the phone while Brandon screamed at the top of his lungs in his playpen. It was like she didn't even hear it… like she had learned to tune him out."

"She'll never win Mom of the Year; that's for sure," Brant sighed.

"I feel sorry for Brandon," Jennifer snapped back. "I couldn't imagine having to depend on Brianna Clarke for anything."

"Brianna and I talked about enrolling him in daycare," Brant replied, his face full of uncertainty, "because she says she wants to start school in Meridian next semester."

"That might be good for her," Jennifer agreed, "and I heard that Mrs. Wanda Thornton is actually thinking about opening up a home daycare service. She's right down the street from Brianna; it would be very convenient for her, and you know Mrs. Wanda would take wonderful care of Brandon. Do you want me to talk to her?"

"I wish that I could just move him out here," Brant began, "but…"

"But nothing," Jennifer interjected, "clean up this pigpen, and he could stay here. If nothing else, I'll move out here and watch him while you're at work."

"Whoa!" Brant exclaimed. "What about school?"

"We're talking about a baby here, Brant… your baby," Jennifer pled. "My heart goes out to him. Brianna tells everyone that all he *ever* does is cry. Well, when I have him, Brantley, Brandon doesn't cry."

"I can't move him out here, Jen," Brant argued. "I'm never here. You're in school in Alabama, and I won't let you give that up… you love it there."

"I love Brandon more," Jennifer protested, "and he needs me."

"I won't let you drop out of school to move out here and be my babysitter," Brant insisted.

"You could hire a good nanny," Jennifer suggested. "I could help you interview them."

"I could always take care of him," Tommy offered. "As you pointed out earlier… I don't do anything else all day."

"That's really nice of you, man," Brant nodded. "The fact that you would even offer means a lot to me, but let's face it... you aren't cut out to take care of a kid."

"How hard could it be?" Tommy grinned. "He doesn't even walk yet."

"Neither does the remote control, and you can't keep up with that," Brant smiled.

Tommy laughed. "Hey… if Brianna can do it… I can do it."

"He's right," Jennifer nodded. "Anything is better than the situation Brandon's in now."

Brant stood. "Tommy, are you sure that you wouldn't mind? I mean that seems like a big responsibility for…"

"Brant," Tommy interrupted with a sincere grin, "come-on, let's give it a try. We've been talking about how we needed a third roommate…"

"To clean…" Brant scoffed.

"We got this," Tommy assured him.

"Are you sure?" Brant sighed.

"Yes!" Tommy replied confidently. "I mean it; I want to do this. All for one, one for all, Brant. Brandon is one of us now."

Brant smiled. "Alright then… let's do it."

"Should we call and make arrangements?" Tommy shrugged, eager to begin performing his new duties as a full-time nanny. "Should we let Brianna know what we're thinking about doing?"

"Trust me, fellas," Jennifer interjected, "you won't get any arguments from Brianna, so just drive home and pick him up."

Brant looked around. "We should clean this place up."

Tommy scanned the room. "Where should we begin?"

Jennifer rolled her eyes. She picked up a dirty t-shirt off the back of the couch. "You take out the trash. I'll start the laundry."

"What should I do?" Brant asked.

"You're going to the store," Jennifer replied quickly. She took a notebook and a pen from the counter. "I'll make you a list of things you'll need to stock up on for the baby."

As Jennifer examined the contents of the refrigerator, Tommy gathered the laundry.

Brant stood by the recliner, his arms crossed. "I love that girl, Tom," he said softly.

Tommy stopped what he was doing. "It's all gonna work out for the two of you," he said confidently. "I feel it."

"Brianna thinks it's only a matter of time before I ask her to move out here with the baby," Brant groaned. "That's the only reason she hasn't shipped him out here already."

"She just wants to use Brandon to get closer to you," Tommy frowned.

"I know that, but..."

"But nothing," Tommy shook his head. "Sunday, after the game, I'm gonna drive home, and I'm gonna pick Brandon up and bring him here... where he belongs. If Brianna asks to come and visit, we are just going to have to tell her *no*."

"Brianna is Brandon's mother," Brant sighed, "I can't deny her the right to see him."

"She doesn't want to see her baby, Brant. She wants to see you," Tommy sighed.

"I know," Brant frowned, "I've told her a million times that I don't love her... that I'll never love her, but she just won't give up."

"I think that girl has mental issues," Tommy nodded.

"She's got serious emotional issues," Brant shrugged. "I don't think she's ever really felt loved... by her mother or father or anyone else."

Tommy went back to gathering the dirty laundry. He tossed a pair of jeans over his shoulder as he turned toward Brant. "It's all going to work out for the best, buddy. You'll be with the girl you love."

"I wish I could believe that," Brant nodded as he stared toward the kitchen. He looked away, "but right now I can't focus on winning Jennifer back; I have to focus on my son and what's best for him."

"And, right now, that's living here with us," Tommy said confidently.

Brant smiled, "yeah… you're right. I mean how hard could it be for two grown men to take care of one tiny, little, baby boy?"

"Piece of cake," Tommy shrugged.

"Yeah, we can handle it, no problem," Brant concurred as he tossed an armload of laundry toward Tommy.

***

When Brant got home on the following Monday evening, he was surprised to find Tommy and Brandon sprawled out on the couch, glued to the television set, watching a TBS presentation of *White Men Can't Jump*.

"Hey, Brand-o!" Brant smiled as he picked up his little boy and kissed his forehead. "Whaaat has ooh been doin'?" he asked in his best baby talk. "Huh? What has ooh been doin' while Dada was at wook?" He glanced at Tommy. "You tell *anyone* that I just used that voice, and I'll knock a hundred pounds right off of you. You got that?"

"I've been using it all day if that helps," Tommy laughed.

Brant smiled as he turned to the television set. "He can't watch *this*!" he groaned as he scrambled for the remote and punched off the power. "Jen said that she sent him some *Barney* videos… where are those?"

"You take a look at one of them *Barney* tapes and tell me that they won't scar him for life," Tommy insisted. "He's our homeboy, our little man…"

Brant picked up a video from the coffee table, and he eyed the case carefully. "Good call," he nodded.

Tommy stood. "And, by the way, that was the edited for television version of *White Men Can't Jump*… what do you take me for?" He hung his head as he grumbled, "I was just trying to show the kid the classics… educate him right… the best I know how."

"You're right," Brant agreed, "I'm sorry. It's just that Jennifer says that Brandon really likes dinosaurs. I'm sure there are other dinosaur videos for babies. We should find a less…"

"A less *wussy* role model," Tommy blurted.

"Tommy, not in front of the kid!" Brant groaned. "I want his first words to be something I can be proud of."

Tommy reached for Brandon, and Brant let him take him. "If it's dinosaurs you like," Tommy cooed as he lifted Brandon into the air, "then Uncle Tommy will go to the store in the morning and buy you… help me out here, Daddy… what has dinosaurs?"

"Uh… well… there's…" Brant's eyes grew big as he drew a blank.

"What's the name of that movie… you know… uh… ohm… oh… oh… oh… *The Land Before Time*… that's it!" Tommy exclaimed victoriously.

"Yeah, that's perfect," Brant agreed. "Littlefoot *is* a *purple* dinosaur… maybe he won't even be able to tell the difference."

Tommy grinned. "*Littlefoot*, huh? You a big fan?"

"Oh, shut up," Brant rolled his eyes.

Tommy kicked at Brant's shin.

"What was *that* for?" Brant exclaimed.

"Using the *s-word* in front of Brandon," Tommy shrugged.

Brant thought back. "Shut up?" he huffed. "That's what you're complaining about?"

Tommy kicked Brant again. *"What was your son's first word Mr. McLachlan?... Well, the first time he spoke he told me to shut the heck up… isn't that precious?"*

"You kick me again, and he'll see me whip your…" Brant paused, "your…"

Tommy laughed.

"*A-word*," Brant grumbled as he walked toward the kitchen.

"Mrs. Becky would wash your mouth out with soap, son," Tommy shook his head.

"I'm starving," Brant called as he opened a cabinet. "Has he eaten?"

"We had some ice cream," Tommy nodded. "This kid can down some mint chocolate chip like you wouldn't believe."

"Well, that sounds nice and healthy," Brant rolled his eyes as he popped the top on his Dr. Pepper.

"It was that or double fudge," Tommy shrugged. "Mint chocolate chip sounded a little more balanced," he nodded.

"Yeah, okay," Brant nodded sarcastically, "so according to that theory... Neapolitan would be considered extremely nutritious, right?"

"He didn't complain, so you eat whatever you want for dinner, and let me and Brand-o take care of ourselves," Tommy smiled as he cooed at the baby.

"Whatever," Brant laughed as he took a sip of his drink, "just keep in mind that I'm trying to raise a future quarterback here. A couple months with you, and my kid is gonna be ready for the offensive line."

Tommy snorted dismissively. "I'll go to the store in the morning and see if I can find *The Land Before Time*," he said as he set Brandon on the kitchen counter.

"Didn't they make a sequel?" Brant nodded. "Go ahead and get that one too." He reached into his pocket and tossed some cash onto the counter.

"Actually, I think they're currently working on *The Land Before Time* 36 or 87 or something," Tommy shrugged.

Brandon let out a little giggle that made both Brant and Tommy laugh.

"That's right... Uncle Tommy's funny, isn't he?" Tommy smiled as he tickled Brandon's tummy with one finger.

Tommy stared at the cash on the table and then back at Brant.

Brant smiled as he dug in his back pocket. He reached into his wallet and produced two, one hundred dollar bills. "Is that enough?"

"I'll be sure to bring you the change," Tommy smiled slyly.

"That's alright," Brant shook his head, "y'all spend it. I'm sure they have action figures or stuffed animals from the movie. I like Littlefoot... he's bold, adventurous, rebellious... let Brandon get whatever he wants... there's more where that came from."

Tommy danced Brandon back and forth on the counter. "I'll take him to McDonald's for lunch... we'll play on the playground... we'll make a day out of it," he nodded.

Brant smiled, but his smile quickly faded into a frown. "I want to go to McDonald's with you guys," he sighed.

"Brant, you have to work," Tommy replied. "There will be plenty of opportunities for you to take Brandon to McDonald's later. Don't sweat it."

Brant lifted Brandon into the air. He lowered Brandon down for a kiss and then, much to Brandon's delight, lifted him up again. "I'm thankful that you get to hang out with him while I'm at work; I really don't know what I'd do without your help. It's just that I want him to know that I love him, and that I don't leave him because I necessarily want to."

Tommy shook his head dismissively. "It's his bath time," he announced.

Brant followed Tommy into the bathroom. "How warm should I make the water?" he asked.

"Not too hot," Tommy shrugged.

"But, not too cold either," Brant shrugged back.

"Warm," Tommy nodded.

"Not too warm," Brant sighed, "maybe lukewarm."

"I don't want anybody giving me a lukewarm bath," Tommy shook his head.

"I'll keep that in mind," Brant rolled his eyes.

"Call Jen and ask her," Tommy suggested.

"I'm not calling her to ask what temperature to make his bath water," Brant huffed. "She'll think we're stupid. Don't they make books that tell you all this stuff?"

"Do you think the bookstore is still open?" Tommy shrugged.

"How would I know," Brant sighed. "I don't go to the bookstore, but Blockbuster is open 'til midnight… maybe there's an instructional video."

"Good idea," Tommy nodded, "maybe you should call."

Brant eyed Brandon. "He doesn't look that dirty, you know… maybe his bath can wait until tomorrow."

"Brant, call Jennifer," Tommy smiled.

"No," Brant insisted.

"I called her this morning," Tommy shrugged.

"For what?" Brant asked.

"I changed my first diaper," Tommy gulped.

"I'm impressed," Brant nodded.

"You should be," Tommy smiled.

"I am," Brant replied quickly.

"She was very calming," Tommy shrugged. "The experience could have been traumatic, but she walked me right through it. It was like calling a 911 childcare hotline. I was panicking, but her voice remained even and reassuring."

"I guess it wouldn't hurt to call her," Brant agreed.

"She's very helpful," Tommy nodded. "I don't know how she knows so much about taking care of babies. She must have learned a lot watching her mom with Ben."

"Nah," Brant sighed, "Jen was just born to be a mom. It's in her blood, you know. She's a natural."

"Call her," Tommy urged sincerely.

Brant reached for the cordless phone and quickly dialed Jennifer's number.

When Brandon had been bathed and his hair washed, Brant wrapped him in a giant, white towel. Brandon laughed as Brant pointed at their reflections in the mirror.

"That's a stylin' Mohawk you're sporting there, Brand-o!" Tommy said as he pulled his own wet shirt over his head.

"Should we dry his hair?" Brant asked.

"Like with a hair dryer?" Tommy raised an eyebrow.

"Maybe with a towel?" Brant suggested.

"But, if it doesn't get completely dry he could catch a cold," Tommy added.

Brant rolled his eyes as he snatched the telephone off the counter.

***

Instead of the traditional balloons or teddy bears decorating his nursery wall, Brandon had a poster of Roger Staubach hanging over his crib, which sat against the wall in the corner of Brant's bedroom.

He's the only kid I know that, instead of being read the bedtime story *Cinderella*, went to sleep every night with Garth's *It's Midnight Cinderella* on repeat in the CD player.

Brandon's life in Dallas may not have been exactly conventional, but there is one thing I know for sure… he was happy there.

Around the first of December, Tommy came down with a fierce case of the flu that put him down for the count. Wanting to prove to himself and to Brandon that things were under control, Brant found a daycare near the stadium.

On the evening of Brandon's very first day of daycare, Brant's phone rang.

"Brant," Tommy said gruffly when Brant answered his cell phone, "where are you? I've been trying to call you for twenty minutes!"

"I'm in Irving… why… what's up?" Brant asked as he nonchalantly aimed his keyless entry and unlocked the door to his truck while he strolled across the parking lot at Texas Stadium.

"The lady from Brandon's daycare called. They closed thirty minutes ago," Tommy sighed before breaking into a hacking cough.

"What?" Brant exclaimed.

"She said she told you that you had to pick him up by…"

Brant glanced down at his watch. "Dang it!" he exclaimed. "I've been in the film room… I guess time just snuck up on me."

"Well, she's waiting there for someone to come pick him up," Tommy coughed. "Do you need me to…"

"No," Brant said as he jogged toward his truck. "No… you rest. If she calls back just tell her I'm sorry, and I'm on my way. I can be there in five minutes."

"Brant, this isn't working any more," Tommy coughed. "You have to be out of town later this week. What are we gonna do with Brandon?"

"I don't know," Brant sighed as he looked both ways before pulling out of the stadium. "Maybe Jen can come…"

"You know she's in the middle of finals," Tommy replied hoarsely.

Brant slapped the steering wheel as he was forced to stop at a red light. "I forgot about her exams; I'm busy… I have a lot on my mind…"

"Did you have a chance to pick up my prescription from the pharmacy before it closed?" Tommy coughed.

Brant threw his head back against the seat. "Tommy… I'm sorry…"

"Brant, it's okay," Tommy replied quickly, "just worry about getting Brandon."

"We'll stop by a drugstore on the way home and pick you up some cough syrup to get you by until tomorrow," Brant insisted.

"Did you check to see if Brandon was out of juice this morning?" Tommy groaned.

"I don't know… I'll pick some up," Brant said.

"He needs diapers and baby shampoo," Tommy added.

"Okay… diapers, baby shampoo," Brant swerved into the other lane, "and what was the other thing?"

"Juice," Tommy coughed.

"Okay… diapers, shampoo, juice, medicine, and Lysol… not a problem," Brant sighed. He screamed at a fellow motorist as he was forced to slam on brakes.

"Brant, you're trying to do too much," Tommy sighed. "Maybe you should call Brianna and see if…"

"I'm not *that* desperate yet," Brant rolled his eyes as he stepped on the gas.

Tommy cleared his scratchy throat. "Your mom called this morning. She wants to know if she can help; she says she'll take off work."

"She needs to work; her patients need her," Brant replied.

"You're making excuses," Tommy huffed. He covered the phone as he went into a coughing spell, then returned to add, "you just don't want anyone's help because that would be like admitting that you can't handle…"

"What?" Brant snapped. "What? The consequences of my own actions? Is that what you were gonna say? Huh?"

"Brant, calm down," Tommy sighed. "I didn't mean it like that."

"Well, that's what it sounded like you meant," Brant snapped.

"Brant…"

"No one is ever gonna let that rest, are they?" Brant huffed.

"Brant… nobody…"

"Oh please," Brant ranted, "it isn't like you and my brothers don't all have your subtle little ways of reminding me of what a real jerk I was."

"Calm down or pull off the road," Tommy hollered. "You're gonna have a wreck."

"There you go again," Brant snapped. "Let's reference every mistake that Brant has ever made in his life… come-on… hit me with your best shot."

"Okay… here's one for you. How about yelling at your best friend for no reason at all," Tommy shrugged emphatically. "You sound like a crazy man, Brant. I'm hanging up the phone."

"Wait," Brant sighed, "I'm sorry… I'm just stressed out."

"You're just feeling guilty because you forgot to pick Brandon up from daycare," Tommy sighed.

"I love my son, Tommy," Brant declared.

"I know you do," Tommy replied. "I love him too, Brant. We all love Brandon, yet you know good and well that the reason you don't want to ask your mom to come and get him for awhile is that you don't want to admit to her that caring for a child is as hard as she told you it would be when you got Brianna pregnant."

"Brandon needs *me*, Tommy," Brant sighed. "He needs to know that I'm not gonna get so busy with work that I just start passing him around to whoever happens to be free. My gosh, I left him at daycare for crying out loud… he must think I'm a real screw-up. What if he thinks I'm not coming back for him? My son is gonna hate me."

"Brant, you're on your way; I'm sure Brandon is fine, but you eventually have to face the fact that your job is not conducive with raising Brandon on your own. You need some help, Brant, and, believe me, I'm trying to get well, but if I'm still sick when the playoffs start, you're gonna be stuck between a rock and a hard place. Brianna is Brandon's mother. She can…"

"I'll figure something out," Brant jumped in, "but under no circumstance am I sending Brandon back home to stay with Brianna."

***

"I went to work; I made the money; I sent you the money in plenty of time. All *you* had to do was go to the store and buy the gifts, Brianna," Brant yelled. "Why was that too much to ask?"

"Stop yelling at me. I don't have to stand here and take this," Brianna shouted back.

"You're right," Brant huffed. "You can leave at any time, Brianna. You can get out of my apartment, out of my life, and out of Brandon's life for good."

When Brianna didn't budge, Brant slammed his bedroom door.

Mom stood in the living room shaking her head as the shouting match continued, the sheer volume barely muffled by the thin, wooden, bedroom door. Mom kissed Brandon's cheek as she rocked him back and forth.

Brandon cried as Brant's voice carried throughout the apartment.

"Daddy's okay, sweetheart," Mom sighed as she bounced Brandon on her hip, "he'll be right back."

"No, Brianna… there *is* no excuse," Brant hollered. "That was Brandon's Santa Claus money. I made that perfectly clear when we talked on the phone; you knew you were supposed to buy his Christmas gifts with that money… I even suggested a few things I thought he might like."

"Will you let me finish?" Brianna screamed back.

Jennifer reached for Brandon's jacket on the back of the couch. "Mrs. Becky, why don't you and I take Brandon for a walk outside?" she suggested.

"Good idea," Mom agreed.

"Come here, baby," Jennifer nodded, and Brandon reached for her.

"Yes!" Brant shrugged loudly. "Please take all the time you need and explain to me why Jennifer and my mother had to go out on Christmas Eve and buy all of our son's Christmas presents…"

"I went to the store to buy gifts for Brandon," Brianna gulped, "but…"

"But Toys "R" Us was having a huge sale on women's jewelry, and you just couldn't pass it up?" Brant yelled.

"It wasn't like that," Brianna cried.

"Then where's my money, Brianna?" Brant asked as he held out his hand. "You didn't spend it on Brandon, so where is it?"

"Brant," Brianna cried, "please don't be mad at me."

Brant shook his head. "Oh, I'm way past mad…"

"But, Brant," Brianna sobbed.

"Stop your whining; I am so sick of hearing you," Brant groaned.

"I just wanted to look nice for you… for your game and for the Christmas party," Brianna continued.

"So you took it upon yourself to spend money designated for Brandon… on *yourself*," Brant snapped matter-of-factly.

"I'm sorry," Brianna cried.

"Tell me something I don't know," Brant nodded.

"That's not fair, Brantley. You're being mean. I just wanted you to be proud of the way I looked. I wanted to look classy like I knew Jennifer would," Brianna insisted.

"Leave Jennifer out of this," Brant demanded.

Brianna began crying harder as she turned away. "I just wanted to look nice… for you."

Brant exhaled loudly.

"I really am sorry, Brant," Brianna cried. "I mean it. I should have spent the money on Brandon's toys; you're right. It's just that… well, I'm not very good at this whole mommy thing." Her tears flowed harder. "I never wanted to be a mother, remember?" She began to bawl. "Despite what you might think, I didn't get pregnant on purpose."

Brant reached for a tissue and extended it to her.

"Thank you," she nodded as she wiped her tears.

Brant paced back and forth across the floor.

"I can return the dress and the shoes..."

"No," Brant cut her off, his voice softening considerably, "keep the dress and the shoes and the jewelry and anything else you bought."

"Really?" Brianna gulped.

"Yeah, really; you've been through a lot, and I assume you deserve to pamper yourself a little," Brant nodded.

"I know I was wrong to spend that money on myself," Brianna sobbed. "It's just that I haven't found a good job yet, and, well, I'm trying to save up for college."

"It's okay," Brant sighed. "I'm over the money... money isn't the issue anyway. Brandon had a wonderful Christmas, and that's all that matters."

"He seems happy here," Brianna said softly.

"He is," Brant replied quickly, "and I'm happy having him here, but I need to ask you a big favor."

Brianna stopped her sobbing, and her eyes moved eagerly to Brant's. "What is it?"

Brant frowned. "I need you to take Brandon back to Cummins with you... just until the playoffs and the Super Bowl are over."

Brianna shook her head as though she didn't understand Brant's request.

"Brianna, my schedule is going to be insane until the season is over. After all the Super Bowl frenzy, I'll take him right back. It's just that there is going to be so much hype..."

"Sure," Brianna agreed, "I understand."

"You don't sound too excited," Brant sighed.

"No," Brianna shrugged, "it's just that he seems so happy here, and back home... all he does for me is cry."

Brant stared at Brandon's picture on his mirror. "It'll only be for a few weeks... just until Super Bowl mania runs its course," he assured her.

"And then what?" Brianna gulped.

"What do you mean?" Brant asked as he turned to look at Brianna. "Then I'll bring him back here with me."

Brianna's tears returned. "You aren't ever going to build a house out here for the three of us, are you?"

Brant picked up a stuffed animal from Brandon's crib. "No, Brianna," he sighed, "I'm not."

"There's no hope for a future between the two of us, is there?" Brianna cried.

"No," Brant replied quickly. "Brianna, you're craving love, and that's why you're holding on to this false hope that something may develop between the two of us. I don't know why you're so desperate for love; maybe you're looking for the love you never got from your own father. Maybe there are times when you think about the baby you gave up… I don't know. All I know is that… I'm not your guy… I'm sorry, but I can't love you like you need me to."

Brianna shook her head, "but… you and I…"

"No, Brianna," Brant gulped, "there is no you and me."

Brianna turned from him as she cried. "I'm sorry… it's just this is all a little embarrassing for me. I mean I have been chasing you so shamelessly for so long and now…"

Brant lifted Brandon's picture from his dresser as Brianna continued. He stared into the eyes of the little boy he loved more than life, and he couldn't imagine letting him go. Brandon was growing so fast; every day was a new adventure, and Brant wanted to be there for every one of them. Brant glanced over at Brianna and said, more to himself than to anyone else, "it'll just be for a couple weeks."

***

The Saturday morning prior to Super Bowl Sunday, the people of Cummins prepared to caravan to the game that our town had been waiting years for. Even we were shocked that it had come so quickly. All the cars were decorated with shoe polish, blue and silver streamers and other creative memorabilia. The funny thing was that most of the people who were driving to the game, Brant hadn't been able to get tickets for, but they didn't care… they were planning one heck of a tailgate party outside the stadium.

As cars literally lined up in the street outside my parents' house, I walked along the curb reading all the accolades that people had painted on their car windows.

We had everything from GOOD LUCK, BRANT! and COWBOYS RULE! to GET OUT OF OUR WAY! WE'RE SUPER BOWL BOUND!

Kristen Waterford had perhaps the most interesting idea. In giant silver letters on the back of the preacher's Ford Explorer, she had written, HONK IF YOU LOVE BRANT MCLACHLAN! Horns sounded as each new car arrived.

As I admired all of the work and the thought that our town had put into making Brant's Super Bowl extra special, Jennifer drove up. "Don't leave without me," she grinned out the window of her Tahoe. "I'm gonna go see if I can help Brianna get Brandon ready. They're late."

***

"Brianna!" Jennifer called, concerned by the fact that Brianna's front door was cracked open. There were several boxes on the front porch, and Jennifer glanced back at them before slipping inside.

Brianna looked up from the big, brown box that she was packing full of Brandon's things and seemed equally as shocked to see Jennifer as Jennifer was to find Brianna in the midst of packing.

"What are you doing?" Jennifer sighed. "It's time to go; everyone is waiting for you."

"I'm leaving," Brianna replied casually.

"We're all leaving," Jennifer said sarcastically. "Supposedly fifteen minutes ago!"

"I'm not going," Brianna shrugged.

"Well, then don't you think a phone call would have been appropriate," Jennifer fired back.

"I've been busy," Brianna rolled her eyes.

"I see that," Jennifer said as she looked around the room. "What are you doing?"

"Packing," Brianna replied.

"For what? Where are you going?" Jennifer exclaimed.

"I'm moving," Brianna announced without hesitation. "Mom and I are leaving this town."

"And going where?" Jennifer asked.

"Florida, as if it's any of your business," Brianna snapped.

"Were you planning to tell anyone?" Jennifer shrugged.

"As if anyone cares about anything right now except the stupid Super Bowl," Brianna rolled her eyes.

"A lot of blood, sweat and tears went into this *stupid Super Bowl,*" Jennifer scoffed. "A lot of time, effort and energy… it's a big deal for us."

Brianna groaned, "you make it sound so…"

"Exactly," Jennifer interrupted. "Larger than life… whatever you were going to say… that *is* what this game means to this town. Everyone here either watched Brant grow up, grew up with him, or grew up adoring him. Many of us saw the desire that Brant had to play in this game when the football was still too big for his hands. We watched him as a high school freshman as he took on the load of quarterbacking a very talented public high school football team and exceed everyone's expectations. You may scoff at me saying that blood and tears went into this game, but that only makes it more obvious to me that you don't know anything about what Brant has gone through. Two summers ago, this town watched Brant's dreams crumble. If you had seen him that summer, like *I* did… like we *all* did… you would know that he could have used any excuse in the book for not achieving his goals, but he didn't give up, Brianna. Every time that anyone suggested that football could be over for him, he refused to accept it. He got well. First he walked, then he ran, and somehow he made himself a better football player than he was before the accident. He's a champion, Brianna. I've always known that about him; this town knows that, and tomorrow he gets to prove it to the world. Don't tell me that this isn't everything that everyone is making it out to be… because it is."

"Then why don't you go and enjoy it," Brianna shrugged. "The sooner you leave, the sooner Mom and I will be ready to go to Florida."

"What's in Florida?" Jennifer inquired.

"My mom met someone," Brianna shrugged.

"Do you and your mother just move from town to town preying on unsuspecting men?" Jennifer sighed. She stopped herself. "I'm sorry," she shook her head, "I shouldn't have said that."

"Yeah, it's really none of your business," Brianna rolled her eyes.

"When you slept with my boyfriend, you made it my business," Jennifer stood her ground. "You can't just up and take Brandon to Florida without letting Brant know what's going on. I know you haven't told him about this because I talked to him last night, and he still thinks you're coming to the Super Bowl."

Brianna didn't reply.

Jennifer's face turned angry. "Brianna, I asked you a question. What about Brandon?"

"I'm not taking him," Brianna replied casually.

Jennifer looked around. "What do you mean you aren't taking him? Where is he?"

"He's in his room," Brianna said as she finished throwing Brandon's things into a box.

"I don't understand," Jennifer sighed. "If you aren't planning on taking him with you, then..."

"They have good places for unwanted babies, Jennifer," Brianna shrugged. "I am going to drop him off on the way to Florida. That way all of us can forget this ever happened. You and Brant can move on and act like I never existed."

"*Unwanted*? Oh my word!" Jennifer exclaimed, still reeling from the icy calm of Brianna's voice as she spoke of abandoning her child. "How could you say that?"

Brianna frowned. "I don't want a baby, and, apparently, neither does Brant."

Jennifer's mouth fell open. "What? Why? Because he asked you to keep him until after the Super Bowl? Brianna, how could you say that you don't want your own baby?"

"You have no idea what it's like to have a child," Brianna rolled her eyes. "I have to get my life back on track. I have to start a new life... a life of my own. That life doesn't include a baby that will always hold me back," Brianna explained. "I gave Brant everything, Jennifer. I love him, and he doesn't return that love... it hurts."

"You don't love him," Jennifer shook her head. "You don't even really know him."

"I do love him," Brianna retorted.

"You may love his money, his body… the idea of having a guy like him, but that's not love, Brianna. You don't even know what it means to truly love someone. You don't even love your own baby, and there will never be a love in your life greater than that one. The only person you love is yourself."

Brianna nodded. "You're right. I don't love this baby. I gave Brant this baby because *he* wanted him. It may have even crossed my mind, after the fact, that this baby would make Brant love me; obviously, it didn't. For some reason he's still crazy about you. I guess that I was wrong for thinking that Brant was the man for me, so I'm certainly not going to stick around here to be his babysitter and still not have him in my life."

"I was right… you really have no idea what *love* is," Jennifer shook her head. "You don't love Brant. You don't even love Brandon. You came to this town; you got my boyfriend addicted to prescription painkillers; you got him drunk, so that he would sleep with you, no doubt intending all along to get pregnant…"

"You're wrong!" Brianna snapped.

"Oh, please," Jennifer rolled her eyes.

"No," Brianna protested. "Jennifer, you're wrong. I wanted to steal your boyfriend; I wanted to have the upper hand, so I took him to bed, but I never meant to get pregnant. In fact, I wanted an abortion. It was Brant who convinced me… begged me… to have the baby."

"What?" Jennifer swallowed.

"Oh, I guess he didn't tell you," Brianna smiled wickedly. "Yeah… that's right. I never wanted to be a mother in the first place, but Brant promised to be here for me and take care of me and the baby. I should have known it was all a lie; I should have known that he wouldn't stand by me… all he was trying to do was spare his conscience."

"You told him you wanted an abortion?" Jennifer said slowly, as she tried to absorb the words. A knot formed in Jennifer's throat. She took a deep breath as she tried to think both quickly and clearly. "I need to call Brant and let him know what's going on," she said as she fanned her face with her hand.

"He's busy playing football hero… you'll never be able to get in touch with him," Brianna snickered.

Jennifer rubbed her hands together, not knowing quite what to say or do. "Brianna, until you came here, I never understood what sheltered little lives we live here in Cummins. We're all one big family here…"

Brianna crossed her arms. "A family that you've all made it perfectly clear I'll never be a part of. That's why I'm going with my mother."

"That makes sense," Jennifer nodded after a moment. "I mean, you're right that you need to go and find a life of your own. You need to find a place where you fit in, and where you'll be accepted for who you are. You deserve to find someone who will love you… every girl does. You deserve a man who will love you the way Brant loves me. So… go to Florida, Brianna, and make a life for yourself… but give Brandon to me… because my life is here… with his daddy."

"You don't want the baby Jennifer," Brianna shook her head dismissively.

"Yes I do," Jennifer replied boldly.

"Why would you want to burden yourself?" Brianna shrugged.

"Brandon isn't a burden; he's a baby," Jennifer snapped. "Brant loves him, and so do I."

"Brant has a very long and busy career ahead of him," Brianna sighed. "He's not ready to be a dad."

"Unlike you, he realizes that whether he's ready or not… he *is* one," Jennifer shrugged.

Jennifer hurried toward Brandon's room.

"Where are you going?" Brianna called after her.

Jennifer gently picked the sleeping baby up out of his crib. Her eyes watered as she looked at Brandon's face and saw Brant.

"You really want to take him?" Brianna stared at Jennifer.

"I'm not leaving here without him," Jennifer gulped.

"I'll put his things in your car then," Brianna said coldly.

Jennifer and Brianna loaded all of Brandon's belongings into the back of Jennifer's Tahoe. Jennifer strapped Brandon into his car seat, and, without ever looking back at Brianna, she pulled away with tears streaming down her face.

About half a mile down the road, Jennifer stopped the car, suddenly overwhelmed by what had just happened. She got out and moved to the back seat. She held Brandon's hand and twisted his beautiful, blond hair around her finger. His personality was bubbly and friendly, his eyes so full of life and wonder. He seemed to understand what was happening even more clearly than Jennifer did at the time. He smiled as he held his hands up to her, and, as that familiar smile touched her heart, she cried, "can you say *Super Bowl*, Brandon McLachlan?"

Brandon giggled, and Jennifer kissed his tiny cheek before pulling back onto the road.

***

Ben and Kristen played quietly on the hotel room floor as Jennifer rocked Brandon to sleep. Kristen mimicked Jennifer by rocking her baby doll in her arms.

Jennifer watched the two children, and her mind drifted back to a time when she and Brant had played together as kids. She nodded toward Ben and Kristen, and she and I both smiled.

"Look familiar?" I gulped.

Jennifer nodded slowly. "It takes me right back to a time when my life was perfect," she whispered.

"It will be again," I nodded slowly.

Jennifer glanced down at the sleeping baby and then back at me. "Yeah," she said with a loving smile, "yeah… it will be."

"He's finally asleep," I whispered.

Suddenly, the phone rang loudly, and I jumped. "Shhh," Jennifer cringed.

"Grab it, Ben," I sighed.

Ben snatched the phone off the hook. "Hello?" he said softly. There was a brief pause; his face lit up. "Hey!" he practically yelled.

"Ben," Jennifer sighed as Brandon opened his eyes.

"It's Brant," Ben said excitedly.

"Oh," Jennifer smiled as she jumped up and handed me the baby. She grabbed the phone from Ben and slid down the wall to the floor.

As Jennifer talked I could practically hear the battle going on inside her head… *to tell him or not to tell him.*

"Is Brianna there with you?" Brant asked. "How's Brandon?"

"Brandon's fine," Jennifer replied. "He's asleep. He's had a long day."

"How's he liking all of this Super Bowl hype?" Brant laughed. "I guess I need to talk to Brianna and arrange to see him in the morning before the game."

"Brianna isn't here," Jennifer blurted. "I brought Brandon with me."

"She didn't want to come to the game?" Brant inquired with a hint of unconcern.

"Well, I wasn't going to tell you this until after the game, but..." Jennifer began as she shooed us all out of the room.

I ushered the kids outside.

"I'll take him to my parents' room," I called quietly.

Jennifer shook her head as she motioned for me to bring the baby to her.

I placed him in her arms.

"You okay?" I mouthed.

She nodded, and I eased the door closed behind me as I left.

"So she was just going to up and move to Florida without telling anyone?" Brant exclaimed when Jennifer was done with her story. Brant's voice turned angry. "How in the world did she think she could get away with that?"

Jennifer didn't seem to be listening. "How come you never told me that Brianna wanted to have an abortion?" she asked.

"She told you that?" Brant sighed.

"I don't understand how anyone could not love this precious little boy I'm looking at right now," Jennifer shook her head.

"I have to see him," Brant said suddenly.

"He's doing great, Brant," Jennifer promised. "He and I seem to be bonding. He really likes me."

"Of course he does." Brant said as his anxiety seemed to settle. "Does he need me? Does he miss me?"

"He needs you *and* misses you," Jennifer smiled, "and so do I, but we both think that we can suffer through together until the morning."

"What made you go over there when you did?" Brant contemplated. "It was a miracle, Jennifer. If you hadn't gone to check on Brianna when you did... who knows where Brandon might be right now..."

"Let's not even think about that," Jennifer insisted. "The fact is... he's here... I've got him... and honestly..." Jennifer stopped in mid-sentence.

"What is it, Jen?" Brant urged.

"Honestly, I feel like this is the way it's supposed to be," Jennifer said confidently.

"Me too," Brant nodded.

"I love you, Brantley," Jennifer smiled broadly.

"I love you more," Brant replied. "I don't deserve you, but I sure love you."

There was a long pause on both ends of the phone.

"Wow… it's hard to believe, huh?" Brant spoke the words they were both thinking. "Brianna is gone; she's out of our lives."

"I'm glad," Jennifer agreed. "For us… but especially for Brandon. We can finally all move on."

"Speaking of moving on," Brant replied quickly. He laughed. "Let's make this official."

"What do you mean?" Jennifer laughed.

"Well, we'll start simple… will you be my girlfriend, Rocky?" Brant asked.

"That sounds like a good start," Jennifer grinned. "I would love to be your girlfriend."

"I don't deserve you," Brant sighed. "I need you, but I don't deserve you."

"Well, you've got me! So stop saying that, concentrate on the game, and go get us that ring, Cowboy!" Jennifer said sweetly.

"Kiss the tiny man goodnight for me, okay?" Brant said as he prepared to hang up the phone.

Jennifer glanced at the sleeping baby, her eyes so full of love. "You got it."

***

When we left the hotel the next morning headed to the game, Brandon was bundled in his little Dallas Cowboys jacket; he had on white and blue Nikes and a little navy blue toboggan that had the Cowboys star on the front. His blond hair curled loosely out from under his little hat, and, in his logo-covered attire, he looked like a true football fan.

During the game Jennifer held on to him like a treasured jewel. She kissed him periodically and frequently explained to him everything that was going on down on the field just as if he could understand every word that she said.

He smiled and cooed as if he knew the importance of the game being played. When we clapped, so did Brandon. When Dad got excited, Brandon would throw his head back and laugh as if his pawpaw making a fool out of himself was the funniest thing he'd ever seen.

At halftime Jennifer left Brandon with me while she walked over to the counter at the back of our suite to fix his juice. She stood across the room as Brandon and I relaxed on one of the couches near the enormous glass window that provided us the most spectacular view of any field I had ever seen.

After filling Brandon's bottle, Jennifer started toward us. The cheerleaders on the field caught her eye, and she stopped to watch them.

"You're gawking," she elbowed Christian playfully as he stood at the window.

"Yes I am," Christian nodded reverently.

Jennifer laughed as they began to tussle.

Brandon stared at them for a moment, and his eyes fixed on Jennifer as if to ask why she was not bringing him his apple juice.

"Mama!" he shouted.

Jennifer, her mouth open and her eyes wide, turned quickly, and Brandon stretched his arms toward her. "Mama!" he cried.

Jennifer took him, and Brandon laid his head against her chest as if he knew exactly where he belonged.

"Here... do you want your juice?" Jennifer offered.

Brandon nodded as he reached for his bottle with both hands.

"He called you *Mama*," I gulped.

Jennifer smiled.

Brandon smiled as he pushed his bottle toward Jennifer's mouth.

"Oh... can I have some of your juice?" Jennifer nodded. She pretended to take a sip. "Thank you. It's so sweet of you to share."

Brandon nodded.

"We like to share, don't we?" Jennifer nodded back, her eyes wide and holding Brandon's full attention.

He nodded wildly, and we all laughed.

Jennifer kissed his cheek. "Brandon, where's Daddy?" she asked.

"Where's your daddy, Brandon?" I echoed.

Brandon buried his face in Jennifer's shoulder.

"What are you doing?" Jennifer laughed. "Are you gonna get shy on us all of a sudden?"

Brandon cackled as he wiggled in Jennifer's arms.

"What is so funny?" Jennifer tickled him. "What is so funny, huh?"

"Brand-o," Christian called, "where's your daddy, boy?"

Brandon pointed to the star on his shirt. "Dada!" he exclaimed.

We all laughed.

"That's right," Jennifer nodded.

Brandon nodded back to her. He pointed toward the field. "Dada," he hollered as he shook his finger.

"I love you," Jennifer said as she squeezed Brandon. "Mama and Dada love you so much… yes we do."

***

"I don't believe this," were the words I later learned that the broadcasters used when, with seconds left on the clock, my brother was called upon to make his first appearance of the season. "It's fourth and inches! The Cowboys are down by four… they have time for one more play, and it looks like if the Cowboys are going to win this game it is going to rest on the shoulders of rookie quarterback Brant McLachlan. These are the moments that dreams are made of, America. Can you imagine… nineteen years old… his first NFL snap… and it's gonna happen on the most critical play of the night on football's greatest stage."

"What are they doing?" I exclaimed, my heart racing so fast that I could feel it beating against my chest, as I saw Brant jog onto the field.

"Brant's going in the game!" Christian pointed in utter amazement.

Mom stared in disbelief. "David, is he supposed to be out there?" she gasped.

Ethan smiled as he moved to the window, "yeah, Mom… the old knees of the veteran got them this far… now they're bettin' on the kid with the springy legs."

"Oh, David, I can't watch this," Mom gasped as she turned to Dad and buried her eyes in his ribs.

Dad rubbed her back. "Just jump, kid… just jump," he gulped.

Ben pressed his face against the glass as his father squeezed his shoulders.

"Please, God," Jennifer swallowed hard as she held Brandon close, "I usually don't pray about winning football games, but please… just let him score."

Tommy stared out the window. "This is it; this is the moment he's waited his whole life for."

Jennifer smiled, her eyes glued on Brant. "This is your Super Bowl, baby," she whispered as she pressed her hand to the window and paused to take in the scene, "you can do it, Cowboy."

We all clinched hands as the Cowboys lined up for the game's final play. For a moment no one breathed. Brant took the snap and tucked the ball in his arms as he dove over the pile. After that, everything seemed to be happening in slow motion.

All eyes were on the officials, and the second that they lifted their arms in the air, everyone rushed the field. Confetti fell, and Brant was literally passed from teammate to teammate. They were full of praise, and they shared in his youthful exuberance.

We all made our way onto the field, and Brant ran to us to share his proudest moment with all the people who had been members of his fan club when playing for the Cowboys was just a little boy's dream.

He took Brandon and kissed his cheek. He raised him into the air and exclaimed, "Daddy loves you, Brandon!" He held his baby close as he embraced Jennifer. He kissed her lips, and, as they hugged, Jennifer cried.

"I'm so proud of you," she said, happy tears streaming down her face.

Holding Brandon in one arm, Brant shook Dad's hand. "It happened, Dad… it really happened," he said, overcome with emotion.

"Congratulations, buddy, no one deserves it more," Dad nodded, unable to hide his tears. He pulled Brant into a hug as Mom snapped a candid picture of the three generations of Cowboys faithfuls. "You finally got your ring. It's been a long road, but here you are… you're a Super Bowl champ, son. How does it feel?"

Brant smiled. He handed Brandon to Dad, and turned to Jennifer. "As long as I've been waiting for someone to ask me what it feels like to win the Super Bowl, I've been waiting to ask you this. Rocky, you told me last night to go get us that ring, so I did."

Tommy reached into his pocket, pulled out a little, black box and handed it to Brant. Jennifer gasped.

"Dad's right," Brant grinned. "I may only be nineteen years old, but the road to this Super Bowl has been a long one. Yet, it's been a cakewalk compared to the obstacles that you and I have had to overcome this year. For nineteen years I've dreamed of this Super Bowl; I've dreamed of having someone ask me what it feels like to be a Super Bowl champion. I've dreamed about my Super Bowl ring forever… but for just as long," Brant got choked up as he opened the tiny black box, "I've dreamed of going out and getting *this* ring and looking into your eyes and asking you," he dropped to one knee, "Jennifer Smith, will you marry me?"

A single tear streamed down Jennifer's cheek as she nodded slowly. Suddenly, she snatched the ring, pulled Brant to his feet and flung her arms around him. "Yes, Brantley," she exclaimed, "of course I'll marry you!"

***

Brant and Jennifer's wedding was simple, traditional, but well attended; everyone in Cummins was there.

My mom cried; Jennifer's mom cried; even the preacher cried, but, on that day… all shed tears of joy.

Bro. Waterford presided over the ceremony. "Christ calls you into union with Him and with one another. So, I ask you now in the presence of God and this congregation to declare your intent. Jennifer, do you take this man to be your husband? Do you promise to love him, comfort him, honor and keep him in sickness and in health, and, forsaking all others, be faithful to him as long as you both shall live?" he asked.

"I do," Jennifer replied softly.

Bro. Waterford turned to Brant. "Brantley, do you take this woman to be your wife? Do you promise to love her, comfort her, honor and keep her in sickness and in health, and, forsaking all others, be faithful to her as long as you both shall live?"

Brant stared at Jennifer, his eyes full of tears. Jennifer smiled through her tears as she gently wiped a tear from his cheek. Brant looked deep into Jennifer's eyes as he spoke from the depths of his soul. "I do," he nodded.

Hearing my brother say those words, my life flashed before my eyes. There I was, thirty-two years old. I'd never fallen in love, never dreamed of getting married, yet there I stood as my brother's best man watching him marry his life-long love.

I was content with my life, working and watching my brothers grow up, but, I admit, as I stood in the church on that day, I couldn't help but be a little jealous of everything Brantley had.

He was nineteen years old and married to a woman who loved him unconditionally. He had a gorgeous little boy who was the spitting image of his handsome father. He was rich and destined to be famous. He had a Super Bowl ring! He wasn't content with a life like mine, and I won't pretend that I could have handled a life like his. On that day, as all of Cummins watched Brant and Jennifer promise to love each other as long as they both shall live, we envisioned a bright future for them... one that would last a lifetime.

CHAPTER THIRTEEN

Brant draped his arms over Jennifer, and they swayed back and forth as they stood over Brandon's crib watching him sleep.

Brant kissed Jennifer's neck as he turned out Brandon's nightlight. "Come-on," he whispered, "he's out for the night… let's me and you go see if we can't find something interesting to do. Know what I mean?"

"How romantic," Jennifer rolled her eyes.

"Know what I mean?" Brant repeated with a wink.

"Casanova you ain't, baby," Jennifer grinned.

Brant scooped Jennifer off her feet. She squealed, and both glanced over to make sure they hadn't disturbed Brandon.

"He's still asleep," Jennifer smiled.

"That's my boy," Brant winked. "He knows Daddy's got plans for the evening."

"Put me down," Jennifer giggled.

Brant carried Jennifer out into the hall. She rested her head against his chest as he carried her into their bedroom. "Brantley," she said softly.

Brant answered with a passionate kiss.

"I have something to tell you," Jennifer smiled, and her face seemed to glow as she wrapped her arms around Brant's neck.

Brant lowered Jennifer onto the bed. She reached for his hand and gently pulled him down beside her. He grimaced as he pulled Brandon's toy train out from under him.

Jennifer laughed.

"Oh, you think that's funny do you?" Brant smiled as he tossed the toy onto the floor.

Jennifer nodded as she looked admiringly at Brant.

"What was it you wanted to tell me?" Brant asked curiously.

"That I have the greatest husband in the world," Jennifer smiled.

"Yeah," Brant nodded.

Jennifer playfully rolled her eyes as she reached for Brant's hand. "But not only are you a wonderful, loving husband to me… you are a terrific father to our son." Jennifer's eyes began to water, though she was still smiling.

Brant sat up quickly.

"It's okay," Jennifer laughed at herself as she wiped away her tears. "You know me… I cry when I'm happy." She laced her fingers in Brant's. "Brant…" she radiated, "we're gonna have a baby."

"You're pregnant?" Brant gasp.

"It looks like I'll be taking more than the one semester off from school," Jennifer nodded.

"Oh, Jen," Brant said as he pulled Jennifer into his arms. Their lips met, and they eased back down onto the bed.

"I love you," Brant whispered between kisses.

"I love you too," Jennifer smiled. She lay back on her pillow. "I figured that you and I would celebrate tonight, then I thought that it might be nice if you and Brandon and I drove home in the morning, so we can tell our family the good news in person."

Brant kissed Jennifer's stomach. "Welcome to our family, Morgan McLachlan," he smiled, and the words made Jennifer's night. Brant rested his head against Jennifer's chest.

Jennifer twisted Brant's hair around her finger. "What do you think? Can we go home for the weekend?"

"I can't wait to see our parents' faces when we tell them that you're pregnant," Brant replied excitedly, and somewhere in the back of his mind lingered thoughts of Mom and Dad's reactions the first time that he had announced he was going to be a father.

"They are going to be ecstatic," Jennifer grinned. "You know how our moms are. And my dad… he'll insist on taking us out to dinner."

"Ben'll be pretty excited for us," Brant added.

"Oh… I can't wait to tell him," Jennifer smiled.

"I can't wait to tell my brothers either," Brant replied. "I wish Christian and Ethan were going to be home."

"My mom is going to insist on taking me shopping," Jennifer smiled. "She'll probably want to go ahead and load me up on maternity clothes, though I probably won't show for months."

Brant nodded. "My mom will ask you a bunch of questions like she's some sort of doctor or something. Then, of course, she'll make us a cake."

"Of course," Jennifer grinned, "and your dad'll say he hopes that the baby looks like me because…"

"Because he can only deal with so much curly, blond hair… yeah, yeah, I know," Brant interjected. "He's so jealous."

"Let's just hope he doesn't start washing dishes," Jennifer giggled.

Brant grinned as he closed his eyes and shook his head.

"They're all very predictable, aren't they?" Jennifer laughed.

"Yeah," Brant laughed, "so remind me… if we already know exactly how they're all gonna react… why are we going home?"

"I can't wait to see all their faces when they hear the news tomorrow," Jennifer grinned.

"Me neither," Brant smiled. "The day is gonna be a blast… predictable or not."

They turned to each other and laughed as they began to kiss.

"Hey, Brant," Jennifer asked after a moment, "do you think Morgan is a boy or a girl?"

Brant smiled, and his voice softened, "either one is fine with me."

Jennifer stared admiringly at Brant.

"I love you," he whispered.

***

When the alarm clock sounded the next morning, Jennifer rolled over and turned it off. She stared at Brant as if to ask how he could sleep through the racket. She shook his arm. "Wake up, Brant," she said excitedly, "we have to get dressed to go to Mississippi."

Brant opened his eyes. "Good morning my beautiful, pregnant wife," he smiled sleepily.

"Ooh… say it again," Jennifer smiled as she kissed him.

Brant closed his eyes, a smile stretching across his face.

"Please get up," Jennifer begged. "I can't wait to get home."

"Mama!" Brandon called from the next room.

Jennifer got out of bed, purposely throwing the covers off of Brant. "Come-on, baby. Get up! I'll make you breakfast."

Brant sat up. "No," he smiled, "this morning I'm making you breakfast."

Jennifer laughed. "But, sweetie… you don't cook."

"Did I say *making*," Brant chuckled, "because I meant *buying*… get dressed… we're going to Shoney's."

Jennifer bent down and kissed Brant's lips. "I love you," she whispered.

"Mama!" Brandon called insistently.

"Mama's coming, sweetie," Jennifer called as she scurried off toward Brandon's room.

Brant smiled to himself as he snuggled up to Jennifer's pillow, soaking up the sweet aroma of her perfume.

"Brant, get up!" Jennifer called from the other room.

Brant groaned as he rolled out of bed.

"Thank you," Jennifer chirped as she heard Brant's feet hit the floor.

***

While Jennifer was in the shower, Brant helped Brandon gather a few of his favorite toys for the long drive home.

Brandon ran around the living room in his diaper as Brant tidied up from the night before. "Do you think you have enough toys, Brand-o?" he laughed as he dumped an armload of toys into a toy box in the corner.

Brandon picked up his red and white plastic football and extended it to Brant. "Do you want to take this with you?" Brant asked.

Brandon nodded.

"Okay," Brant smiled as he reached for it, preparing to shove it in the bag with the other toys.

"Play," Brandon squealed as he turned away with his ball.

"Throw it… throw it to Daddy," Brant urged.

Brandon giggled as he slung the football toward Brant, and, losing his balance, he plopped to the floor on his diaper.

Jennifer poked her head into the living room, her hair wrapped in a large, blue towel. "He's got a good arm on him," she said sincerely.

"Yeah," Brant smiled. He scooped Brandon into his arms and kissed his tummy, "but I can see we have a little work to do on his form."

"I'm sure you can handle it, coach," Jennifer nodded playfully.

Brant smiled proudly. He kissed Brandon's cheek and then Jennifer's lips. His eyes full of pride, he rubbed her flat stomach before pulling her into his arms.

"Do you think we should call and let our parents know we're coming home?" Jennifer suggested.

"No," Brant shook his head as he released her.

"Why not?" Jennifer asked.

"Because," Brant shrugged, "we both have big mouths, and, if we call, we'll end up telling them about the baby over the phone, and that's not what you wanted."

"You're right," Jennifer agreed, "let's surprise them."

***

Brant and Jennifer didn't get on the road as early as they would have liked to, and their late start put them right in the middle of heavy Dallas traffic. They stopped for lunch at a McDonald's, and Brandon had a fit to play in the pit of colorful, plastic balls outside on the playground. By the time Jennifer could get her husband to quit playing, so they could leave, they discovered that they would arrive in Cummins much later than they had planned, so they decided to call and let everyone know to be expecting them for a late supper.

"Hey, Mom," Brant said, one hand on the wheel of Jennifer's Tahoe. They chatted for a moment, then he told her that he, Jennifer and the baby were on their way to town, and, though the baby he was referring to was Brandon, he smiled slyly none the less.

"Brant," Jennifer gulped.

"I have to go, Mom," Brant smiled. "I'll be seeing you in about two hours, okay? I love you."

***

Brant pulled down a dark, backroad, as Jennifer grumbled, "isn't there a way to get home by the interstate, Brantley?"

"This way is faster," Brant replied.

"Have you ever used this *shortcut* before?" Jennifer asked as she peered out the window. "This doesn't look like a very good neighborhood."

"You scared?" Brant teased.

"Answer the question," Jennifer insisted. "Have you ever been this way before?"

"No," Brant shrugged, "but I have been wanting to test my theory that this will cut about thirty minutes off of our trip."

Brandon, getting restless from the long drive, began whining in his car seat.

"It's okay, baby," Jennifer said as she reached back to pacify him, "Daddy's just taking us sightseeing in the ghetto. Look, sweetie," she pointed, "that's called *graffiti*… isn't it nice."

"Look what it says up top," Brant laughed, and Jennifer slapped his arm.

Jennifer pointed to an old abandoned house that looked as though it had likely burned down once upon a time. "What are those people doing, Brant?" she asked softly, as though they might could hear her.

Brant glanced over at the men across the street. "Nothing," he sighed as the sight of the drug deal in progress caused him to glance in the rearview mirror at Brandon and momentarily rethink his choice to veer from the main road.

"Let's get out of here," Jennifer sighed.

Brant nodded in agreement as he sped up.

Suddenly, the car slowed significantly, then it just stopped.

"What are you doing?" Jennifer exclaimed as she stared at Brant. "Why are you stopping?"

Brant hit the steering wheel. "I'm not stopping, the car just won't go," he huffed. He pumped the gas, but the car didn't budge.

"You are joking," Jennifer sighed. "Brant, this isn't funny. I know you; this is your idea of a joke…"

"I wish it was, baby, but it's not," Brant shook his head.

"I'm not laughing," Jennifer insisted.

"Neither am I," Brant grumbled.

"Did you run us out of gas?" Jennifer inquired.

"No," Brant snapped, "I did not run us out of gas! What do you take me for?"

"Well, then what's the problem?" Jennifer exclaimed.

"Do I look like a mechanic?" Brant huffed. "I have no idea."

"You ran us out of gas, didn't you?" Jennifer exclaimed.

"No," Brant rolled his eyes, "you just saw me get gas at that Chevron station all of about twelve minutes ago, baby. We're not out of gas." He picked up his cell phone. "No service," he groaned, and he opened his door.

"Where are you going?" Jennifer exclaimed.

"I guess I'm gonna look under the hood," Brant replied.

"The gage is broken, so maybe you just thought you filled us up with gas," Jennifer suggested.

"We're not out of gas!" Brant snapped.

Jennifer frowned.

"I'm gonna look under the hood," Brant grumbled.

Jennifer opened her door and watched as Brant stood peering under the hood. Noticing the dim streetlight overhead, she called, "Brant, do you need a flashlight?"

"Do you have one?" Brant called back.

"Well… no," Jennifer sighed.

"So what if I had wanted one?" Brant shrugged.

Jennifer crossed her arms. "Don't get mad at me," she huffed before lowering her voice and adding, "I'm not the one that ran us out of gas, and I'm certainly not the genius who decided this was the best way to get home."

Brant walked around to Jennifer's door. "You sit tight and lock the doors," he instructed. "I'm gonna go up to one of these houses and see if I can use a phone to call a wrecker."

"I'm not staying out here by myself," Jennifer insisted.

Brant thought. "Okay… get him," he nodded, "and y'all come with me."

Jennifer got out of the car, opened the back door and unstrapped Brandon from his car seat. She looked around. "Of all the places that you could have run us out of gas…"

"For the last time… I did not run us out of gas!" Brant snapped.

Brant took the baby, as Jennifer grasped Brant's hand tightly. "Whoa! I need a little blood flow there, sweetheart," he smiled.

Jennifer loosened her grip only slightly. "I'm scared," she sighed.

"You're fine," Brant assured her, "you're with me."

Jennifer nodded, trying to look reassured.

Brant puckered his lips as he leaned down and kissed Jennifer. "I love you… we'll be out of here in no time."

Brant and Jennifer hadn't taken more than a few steps down the street when two men began strolling toward them from the opposite side of the road.

Jennifer tightened her grip on Brant's hand, and Brant stroked her thumb with his.

The stranger was tall; his head was shaven. He was wearing long, blue jean shorts and a backwards, black baseball cap. He appeared to be in his late twenties, and he had several tattoos, including barbed wire around his right arm and a dagger that stretched down his neck.

His friend followed him. He was shorter, heavier, maybe a little older, and, like his friend, not wearing a shirt.

"Look at that," the shorter of the two men called as Brant and Jennifer walked quickly, looking straight ahead and pretending not to see the two strangers.

"Brant…" Jennifer sighed as the two men approached.

"You from around here?" one of the men inquired as he looked Jennifer up and down.

"Gentlemen, we seem to be having a little car trouble," Brant said as he handed Brandon to Jennifer. "We just need to find a phone to borrow, and we'll be on our way."

"What's your name, sweetheart?" the shorter man asked as he touched Jennifer's shoulder.

Jennifer let out a little whimper.

Brant swatted the man's hand away. "You won't touch her again if you know what's good for you," he said sternly.

"Is that so?" the man laughed.

"I wouldn't try it if I was you," Brant shrugged as he stepped in front of Jennifer.

The man with the tattoos spoke up for the first time. "You got a real smart mouth there, *Blondie*," he said in a deep voice.

"And real quick fists, *Baldy*," Brant nodded as he stood toe-to-toe with the man.

"We just want to talk," one man said.

"We need some help," the other echoed.

"Yeah, man," the first nodded, "what you getting so mad about?"

"We just need to use a phone," Jennifer said softly. "We're not here to cause any trouble."

"Yeah," Brant nodded in agreement. If Jennifer and Brandon hadn't been with him, no doubt the drunken pair would have already been introduced to Brant's quick temper and mean right hook, but, because he felt as though his wife and son were in danger, he wanted to play it smart. "We don't want any trouble," he said. "What will it take for you guys to leave us alone? Money… is that what you're after?"

"I like that shirt," the taller man said gruffly.

"Well, thanks," Brant nodded sarcastically, "Old Navy… fourteen bucks."

"I want it," the man demanded as he crossed his arms.

Brant glanced back at Jennifer. "Okay," he nodded. He quickly pulled his shirt over his head. "It's yours."

"I like those shoes," the shorter man said, staring at Brant's feet.

"I don't believe this," Brant sighed.

"I need them," the older man grunted.

"Too bad they're not your size," Brant shrugged.

"Take them off," the taller man ordered.

"No," Brant shook his head.

"Give him the shoes, Brant," Jennifer cried.

Brant glanced at her, and she nodded insistently. Brant slid the shoes off of his feet and kicked them toward the men. "Guaranteed to make you run faster and jump higher," he said sternly. He took Jennifer's hand. "Nice doing business with you boys," he said as, his eyes still on the men, he started toward a house in the distance.

"*Brant*?" the man who was now wearing Brant's shirt pondered. "You ain't that football player, are you?" He stared at the ring on Brant's finger. "You are… ain't you? I heard about you on the news. Yeah… that's a real nice ring you've got there."

"We want it," the chubby man pointed.

"Right!" Brant laughed as he continued down the street. "Doesn't everyone!"

"Give us the ring," the shorter man yelled as he moved down the street next to Brant, visibly agitated by Brant's refusal.

Jennifer gripped Brant's arm. "Give him the ring," she gulped.

"No way," Brant shook his head as he stared at the men.

"I think you better listen to your girlfriend there," one man said.

"Give us the ring, and we'll leave you alone," the other added.

"You've both had a little too much to drink tonight," Brant huffed as he started past the two men again with Jennifer and Brandon tucked under his arm. "Do yourselves a favor and go home."

The younger man stepped in Brant's path. "Give me the ring, or you'll be sorry."

"Get in my way one more time, and you'll be sorry," Brant fired back.

"Give me the ring!" the stranger shouted.

"Listen, buddy," Brant said sternly as he stared back at the man who stood three or four inches taller than him. "You've got my shirt; you've got my shoes. Brant took off his watch. Here you go. Take this too. Pawn it… buy more booze… do whatever you want with it," he shrugged, "but there are three things you aren't getting your hands on. One is my wife, the other is my son, and the third thing is my Super Bowl ring. Are we clear?"

The man grabbed at Brant's arm, apparently intending to take the ring by force, and Brant's natural instinct was to swing.

"Help! Someone help us!" Jennifer shouted as punches were thrown.

Brandon shrilled as he watched his daddy struggle with the two men, and he sensed his mom's mounting fears.

Brant fought the man with the barbed wire tattoo to the ground as the shorter man watched nervously. He reached into his pocket, and Jennifer gasped as she watched him remove a small, black handgun.

"Brant!" Jennifer shrilled.

"Let him go," the older man demanded as Brant pinned his friend to the asphalt.

Brant, not so much as looking back, continued to swing.

"Brant, listen to him," Jennifer screamed. "Do whatever he tells you; he has a gun."

Brant spun around, his heart jumping into his throat as he stared at the gun pointing back at him.

"Don't shoot me," Brant gulped as he held his hands up in submission. "I'll give you my ring… just please don't shoot us."

His nose pouring blood, the taller man peeled himself off the ground. He wrapped his arm around Brant's throat and jerked his head back, so that Brant was staring at the gun.

"Don't hurt him," Jennifer begged, her voice shaking. "He'll give you the ring, just please don't hurt him."

Brant slid the ring off of his finger as he stared into the eyes of the man holding the gun.

The younger man took the ring.

"Very good," the gunman smiled, "now get his wallet."

The man reached into Brant's pocket and pulled out his wallet. He tossed it to the man with the gun who opened it and pulled out the thirty-two dollars that it contained before tossing the wallet to the street. "Thirty-two bucks?" he scoffed. "That's all you've got… thirty-two bucks!"

"I'll get you more, I swear," Brant replied quickly.

"We get lucky enough to rob some fancy pants, professional football player, and all you have is…"

"I'll get you as much as you want," Brant panted. "Please, just let us go."

The gunman turned to Jennifer. "Don't look so scared," he said as he gently stroked her arm.

"Don't touch her!" Brant screamed.

Jennifer backed away as Brandon began to wail. "Help us!" Jennifer cried loudly. "Please… somebody…"

"I'm not gonna hurt you," the man said as he slid the gun back into his pocket. As he reached for Jennifer, Brant began to swing his elbows in an attempt to free himself from the tattooed man's grasp.

"Brant!" Jennifer cried, her voice pleading for help.

Brant exchanged screaming words with the gunman as he fought to go to Jennifer's defense.

"Calm down," the man with the tattoos demanded as he and Brant wrestled in the street, "we aren't gonna hurt your girlfriend."

The man with the gun laughed. "Here you go," he said as he reached into his pocket, "you ought to be able to control him with this." He carelessly tossed the gun toward his friend, and it fell onto the pavement.

Hit with a surge of adrenaline, Brant jerked free and buried a punch in the stomach of his counterpart as he crawled toward the gun. As he reached for it, he was tackled to the ground again. Both Brant and the man in the hat lunged for the gun. There was a brief struggle. Both got their hands on the gun, and they fought to see who would gain control of it as they rolled in the street.

"Jen… run!" Brant demanded.

Jennifer stood, frozen in fear.

"Run," Brant barked as the struggle persisted.

Jennifer turned to run. Then, suddenly, the night air was filled with the sound of a single, deafening shot.

Jennifer spun, her head reeling. "No!" she screamed as she ran into the street and dropped to her knees.

Brant rolled over on his side, his eyes wide with panic.

"Brant!" Jennifer shrilled.

"What did you do?" the chubby man shouted.

The younger man stood. "I… I…" he stuttered as he stared at the splattered blood on his hands.

"What'd you shoot him for?" the shorter man yelled.

"I didn't mean to… it was an accident," his friend panicked. "If you hadn't tossed the gun…"

"Oh, so it's my fault…"

"Brant," Jennifer cried as she shook his shoulders and begged him to respond.

Brant coughed blood onto the pavement.

The shorter man bent down next to Jennifer. "You got him pretty good," he nodded to his friend.

"We've got to get out of here," the tattooed man with the gun sighed.

"Brant… hang on," Jennifer begged. "I'm gonna get help. You're gonna be okay."

"Jen…" Brant tried to speak but couldn't. He closed his eyes. "Rocky," he cried weakly.

The sound of a siren in the distance alarmed the two men.

"Run!" the older screamed.

As they started away, Brant's ring fell to the ground with a ping. Instinctively, Jennifer grabbed it as it bounced on the asphalt and immediately slid it onto her thumb.

Jennifer pressed her shaking hands against the bullet wound in the middle of Brant's chest. Blood oozed through her fingers, and she cried loudly. "Brant," she screamed. "Brant, can you hear me? Answer me, baby. Please!" There was no reply. "Brant!" Jennifer yelled, shaking her head. "No... no... come-on... hang on..." Feeling helpless and alone, she draped her body over Brant's, and time stopped.

Brandon howled with tears as he tugged at Brant's shoulder, begging for his daddy.

Before Jennifer even realized that anyone else was there, a policeman had his hand on her shoulder.

"Don't leave me," Jennifer cried as the policeman rushed back to his car.

"I've got to call for backup and get him an ambulance," the policeman told her.

He returned quickly and lifted Brandon up out of the street. He held him closely, and the way that he consoled the screaming baby made it obvious that the officer had kids of his own.

"Can you tell me which way the shooter went?" he asked as he knelt next to Jennifer who was trembling and disoriented.

Jennifer cried as Brant lay motionless in the street. "He's gonna be okay, right?" she insisted as she tried to catch her breath between her heaving tears. She saw the blood around the edges of Brandon's white tennis shoes, and she could no longer breathe.

The policeman held Brandon in one arm as he put the other around Jennifer. "No... he's gone, sweetheart... I'm sorry," he sighed, his eyes full of compassion.

"No," Jennifer cried. She fell on top of Brant. "Brantley! Brant, please don't leave me! I need you!" She put her bloody hand over her mouth as she turned back to the officer.

"I'm sorry," the policeman gulped.

Jennifer's hand shook. "But... but... we were so happy... he is my life... and... and... what about the baby... I'm pregnant... I need him," she said, her voice cracking.

The policeman pulled her into his embrace once again. "Is there someone I can call for you?" he asked.

Jennifer tried to think. "I can't remember my parent's phone number," she panicked.

"We'll think of it," the policeman assured her as he held her close to him. "You're in shock… it'll come to you."

***

Shock was the only word that could describe what Jennifer and the rest of us experienced that night. For little more than thirty-two dollars and a pair of Nike tennis shoes, my little brother lost his life.

I remember getting the call from my father that night, and, from the second the phone rang, life became a nightmare that I never woke up from.

That was the first time that I had ever known what *hate* was. As wrong as I knew it was to feel hatred toward another human being, I couldn't help myself.

Though the investigation is considered ongoing, the police never found Brant's killer. I'd give anything to look into his eyes and just ask *why,* but I've never been given that chance.

While the fact that whoever killed my brother is still out on the street is a hard reality to face, it has not been the hardest part of losing Brantley. I know that someday my brother's killer will have to answer for what he did. Someday he will have to pay for what he took from my family and from the world.

The most difficult part for me has been watching Jennifer carry on with a strength that I don't even think she knew she had. She has her good days and her bad days. As with anyone who has ever experienced tragedy in life, she has times when she is certain that she can't go on, but her faith in God, and her love and devotion toward her two sons always pulls her through when she doesn't feel as though she can go on living another day without Brant. Her devotion to Brandon and to Morgan gives her the strength to get up on the mornings when she doesn't think she can get out of bed. Her faith in God assures her that, though she may never understand it, this is all a part of God's plan, and He will never give her more than she can handle.

***

There isn't much that I can say about Brant's funeral because there isn't really that much that I can remember. The day is just all one big blur. I sat there with a blank stare on my face with my brothers on each side of me, both trying to be strong, but both unable to contain their grief. Every now and then, Jennifer would let out a wail that would send a shiver down my spine, and her dad would hold on to her just a little tighter each time.

I remember Bro. Waterford breaking down before the service even began, as Brant's voice came through the loudspeakers and Kristen ran crying from the sanctuary. As a tape of Brant singing Garth Brooks' *The Dance* played over the loudspeakers, hearing Brant's voice was almost unbearable. The words that were coming out of his mouth were so beautiful, yet so ironic, and anyone in the room who had maintained any composure up to that point, lost it.

I remember looking behind me and seeing Peggy Jackson resting her head against Rick Jackson's shoulder. He kissed the top of her head as they both cried.

There were old men with handkerchiefs, and big, burly football players who wept openly.

I remember that, as they got ready to wheel the casket out of the church, I jumped up, my throat burning and screamed, "wait! Does he have his ring?" I remember seeing all of the sympathetic stares and seeing my dad nod to me reassuringly as I watched him age in an instant.

I don't remember anything else about that day. As I watched them put my best friend in the ground, I wondered what my purpose in life would be from that point on. I knew that I would have to find something else to do with my life because, right then, it felt like my reason for living was gone. Everyone defined me, and, in fact, I defined myself as Brant's big brother. Without him, I was lost.

I went home to an empty house and began to think about the meaning behind my brother's short life. Over and over again I would ask myself why my brother had turned down that street that night, why he hadn't willingly given up his ring, why my brother had to die. The first two I could answer; the other I am still asking myself today.

It was there in my little, white house that I started writing this book. I stopped time and time again before I produced a final product because I feared that I wasn't skilled enough as a writer to capture the picture of my brother that the world needed to see. It didn't take me long to realize that Brant didn't need the help of any fancy words to make his story special, so, day after day, everyone that knew Brant came and told me stories that helped make this book complete. Just like everything else in Cummins, it was a group effort.

Four years after Brant died, I was standing in my front yard with two little, blond-haired boys at my feet. I handed Morgan his little, red and white, plastic football, and, as he hurled it into the air, I could have sworn that the sun shone a little brighter. At that moment it hit me that Brant needed me more than he ever had, and I wasn't about to let him down.

My dad never coached another football game after Brant died. For years we tried to get him back involved in the sport he had loved so much, but he would simply shake his head, grimace, and say that football would just never be the same game to him.

After the funeral, my mother begged Christian and Ethan to stay in Mississippi, and they both did for the remainder of the summer. They both eventually returned to school and graduated from the University of Alabama and Duke University respectively. Today, Mom watches a lot of home videos and looks at a lot of old pictures. In prayer she found closure, and she's dealing with Brant's death in a healthy way; she just wants to see his face every day, and no one can blame her for that. Sometimes she is so caught up in a movie or a photo album that she doesn't hear me come in, and I stand silently behind her, watching, and always, no matter how many times it happens, end up having to wipe my tears away before joining her in the living room.

Following Brant's first season with the Cowboys, the NFL was able to convince the Supreme Court that, due to reasons that had absolutely nothing to do with my brother, its age limit should be reinstated. In 2004, Ohio State running back Maurice Clarett made national news when he challenged the ruling. Clarett was able to convince a trial court that underclassmen should be eligible for the draft, but he did not succeed in convincing the Supreme Court, and his appeals were denied. I don't profess to know the answer to this ongoing controversy; I can only say that I'm thankful that Brant was able to achieve his dream before he died. I don't know why the courts listened to his argument and have denied others; I only know that things happen for a reason.

Today, Ethan is still in medical school in North Carolina where he lives with his wife, a first grade teacher named Hannah, and their daughter, Emily.

Christian gave up playing football not long after Brant's accident. It was a decision he spent many hours pondering, but, ultimately, he decided that he wanted more free time to spend with his family, especially Jennifer and the boys. He came home on the weekends and during the summers, and it was during that time that he and Jennifer's friendship began to blossom into more. At first, the feelings that seemed to be developing between them seemed taboo, and they both shied away from them. In each other they found comfort and security, yet, for Jennifer, the thought of giving her heart to another man seemed unbearable, and, for Christian, the thought of falling in love with Jennifer seemed like the ultimate act of betrayal. As time passed, however, there came a time when, for both of them, building a life together felt like the right thing to do.

Jennifer is still the most amazing woman that I have ever met. She is raising two sons to know exactly who they are and how much she and the rest of us love them. Brant left her way before she was ready to let him go, but he left her with two bright-eyed little boys to introduce to the world. She remains determined, despite all that has happened, to instill in them the genuine love of life that made their daddy so special.

Tommy still hangs around Cummins at his parents' place. He's the same good guy that he's always been; he has a heart of gold and miracle cures for skinned knees and sad faces.

Brandon is five years old now, and Morgan is three. They brighten all of our lives just a little more every day. To see Brant, all anyone has to do is look at the boys. Brandon has Brant's features, right down to the golden hair and the wide smile. Morgan looks just like his father and has Brant's outgoing personality; he is a hard-charging three-year-old who can match his big brother step for step. When he laughs, I hear Brant, and when he runs, I see Brant back on that old football field at the high school. Morgan is, no doubt, a quarterback in the making. He has a football jersey he won't take off, a Nurf football that he rarely lets out of his sight and a plastic, Cowboys helmet that he begs to sleep in every night. Brandon started playing football at the park this year, so I took up coaching there, and Dad often joins me. Brandon doesn't have any memory of the horrible way that his father died, and we're all thankful for that. Both he and Morgan know that their daddy was special, and they have just started asking lots of questions about him. In some way I hope that this book can answer many of them. We'll just have to wait and see where the boys' football careers lead, but, as far as we are concerned, the McLachlan family has two more little superstars on our hands… and everything to look forward to.

Brantley:

Brantley,

You made me laugh the most; you made me cry the most. You were an angel sent to me straight from Heaven, and I thank God for every single day that He let you stay here with us. You blessed my life with every smile and every hug. I will never forget the way that your voice sounded so sweet when you sang… and so especially sweet when you told me that you loved me. You may be gone, but you will always be my baby. I love you with all my heart.

Love,
Mom

Brant,

When I sat down to write this, summing up everything that I wanted to say to you seemed impossible. I crumpled up page after page before Jennifer and the boys stopped by to pick up what was supposed to be my final draft. The boys were running around, oblivious to the fact that I was frustrated because I couldn't seem to find the words to put what I wanted to say down on paper. Just as I was about to reach the end of my rope, Morgan scurried up into my lap, howling with laughter. I looked down at him, and it was scary just how much he reminded me of you. Then, as if he was telling me what I had been trying to say all along, he uttered three simple words. Brant, you were *my* son, *my* quarterback, *my* Super Bowl champion and so much more, but the words that say it all are simply, I love you.

Dad

Brant,

My life has been blessed through the years by two very dear people. I never thought that I would ever relive the pain that I felt when Half-pint died, but the day that you died I felt empty all over again. You were my best friend, Brant, and I'll miss you for the rest of my life. Time does heal the pain of loss; I learned that with Sarah, but the emptiness never quite goes away. Yet, I've been taught over the years to focus on the good…to remember what time we did have together, so I want to say thank you for all of the advice, all of the laughs and all of the good times we shared. Today I know that Heaven is smiling! Our friendship is a treasure that I will hold tight to forever. Take care of my baby up there, Brant, and I promise to see that yours are always taken care of down here. I love you, bro.

I miss you,
Tommy

Brant,

Back when we lost you, I was still a little boy. I thought that you were going to miss out on my life that I so badly wanted you to be a part of. I have since come to realize that you've gotten to see me grow up; you just have a better view than everyone else. I hope that I make you as proud as you always made me. I didn't used to think that they played football in Heaven, but now I know that they do. I know now that all the angels play football and sing country music. I know that I will see you again one day, but until then you will be in my heart. I miss you.

Your little buddy always,
Ben

Brant,

We were always three, but on that fateful day, Christian and I stood together in a cemetery, feeling alone, as though we would never be whole again. Without you we are missing so much. Christian was always the strength; I was the brains, and you, Brant… you were the heart. One day at a time, Christian and I will get through, but life will never be the same without you.

Love,
Ethan

Brant,

I guess we all have visions of the way our lives will turn out. The day you died mine took a very unexpected turn, and my mission in life was redefined in a way that I never envisioned. Jennifer is an amazing woman, and, together, we are raising two very special little boys. Being a father to Brandon and Morgan has given me a purpose in life that is more precious than anything I have ever done or will ever do. I miss you more than words can say, but if I could say just one thing to you it would be that you inspired me so much in the way that you lived your life. Thank you for all the smiles and all the laughs and nineteen of the best years of my life. You taught me so much about football and, more importantly, about life. You may be gone, but *no one* will ever forget you. Doesn't everybody wish that they could say that when it's all said and done? The only reason that I can think of that you were taken away from us so suddenly is that the big man upstairs needed some comic relief up there. All I can say is that He picked the right guy, Brant.

I love you.
Christian

Brant,

There is never a second that passes by that I don't feel your hand in mine, smell your cologne close to me, see your beautiful eyes and your captivating smile and hear your angelic voice and your heartfelt laughter. My lips miss your kisses, and my heart misses your love. I'd give anything to have one more minute with you, so that I could tell you just how special you made my life and just how special you continue to make it every day. Our sons continue to fill my life with the simple joys that I no longer take for granted, and every day, as I look into their eyes, I thank God for them and for you. When Jordan asked me to write you a letter that would be included in your book, I wasn't really sure what to say. I feel like I'm repeating myself here because I talk to you every day as if you were right here beside me, and, somehow, you make me feel like you are, and that you hear every word that I say. The day that Christian asked me to marry him, I felt you there with me, not only telling me that saying *yes* was right, but giving me the courage to say it. Thank you for that. Christian has been wonderful. He takes terrific care of me and the boys. They absolutely adore him. They need him around, and so do I. I love Christian as my husband, my partner and my friend, but soulmates only come along once in a lifetime. I love you, Brant.

Forever yours,
Jennifer McLachlan

Brant,

Some people can live a lifetime and only impact a few. Others leave behind a legacy that will never be forgotten. You touched more people in more ways than you could ever have imagined possible. You wouldn't believe all of the book offers that we got after you died. Everybody wanted to tell the story of what could have been. I took on this project in order to make sure that your story was told the right way. I didn't want to write a book about your death; I wanted to write a book about your life. I didn't want to tell the story of a kid who died too young… instead, I wanted to tell your story… the story of a kid who *lived* his dream. In many ways writing this book has helped me deal with your death, and, for that, I am thankful to you yet again. Initially, I was worried that I wasn't capable of bringing this book together the way it needed to be done, and that is why this project has taken me so long to complete. All of the fancy writing classes that I took for my degree made me believe that I had to craft this story, delicately choosing the perfect words and piecing them together in a set order, but, ultimately, as we all gathered to share the memories that would construct this book, it became apparent to me that you could speak for yourself. All I needed to do was tell your story… *the Brant McLachlan story*, so here it is, Brant. I love you.

Your big brother,
Jordan

HIS HEART I HOLD

CHAPTER ONE

Jennifer McLachlan

In the town where I grew up, life consisted of three simple rules: worship Jesus, love your family and live for North River High School football. I wasn't born yet when word spread through town that North River High School's beloved football coach was expecting triplets, but I'm told that there was instant chatter of the role those three boys would play in the future of North River football. The coach's wife, who was also my mother's best friend, gave birth to her triplets within days of my mother delivering me. I may not have been aware of the hype that surrounded the McLachlan triplets before they even arrived, but I was there for every moment of their journey into the ranks of high school football glory. Long before they suited up for a varsity game, they became known around town as the McLachlan triple threat. Brant threw the touchdowns; Christian scored them, and Ethan kicked the extra points.

Football was a way of life in our town; players became heroes of the gridiron. Boys in football jackets got free cokes at the Country Mart, and, during the four years that the McLachlan boys wore the North River uniform, the light never shone brighter on our school or our town.

Brant McLachlan became more than a small town quarterback; he became the hope of a town. With a personality to match his flashy style of play, Brant became larger than life on Friday nights. When he was on the field, the whole town walked with a certain swagger. We didn't expect to just beat our opponents; with Brant at the helm, we expected to slaughter them. On a field full of high school boys, Brant McLachlan was in a league of his own.

As the captain of the varsity cheerleading squad, I decorated my fair share of signs and passed out countless pep bags full of candy. I led the cheers; I rallied the crowd, and, on homecoming night, I was honored to be crowned queen! I even managed to obtain the cliché; I dated the star quarterback. In fact … I married him.

Brant was my best friend. We were inseparable from the time we were babies, and, while most people don't have the luxury of knowing their best friend for their entire life, I did. Brant and I were sandbox soulmates, and it is impossible for me to imagine my life without him because he was so much a part of it. For almost twenty years, there wasn't a single significant event in my life, or insignificant one for that matter, that he didn't experience with me.

Brant seemed, to the masses, to personify perfection; he was a handsome, blue-eyed, blond-haired star quarterback with a personality that charmed; he had a bright, infectious smile readymade for a toothpaste endorsement, and the world was ready to open its arms to him. Yet, it was his imperfections that made him so endearing because, no matter how many times he messed up or how costly his mistakes were, his heart always belonged to me. Each of the struggles we went through were molding my childhood playmate, my high school sweetheart into the man that Brant was becoming. Others saw a boy who had the ability to light up a room when he walked into it, but all I cared about was the way my heart lit up every time I walked into his arms.

I remember cheerleading camp and hiding out talking to Brant on the phone after the coach called for lights out.

I remember the fake, blue, Sharpie tattoo of his #13 that he drew on the small of my back that cost us both a spanking when my daddy saw it.

I remember sitting in church, our little legs dangling off the pew, pressing on hymnals, writing on church bulletins with those tiny, little, yellow pencils and passing our notes back and forth until we felt the subtle pinch of our mothers' fingers on our legs.

I remember Dr. Pepper floats in the summers and triple dog dares on the playground.

I remember Brant's head on my lap while we watched TV and how I would twist his blond curls around my finger.

I remember tents made out of covers in the middle of the living room floor ... just me and the boys.

I remember playing outside until dark and the way we giggled when Brant's oldest brother, Jordan, chased us around the yard with the water hose.

There were trips to the store with my mama and riding in the buggy long after we were way too old for it.

I remember riding in the back seat on the way to Tuscaloosa in my mini cheerleading uniform, sitting next to a little snaggletooth Joe Namath.

There are pictures of Brant and me to fill dozens of photo albums, but it's the mental images that play inside my head like a montage of memories that I hope never fade. *I heart Jen* drawn in the sand at Orange Beach. Tea parties in the tree house. Playing football in the pool. Catches made jumping off the diving board into the deep end. Cherry popsicles on the pool steps. Bonfires at his daddy's hunting camp. Disney World the summer we turned five. Football games in the hallway on rainy days. Inside jokes. Chasing lightening bugs. Picking Dandelions and the magic of blowing the seeds into the air. Laughing so hard we had to lean on each other for support. Riding shotgun the day he got his very first truck. Decorating Christmas cookies on Christmas Eve in our Christmas pajamas. Carving our initials in a tree down by the creek. Carving pumpkins. Wrestling. Laughing until we cried. Shamelessly informing him the day my mama made me start wearing a training bra for the first time. Backyard fireworks on the Fourth of July. Brant and Christian always fighting over who got to be which Ninja Turtle. Holding his hand. Running and jumping into his arms without hesitation, always trusting him to catch me. Buying M &M's on sale after Easter, Halloween and Christmas because they were his absolute favorite. Every song Garth Brooks ever sang. Being seventeen and kissing him for an hour sometimes while contemplating compromising everything that I knew we both believed. Knowing what the other was thinking before they said it. The song he sang to me on graduation day. Being his favorite duet partner even though his vocal abilities were far superior to mine. The perfect proposal. Our wedding night. Finally waking up in his arms in the mornings.

There is no smile that will ever compare. There is no sound that I miss more than the sound of his voice when he said my name. Though my life continues to be filled with blessings, nothing brings me the unfiltered joy that it did when Brant was alive. Even in my happiest moments, there is always that part of me that wishes I could share my every thought and feeling with him, the way we used to. The pure, unadulterated moments of sheer joy that were so frequent between Brant and me seem like a fairytale dreamed up by an innocent, young girl who doesn't exist any more. There are times when I fear that the girl that I once was wouldn't recognize the woman I've become. Then I look into Christian's eyes, and I see the person I want to be.

CHAPTER TWO

To Make You Feel My Love

Jennifer McLachlan

Sometimes you see someone, and it is impossible to imagine that they will have any impact on your life, then, in a moment, they become tied to a life that they forever changed.

There is a face that haunts my dreams some nights; I don't know his name or his story or what events transpired in his life that turned him so cold. I only know that our lives became intertwined the night he fired the fatal shot that robbed me of a future with my husband, my sons a future with their father and Christian of an adult relationship with his brother.

Sometimes I hear Brant's voice, begging the stranger to spare his life; his cries are so gripping, so real that it's hard for me to remember now if my mind is playing tricks on me, or if this gut-wrenching moment actually occurred.

Brant and I were excited to be heading home to Mississippi. It was to be a reunion of sorts; everyone we considered family would be there, home from work or school, and we had *big* news! I was absolutely giddy to share with my loved ones the news that I was expecting. I had dreamed of this day since I was a little girl.

When Brant and I were kids, the assumption that we would get married one day was so commonly accepted that, even as a child, I planned the life that we would share one day. We would get married; Brant would play professional football, and we would have two children, who, regardless of their gender, would be named Brandon and Morgan.

Though it had never been part of my plan, Brandon McLachlan arrived soon after our high school graduation, a precious, blond-haired miracle whose conception may have been the biggest mistake of Brant's life, but whose birth was nothing but a blessing to both Brant and me. God answered the prayers that I prayed at that time in my life and graciously provided me with a heart prepared to love a child whose mere existence had once shattered my heart.

From the time that sweet baby boy was born, he was the spitting image of his daddy, and, though I remained devastated that the day I had dreamed of forever had been stolen from me by a moment of reckless behavior and bad judgment, I instantly felt a connection to a child I could not help but love.

Brandon and I began to form a bond that was strong and undeniable. I watched as God opened doors for Brandon to become a bigger and bigger part of my life. Though I didn't believe it was possible, I loved Brandon like my own, and I know now that was because God knew that, very soon, he would be mine.

Brant and I cried tears of sheer joy the day the adoption became final; I will never forget my baby boy asleep in my arms, and the man I loved praying a beautiful prayer of gratitude for the grace that God had bestowed on him.

God filled me with a forgiveness throughout that delicate situation that only He could have; Brant had undeniably broken my heart, but our shared faith, both in God and in each other, allowed me to forgive him more easily than I ever thought possible.

We had moved on from what we believed would be the most difficult season in our relationship. Life seemed perfect in that moment as we prepared to head home to share the news of my pregnancy. The sun shone brightly on me that day in Texas as I walked outside to our SUV to head home to Mississippi. I was married to the love of my life, carrying a curly-headed, blond, spitting image of him on my hip and pregnant with the child who would make our little family complete.

The family reunion I was so excited about *would* happen that night, but not at all in the way it was supposed to. Brant, Brandon and I never made it home that night. I remember being in a cold hospital room, the gunshot that had ended Brant's life still ringing in my ears; Brandon's innocent screams still piercing my heart, and Brant's blood staining my hands. I don't remember the details very clearly, but I know that all my loved ones arrived. There were tears, screams and long, silent embraces that said all there was to say that night.

The feeling of loss that consumed our family was indescribable. I remember a nurse warning me with a pitying frown that my unborn baby, my Morgan, would need a miracle to withstand the trauma and stress I was experiencing so early in my pregnancy.

I watched as a nurse handed Brandon to my mother. They had cleaned him up; he was wearing a diaper and a tiny hospital gown and crying softly for his daddy. I knew that Brandon would one day forget witnessing his daddy's murder, and I silently prayed that my baby boy would forget every heartbreaking detail of that tragic day, though I knew I never *ever* would.

***

Kathy Smith

Becky McLachlan and I have always been so alike that our friendship seemed only natural. We grew up, got married and dreamed of having babies around the same time. Becky and her husband, David, had their oldest son, Jordan, right away. Many years later and several very difficult miscarriages later for my husband, John, and me, the dream of raising our children together seemed far fetched.

Becky and David eventually decided they wanted to make their family of three a family of four ... one last child to fill that role as baby of the bunch. Becky got pregnant, and, miraculously, so did I! As Becky, David, John and I continued to pray that I would be able to carry my baby to term, Becky got some pretty unbelievable news. My best friend wasn't going to have a family of four after all; the McLachlans were about to go from a family of three to a family of six... she was carrying triplets!

Becky and I prayed constantly for my baby and for hers. In moments when I was holding on to hope for my own child, Becky always knew just when and how to lighten the mood. I will never forget how many times, as she swelled into nothing short of a beautiful, beached whale and struggled, breathlessly and miserably, to waddle to the couch, only to need assistance just to sit down, she joked that I could always just have one of her extra babies!

The day that my daughter, Jennifer, was born, I felt like God had blessed me beyond my wildest imagination. She was absolutely perfect. The baby I had spent years praying for was finally in my arms. Two days later, Becky gave birth to three, healthy baby boys.

Like I said, we had joked often that God had blessed Becky so unexpectedly and abundantly that I could always have one of her babies if it wasn't in God's plan for me to have my own. The funny thing is… I did get one of those babies!

Brant loved my daughter from the moment we placed Jennifer and him in the crib next to each other. They played so sweetly together as babies; he was protective of her from the very start. I am convinced he taught her how to crawl, demonstrating and then looking back for her to follow; he shared his Cheerios with her, always making sure she got the last one; they held hands in their car seats; they held hands the day they walked into kindergarten for their very first day of school.

I think every daughter's mother dreams that one day her daughter will meet her very own Prince Charming. It isn't very often though that you get the chance to help raise the boy your daughter will marry. I loved Brant like my own son. I changed his diapers; I spanked his bottom; I bandaged his knees; I gave him his first haircut; I pulled his first tooth; I helped with homework; I fixed his favorite foods; I hugged that sweet, funny, little boy to pieces.

The truth is, I was his second mother, long before I became his mother-in-law. God blessed my life with the mate he chose for my daughter, and, at that hospital the night we lost Brant, we grieved as one big family, each feeling the pain and immeasurable loss of the other.

***

Christian McLachlan

I was the last to make it to the hospital the night my brother was killed. My dad looked like a broken man as he met me in the hospital parking lot. He threw his arms around me so tightly, and I did the same to him. It was a silent embrace, like so many that night, because there really were not words that could express the loss we were all feeling. Dad kept his hand on my shoulder as we walked inside the hospital, and I secretly hoped he wouldn't let go because I was almost certain that his arm was all that was holding me up.

I walked like a teary-eyed zombie into the waiting room where my family was gathered, and my heart sank when I saw my mother. The doctor who had seen it all… the woman who had devoted her life to saving lives… would have to bury her youngest son.

My whole body was shaking as my mother held me, my throat burning before my tears poured forth freely.

My brothers hugged me at once. I was thankful that my big brother, Jordan, was there and Tommy Jackson, who was like a brother to all of us. Because, honestly, it was that embrace between Ethan and me that I wasn't sure I could take. It felt the most right and the most empty at the same time. It's something I've tried to explain before, and the explanation seems lost on those who weren't born multiples.

The long, silent embrace between my brother and me was so incredibly painful. I think both of us wanted to speak but just couldn't find the words to say. It was Ethan who finally broke the silence and whispered through his tears, "Christian, Jen's pregnant… they think she might lose the baby."

I couldn't find the words to admit that I already knew Brant and Jennifer's little secret. I didn't tell anyone that Brant had called me that morning, swearing me to secrecy, but so excited that he just couldn't help but tell someone. *If I had only known that would be the last time I ever heard my brother's voice.* Nor could I tell them that Jennifer had called me only five minutes later, practically squealing with joy and making me promise to act surprised when they delivered their baby news!

"Where is she?" was all I could manage, and I could feel the tremble in my own voice.

I remember seeing Jen for the first time after my brother died, and that was the moment that all the hurt, all the pain, all the anger, all the deep feelings of loss I had felt that night seemed to settle into a clear understanding that my life would never go back to normal ever again.

***

Jennifer McLachlan

My pregnancy with Morgan was not the joyous experience I had dreamed of. I never felt radiant. I never glowed. I was sick, scared and, though I was never by myself, I often felt alone. Given the extremely complicated pregnancies my mother experienced before she was able to have me and my younger brother, Ben, I was terrified every moment of every day that I could lose my baby… Brant's baby.

I lived in absolute fear that I could lose the only opportunity I had at holding on to a little piece of the love that Brant and I shared.

Morgan and I made it through the funeral. We made it through seeing Brant's brothers arrive back in town with a U-Haul containing the contents of the home in Dallas where Brant and I were building a life. We made it through the weeks that followed, the weeks when I didn't want to get out of bed for days at a time. I didn't feel like eating; I ate only for Morgan. I couldn't sleep because nightmares startled me awake. I had dreams about Brant's murder; I had dreams that I lost our baby.

I was staying with my parents then, and, though they were a tremendous help with Brandon, I noticed that they were slowly forcing me to do more and more for him, and I knew that was because caring for him was my only motivation to get out of bed.

The day my ultrasound revealed that I was carrying a son, I was so overcome with a variety of emotions that I passed out in the doctor's office. An entire support system had gone with me to my appointment, and when I collapsed, thankfully, it was right into Christian's arms.

Throughout my pregnancy, I suffered traumatic nightmares. I would wake up in the middle of the night, feeling for Brant next to me. Then it would all come back in flashes. It wasn't just a night terror; my reality had become one, big, waking nightmare. I was about six months pregnant, awake in bed at night, when I picked up my phone and began scrolling through my contacts. I hesitated for a moment when I remembered what time it was, then, unsure of what else to do, I dialed Christian's number.

I remembered how he had held me on the night we lost Brant. He and Brant wore the same cologne; it was the reason I wanted to push him away and never let go at the same time. Our faces pressed together; our tears mixed; we never said a word to each other that night because there just are not words for a hurt that bad.

Toward the end of my pregnancy, I ended up in the hospital, fighting for my life and the life of my unborn child. My family wanted to be there to support me, and, as much as I wanted them all there, it was just too difficult. I wanted to be alone. I wanted to talk to Brant and not feel judged.

One day, like a Godsend, right at the moment I was wishing somebody I loved would walk through the door, Christian came to me, and I will never forget the words he said. Standing in the doorway in jeans and a vintage, University of Alabama t-shirt, he shrugged and sighed, "I'm sorry, Jen… I know you said you wanted to be alone… I just didn't know where else to go."

I patted the side of my hospital bed, and he crawled in next to me. I had an IV in my hand, but I instantly grasped Christian's hand with my fingers and squeezed it tightly. Both our hands rested on my pregnant belly. In that moment, I know he felt like I was being strong for him, but the truth was, I had never been so glad to see him in my life. As I prayed for God to give me strength I didn't have, Christian appeared out of nowhere, like an angel… like a tearful… broken… perfect… angel.

***

Ethan McLachlan

When my brother died, it felt like the world fell apart and no decision seemed easy any more. My parents were shattered, and my dad quit his job at the high school because he said his heart just wasn't in coaching.

I had met and fallen in love with Hannah during my first year of college in North Carolina. Suddenly, I wasn't ready to go back to school following my brother's death, and I felt a distance begin to grow between Hannah and me. She tried to be supportive of me and give me time to grieve, but the strain on our blossoming relationship with undeniable.

I vividly remember our trip to Dallas, introducing Hannah to Brant and Jennifer for the first time; Brant took us all out to dinner at a really expensive steakhouse where I ate the best steak I have ever had in my life. Double dating with my brother and Jen seemed right. We had a blast, laughing, telling stories and getting to know the woman I would eventually marry.

Hannah didn't grow up in a small town; she didn't have a circle of friends who had been her family since childhood. She stood by my side at my brother's funeral, and she was overwhelmed by the outpouring of love shown by our town. As tight as my, small but special, social circle is, I imagined it would be a hard one to break into for outsiders, so I did everything I could to try and make Hannah feel a part of the group and help my friends accept her. Christian was really the one who stood by me and encouraged me to focus on my relationship with Hannah and go back to North Carolina to school.

Ever since I was a child, I wanted to be a doctor just like my mother. I wanted to help people… to save the sick, injured and afflicted… but there were dark days after my brother's death when chasing my dream didn't seem worth it. I could save a million people in my lifetime… but I could never save him.

I knew that I had to find focus in my life again. I had to keep living, and, for me, going back to school and working on my relationship with Hannah was most important. There were days when I was sure I was forcing my relationship with Hannah to work because it *had to be her…* she had met my brother; he had met her… I wanted it to be her… in his lifetime, I just wanted Brant to have seen me with the one I would spend forever with. Looking back, I don't really think I would have felt that way if Hannah hadn't been the one.

Hannah didn't want a big wedding, or maybe she just knew that I couldn't fathom getting married without Brant standing next to me, so we skipped the ceremony and just made it official.

I remember the day that Hannah told me that I was going to be a father. I was beside myself with excitement, yet there was this little part of me that felt like the timing was all wrong. I explained to Hannah that I didn't want to tell my family that she was pregnant until after Jennifer and our nephew were out of the woods.

For me, news of my child was a light amongst the darkness. My daughter, Emily Jane McLachlan, was born nine months later, and she healed her daddy's heart in a way that she could never understand.

***

Jennifer McLachlan

The day that I went into labor, I felt like I was having a baby and a panic attack simultaneously. Despite everyone begging me to calm down for my sake and that of the baby, I was a mess of emotions, and nothing anybody could say or do would change that.

The only person I needed, the only person I wanted, the only person I had ever dreamed of spending this day with… wasn't there… and he wasn't going to be there… not for the birth and not for a single day of our baby boy's life.

I gripped Christian's hand, and, though I knew I was squeezing hard enough to break bones, he never flinched; his eyes never blinked. "What am I going to do?" I screamed at him. "I really can't do this without Brant. What am I going to do?"

"You can do this," Christian nodded confidently. "One day at a time, you can do this… right now all that matters is having this baby."

"I need him here holding my hand," I cried as I was gripped by another merciless contraction. As painful as the contractions were, nothing could compare to the heartache I felt in that moment. "Christian," I panted after I caught my breath, "this isn't fair. He was supposed to be here. I need him."

"I know," Christian swallowed. "And I know I'm not him, Jen, but I'm right here; you're not alone, and I know you can do this."

"Don't leave me, Christian," I cried without hesitation. I stared into his eyes and saw a man who was so much stronger than he knew.

***

Christian McLachlan

When Jennifer went into labor, I have to admit that I was scared out of my mind. When she took me up on my offer to be by her side during the birth, I was beyond terrified.

There I was in the delivery room, determined not to look, throw-up or pass out as my best friend experienced the miracle of childbirth right before my eyes.

My favorite little tomboy had grown up into an amazing woman who was about to give birth to a baby whose health and wellbeing I had prayed for more than I had ever prayed for anything in my life.

As I stood by Jen's side, I was determined to stay strong for her because I had promised her I would. Once everything began, I just went into auto-pilot.

As the doctor placed the baby in Jennifer's arms, I stared down at her in awe. My knees felt weak and my heart absolutely raced, but I had never been so proud of anyone in my entire life.

Jennifer looked up at me, and a faint smile broke through her tears.

"You did it, Jenny," I whispered. "He's absolutely perfect." I leaned down and pressed my lips hard against Jennifer's forehead. "You did it."

As Jennifer and I both stared at the bundle of pure love and innocence she held in her arms, we both felt the weight of my brother's absence and the calming peace of his presence.

"I can feel him," Jennifer nodded at me, and her smile grew as her tears flowed. "I can feel him here with us."

"Me too, Jenny," I nodded. "And I know that if he could, he would tell you that he loves you, that he's proud of you and how lucky Brandon and Morgan are that you're their mother."

Jennifer nodded as she reached for my hand and squeezed it gently. She looked at me like there was so much she wanted to say, then, spent, she simply whispered, "thank you."

***

Jennifer McLachlan

I think I realized how much I would miss Christian when he went back to school, but I also knew it was something he had to do. He had been commuting back and forth between school and home for months, but he had been home for a full week leading up to the baby's birth, being so attentive in catering to my every need and demonstrating acts of true friendship in the most difficult circumstances.

We talked on the phone every morning and every night. We talked about his classes, about football, about milestones each of the boys reached. We talked about the mundane just to hear each other's voices. We shared gossip we heard about people we went to high school with. We made jokes, and we laughed again. We tried just finding normal again.

When Morgan was old enough that I felt good about traveling with two babies on my own, the first road trip we took was to Tuscaloosa, Alabama, to visit Uncle Christian.

One night I remember dressing both boys in little Alabama football outfits my parents had gotten them and walking down the street with both boys in the stroller. Christian and I were both laughing and racing to finish our ice cream cones as they melted. That's when it happened… a car backfired, and it sounded exactly like a gunshot.

I released a guttural shrill as I dropped my ice cream cone onto the sidewalk and relived the nightmare that played like rapid fire images inside my head. *Brant was on the ground. There was blood pouring from his chest, pooling all around him. My world was spinning out of control.*

I can imagine that passersby, unfazed by or even oblivious to the sound, stared curiously, perhaps some even judgmentally, at me as they passed, but all I know for sure is that Christian wrapped me up so securely in his arms that I felt my present reality start to seep back in.

There was so much love in that embrace, so much understanding and empathy that it was tangible. "You're okay, sweetie," he assured me in a voice that sounded so much like his brother's that I could hardly breathe. "I've got you."

***

Christian McLachlan

Jen would drive to Tuscaloosa, and, when my schedule allowed, I would drive home to Mississippi. I wasn't sure what was going on between the two of us. We had always been extremely close; frankly, she had always been like a sister to me. Our friendship was undeniable; that we felt a closeness to Brant when we were together was equally undeniable. There was something about just being near her that was comforting for both of us.

It had been well over a year since we lost my brother, and I had done everything I could to be the supportive friend that Jennifer needed me to be and the present, loving uncle that her boys needed me to be.

I don't know when it happened; I don't know when exactly I went from loving her… to being in love with her.

***

Jennifer McLachlan

It was a cold night and Christian had come home from school to visit. It had become increasingly difficult for him to fit in time to come home, given the intensity of his school and football schedules, but he always seemed to make a way, even if it meant he could only be there for a couple of hours.

I remember the moment, sitting in front of the fireplace at my parents' house. Brandon and Morgan were out enjoying some quality time with both sets of grandparents.

Christian is smart and funny and really sweet, and there was such a history there that we knew how to make each other smile. I knew things about him, and he knew things about me that took us right back to simpler times. That night I remember truly, honestly laughing from a place deep inside of me for the first time since Brant died.

Then, somehow, I ended up in Christian's arms, looking into his eyes, and it happened before either one of us could stop it. I kissed Christian, and while my lips longingly trembled against his, my heart was pierced at once.

We both pulled away from the kiss and stared back at each other, our eyes admitting we had each felt the betrayal in that forbidden kiss.

I remember the disbelieving way that Christian looked at me, and the sincerity with which his soft but numerous apologies spilled forth.

I recall the fear in the pit of my stomach, the shame, the guilt, the breathlessness and... the passion in the kiss that followed.

CHAPTER THREE

Christian McLachlan

As I stood out on the football field today watching the team I coach run through the drills I've taught them, I watched my life flash before my eyes. As a little boy, I stared out at that very field watching the boys who went before me and dreaming of the day when I too would put on a blue and white jersey, step onto the field on Friday nights and hear the crowd yelling my name! Those days came; for a moment in time, we were heroes, and the town revolved around us.

Now I coach the same boys who stood by the fence hoping to fill my shoes one day, and the experience leaves me with mixed emotions.

My dad was always my football coach, he and my oldest brother, Jordan. Dad and Jordan coached me, Ethan and Brantley throughout our high school years. I knew that one day, I would come back home and take over coaching my beloved North River Eagles.

Of course, in my mind, that didn't happen until after I spent four years playing college ball at the University of Alabama and took my shot at playing professionally. Fate didn't play out the way an eighteen-year-old boy had it all planned though.

Don't get me wrong, I love the role of coach in a town where people live for Friday nights; I thrive on having the opportunity to build young men first and football players second. I like to think that each boy who plays for me is taught in the tradition of the great Paul "Bear" Bryant.

My dad played football for Coach Bryant at the University of Alabama, and, though he moved back home to Mississippi to raise his family, it was common for him to take my brothers and me to Tuscaloosa on Saturdays to watch his Crimson Tide.

We were proud, small town, Mississippi boys who said *Roll Tide* and sang a mean *Rammer Jammer.* I fell in love with Alabama football at a young age, and, from the time I was a kid, there was nothing I wanted more than to attend the University of Alabama, put on that crimson and white jersey and play Alabama football… and I got that chance.

I recall with mixed emotions the pride that I felt when I stood on that field on game day. In Tuscaloosa I discovered an identity that I had never known before. It's that identity that I miss most now… because in *this* town, on *this* field, I will always be one of three.

When I was growing up, even in high school, that identity was a blessing. I had two best friends who shared everything with me, and it is only now that I must face this town without them that I have moments when I wonder if I made the wrong decision by coming back here to start my life over again.

The day I decided to give up playing Alabama football, I knelt on my knees on the locker room floor and, as I prayed for God to show me the answers I was desperately searching for, I wept like a little boy who knew he had to choose between everything he wanted and everything that the people he loved needed. I clenched my jersey in my hand as I thought about all the blood, sweat and tears that had gone into earning that coveted uniform, but I knew what I had to do.

I walked away from my football career that day, and, in my heart of hearts, I know that was the right thing to do. Yet, even watching a game on television, I stare into the sea of crimson and white and can say, without a doubt, that the sight doesn't even compare to the view from the field. The fight song makes my heart pound and floods my head with memories of the traditions I was once a part of.

Catch me on a good day and Big AL makes me smile while thousands of waving pom poms bring back the best of memories, but catch me on a bad day, and I'm the guy whose eyes well up with tears at the sight of a kid in a Bama jersey strapping his helmet on before taking the field.

I wonder what my final two seasons could have been like, and sometimes I even dream of hearing broadcast legend Eli Gold calling my name on the radio as I score the winning touchdown, but in that dream he ends his commentary with a mention of my brother, professional football star Brant McLachlan, the starting quarterback of the Dallas Cowboys who is well on his way to leading his team to another Super Bowl. Because *that* is the way it was supposed to be.

I am struck by a vision of the jersey in the glass case that hangs on the wall in the gym at the high school I once attended and where I am now employed.

#13

There is a record book full of records that no one will ever touch. There is an emptiness that looms over this town, and, even amongst the cheers on Friday nights, there are shared memories of a time when we witnessed greatness blossoming before our very eyes; there is a part of all of us that wishes we could go back to a time when the hopes of our town rested in the hands of a quarterback who commanded the field with a confidence that reflected the fact that he was perfectly comfortable carrying the expectations of a town on his shoulders.

On Friday nights when Brant was here, this town felt invincible because there was a peace of mind that came with putting the football in Brant's hands. At that point, it was just time to sit back and enjoy the show!

Our town hasn't been the same since Brant died. My dad gave up coaching, and a team that was once a dominant force to be reckoned with now struggles to even make the playoffs.

I made the decision to begin coaching alongside my brother Jordan, and, though I love it, I don't feel like it's something that I'm necessarily ready for.

In my heart, I'm still a player, and I find myself a little jealous of the boys I'm in charge of coaching. I see their dreams, so alive and so promising, unhindered by events beyond their control.

They're kids; they will each face a single moment in their life that forces them to grow up; I can tell them this with certainty; the lives they are planning as they walk the halls of North River High School can change in an instant. I hope that each one of them realizes how special this town is, but I also hope that they realize that there is a whole world outside the confines of Cummins, Mississippi.

The boy who wore the jersey that now hangs on the wall… he knew that.

That jersey in the glass case represents everything that I love about this town, but it also represents everything that I hate about it too.

It is a throwback to a time when everything was right in my life. It takes me back to a time when my brothers and I were three kids having fun and living large in a town that coined the phrase high school glory days.

Yet, that jersey is also a reminder that those times couldn't last. My brothers and I couldn't be high school football heroes forever, nor did I want us to be, but I never dreamed that growing up was something I would have to do without my best friend.

In a town where football is a way of life, amongst a host of talent, Brant stood alone as the star, but Brant, Ethan and I were the McLachlan triple threat on the football field and off. They were my brothers, my best friends, my teammates, my roommates, my partners in crime, and, in Cummins, Mississippi, I will never be anything other than a third of the McLachlan trio.

Most of the time I long for that identity, but there are moments when it just hurts too bad because the triple threat, the trio, the three musketeers… just doesn't exist any more.

I never thought that I would end up as one of those guys standing on the sidelines of a high school football field dreaming of a return to the good ole days, and I certainly never dreamed that I would be back here in my early twenties trying to salvage North River's once rich football history.

As I huddled my team up and dismissed them, I saw my wife walking onto the field. Brandon and Morgan held Jen's hands as they walked, and, as always, I was struck by just how much those two, gorgeous, blond, little boys look like my brother.

Jennifer let loose of their little hands, and they raced toward me with priceless grins on their faces. As I knelt down and they ran into my open arms, I smiled up at their mother. She was absolutely beautiful without a trace of make-up on, standing there on that field that held so many memories, her long, brown hair blowing in the breeze, exactly the way I remembered it.

I was instantly transported back to high school. In my mind, she was wearing her cheerleading uniform, and she was tucked under my brother's arm… right where she belongs.

CHAPTER FOUR

Cowboys and Angels

Jordan McLachlan

I was a thirteen-year-old, only child before my three brothers were born. Christian, Ethan and Brant were truly my *baby* brothers. Given the age difference between us, we weren't peers; there was no sibling rivalry, no real sense of shared experience, no arguing, fighting or competing. I got to enjoy a really special relationship with each of them as a role model, mentor, big brother and coach. As the oldest brother, I was protective; they were my little brothers, and I unashamedly adored them.

Christian dreamed of playing college football at the University of Alabama since he attended his first college game as a child. It's hard to describe game day in Tuscaloosa, Alabama. It's really not something you can understand until you've experienced it firsthand. It's more than a football game; it's tradition. My brothers and I may have grown up in Mississippi, but our roots were firmly planted in Tuscaloosa.

Christian always wanted to be just like our dad, so it didn't surprise me at all that he wanted to follow in Dad's footsteps by playing football for Alabama.

In the interest of full-disclosure, I should note that I played my college ball at Southern Mississippi. I always wondered how Ole Miss legend, Archie Manning, felt when his son, Peyton, chose to cement his legacy at Tennessee instead of Ole Miss, but, having met Mr. Manning on a couple of occasions, I feel certain that he was every bit as supportive as my dad was.

Unconditional love is best defined in my mind by a diehard Alabama alum who was willing to put on black and gold for a couple of years to support his son. I am pretty sure those shirts and hats disappeared as soon as I graduated, but I have pictures to prove they existed. I also have pictures to prove that the year Alabama showed up on our schedule, my father showed up to the game in a crimson shirt with the words GO, JORDAN emblazoned on the front in houndstooth lettering!

I had always desired to follow in my dad's footsteps, but when I didn't receive a scholarship offer from Alabama, I had to make the decision that was best for me. Then, as I like to say of my little brother… *along came Eli…* following in dad's footsteps!

Christian was a standout athlete who worked hard and got his chance to chase his dream. Seeing my little brother in an Alabama football jersey was such a proud moment. He was always a hardworking, dedicated player, and I know how much playing at Alabama meant to him.

But, as you can probably imagine, being a Division I student athlete doesn't leave you with a lot of free time on your hands. Between school and football, it was difficult for Christian to spend as much time with Jennifer and the boys as he felt they deserved.

I realized, as all of us did, that the state of Christian and Jennifer's relationship had been slowly redefining itself after Brant died, but when Christian made the brave and, I believe, truly admirable decision to quit playing college football… that's when I knew that he had fallen in love with her.

***

Becky McLachlan

Christian and Jennifer have always had something in common. They are both two of the most selfless people I have ever known. Growing up, I felt that the two of them constantly provided Brantley with the balance he needed.

Brant was always my handful… my precious boy so full of life with personality to spare. He was born a star, shining bright in everything he did. And, oh how his star burned brightly in the short time he had here with us!

I always knew that Brant would marry Jennifer; it was a love that was special and undeniable, but the day that Christian and Jennifer gathered us all around to tell us that they had fallen in love, I can't say that I was shocked that those two had gravitated toward each other after we lost Brant.

I knew that one day… eventually… hopefully… as was my prayer for her… the day would come when my sweet, young daughter-in-law would marry again, and I can't tell you how much it meant to me and our entire family that she and Christian fell in love.

I knew that my relationship with Jennifer was so strong that I could never truly lose her, despite whatever changes time would bring for all of us. She was always the daughter that I never had, and nothing could have ever changed the deep love and respect I have for her. But, as I told her on the day she married my Christian, I feel beyond blessed that she remains a part of the McLachlan family… right where she belongs.

Jennifer and Christian agreed that a big wedding ceremony wasn't something they wanted. The event was a very private one, and, though many tears were shed for so many reasons on that day, I could not have been more proud to watch those two beautiful souls unite and become the couple that would raise my grandchildren and keep Brant's memory alive.

***

Jennifer McLachlan

It hits me hardest in the simplest moments and at the most unexpected times… a song on the radio, the sound of the kids laughing in the back seat of the car, the roar of a football stadium, a random photograph, the smell of Honeysuckle or just reaching for a handful of red and green M&M's at my parents' house on Christmas Eve. There is a memory of Brant in every single thing I do; some days I find that incredibly comforting; other days it seems unbearable.

Every day I long to have Brant's arms around me… to feel his touch… kiss his lips... and sit for hours holding his hand and talking about nothing and everything all at once.

I miss his jokes, his voice, his laughter, the way he sang, his happy-go-lucky approach to things, his ability to make me feel like the happiest girl in the world.

He completed me like nobody else ever will. He was my soulmate, my best friend, that once in a lifetime love that no one else can ever compare to. My love for him is tied to my childhood and contains within it nostalgia that is often lost in adulthood.

There are times when I get so angry that I wish I could escape myself…. times when I feel like such a fraud behind my white picket fence that I wonder if the girl I was would even recognize the woman I have become.

My anger is usually directed at the shooter, a nameless, mystery man who, without regret or remorse, broke my heart into a billion little pieces and never looked back. I get frustrated by circumstance… just that a stranger could take so much from me and my family and go on living like it never happened.

But, I'm the first to admit that the brunt of my frustration has, on more than one occasion, been directed at Brant himself. I've yelled at him for leaving me; I've chastised him for daring to take some ridiculous shortcut instead of staying on the main road that night; I've called him stubborn and reckless; I've blamed him for putting us in a position to cross paths with those men that fateful day. Then, inevitably, I fall exhausted onto my bed, and I think about the man I loved. *Stubborn. Proud. Reckless. Loud.* Those are words to one of our favorite songs… words that made the guy I lovingly called my *Cowboy* exactly who he was.

Some people probably assume that I have lost my mind a lot of the time. People at the grocery store or at the park… they probably think I talk to myself because I like to talk to Brant as though he is standing next to me.

"You'll never guess who I ran into today," I might say to him as I sit alone in my car.

"How about that, Cowboy?" I might say in the middle of a football game, earning me a little sympathetic side-eye from everyone else in the room.

"What do you think? Is it a spaghetti night or a taco soup night?" I ask aloud as I browse the grocery aisles. "You're right, the boys would probably rather have spaghetti."

When people are around I usually try to keep my comments to a minimum because I really don't appreciate the cynical looks, nor do I blame people for them because I would probably stare at the crazy lady conversing with herself too if I was in their shoes.

However, when I'm alone, the conversations can go on and on. I tell him everything about my day because there are some things that I only feel comfortable sharing with him. We usually talk in the shower because it's easier to hide my tears there.

I can tell him anything; I can talk about how I really feel, and he'll love me anyway. I can admit what a dork I am sometimes, and it's okay because he already knows. I can tell him about embarrassing things because we have no secrets. His heart is my safe place; it always has been, and I don't want that to ever change.

Some people would probably argue that, by talking to Brant, I am denying reality, not accepting the fact that he is gone, or that I'm blocking out his death and living in a fantasy world where Brant is still alive. That is not the case; I have a good grasp on reality; I know he's never coming back… but, I guess, I just don't want to lose touch with someone who is so much a part of me.

***

Christian McLachlan

For a short time after Jen and I got married, she and the boys moved to Tuscaloosa, so I could finish school. I had given up football, but Jen and I both agreed that it needed to be a priority for me to complete my degree.

While we were living in the small apartment we shared in Tuscaloosa, Jen went through a pretty rough bout with depression. She had been through so much, and I was committed to doing anything that needed to be done to help her get through this next hurdle. The boys kept her going; making sure that Brandon and Morgan were happy, healthy, vibrant little boys was her priority, even as she struggled with nightmares and doubts about our marriage and our future.

Given everything that Jennifer had been through, I was determined to extend to her the utmost patience, even as my insecurities mounted. I felt like she deserved patience and understanding, especially from me, given that I had taken a vow to love her through good times and bad.

"Jen, do you know what it's like to see someone you care so deeply for hurting so badly, and there is nothing you can do or say to make the pain go away?" I said to her one night, after a day that hadn't brought out the best in either of us.

She stared at me with cold eyes that I didn't even recognize. "Chris, I can't do this right now. I'm not up for another sparring match with you… I don't feel like defending my feelings."

I slid my text book aside and began helping her fold a basket of laundry that was sitting on our bed. I glanced over at her, and tears were streaming down her face as she folded her favorite nightshirt, a t-shirt that used to belong to my brother. "Jenny…" I sighed.

She shook her head, cutting me off. "What about you?" she said loudly. "Since my emotions are so disturbing to you, I have a question for *you*. Do you know what it's like to crawl on your hands and knees in the street, absolutely helpless as you watch your life slip away? I'm sorry I can't put on a happy face every time you would like for me to."

I swallowed, determined not to raise my voice. "The difference is," I said, "there was nothing you could do to save him. I feel you slipping away from me now, and, though there has to be something I can do or say to save our marriage, I don't know what that is."

"You *say* all the right things. You *do* all the right things," Jennifer snapped at me. "You're gonna stand by me forever out of some heroic sense of duty, all because I'm too scared to let you go. But, I can't do this, Christian… I can't let you spend the rest of your life being robbed of the life you deserve while you stay with me… being my safety net."

"I love you, Jennifer," I said too harshly. "I'm not trapped in this marriage… nobody forced me into it, and nobody can make me stay. For the record, I didn't marry you out of some archaic notion of duty; I married you because I fell in love with you. We didn't do anything wrong here, Jen! Don't think I don't know how you feel! Don't think I don't think about him every time I touch you, every time I kiss you! Don't think I don't still feel guilty... but that's crazy, Jennifer... we're not cheating on anybody here!"

"Then why does it feel that way?" she cried.

"Sometimes I wish that I could trade places with him," I confessed, "because that is the only thing I could give you that would save the girl I used to know... give you back that spirit... recreate the way you danced... the way you radiated joy to everyone around you. I would do anything to save that girl, Jenny... because I love you."

"Christian, I need you to hear something," Jennifer cried.

It had been a long day, one of those days when I felt like my love was just never going to be enough, as much as I wanted it to be. "I'm gonna go for a drive," I sighed.

"No," Jennifer shook her head as she ran around the bed and grabbed both of my hands in hers. "Christian, you have to know that I love you too... that's the problem... I do... *I love you*, and that scares me to death."

I stared at her, not knowing what to say. It seemed like the same conversation we had been having for weeks.

"I don't know how to explain to you how this feels for me," she shrugged as her tears flowed. "But, I can't let you walk out of here thinking that I don't love you... because I do... I love you so much... and it's like I want to, but I don't want to... I need to, but I can't... just the thought of hurting him... the thought of disappointing him... I just... I don't know... I keep fighting the feelings inside of me because I'm scared to death that they could even exist!"

"I know... I know, Jenny... I do," I pulled her into me, and my tears began to flow as freely as hers.

Jennifer buried her face in my shoulder, gripped her fingers into my t-shirt and held on for dear life. "He was more than my boyfriend, more than my best friend, more than my husband," she sobbed. "It's a bond that death can't break, and sometimes it just feels like I'm going crazy..."

"He'll always be a part of you," I said, feeling her body tremble next to mine.

"The thought of me loving someone else would crush him, and I could never hurt Brant," she cried, nearly hyperventilating.

"Jen, we worked through this," I shook my head, feeling exhausted and defeated. "We had these conversations before we got married. He'd want you to move on… and find happiness again."

Instantly, she moved away from me, and I wasn't prepared for how badly that would sting. She stared at me, her eyes so defensive, as though she was taking sides in a competition that was non-existent. "Is that true, or is that just something we say to make ourselves feel better for what we've done?" she gulped.

I felt anger in that moment. Not even at her really… more at myself… that her words could arise in me anger *at my brother*. I was standing there staring at my wife and somehow felt jealously toward my dead, murdered brother. I had often suggested that we speak to a professional about her grief, but, in that moment, I was sure that if anybody needed psychiatric counseling, it was me. "Jennifer, the day you lost your husband, I lost my brother!" I screamed at her, and I hated myself for it. I instantly lowered my voice. "We found comfort in each other," I sighed. "Neither one of us intended to fall in love with the other… we didn't set out to hurt Brant."

She nodded and tucked her hair behind her ears.

"I didn't want to steal his wife," I shrugged. "It's not like I'm over here cheering because I got the girl… it just happened… life happened, Jen, and we had to deal with it the best way we knew how… and the best way for us to cope was together… *is* together."

"I want to learn to live again, Christian. I do." She turned to the mirror and kept fixing her hair in what could really only be described as a nervous fidget.

I stood behind her and wrapped my arms around her. "Then lean on me instead of pushing me away," I begged her.

To my surprise, she slowly spun around and wrapped her arms around my neck. I lifted her into my arms, and she ran her fingers through my hair. "Did anybody ever tell you how special you are?" she smiled, as she wiped her tears away. Then she caught me off guard again. "You're so special, and you deserve a wife who can love you the way you deserve… but…"

"But nothing," I cut her off.

"Look at you; you could have any girl you wanted," she smiled.

"I only want you," I gulped.

"Christian, hear me out," she insisted as I set her back on her feet. "You deserve to be somebody's everything…"

"No," I argued. "I don't want to hear that I deserve better… that I deserve more… that somehow your bad days aren't ours to navigate together… you are my wife…"

"Chris, I really thought I would be stronger than this when I agreed to marry you… that time would heal this pain like people say…" Jennifer confessed.

I sat down on our bed, trying to extinguish my mounting frustration. "Jennifer, all of those people who you think are so strong… they are just like you… they deal… they put on a brave face… they have faith… they put one foot in front of the other day after day… they cope… but you don't see their private agony. They have their moments, just like you do. We are all human… we are allowed bad days. Loving Brant is okay! I know that you love him! I knew that when I married you, and I never assumed that you would stop! I don't want you to stop… I love him too!"

"I've just been thinking that maybe if I took the boys back to Dallas," Jennifer began, not looking at me.

"What?" I exclaimed, confused.

"Christian, I want to be with you… I do… and maybe in time…" She still wasn't looking at me. "People keep telling me that I'll feel better in time, but they're wrong! I miss him *more* every day… every day the pain just gets deeper, and it isn't fair to you. You don't deserve this…"

"I don't deserve what?" I said, exasperated. I reached for her, forcing her to look at me. "Do I deserve to have my heart broken by the only woman I have ever loved because she wants to run off in search of some past life in Texas… one that simply doesn't exist? He's not in Texas, Jen! You spent eighteen years with him in Mississippi… let's just move home! I can commute for night classes maybe, rearrange my schedule… I'll figure it out!"

"You're a saint, Chris, but I've tried everything… you're right; it's not the place; it's not you… I just want to wake up one morning and feel whole again," she said honestly.

"You've always been whole, Jen," I corrected her. "You are a person who people love, admire, respect and look up to… and that's why my brother loved you. Jennifer, he never completed you… you accomplished that all on your own… that's why you could love him as completely as you did."

"You say all the right things, Christian," she sighed. "You say all the perfect words I need to hear… you do everything I need you to do and more, and I love you… I do… but sometimes I think it's harder because it *is* you."

"Who else could it be Jennifer?" I shrugged. "Brant died… it was awful; it was tragic; it still hurts every single day… but look at you… you're so young; you have your whole life ahead of you! Just tell me… if not me then who? If you went out, and you found somebody new… somebody from somewhere else who didn't even know Brant… ask yourself, would that person ever understand the bond that the two of you shared? Would he be able to deal with your bad days when you miss Brant so much you can hardly function? Would he know what to do or say when you wanted to talk about all the times that you and Brant shared? Would he get the inside jokes? Could you communicate without words because so many of your memories are his memories too? Would he understand the girl you were, the things you've been through and the woman you've become? Could he deal with there being more framed photographs in his house of you and Brant than of you and him? Could he love you unconditionally, even though another man will always own your heart? If you think that guy is out there, Jennifer… then go find him…"

"I'm looking at the only other man I could ever love," Jennifer said with so much conviction that it hit me right in the heart.

"So maybe we didn't choose each other," I shook my head. "Maybe this is just the way it had to be."

"I know that God sent you to me," Jennifer cried. "Brant is my angel in Heaven, and you… *you* are my angel right here on Earth… do you know that?"

"I know it's not easy, but we're gonna be okay," I promised her. "I don't know that time ever heals the wounds of such profound loss, but I do think that time eventually lessens the sting a little. I think, at this point, we just need to keep being there for each other and trying to weather the storm. I don't know the answers any more than you do, Jenny, but I know that we can do this… together."

"That's because when I try to push you away, you just hold on tighter," Jen laughed through her tears.

"Yeah," I whispered as she kissed my cheek. "And I promise you that, on the really bad days, I'll always hold on tight enough for the both of us."

***

John Smith

David McLachlan and I go way back. He's a good man who has done a lot for me over the years. We've spent many a prayer meeting praying for our children, both before they arrived and many times after.

David and Becky did a wonderful job raising their four sons. Jordan and the triplets were always well-behaved, hardworking and respectful young men. The McLachlan triplets spent as much time at my house when they were growing up as they did at their own. Christian, Ethan and Brant were a part of our family long before Brant married my only daughter.

Brant was a charmer. My wife always said that he was a special, little ray of sunshine. He was special alright; he drew you in with his confident, mischievous personality. He was hilarious; he could make you laugh even when you knew you probably shouldn't. David always said, you never knew whether to spank Brant or hug him, and that was about right! He had this spunk about him that you just couldn't help but fall in love with.

He and my daughter were inseparable and incredibly generous playmates. I sat in my recliner many evenings watching a tot-sized, future NFL quarterback rocking Cabbage Patch Kids and brushing Barbie's hair. Likewise, my young daughter, who loved playing house and taking care of her baby dolls, could transform into a tomboy who could catch a football and play ninjas or cowboys with the best of 'em. The love between those two was really a beautiful thing to get to witness.

I always believed that the sweet, funny, curly- headed, blond munchkin who, on many nights, crawled into my lap for story time before bed, would one day be my son-in-law.

The day Brant married my daughter, I knew I was giving her away to the one she was destined to spend her life with. It seemed so natural, and I had known Brant and his family for so long, that I really didn't get caught up in the emotion of it all. Having Jennifer leave my house to start her life with him seemed only right. It was with great pride that I placed her hand in his that day, kissed them both and wished them a long and happy life together.

It was no secret to anybody that Brant hurt my daughter during their final year of high school by getting mixed up with another girl. But, what most people probably don't know about that situation is that Brant came to me soon after and asked me to forgive him and to pray with him.

Forgiving Brant was easy for me because, though he had made a mistake that hurt my baby girl, I knew the heart of the kid who stood before me. I thought of him as my son as much as she was my daughter. I shook his hand; I put my arm around him; I told him exactly what I thought about what he had done, then I told him about mistakes I had made in my past that had hurt my family and how I had to overcome those to become the man I wanted to be.

I will never forget how he listened respectfully to me pouring out what I believed to be secrets I was sharing with him and acted as though he was shocked by the details of my mistakes. I could see it in his eyes though; everything I was telling him, he already knew and had probably known for years. That was the kind of relationship that Brant and Jennifer had; they shared everything; they were a team.

I put my arm around Brant, respecting him so much in that moment for coming to me at all, and we prayed together. We prayed for him and for Jennifer and their relationship and for the baby who would become my first grandchild.

My heart feared for my daughter the night that Brant was taken from us; I wasn't strong enough to deal with losing a child I loved so dearly or to cope with my daughter's broken heart, but I knew somebody who was strong enough. So I prayed.

Jennifer's pregnancy was so complicated that I wondered if she could survive losing her and Brant's baby. Her mother and I suffered the tremendous loss of multiple miscarriages before Jennifer was born, but I had no idea what it would be like to lose your one and *only* chance at having the child you had always dreamed of with the love of your life.

In my mind's eye, I clearly saw my daughter and my future son-in-law toting around Cabbage Patch dolls at our vacation campsite in the Smoky

Mountains. They fed them; they rocked them; they even put jackets on them before allowing them to ride in the back of the truck while looking for deer in Cades Cove. In so many of the pictures in our vacation album, Brant and Jennifer are posing with those dolls, beaming with pride over their pretend family. In one of my favorites, Brant has one of the dolls sitting on his shoulders and is holding both of its cloth hands the way you would a real baby. I was always amazed by Brant's willingness to participate in this form of play; it was one of the early signs when I knew that Brant loved my daughter.

The day Morgan was born and they told us that he was a perfectly healthy baby boy, and Mama and baby were both doing just fine, it felt like a weight that had been sitting on my heart for nine months had been lifted.

During Jennifer's pregnancy, and even more-so after Morgan was born, I noticed how much my daughter was depending on Christian. Watching them together was like witnessing two lost souls finding each other. Over time, their friendship began to blossom into something more. The day that Christian asked Jennifer to spend her life with him was the first day that I really felt like my daughter was going to be okay.

Of David's four sons, I always saw Christian as being most like his father. David is a dependable, respectable and Godly man whom I have always admired. Likewise, I watched Christian grow into a man I was proud of. Christian's always been sweet, steady, loving and dependable, but it wasn't until I got an up-close view of his newly defined role in my daughter's life that I began to truly understand and appreciate the man Christian is.

One evening, Kathy and I had been over at David and Becky's house eating dinner and spending time with our two grandsons before returning home. As soon as we got out of our truck in our driveway, we could hear Jennifer's tearful screams coming from inside the house. Terrified, Kathy and I ran to the door and rushed inside.

"Come-on, Jen! Stop it! You're scaring me!" Christian begged her.

"Leave me alone!" Jennifer screamed at Christian, her eyes insisting that the conversation she was having was a private one. "Leave me alone!"

"Jen," Christian reached for her, "sweetie… you had a dream… he's not here. I don't know what you think you saw or what is going on, but, you have to trust me!"

Jennifer moved toward Christian and slammed her open palms against his chest so hard that he took a step back.

"Jennifer!" her mother gasped, utterly shocked.

"Just because *you* can't see him doesn't mean he isn't here!" Jennifer screamed at Christian, ignoring us.

Christian closed his eyes, gathering his thoughts.

"You don't believe me!" Jennifer accused.

"I believe that you think that you saw Brant," Christian frowned. "But, you were napping on the couch, and…"

"It wasn't a dream," Jennifer insisted. "I'm not a child; I know the difference!" She began running around the room, looking behind furniture. She ran into the kitchen; she even opened the doors to the pantry and laundry room to check inside. "Do you see what you've done to me?" she hollered, ignoring all of us. "They all think I'm crazy! They don't get it! And why… *why*? Because you had to try some *stupid* shortcut… then you had to shoot off that smart mouth of yours! I *always* told you that your mouth was going to get you in more trouble than you could get out of one day!" She stopped screaming and started sobbing. "Then you had to try to be the hero and reach for the gun! Why couldn't you just let them take our things and go?" She fell to her knees. "I'm sorry; I didn't mean to yell at you… please come back… where did you go? I miss you already, Brantley!"

Christian and I both rushed to her. I could see the fear in Christian's eyes as my daughter spiraled further into what I can only describe as a nervous breakdown.

"Stay away from me," she screamed at Christian as he pulled her to her feet.

"No," he said with gentle confidence. "Come here; let me hold you."

"Let go of me, Christian," Jennifer insisted.

"Calm down, and if you still want me to let go then, I will," Christian promised.

My eyes filled with tears. "Please, Jennifer… sweetheart. We all just want to help you."

"Nobody can help me," Jennifer cried as she jerked free of Christian. "I want Brant! I only want Brant!" She made two tight fists as her tears consumed her, and she began pounding them as hard as she could on Christian's chest one after the other.

"Brant's not here, Jenny," Christian said gently, flexing his chest as she continued hitting him, one fist after the other then with both at the same time.

"Jennifer Leigh, please!" Kathy insisted as Christian stood unflinching.

"Why did I yell at him? I didn't mean any of that… it wasn't his fault!" Jennifer blubbered as she continued to pound repeatedly on Christian's chest. "It isn't fair! It isn't fair."

"Jennifer, I want you to listen to me," Christian said as he forcefully, yet ever so tenderly, took her wrists in his hands. "Stop this." Jennifer breathed heavily as she focused on Christian's eyes. She melted into him, holding tightly to him and heaving in tears, as she struggled to catch her breath.

"Sometimes I have trouble remembering exactly what his laugh sounded like, Chris," Jennifer bawled, coughing breathlessly as she held desperately to Christian. "My memories are fading… I don't ever want to forget that… that was my favorite sound in the world."

"It's okay… you won't forget," Christian whispered softly as he slowly sank down the wall, taking Jennifer with him without ever letting go. They sat there on the floor for what seemed like forever, her head against his chest, and his arms wrapped tightly around her.

"Why did you wake me up?" Jennifer cried pitifully. "I didn't want that dream to end. That was the best dream I've ever had. "

"I'm sorry," Christian whispered as he held her tighter.

I looked down at Christian, and his eyes met mine. I pursed my lips in a silent thank you, and he offered me the most sincere smile in return. I think that, in his own way, he was letting me know that Jennifer was going to be okay. My respect for that young man grew immensely that night. Watching him stand by my daughter even when it could have been argued that she didn't deserve it, told me all I ever needed to know about the man Christian McLachlan is.

***

Jennifer McLachlan

I have always been a sensible, practical girl, but there were certainly some growing pains in my relationship with Christian that I am a little embarrassed to even admit.

For example, I took a long nap one day only to wake up wholeheartedly believing that I had been talking to Brant. *I had seen him; he was standing there with me in all his handsome glory.* In my dream he was smiling at me, and it was so real that, when I woke up, I couldn't seem to let him go.

I acted so inexcusably awful toward Christian, but, in my mind, Brant was there; I could see him, and Christian was the crazy one! I yelled at Christian; I said awful things to Brant because I was angry at him for leaving me. Everything just seemed so messed-up. Then I started hitting my husband as if he was my punching bag. I have trouble even admitting that now because I am so shocked and sickened by my own behavior. Sometimes, when I think about the tone I used toward him or just the way I looked at him, it makes me physically sick to my stomach.

The thing that stands out most to me about that evening, other than how deplorably I behaved, is that when Christian stopped allowing me to take my frustrations out on him, I crumbled into him feeling the weight of everything that had just happened and wanting to tell him a million times over how sorry I was and how much I loved him. As we sank down to the floor in an embrace that was all that was holding me together in that moment, I could feel his heart beating against my cheek, and I knew that, despite the calmness in his voice and the steadiness of his hands, he was scared too.

My parents slipped out of the room, giving us the time we needed and leaving us to sit there alone for an hour, neither of us speaking a single word. Christian and I were good at that. I truly believe that sometimes it's the things that never have to be spoken that mean the most.

My sweet husband pressed his lips against my forehead and let them linger there. I have heard that a kiss on the forehead can erase memory, and, as I felt his lips against my face, I wished for certain memories to fade, while hoping that others could last forever. Then Christian's lips moved to mine, and, without saying a word, he told me of the unfailing steadfastness of his love for me, his devotion to me… his devotion to us.

***

Christian McLachlan

Jennifer's long, brown hair fell over her shoulders as she walked into the kitchen wearing only an oversized, football jersey and a rolled-up pair of my boxer shorts. I smiled as I watched her open the freezer door and remove a carton of chocolate ice cream. "Late night chocolate craving," she smiled as she offered me a spoon. "Join me?"

"Anytime," I smiled.

Jennifer took a bite of ice cream, playfully licking her lips as she savored the rich chocolate taste.

"The boys are asleep," she told me, coyly.

"That's good," I grinned, "because if they were to see us indulging in sugary treats after bedtime it could corrupt their entire world view."

Jennifer took one more bite of ice cream and tossed her spoon in the sink.

She danced over toward me in a playfully flirtatious mood. Jennifer had always been a beautiful girl, but since giving birth to Morgan, her body was… well… *smokin'*! She was more beautiful than I had ever seen her, but that could have had a lot to do with the fact that she was looking at me with eyes I had never seen from her before.

"Kiss me, Chris," she whispered as she ran her hands through my hair.

She didn't have to ask me twice! I took her in my arms and kissed her neck, then her cheek, then her lips. "You're amazing," I told her before I kissed her again. She ran her fingers up my back, gathering my shirt and tugging it over my head. She threw it onto the floor and jumped up into my arms. She wrapped her legs around my waist as we kissed, and I carried her toward our bedroom.

She giggled as I jostled her in my arms, growling at her playfully. She was kissing my shoulder as we passed by a bookshelf in the living room and started down the hallway.

I could instantly feel her mood change as I held her, and I knew that a single photograph had most likely just derailed the evening I was planning. Suddenly, she rested her chin on my shoulder and dangled her arms down my back.

"What's wrong?" I asked her as I eased her onto our bed and lingered on top of her, tenderly kissing her cheek.

"I'm sorry," she shook her head. Then, in a sweet gesture that felt more like a consolation prize in the moment, she kissed my lips again. "Please just hold me."

I brushed a strand of her hair away from her face before I rolled away from her. We both crawled under the covers, and she snuggled next to me. We were quiet for a long moment, and I knew she probably sensed my disappointment. "You don't have to be sorry… you don't *ever* have to be sorry," I whispered.

***

Ethan McLachlan

I was excited to be visiting my hometown while I had a break from school. My daughter, Emily, was sitting on my shoulders, occasionally accidently smacking me in the face with her blue and white pom poms as she cheered on the North River Eagles.

Morgan was perched on my dad's shoulders, all of us watching Christian in his role as high school football coach one Friday night.

The stands were full of people showing their town pride and school spirit by wearing blue and white. The cheerleaders cheered; the signs were all hung; the old scoreboard shone bright in the night sky.

Brandon wore his royal blue North River Football sweatshirt as he played at our feet next to the fence, running back and forth between us and Jennifer, who was sitting in a chair close by feeding him his Friday night favorite of nachos and cheese every time he bounced over.

I held on to my daughter's tiny feet as I faintly heard her jabbering with her cousin.

"Mo," she called him lovingly as they held hands, forcing their pawpaw and I to stand a little closer than we would have otherwise.

"Emmy!" Morgan practically sang out to her as the crowd cheered, and when he laughed my dad and I caught glances. Dad's eyes immediately left mine and returned to the field, but I knew he had heard it too. In that little boy's innocent chuckle, we heard a laugh so familiar that I could hear it clearly above the noise of the game and the fans in the stands.

"Go, Daddy!" Morgan screamed excitedly, pointing out at the field toward my brother. He clapped his hands, and, then, so did Emily.

"Yeah, there's Daddy," my father said, rubbing my nephew's little leg with a tenderness that Morgan couldn't yet understand.

I smiled up at my nephew, who had moved on to playfully poking at his cousin after she had stolen his camouflage, Alabama baseball cap that she was now wearing herself.

All the while, there was a constant parade, for lack of a better word, of friends and acquaintances who came by to speak to my father and comment on just how much Brandon and Morgan looked like Brant. Each member of our small community, as we were accustomed to, told stories of days gone by. At first, all the stories were a little hard to digest, but, over time, I had come to really appreciate them. Only by moving away had I learned that it wasn't the norm to grow up in a town where everybody had a personal story about the local high school quarterback. I could tell that the stories were still too raw for my dad, despite the years that had passed since Brant's murder, but I had learned to really value them. In fact, I started writing many of them down. Because, while you think you won't ever forget, you do forget things, and sometimes it is just really nice to be able to go back and remember.

Morgan swung his legs atop my dad's shoulders, his curly, blond hair blowing in the slight breeze as he grinned, so blissfully unaware that the father he would never know was once cast as the leading man, playing Friday night hero for an entire town, right on that very field.

***

Jennifer McLachlan

Christian and I started going to a therapist once a week. I wasn't a big fan of the idea at first because when I think about therapy, I automatically attach a certain stigma to it, and I certainly wasn't ready to put myself in that category.

However, Christian said that he thought that we should go and talk about our problems with a neutral third party because he didn't want our marriage to fall apart because we were too embarrassed to deal with our very real issues. He was right, and I agreed to attend; we were essentially in marriage counseling, though it seemed most of the time to feel more like grief counseling.

One of the first exercises that our therapist had us do was to write about the most memorable or meaningful moments of our lives. The first night, as I sat down to write, I hated the assignment. I had no desire to sit with a pen and paper and recount the horror of the night that had changed my world forever. I had already tearfully told that story to the police and all of my family. I had relived it in vivid detail, so that Brant's oldest brother could write the story of Brant's life, and I had no desire to go there again.

My head was flooded with images of blood, and, though thoughts filled my head as I tried to write about the gunshot that had shattered life as I knew it, nothing seemed to be going on the paper.

I willed thoughts of that night away, abandoned the assignment, planned immediately to cancel future sessions with the therapist, went into the kitchen, took a gallon of chocolate ice cream from the freezer, grabbed a spoon from the drawer and crawled up on the counter wearing one of Brant's old t-shirts.

As I sat there, I thought of other moments… meaningful moments that I could have used to complete my assignment. I thought about writing about Brant's spectacular marriage proposal, or my magical wedding day with him. But, then I imagined my therapist looking at me and then at my poor husband and then back at me, only to tell me that she had never had a woman show up to marriage counseling with one husband only to complete her most memorable moments assignment with stories of another.

I shook the fog from my head and decided all over again that the assignment just wasn't for me. I was sure that Christian would write something incredibly sweet and moving and leave me looking like the weakest link anyway.

Out of nowhere, my mind drifted back to a Saturday in October... Alabama was playing Tennessee, and I was sitting next to Brant on the couch as he and Christian argued over a past game in that rivalry and whether it had been played in Tuscaloosa or at Legion Field in Birmingham. I personally could not have cared less *where* the game was played, since they both seemed to agree that we had won the game.

In typical Brant and Christian fashion, before Google and smart phones put answers at our fingertips within seconds, they argued well into the second quarter before their dad found the answer in the form of an old newspaper article in his study. It turned out that Brant was right; football stats and trivia were his thing; I'm not sure why anybody ever doubted him, but he proceeded to gloat until halftime, at which point he and Christian went outside to play what was supposed to be a little game of Two-Hand Touch, but, given the competitive tension that had been mounting between them for an entire half of football, quickly turned into a game of back yard... *tackle... personal fowl... late hit... shoving match... somebody please throw a flag... oh my, I think they're really fighting!*

"Seriously, you two?" their daddy scoffed as he and Jordan pulled them apart.

Ethan and Tommy cackled like it was the funniest thing they had ever seen. I admit that it *was* pretty funny, given that during their *fight* neither one of them had actually hit the other. They pushed and shoved and tackled and taunted... but nobody had actually tried to hurt anybody.

I remember standing on the back porch rolling my eyes as Brant continued to kick in Christian's general direction despite his lack of anything resembling an actual effort to break free of his daddy's grasp.

"Oh, you want some of this? You better be glad he's holding me back!" Brant taunted, even after his daddy had popped him across the back of the head and let him go.

"Nobody is holding you back, moron!" Christian threw his hands up. "Bring it!"

"Give it up, guys!" Tommy laughed. "I smell food! How's the grillin' comin', Coach?"

"It'd be going a little better if I hadn't had to stop what I was doin' to break up those two knuckleheads," Coach McLachlan quipped.

I don't really know why that particular memory popped into my head at that moment, but it did make me smile!

Brant and Christian shoved playfully all the way back inside the house. Brant grinned as he put his arm around me and reached for a cookie his mama had just taken out of the oven. "Don't make me hurt you in front of Rocky!" he chided his brother with a grin.

Suddenly, my mind flashed back to my assignment. I thought about the night that Brant died. It wasn't the fear, the hopelessness or the horror of watching Brant's life slip away that grabbed me then. It was a nickname that stood out instead… and, suddenly, I was ready to write about a deeply meaningful moment in my life.

When Brant was shot, it was sudden, and there was no time for a speech in which he told me of the depths of his love for me, yet the last word I ever heard him say will remain with me forever because, in a single word, he was able to say that he loved me and that he'd always be with me, in a way that only I could understand. As his life slipped away, he cried out my name, a nickname that he'd given me, a nickname that, to this day, only he and I know the meaning of. There was a lifetime of history in that single name, and there are days now when I would give anything just to hear him call me *Rocky* once again.

CHAPTER FIVE

Jennifer McLachlan

I was about two inches taller than Brant the day we walked hand-in-hand into kindergarten on our first day of school. We were so proud to be such big kids with backpacks and lunchboxes and supplies like crayons, scissors and paste that we had picked out ourselves at the Walmart in Meridian.

Brant was so pumped about the football on his new thermos, and I thought my crayons were extra special because they had a sharpener right in the back of the box. I could not wait to show those things off to all my new classmates.

We sat down at our little kindergarten table, waved goodbye to our mamas and started our very first day of school. I was so excited to see the coloring sheet my teacher had left in front of me. I dug out my crayons and began work on my masterpiece.

That's when little Lizzy Highsmith reached into my prized box of Crayolas, took out my violet blue and snapped it right in half.

I fought back tears; I was done with kindergarten and ready to go back home. I was so proud of that box of oddly named crayons, and, at the store, I had promised my mama that I would take excellent care of them if she just bought the more expensive box… the one with the sharpener right in the back. Now, there I was; I had been in kindergarten for fewer than twenty minutes, and violet blue had already met a violent and unnecessary end in the grubby, little hands of one Lizzy Highsmith.

Brant knew I was about to cry, and he quickly dug through his box of crayons. "Here, you can have mine," he said, instantly restoring my faith in kindergarteners. Then, he looked right past me at Lizzy Highsmith and, though she was probably twice his size, he squinted his blue eyes at her and said matter-of-factly, "if you were a boy, I'd punch your lights out!"

From our first day of kindergarten to the day we graduated high school, Brant was there making every day better than it would have been otherwise. From king of the playground to four-time State Championship winning, starting quarterback and every day in between, Brant was there lighting up my day with his smile, filling my heart with his infectious spirit, amazing me with his talent and proving time and time again that nothing would ever change the fact that our lives were meant to be irreversibly intertwined.

One defining moment in every girl's life centers around her first kiss. Brant and I shared countless kisses throughout our childhood, but I don't count any of those as my first *real* kiss. From the time that we were toddlers, a smack on the lips was more common than a high-five between the two of us. Later, during the years when we were twelve, thirteen and fourteen, we shared many kisses, all very innocent and experimental. Neither one of us really knew what we were doing, but we tutored each other on occasion.

The first time that we decided that we needed to try a French kiss is a day that I'll never forget. Looking back on it now, it is hilarious to imagine two thirteen-year-old kids caught in an awkward moment between childhood and adolescence. It was nothing for us to share a bed as kids, and, in our first year as teenagers, we still thought nothing of it. Our mamas and daddies weren't worried about it yet; in their eyes Brant and I were still innocent products of overprotective parents, but the reality was, Brant and I were getting older, and things were changing.

We were wrestling playfully in my living room floor one day like we always did, and I didn't think anything of sprawling across Brant and pinning him to the floor, holding him down for the count, but, when I looked into his eyes, I saw a different person than I had ever seen before.

He was still my best friend, still the boy that I knew everything about, still the guy I had a childhood notion of marrying when I grew up, but there was something else. That was the day that I noticed how blue his eyes were, and that he was cuter than any other boy I had ever seen.

He put his hands on my waist and lifted me off of him, and, instead of fighting back, I was impressed by how strong he was.

Stunned, I crawled over to the couch, and he followed me. I told him that I thought we should kiss like *real* girlfriends and boyfriends do. That phrase alone makes me laugh now, but he knew exactly what I was talking about.

"Tongue?" he exclaimed.

"You wanna?" I shrugged.

"Fine," he agreed. "Just don't tell the guys!"

I smiled, fondly remembering my tree house, my baby dolls, my tea set and my six-year-old boyfriend feeding our Cabbage Patch Kid a bottle of milk that disappeared as he tilted it. Even at thirteen, though most of my classmates had outgrown it, I still liked to play with dolls sometimes, and, though nobody knew about it, I could still convince Brant to play along when we were alone. "Remember how you told me not to tell the kids at school about how we play dolls?" I retorted. "I never have, so I'm not gonna start telling secrets now!"

"That sort of information is a linebacker's dream!" Brant exclaimed. "I can't have that sort of thing getting out!"

I pointed out that I wasn't the only one who was supposed to be keeping secrets. "You promised me in the fifth grade that you wouldn't tell the guys about that weird video they made all us girls watch during P.E..!"

"I wish *you* hadn't told *me* about that video!" Brant scoffed.

"You told me about the video *you* had to watch," I retorted.

"Mine wasn't *as* gross," he insisted.

"Well, it still ain't happened," I said proudly.

"You're still not a woman yet," he chastised me, clearly remembering every detail I had told him about the video that had traumatized my fifth grade self.

"I don't even want to be," I grumbled.

"I don't blame you," he said confidently.

"Don't tell anybody, okay?" I sighed.

"Cross my heart," Brant nodded as he crossed his chest with his finger.

"French kissing can be another secret," I told him.

"Okay," he agreed as casually as if we had just decided on what snack to buy out of the vending machine.

"Pinkie promise," I smiled as I held my finger out to Brant.

Brant and I were growing up, and it was an adventure that we were determined to pioneer together. The first time that he stuck his tongue in my mouth, both of us burst out laughing. I told him that he must be doing it all wrong, but he insisted that he had seen it in the movies and knew what he was doing. Take two was a little better at best, and I about decided that if *that* was romance, I would rather wrestle. The third time was not a charm because when Brant started running his hands up my back as he kissed me, I lost all track of what I was supposed to be doing with my mouth.

"What do you think you're doing?" I snapped at him.

"What am I supposed to do with my hands?" he asked seriously.

I thought about it for a second; it was a good question. "Maybe you should put them in my hair?" I suggested with a shrug. "They do that sometimes on TV on the soap operas."

For Brant and me, the art of the French kiss was no different than his football or my dancing; it took dedication and practice. It didn't take us long before we found a method that worked for us. It was undeniably mechanical at first, but with each passing day we discovered the passion that would fuel every kiss that we shared from that point on.

The kiss that I consider my first was actually far from it, but my sixteenth birthday was the first time I feel like Brant and I stopped being kids experimenting with things we didn't understand and shared a kiss between a young man and a young woman for the very first time.

It was spontaneous and magical. My party was over, and Brant and I were alone on my parents' back porch. He looked into my eyes, and I knew he was about to kiss me. There was no awkwardness, no giggling, just two kids very much in love.

Two nights later, I repaid the favor on his sixteenth birthday, and, though I didn't think it was possible, I think that kiss was even better than the first.

I don't know when he figured it out or how… but, oh boy, did he figure it out!

Now, at some point between our experimental kisses at age thirteen and our first real kiss at my sweet sixteen, came the WWF Royal Rumble in the middle of the McLachlans' living room floor that turned into The Ultimate Warrior and Hacksaw Jim Duggan's worst nightmare.

We were all there… me, Brant, Christian, Ethan and Tommy.

Christian was playing Macho Man Randy Savage. He was shirtless and wearing sunglasses and a glorious, gold, plastic crown.

Christian had always been a huge Macho Man fan! Brant could do a perfect impression of the Macho Man's Slim Jim endorsement, and Christian would ask him to do it repeatedly. Christian had a giant Wrestling Buddy, which was essentially a huge, stuffed, Randy Savage doll that Christian slept with… or maybe he didn't, but I always like to say that he did! He was always trying to convince me to take on the role of his wife and play the sexy Miss Elizabeth to his Macho Man! "Not in a million years," my fifteen-year-old self told my future husband that day.

Ethan had on the classic red and yellow Hulk Hogan tear-away tank with a silly bandana.

Tommy had on a blue, button-down shirt and an old, toy, sheriff's badge that said "Ethan" on it. He carried a black billystick and proclaimed himself the Big Boss Man.

I was wearing short denim shorts and a white tank top; my only prop was a foam two-by-four that Christian had bought at the Mississippi Gulf Coast Coliseum the night we went to a live taping of SummerSlam.

Brant experimented with a shockingly accurate impersonation of Ravishing Rick Rude before jumping off the sofa, otherwise known as the top rope, and landing on top of Tommy while proclaiming himself Superfly Jimmy Snuka. Then he danced around for a minute, flapping his arms like a bird and calling himself KoKo B. Ware before lamenting the fact that he didn't have a readily available blue and yellow macaw. He tossed around toy money in Million Dollar Man Ted DiBiase fashion for a minute and toyed with the idea of playing Mr. Perfect, before declaring that choice too obvious.

Then Brant finally made his decision. He took his shirt off, slapped some paint left over from Halloween onto his face, tied some neon strings around his biceps and called himself The Ultimate Warrior.

I had been outside every day that summer; I had a nice tan and legs that had been to a lot of cheerleading camps and dance classes that year. I circled the living room in my denim cut-offs, imitating my Hacksaw character to the fullest, though I doubt the real Hacksaw Jim Duggan ever took a double take at The Ultimate Warrior. He was just so cute; he hadn't cut his hair all summer, and his blond curls were wild and messy.

Tommy threw me over his shoulder and toted me around the living room as I insisted that he put me down, reminding him that Hacksaw and Big Boss Man were allies. Not that day I guess; he marched me around playfully smacking me with that stupid baton as he rambled on and on about his beloved Cobb County, Georgia.

When Tommy finally put me down, Hulk Hogan and The Ultimate Warrior were engaged in a classic test of strength in the middle of the ring. We'll never know how it ended, because before one could take down the other, Macho Man flew off the top rope, landing between them.

We all began fighting Royal Rumble style. I swung my two-by-four with vigor, hitting Christian across the back and Tommy right in the face. I was laughing so hard at his fake injury antics that I didn't even see Brant swoop in and body slam me to the mat. On my back on the floor, I fought back with a pretend right hook, followed by a pretty well-executed, fake left hook. Brant fell to the side, allowing me enough time to jump up and prepare my famous, three-point stance clothesline.

We all stopped long enough to show a little concern when Tommy picked Christian up and the piledriver that followed didn't exactly go as innocently as planned.

"Tommy, you could have broken his neck!" Ethan exclaimed.

"Christian, you okay?" Brant asked seriously as he knelt next to his brother.

"Sorry, dude!" Tommy gulped.

"I'm fine!" Christian groaned, rubbing his shoulder. To prove to us that he was indeed okay, he yanked Brant to the ground with a laugh. That was our cue; we all piled on, and the match continued.

We were all laughing and having a grand ole time, but our fun was about to come to a screeching halt… at least for two of us.

Brant had me pinned to the mat. I was flat on my back, and he had pinned my legs to the ground, so that my knees were right up next to my ears. I was giggling furiously, barely able to breathe. I could feel my denim shorts rise a little higher than intended, but I was stuck in such a silly position that all I could do was laugh and grin up at him. Brant winked at me playfully, and I knew he was about to let me up, but, right before he did, he smacked me hard, right on my bottom. And *that* was the exact moment that my daddy and his daddy decided to stroll around the corner.

They both froze for a moment, and the looks on both their faces made my heart race. I was embarrassed; I was humiliated, and, as, Coach McLachlan marched over and snatched his son to his feet, a little fearful for my boyfriend.

"*Ooooooh*," came the less than encouraging sound effects from my friends. "Y'all are in big trouble!"

"Get up, little lady," my daddy stared down at me.

Coach McLachlan backed Brant into his office.

I shot to my feet and straightened my clothes, pulling my denim cut-offs down, making them as long as I possibly could.

"Daddy, it wasn't anything like it must have looked like," I pled my case, trying my best to listen to what was going on in the next room and freaking out a little bit that I didn't hear my big-mouthed boyfriend saying a single word.

Next thing I knew, my mama and Brant's mama were standing in the room, looking around curiously, wondering why Macho Man, Big Boss Man and Hulk Hogan were huddled up, straining to look back and forth between my daddy and me and Coach's office.

"What's going on?" Mama asked.

"Where's Brant?" his mama asked, directing her question to the boys.

"I'll tell you both what's going on," Daddy said, shaking his head.

"Brant's in the study with Dad," Christian added with a shy nod. "You… umm… you may want to check on him." He pointed toward the study as his eyes moved to the floor.

"When David and I walked in," Daddy continued, his eyes now piercing my mother, "your daughter in her little Daisy Dukes that you let her out of the house in had her ankles pinned behind her head and a certain shirtless, war-painted, fifteen-year-old boy was playing bongos on her little booty!"

"Oh my word," I sighed as I buried my face in my hands. I didn't think I would ever be able to look at any of those people ever again.

"Jenny?" Mama gasped.

Brant's mama nodded her head slowly. "Oh yeah, I better go check on him *indeed*," she nodded as she scurried off. "David? David?" she called as she hurried toward the study. Christian, Ethan and Tommy moved quickly in a pack behind her. "Stay!" she barked at them.

The next thing I knew, Brant and I were sitting silently in his daddy's office before a panel consisting of all four of our parents and Bro. Waterford, our pastor. Horrified, humiliated, embarrassed, traumatized and, at the time, ungrateful for the wealth of advice coming my way, I sat next to Brant, who was still awkwardly dressed as The Ultimate Warrior, being lectured on the birds and the bees.

CHAPTER SIX

The Thunder Rolls

Jennifer McLachlan

Christian and I had just kissed the boys goodnight and put them to bed. Fresh and clean after their baths and adorable in their matching pajamas, they were absolutely my reason for living. The way they kissed and hugged Christian and me as we put them down to bed was what kept me going. That night, I gathered them both in my arms and snuggled them close, soaking in their sweet scent. As was our nightly routine, Christian picked a book from their bookshelf and read to all three of us. The boys loved to hear him read their stories. They listened quietly or giggled when he gave all the characters funny voices. Brandon and Morgan thought that Christian hung the moon, and I absolutely treasured every moment of it.

I held Christian's hand as we walked down the hall to our own room. "I saw a game in a magazine that I think we should try," I told him. "It's sort of a *get to know you* questionnaire for couples before they get married."

"We are *already* married, and I've known you all my life," Christian laughed as I crawled into bed and opened my bedside drawer, pulling out a magazine with one page folded down. Seeing that I wasn't giving up, he gamely added, "but hit me with the first question."

"How many people have you ever kissed?" I read aloud.

"Only one that matters," he replied with a corny smile.

"Oh please," I scoffed, "I can name like six to eight just off the top of my head, buddy."

"You remember names?" he joked. "I don't even remember names!"

"Oh I know names," I grinned. "Would you like me to refresh your memory about the time..."

"We'll go with eight then," Christian smirked, interrupting me before I could bring up the story we both knew all too well. "And what about you, Miss Jenny?"

"Two," I shrugged.

"I already knew that," he nodded.

"The next question asks about sexual partners, and we can actually skip it," I shook my head.

"Your answer is two. My answer is one," Christian answered breezily. "Next question?"

"Maybe this wasn't such a brilliant idea," I swallowed as I read the next question to myself. "It's asking about where you lost your virginity and if you are still in touch with your partner."

"Well, I would assume that you remember the when, where, why and how of my answer," Christian scoffed.

"Of course," I blushed.

"And *you*?" he followed up.

I rolled my eyes, scolding myself for failing to read the questions *before* I decided we needed to take some stupid quiz in a magazine. "I'd have to say... with Brant... in our honeymoon suite in..."

"I'd have to go ahead and call you a liar," Christian interrupted with an evil chuckle. His mouth opened wide and his eyes big and accusatory, he pointed at me.

"What?" I laughed.

"Oh, I think you know," he poked at me until my cheeks turned a bright red. "Let's not rewrite history here, Jen. I'm recalling something about you still in your wedding dress after the ceremony at..."

"Oh my word... he told you that?" I gasped as I slapped Christian's arm.

Christian was cracking up as I covered my red face with my hands.

I slapped Christian again, then my eyes turned skyward as I wagged a scolding finger in the air but couldn't find the words to say.

"Come here you wild and crazy girl," Christian laughed as he pulled me close.

I fell easily into his arms that night. "I love you," I said.

"I love you too," he said with sweet sincerity.

When he kissed me that night, I felt alive again. I looked into his eyes, and I saw so much hope and love in my future. Christian began undressing me, and, for the first time in a very long time, I didn't feel like anything was holding me back.

Then came a little tap on the door and the soft, pitiful cry of, "Mommy? Daddy?"

"Brandon, Mommy's coming," I called as I hurried to throw my clothes back on.

I rushed to the door and scooped up my crying son. "I got scared, Mommy," he cried as he clung to me. "I got scared, Daddy," he repeated as he lunged for Christian.

My heart ached at the sound of his sobs. I watched Christian holding our son, tenderly stroking his back and whispering comforting words of assurance. I walked to the boys' room to make sure that Morgan was still asleep. I peeked in and saw him sleeping peacefully.

"I had a bad dream, Mommy," Brandon sobbed when I walked back into my room. He was already sitting up in Christian's lap, sipping water from his sippy cup and looking more content, but there was something about those words from that child that tugged at my heart in a raw and painful way.

"What kind of dream, baby?" I asked him against my better judgment.

"Bang! Bang!" he cried.

I'm pretty sure my heart stopped for a moment, and I know by Christian's reaction that my face went as ghost white as I felt like it did.

Christian got up with Brandon in his arms and helped me sit down on the bed. "It's okay," he assured me. "Brandon, what are you talking about? Are you talking about the loud cars that blew up on the TV at Uncle Tommy's house today?" Christian asked him.

Brandon nodded. "I don't like that movie," he shook his head, his eyelids already getting droopy again. He cried for a moment or two as Christian rocked back and forth with him, and, in no time, he was asleep on Christian's shoulder.

Christian tip-toed into our room after tucking Brandon back in bed, only to find me balled up in the center of our king-sized bed, crying my eyes out. He picked me up and held me tight, snuggling me close to his chest, just as he had just done for our son.

He didn't say a word; he didn't try to argue with me that I was wrong, and that Brandon's nightmare had not been a traumatic flashback to an event that only he and I witnessed.

I tried to stop crying, but the flood of emotions just poured forth. As I held on to Christian, so grateful for him and thankful for his unending patience, I began my one-sided dialogue with Brant. "It scares me so badly that he could have memories, even subconsciously, of what happened to you. I still hear his screams from that night, Brant. I see it all; I remember it all, and I don't want him to know that fear."

Christian kissed the top of my head. "Brandon's fine, Jen," he assured me. "He saw some action thriller on the TV when I stopped by Tommy's house with them this afternoon. That's all there was to it. It was my fault; I should have turned the TV off, but we were there for such a short time that I didn't even realize they were seeing it."

I nodded, praying that he was right.

Christian hugged me and rolled me gently onto my pillow. "Let me get you a tissue," he said sweetly as he got out of our bed and walked around to my nightstand. He took a tissue from the box on the table and handed it to me. The magazine we had been reading from earlier was still on top of my nightstand, and he opened the top drawer to place it back inside. He glanced into my drawer and then over at me, then back in the drawer. I had no idea what he was doing at first, then, suddenly, realization sank in, and I let out a defeated sigh.

"What is this?" he asked disbelievingly, holding up my packet of birth control pills.

"Christian," I said, sitting up slowly, searching for the right words to say, knowing that no matter what I said or how angry I got at him, I was the one in the wrong here.

He opened his mouth to say something but stared at me with a stunned expression instead, when the words just wouldn't come.

"I can explain," I said, only to have something to say.

"Me too," he nodded. "I'm a fool, and you lied to me…"

"No," I cried, my heart breaking, realizing that no matter what I said, what explanation I gave, or how genuine my reasoning, I *had* lied to him.

My mind flashed back to a session with our therapist. Christian had opened up to me about his desire to have a child… particularly a son. Though circumstance had given him two, little boys he loved unconditionally and was wholeheartedly devoted to, he still longed to have a child that was biologically his.

I remember being blown away that I wasn't the only one in my circle of friends who had named my babies long before they arrived. Christian confessed to me that he often thought about having a son and that if he ever did, he would love to call him *Connor*. I had no idea that guys even thought like that, and I was so touched in that moment that I hoped that one day God would bless me with the opportunity to be baby Connor's mommy.

But things had been difficult for Christian and me. I continued to struggle daily with depression. I was plagued with feelings of guilt for loving Christian. I felt inadequate at providing him the relationship and the marriage that he deserved.

I knew that I loved Christian, but I often wondered if I loved him enough to let him go. I wanted a life for him that I didn't feel capable of giving him, and I knew that if we had a biological child together that my relationship with Christian, and, selfishly, with Brant, would change. Like most things in those days, that scared me. Morgan was my miracle baby… the perfect gift of a perfect love… and I wanted to hold on to that sacred bond that I shared only with Brant for just a little longer.

"You lied to me," Christian said, tossing the little packet of pills at me with so much hurt in his eyes. "A lie of omission is still a lie, Jennifer. I'm you husband… this decision impacts both of us."

"I know," I sighed, not even sure how to defend myself.

"You really don't have anything to say do you?" Christian asked angrily. "Why don't you just look me in the eyes and say, 'Christian, I don't want to have your baby because then you and I would share as many biological children as Brant and I… and I have to make sure he always keeps the upper hand.' Just say it… just be honest."

"No," I cried.

"Yes," he shrugged. "Admit that you don't want another baby because you don't want anybody in this nosey, little town to get the impression that you're happy."

"How dare you!" I shot back at him. "I put on my happy face to go out and face the world. I try to be strong and put on a smile for everybody. You know that! Besides, I don't care what anybody in this town thinks! I don't owe them anything! And for the record, Morgan doesn't owe them anything either. I am so sick of them putting such high expectations on my son! Just because he looks just like Brant doesn't mean he'll grow up to be the next great quarterback around here! It's like just because he's Brant's child everybody expects him to grow up living in the shadow of someone else's dream. He's a baby, Christian."

"Just not the baby we're talking about right now," Christian said sternly.

"Did it ever occur to you that I was trying to protect you?" I sighed.

"Protect me?" Christian scoffed. "I don't believe that for a second, Jen. This is the deal I signed up for. I think you're trying to protect yourself. I think you're still scared of moving on."

"Maybe I am," I nodded.

"Then maybe that's our answer," Christian shrugged. "Maybe that's what you should have told me instead of hiding birth control pills in your drawer."

"I'm sorry," I sighed, but it came out whiney, even to my ears.

"Me too," Christian frowned. He walked to his closet, pulled on a t-shirt and slid on some shoes.

"Where are you going?" I begged him.

He shrugged. "I'm your husband, your partner, your friend, your sounding board, your provider, your protector, the arms you dance in and the arms you cry in. Sometimes I'm your doormat; sometimes I'm your punching bag; sometimes I'm your babysitter; sometimes I'm your safety net, and sometimes, when I get lucky, I'm even your man between the sheets for a night, but the one thing I never ever am… is the guy you want to be with."

I should have jumped up and stopped him. I should have begged him to stay. I should have done something for the man who had done so much for me. But, at his words, shields went up and my defenses were on high.

My need to defend Brant was misguided, but, for me, it was as automatic as breathing.

"We shared *everything*," Christian shrugged as he slid his wallet into his pocket, "our toys, a bedroom, a wardrobe, homework, a love of football, even a birthday… but I won't share his wife."

"Don't do this," I begged. "Don't make me choose." I crossed my arms so defensively, determined to prove to Christian and myself that I was strong. "You won't like my choice."

"It's been four years, Jennifer," he pursed his lips, and I watched as a single tear rolled down his cheek. "You made your choice a long time ago." He slid off his wedding ring and placed it in my palm, forcing my fingers closed around it. "I'll never *ever* walk away from Brandon and Morgan," he said sternly, "but I think it's about time we admit that this isn't working, and no matter how much I love you… it never will."

"It never gets any easier for me," I cried, feeling like I was falling apart. "If anything it gets harder. He's gone longer… I miss him more. I think that when people say it gets easier with time that what they really mean is you just become a better actress. I go through my day being what other people want me to be, what other people need me to be."

"All I needed was for you to tell me the truth," Christian said pointedly. "*I've* never lied to you; *I've* never hurt you…"

"Stop right there," I demanded, my defenses on high alert. "You don't get to do that! You don't get to compare yourself at 23 to Brant at 17… that's not fair… he made a mistake… do you think that makes you a better man in my eyes? He never got that chance, Christian… he never got to be 23… he never got to be an adult who made adult decisions, so your snide remarks don't impress me… they don't earn you any points with me… they make me sick."

Christian held up his hands in surrender. "I wasn't even talking about that, Jen," he said slowly. "I can't win here…"

Christian walked out of our house that night, and, when I heard the door close and then this truck pulling away, I felt like a failure.

"What have I done, Brant?" I cried, burying my face in my hands. "How could I let him just walk out of here? Are you mad at me right now for hurting him, or can you feel my love when I fight for what we had no matter the cost?"

I reached for a picture frame that was sitting on my dresser and sank down to the floor. I stared at that little girl I envied… four years old, wearing a purple party hat and grinning over the lit candles of a My Little Pony birthday cake, without a care in the world. Brant and Christian were on either side of me, both of them with their arms around my shoulders, all our faces radiating the pure joy of a beautiful friendship.

In Brant I saw my own children, their sweet eyes identical to his, that mischievous smirk I so commonly found on Morgan's face. Then I glanced over at three-year-old Christian just two days shy of his fourth birthday, and my heart pounded. My hand moved to my flat stomach, where I lovingly cradled the biggest lie I had told all night.

I pulled from underneath my nightshirt the wedding ring that I wore on a chain around my neck. I brought it to my lips and kissed that symbol of never ending love. Then I looked down at Christian's wedding ring in my hand and knew that I had made the biggest mistake of my life. I hugged the picture frame close to my chest, clinging desperately to the two men I loved.

***

Tommy Jackson

Christian lay on the weight bench in my garage looking up at me with angry intensity as he bench pressed rep after rep.

I stood there spotting him, still unclear why we were in my garage at nearly midnight getting in a workout that felt more like a meltdown.

Christian was sweaty when he stood from the weight bench and moved directly into free weights.

"Will you please stop and tell me what is going on?" I begged.

"My wife loves my brother," Christian popped off breathlessly, "but, that's not news to anybody is it?"

"Christian," I sighed. "What happened tonight, man? Why are you *here* instead of home with Jen and the boys?"

Christian stopped lifting weights for a moment. "Do you remember our infamous camping trip?" he asked me.

"Of course," I smiled. "Our camping trips pretty much defined my youth. Which trip? The time Ethan set the grass ablaze trying to start a fire? Or the time Brant discovered all the snacks I had shoved into my backpack despite the fact that our tent was in your back yard? Or the time we stayed up all night telling ghost stories with that flashlight, and you got so scared that…"

"Remember camping at Lake Windy Pines?" Christian said, pointing me toward the exact memory he had been referring to.

"Sure," I shrugged, "four sixteen-year-old boys sitting around a campfire wondering when exactly it was that our resident tomboy had turned into the natural beauty who stood before us…yeah, of course, I remember."

Christian sat down on the weight bench again. "And why do you think it was that you nor Ethan nor I had any interest in going after that girl? She was perfect. Spunky. Funny. Beautiful without a lick of effort. Cutest little freckles on her nose. Pretty hair. Sweetest eyes. Cutest little figure. Football-loving. God-fearing. She was like a little country queen illuminated by the firelight that night."

"That was a long time ago," I sighed. "We were smart enough to realize that she only had eyes for one of us then."

Christian lay back on the weight bench and jerked the barbell back into action. "And you and Ethan were smart enough to keep realizing it," he huffed as he brought the weights down to his chest and back up again.

"Chris, how many of those are you gonna do, bro?" I sighed.

He ignored me and continued to power through yet another round of bench presses.

I didn't say anything for a long time. I spotted him as he began to struggle under the weight of the barbell and, maybe even more so, the weight of his own thoughts.

"Do you know that sometimes I hate him so badly that I can barely stand it?" he panted with an angry laugh. "Do you know that I hate that I look like him, sound like him… because none of those things are lost on the woman I love?"

"Christian, you don't hate Brant," I urged, trying to force the barbell back onto its rack.

"I look like him, but I don't look enough like him, you know?" he said, standing up from the weight bench and moving immediately to the punching bag hanging in the corner. He slid on my boxing gloves. "Not enough blond in my hair, no dimples in my grin, not enough arrogance in my voice or confidence in my laugh. Hard to hear, right? Turns out I'm not the saintly do-gooder that everyone assumes I am… I'm no hero… I'm just a jerk… a jealous monster who blames all of the problems in his life on his poor, dead brother."

"You're not a monster… and you're not a saint," I shook my head. "You're just human. You're allowed to have feelings… you're allowed to hurt… just like everybody else."

"I didn't mean to say that I hated him," Christian sighed.

"Right now you're talking to me, Chris," I shook my head. "I know how much you love him, so just get it off your chest, man. Say whatever you need to say; pound it out. I got your back, bro."

"I love him, and I miss him like crazy," Christian screamed as he annihilated my punching bag. He breathed heavily. "It's not his fault that I'm not good enough for his wife."

"It's not like that," I assured him. "I see how she looks at you, Chris. You're her rock."

"And what about me?" Christian screamed. "Who's supposed to be my rock? I'm not okay here, people; I miss my brother!"

"I know you do," I nodded, feeling on the verge of tears for my friend.

"I put my all into this relationship day in and day out," Christian attacked the punching bag again. "I give Jennifer and the boys everything I can," he panted. "I do all that I know to do, and I just ask myself what it is that I'm missing, what it is that I'm doing wrong… and you and I both know that, at the end of the day, the answer to that question is simple… I'm just not Brantley."

"But she loves you!" I exclaimed.

"Yeah, I know… and she loves you, and she loves Ethan!" He flopped himself into a nearby folding chair and added, "I mean she may call me her husband, but you and Ethan aren't sleeping with her and neither am I."

"What?" I asked confused. "Are you seriously sleeping on the couch these days?"

"Oh, no," Christian shook his head sarcastically, "she loves to cuddle."

"But I thought you said y'all had talked about having another baby?" I recalled.

"We did!" Christian huffed. "We talked about it, and then, apparently, she ran right out and got herself on birth control pills!"

"What?" I sighed.

"She lied to me," Christian exhaled.

"Jen?" I shook my head disbelievingly.

Christian moved back to the weight bench and began lifting again. He had done ten reps or so before he spoke again. "This is certainly not about sex," he confessed. "It's just that even when I do sleep with her, I think she feels like she's cheating on him. In fact, I'm sure she feels that way because, believe it or not, I still feel guilty sometimes myself."

He increased the speed of his reps until he was pouring sweat and panting loudly. "He's dead, Tommy!" he screamed. "He's dead… he's never coming back… and he still gets the girl!" With adrenaline-filled rage, Christian hurled the entire barbell crashing into the garage floor and struggled to catch his breath.

Christian was a rock, but the guy who had been so strong for everybody else had finally reached his breaking point. "I miss my brother," he panted. Tears poured. "I miss him so bad," he cried. "I just want things to go back to the way they were when Brant was here. I miss him, Tommy. I miss him." Then he fell back onto his back on the bench and began to weep loudly.

I knelt down and put my hand on his shoulder, tears dripping from my own eyes as I witnessed my friend's pain. "I know, buddy," I said, squeezing his shoulder tightly.

When he was all cried out and panting, Christian sat up, and I handed him a water bottle. "Thanks," he said softly.

"Do you need to stay here tonight?" I asked him.

"No," he answered after a moment. "I think that I just need to know that you and Ethan won't hate me if I decide I have to walk away."

"You're serious, aren't you?" I gulped.

"Yeah, I'm serious…" He squirted water on his face. "I don't think I can do it any more."

"You know that whatever you decide, I have your back," I nodded, "because I know that you've always got Jen's."

Christian nodded and stuck out his hand. I grabbed it, and pulled him into a hug. "Thanks, man," he sighed.

"Hey, Christian?" I asked as I walked him to his truck. "Are you going to be okay? Where are you going?"

"I think I'm gonna go home and check on Jen," he said as he got into his truck. "Maybe I should just sleep on it and try to figure everything out in the morning."

***

Christian McLachlan

It was past midnight when I left Tommy's house, and I instantly knew who else would be awake. I dialed Ethan's number as I drove, and I knew how he would answer the phone when he saw the caller ID.

"Happy Birthday, bro," came his voice after only one ring.

"Happy Birthday to you too," I smiled. "I miss ya, man."

"I know you didn't call at midnight to wish me a happy birthday, since we'd both just assume no one acknowledge this day at all," my brother said knowingly.

"I'm not really sure *why* I called," I replied honestly. "I was just driving around… thinking about maybe stopping by the cemetery." I pulled my truck off the side of the road and put it in park. "I guess I just need some advice."

"I'll do my best," Ethan replied.

"I walked out of my house earlier after handing Jennifer my wedding ring," I exhaled, glad to have put it out there.

"What happened?" Ethan asked, and I appreciated the lack of judgment in his tone.

"Brant happened," I quipped, not wanting to get into a deeper explanation. Ethan didn't say anything back, silently chiding me to say more. "I've given her my whole heart…"

"Yes, and you can do that because you have your whole heart to give her," he said instantly understanding what I was saying, though I hadn't said much at all.

"I'm listening," I swallowed.

"She's giving you all she has left, Christian," Ethan sighed. "Part of her heart died, but she's given the rest of it to you."

"That's a really nice way of looking at it," I replied after a moment. "So, you're saying, if we're both giving all we have to give… we're both giving equally."

"Christian," Ethan said bluntly, "you'll never ever be what he was to her… but you're not supposed to be! He was her first friend, her first love, her first kiss, her first time… there is no competing with that!"

I sighed. "Yeah, that's a lot to compete with."

"There's a flipside," Ethan promised. "He wasn't what you're gonna be to her. You and Jen are writing your own story, creating a history of your own. The guy who stood by her on the hardest day of her life… that was you. The man whose hand she held as she gave birth to her first child… that was you. You may not have taken her to prom or given her your class ring, but you guys already have some pretty unbelievable moments under your belt."

"You mean… *Brant's* funeral and *Brant's* baby?" I scoffed. "Those are really the only examples you can come up with? The possessive in both of those sums up my entire problem! Why didn't you just wish me a Happy Brant's Birthday while you were at it?"

"Are you done yet?" Ethan grumbled.

"Don't ever go into psychiatry, man… I'm like hanging by a thread here!" I exclaimed. Then, rolling my eyes, I said, "sorry, in case you can't tell, I'm just not in the best place tonight."

"The Jennifer that he loved was not the Jennifer you're in love with," Ethan said, mostly ignoring me. "That's all I'm saying. The two relationships are completely separate, and they need to stay that way."

"She lied to me," I exhaled.

"And you handed her your wedding ring?" Ethan replied.

"Can you just maybe *pretend* to be on Team Christian for a minute here?" I huffed.

"Christian… been there, done that, wearing the t-shirt right now!" Ethan retorted.

I smiled.

"Look," Ethan said, "from the outside looking in, you and Jen have done a really inspiring job dealing with a lot of growing pains in your relationship. I think you are both incredible people who love each other very much. I don't know what she lied to you about, and I'm not sure I even need to know because I know you, and, if handing her your wedding ring had been your final decision, you wouldn't be sitting in your truck on the side of the road wanting me to tell you to fight for your marriage."

I cranked my truck. "Would you think less of me if I did walk away?"

"No," Ethan replied confidently. "But I know you, and I know you won't."

"Ethan, will you pray with me?" I asked my brother.

"Of course," he replied.

For twenty solid minutes, Ethan and I prayed together… for me, for Jen, for our unique situation and for our marriage.

"Who's supposed to be *my* rock?" I had cried out earlier in the midst of my grief. Where was I supposed to find the strength to be strong for Jen in moments when my own pain drained me of my strength, and I felt I had nothing to give?

As Ethan and I poured our hearts out in prayer, I was thankful to have a father who taught his sons to pray, grateful to have a brother who answered his phone in the middle of the night and, ultimately, reminded that I already knew the answer to my own question.

"The LORD is my rock, my fortress and my savior; my God is my rock, in whom I find protection. He is my shield, the power that saves me and my place of safety."

***

David McLachlan

Phone calls in the middle of the night are every parent's worse nightmare, but once you've lost a child, the sound of that phone ringing at an hour when nobody is calling to tell you anything good, will stop your heart.

I picked up my phone, and I heard the sheriff's voice. "Christian wrecked his truck."

"No, no, no, no," was all I could say as I hurried out of bed, fearing the words he would say next and knowing all too well how final they could be.

"He hit his head, and they've taken him to the hospital, but he's alright," the sheriff said.

My heart started beating again. "What about Jennifer and the boys?" I asked.

"He was alone," the sheriff replied, "but I just called her to let her know."

I thanked the sheriff for calling and immediately dialed my daughter-in-law.

Jennifer and I arrived at the hospital with the boys both asleep in their car seats. With Brandon asleep in my arms and Morgan asleep in hers, we rushed inside. My wife was waiting for us. She gently took Morgan into her arms. "He's right through there, and he's fine," she pointed, urging Jennifer to go ahead. "We've got the boys; take all the time you need."

***

Jennifer McLachlan

It was strange, but the moment I saw Christian sitting there on that table in the ER, his head bandaged right above his left eye, I felt the strength of a woman who was slowly emerging from the fog that accompanies losing the one you love.

I rushed into Christian's arms so thankful he was alive and that the words I said to him earlier that night would not be the last words I ever said to him. I put my hand on his cheek, ever so gently caressing his bruises.

"I'm so sorry, Jen," he said, stroking my hair and staring into my eyes. Tears rolled down his face, and, while I could tell that he was in pain, there was no doubt in my mind that those tears came straight from the heart.

"You don't need to apologize for anything. That's my line tonight," I said softly. "I'm so sorry that I wasn't honest with you." I reached into my pocket, took out his wedding ring and slipped it back on his finger. "I promise that I will never give you another reason to take this off again."

Christian adjusted the ring on his finger. "Jen, I'm so sorry for…"

I shook my head to stop him, so grateful for a husband who kept trying to apologize to me despite the fact that, in my heart, I knew his actions had been completely justified. "Stop," I whispered. "I'm the one who messed up… I'm the one who needs *you* to forgive *me*."

"Well, you know what they say," Christian offered me a little smile. "If you can't handle someone at their worst, do you really deserve them at their best? I'm a blessed guy to have a woman like you in my life. I never should have walked out that door. I was coming back, Jen, I swear… I was coming back home to you and our boys."

My eyes welled with tears again. "I'm not proud of the way I acted tonight, Christian," I said confidently. "Nobody deserves to be made to feel like second best… especially not a man as amazing as you." I kissed the ring on my husband's hand. "Just promise me you'll never take this off again."

"I promise," Christian nodded. He took my hands and held them both in his. "I have to tell you something," his voice cracked.

"Me first," I shook my head. "There's something you have to know."

"You need to hear this," Christian swallowed, and tears ran down his cheeks.

Before this conversation went any farther, I needed to tell my husband that I was pregnant, but I could tell something was really weighing on him.

"I saw him, Jen," Christian whispered, choking on his tears. "He was there."

At those words, my bottom lip trembled. I stepped into Christian's arms and rested my head against his chest as I lovingly rubbed his back with my hand. Slowly, I lifted my teary eyes to meet his.

"I fell asleep while I was driving," he cried. "I don't know how it happened; my dad taught me better than that. I was too tired to be behind the wheel, but I was just trying to make it home, and there wasn't very far to go. It happened so fast, and it was just for a second."

I was crying, somehow already knowing that this story was about to change my life.

"When I woke up, I had veered off the road, and I was about to hit a tree," Christian told me through his tears. "It all happened in a flash. I didn't even have time to react. I didn't touch the steering wheel, Jen… I didn't touch it. My truck just jerked to the right all of a sudden and went into some bushes."

I was blubbering by then, and I couldn't even look at Christian.

"I guess I hit my head; I could feel myself blacking out," he said softly, "but I saw him... plain as day... no bright lights... no halo...no white robe... he was just sitting there right next to me like this happened four or five years ago. He smiled at me, Jen."

I wiped my eyes, smiling through my tears. "Christian," I exhaled, "I think that's exactly what I needed to hear."

"I reached for him," Christian gulped, "and he *winked* at me... that same famous wink he used give everyone... and just like that... he was gone."

I laughed and cried at the same time, and so did Christian. We knew that wink well. Leave it to Brant to be such a charming guardian angel. I held Christian tightly, thanking God for the guardian angel He had sent my husband that night.

"I think I'm free to go," Christian said, easing himself down from the table. "Let's go home."

"Yeah," I smiled up at him adoringly, awaiting his reaction, "let's get out of here and take our three babies home."

Christian stared at me. "Are you joking?" His mouth fell open.

"No," I shook my head. "Christian, I'm pregnant; we're gonna have a baby!"

"But..." he still looked stunned.

"I forgot to take it," I admitted with a shrug. "I was too scared to take it after that, so I just stopped."

"You're really pregnant?" His smile widened with each passing second.

"I just found out," I grinned at him.

Christian picked me up and spun me around. I giggled and cried at once. His excitement meant the world to me.

Suddenly, Christian put his hand against the wall and lowered me back to my feet. "They probably don't recommend that you spin your pregnant wife around when you're still bleeding from the head, huh?"

I couldn't help but laugh out loud as I helped him sit down in a nearby chair. "Dizzy?" I asked.

"Little bit," Christian sighed, but he couldn't stop grinning.

I bent my knees, so that we were face-to-face. "I know you don't really like to celebrate your birthday," I smiled, "but, Happy Birthday, Christian."

Christian kissed my lips, then my stomach. "Best birthday present *ever*!"

Christian and I walked hand-in-hand toward his mother's office, only to find our two sons, bright-eyed and bushy-tailed as they bounced around in their pajamas.

Christian's mom picked up a small birthday cake with a single candle from off of her desk. "Happy Birthday, Christian!"

"Happy Birthday, Daddy!" Brandon jumped up and down.

"Cake!" Morgan shrieked as I lifted him into my arms.

"I don't know that you're gonna get any birthday cake at 3 a.m., buddy," I chuckled.

Christian took Morgan from me. "Why not? You only live once!" he smiled with a shrug.

"Please?" Morgan begged.

"Okay, you can have some of Daddy's birthday cake," I grinned at my son.

Before Christian had a chance, Morgan leaned toward the cake and blew some rather moist air, spitting the candle right out.

"And just like that, you can have the whole thing," Christian joked as he ruffled Morgan's curly, blond hair.

With two, little boys sugared up but tuckered out, Christian, the kids and I started our journey home.

As my babies and my birthday boy slept, I stared out my windshield at a star-filled sky, and I couldn't help but think that it looked like quite a spectacular birthday party! "Happy Birthday, Cowboy," I whispered, blowing a kiss toward the sky.

I watched as one star shone brighter than the rest.

"Thank you for everything. Thank you for our life together," I said. "Thank you for these boys. And thank you for being there for your brother today."

I glanced over at my sleeping husband, a little bruised up but just fine.

"He's the answer to my prayers," I smiled, as I continued driving down the road memorized by the starry night sky. "Thank you for showing me that he's the answer to your prayers for me too."

That's what that whole night felt like. I finally felt like, beyond a shadow of a doubt… I had Brant's permission… his blessing.

I moved my hand to my stomach and glanced into my rearview mirror at my two, sleeping babies. "I have to move on with my life," I said with more confidence than I had felt in a very long time. "But that never ever means goodbye. There are no goodbyes in a love like ours."

I blew one final kiss out my windshield. "I'll see you again one day."

CHAPTER SEVEN

Christian McLachlan

Growing up, my brothers and I were obsessed with football, Teenage Mutant Ninja Turtles, PEZ dispensers and the World Wrestling Federation.

Those cleverly named heroes in a half shell known as Michelangelo, Leonardo, Raphael and Donatello were constants throughout our childhood.

We wore the costumes; we owned the action figures; we watched the cartoons; we ate out of Ninja Turtles themed cereal bowls and had lots of pizza parties where the word COWABUNGA was used frequently.

Much to Ethan's chagrin, Brant preferred the blue mask belonging Leonardo but insisted on using the dual nunchucks which were the weapons of choice of Michelangelo. As often happened in our house, Brant usually got his way because it was easier just to let him play Michelangelo in a blue mask than argue with him over his distaste of the color orange or his complete monopoly of the nunchucks.

I will never forget the time my dad got us all ringside seats to WrestleMania. Brant, the master of The Sharpshooter, was sitting on my dad's shoulders when The Hart Foundation made their way to the ring for the nights' main event, tag-team bout.

Bret "The Hitman" Hart, in his signature, mirrored sunglasses, was Brant's all-time favorite wrestler. And, on that night, "The Excellence of Execution" as he was known, stood in front of us in his pink and black tights and leather jacket, close enough to touch and, as was his tradition, took off his glasses to give to a kid in the crowd. They were sweaty; they were gross, and, when he slipped them on my grinning brother's face, he couldn't have chosen a kid who was more pumped.

Brant threw his arm in the air, repeatedly pumping his fist and leading a victory chant as he rallied the already rowdy crowd. He won hearts among that crowd that night and even managed to score a post-match high-five from Bret Hart's tag-team partner, Jim "The Anvil" Neidhart.

We loved Halloween at the McLachlan house. One year Jennifer's mom made Brant and Jen these amazing yellow and black, splatter painted costumes, so they could go Trick-or-Treating as The Rockers, WWF superstars Marty Jannetty and Shawn Michaels!

Shawn Michaels was Jennifer's all-time favorite wrestler. I will never forget when her beloved Rockers broke-up on national television, their feud coming to an end with Shawn Michaels super kicking his former partner before throwing him through a glass window at Brutus "The Barber" Beefcake's barbershop.

That's when Shawn Michaels began his transformation from a good guy to a bad guy known as "The Heartbreak Kid"… and yet, bad guy or not, he was still always Jen's favorite!

My favorite Halloween costume ever was the year that Ethan, Brant and I dressed up as Demolition. The two-man WWF tag-team known as Demolition had recently added a third member, and the McLachlan triplets were not about to miss our opportunity to go all-out for Halloween as Ax, Smash and Crush. Jordan spent forever perfecting our face paint for those costumes, and the pictures from that Halloween made every minute of it worth it!

I remember Christmas mornings, all of us in matching red, plaid pajamas, waiting eagerly at the top of the stairs for Dad to get the video camera turned on. Every year he would capture our excited faces as we raced down the stairs to see what Santa had brought us.

I remember balling up wrapping paper and having epic wrapping paper wars long after our presents were opened.

I remember how Jordan would pull my brothers and me around the living room in empty boxes, and Dad would always quip that Santa could have saved himself and the elves a lot of time and money if he had just dropped some extra boxes by our house when he was done with everybody else.

I remember jumping up and down on giant sheets of bubble wrap with Ethan and Brant and truly wondering if life could get any better than that!

I remember *three*, red tricycles one Christmas, *three* blue and yellow Pogo Balls another, *three* Big Wheels, *three* dump trucks, *three* Army tanks, *three* inflatable punching bags, *three* Etch A Sketches, *three* Huffy bicycles, *three* Magna Doodles, *three* light-up, He-Man Powerswords, *three* Nerf guns, *three* Game Boys and *three* Super Soakers.

Football, wrestling, hunting, fishing, camping, video games... whatever it was that we were doing, my brothers and I did it together.

There is a piece of Ethan and me that is forever missing. We're triplets after all... by definition we are defined in terms of three, and I have definitely found that to be true. Ethan said once that I was the strength, he was the brains, and Brant was the heart. I don't really think there is a better way to put it than that. Brant was pure heart, pure passion... confident in what he wanted, driven to achieve it and always accomplished it with a natural charisma that defined his larger than life personality.

Don't get me wrong; he was stubborn, bullheaded, good-naturedly arrogant and comically egocentric.

For example, one time when I was seventeen, I was going hunting with my dad and my brothers one afternoon, and the pants I had planned on wearing were nowhere to be found. I searched my closet, the laundry... they weren't there. I ran down the stairs from my bedroom calling, "Mom, I can't find my new camouflage pants! Have you seen them?"

My mother was sitting at the kitchen table with Jennifer, drinking her coffee and reading the newspaper as she nonchalantly wagged her finger toward the front door. "They just walked out of here," she said casually.

I didn't need any further explanation, and I rushed outside with Jen following behind me, sensing an argument.

Ethan and Tommy were loading the toolbox of my dad's truck, and Brant stood in the truck bed, wearing, despite the cold temperature, nothing but my new camo pants.

I hastily made my way over the tailgate and gave the thieving rascal a shove. The grin on his smug, little face told me that he was fully expecting it.

Mom walked outside as Brant and I argued over his notion that pants I paid for myself and hung in our shared, bedroom closet somehow fell under some "finders keepers, losers weepers" clause.

I shoved him; he shoved me and so on and so forth.

"David, are you going to do something about that?" Mom asked with very little actual concern in her tone.

"If I didn't need 'em *both* for Friday night's game," Dad grumbled, "I'd pull up my lawn chair, get you to pop me a bag of popcorn and watch these two goobers do whatever it is that they do!"

"Break it up, and let's get the truck loaded!" Jordan scolded us as Brant jumped over the side of the truck and I followed, landing on him hard enough that we both fell to the ground.

"You're getting *your* pants dirty!" Brant hollered with such humorous inflection that I couldn't help but laugh.

"Are either of you going to help us load this truck?" Ethan called.

I put Brant in a headlock and demanded that he go change into clothes that actually belonged to him.

Brant, always a scrappy pest, managed to get to his feet, and he was laughing as he elbowed me hard in the stomach.

"Dude!" I exclaimed, doubled over as he caught me in the ribs. "Seriously, Brant! That hurt!" I popped him in the shoulder.

"Enough, you two," our dad rolled his eyes as he single handedly separated us. "Get in the truck now if you're going with me." Then he looked at us, apparently for the very first time, and his forehead wrinkled, and his lip curled. "Brantley, where's your shirt? Christian, son… pants?"

"He has my pants!" I replied matter-of-factly, shoving my brother again.

We stood there, me in my boxers, wearing a camouflage hoodie, and Brant wearing my camouflage pants, two fools making up one complete outfit.

Jen stepped in with a chuckle. "Do you mind if I grab a goodbye hug from him before y'all get back to scratching and clawing each other or whatever it is you do?" she directed at me.

"Go for it," I shrugged sarcastically. "You'll probably have better luck getting him out those pants than I would anyway," I joked.

She did not appreciate my humor in the least. Jennifer spun around and pointed a sassy finger at me. "You best watch who you're talking to," she warned me.

We all laughed.

"Hope you get a big buck, babe!" Jen said, kissing Brant's lips.

She turned back to me and looked me up and down. "Hope you... *find some pants*?" she shrugged.

"Yeah," I sighed. "Love ya!"

"Love you too," she laughed as she walked toward her SUV.

Jordan slung a pair of camouflage pants at me, as the camouflage hoodie he had thrown at Brant landed on top of his head. I flung my arm around my brother's neck as we walked toward the truck. "You, I hate," I grinned at Brant.

His only response was to plant a long, obnoxious kiss right on my cheek.

When I remember my brother, I remember someone so full of life and so in love with living.

We laughed all the time, and, though we competed, pushed, shoved and got on each other's nerves, I had his back, and he had mine.

There was a loyalty there that nothing could shake. We always had each other's back; if he got into a fight, I had his back one hundred percent, even if I pulled him aside afterwards and said, "look, man, I think you were probably in the wrong there".

That was the nature of our relationship... no questions asked... loyal companions, best friends, brothers, teammates.

Sometimes Jordan joked that I was the good angel on Brant's shoulder, and Brant was always the little devil on mine. We laugh about that because I probably would have gotten in less trouble without Brant there to encourage me, but I also wouldn't have nearly the memories that I do.

My brother was a dreamer, a competitor, a fighter and his spirit inspired me more than he will ever know.

Editing books, particularly biographical and autobiographical ones, has always struck me as an odd process. I heard an industry bigwig say once that editors are responsible for cutting out things that aren't crucial in advancing the story the book is focused on telling.

In layman's terms, I take that to mean that editors get to decide which parts are important enough to keep and which parts aren't. Who's to say which parts of a person's story are worth deleting though?

I sat at my brother Jordan's kitchen table after Brant died, having to relive a story that I would have just assumed forgotten, only to learn upon the publication of my brother's story that the chapter had been cut out.

I think Brant and I probably tussled in the womb, hitting and kicking in our shared space. That never changed. He shoved; I shoved back.

He kicked me as I walked past his bed because he knew I was going for the last piece of pizza in the box sitting on the desk in our room.

I knocked the controller out of his hands when he started beating me at Nintendo.

Not to mention the countless WWF moves we practiced on each other. From Jake the Snake's famous "DDT" to the Undertaker's classic "Tombstone", we emulated all the moves, and they were just as fake as the ones we watched our favorite wrestlers performing on TV.

We pushed and shoved, played tackle football with no pads or helmets and hosted our own Survivor Series and Royal Rumbles in the living room floor… but, never in my life had I ever actually hit my brother out of anger… not until that day.

It wasn't my proudest moment.

A new girl had moved to our little town, and all the guys at my school were intrigued by this girl who wore lots of makeup and big jewelry and seemed more mature, worldlier and shapelier than any other girl who had ever wandered into our neck of the woods.

I'll admit that I took my fair share of glances at her. Her outward beauty didn't go unnoticed by any of us guys at North River High School that year.

But, just as with most girls I had ever met, she was instantly attracted to Brant. It started out as innocent flirtation on his part; we were all a little mesmerized by her mere presence, so none of us really blamed him for enjoying the attention.

Long story short… things happened… mistakes were made… and Jennifer's heart got broken the day that Brant had to tell her the unfathomable news that he had gotten some girl pregnant.

Jen was devastated, heartbroken and incredibly angry at and disappointed in my brother. I did my best to be a good friend to her during that time because I knew how badly she needed to know that her friends and my family were sticking by her through that very difficult situation.

Jennifer and I were just talking about it recently, in fact… the punch that bothers me more now than it ever did then.

"I can't stop thinking about it," I confessed to her.

"I don't like to think about it," she shook her head. "You hit him so hard..."

"I know, Jen," I sighed, "but he hurt you, and it was just unreal to me that he, of all people, could do something like that."

"I know that you were defending me," Jennifer nodded, "and I appreciated it, but to see the two of you fighting... I could deal with anything, but not that."

"I was angry, Jen," I said honestly. "You deserved better than what he did to you, and I wanted him to know that."

"He already knew," Jennifer said confidently.

"I know he did," I admitted. "And if I could take it back, I would." Suddenly, I had a vision of my brother standing there; his eyes flashing at me as he slowly moved a handful of blood away from his nose.

"Well, it's not like he didn't hit you back," Jennifer sighed.

I snickered. "We're guys, Jen. A guy punches you, and you swing back..."

"I told him afterwards that he had no right to hit you back," Jennifer confessed.

A surprised chuckle escaped my lips. "Jenny, don't you think I gave him that right when I bloodied his nose?"

"The whole thing still bothers me," Jennifer admitted. "You hit him; he hit you... I was screaming because I couldn't believe the two of you were *actually* fighting."

"Brant and I were over the fight before the bruises healed," I promised her.

"Still, I hated it," Jennifer declared, crossing her arms. Then she grinned. "I still remember having to ride home in the truck with your dad. You and I were sitting in the front seat with your dad, and Brant was all laid out in the back. You kept whining about your hand..."

I laughed and rolled my eyes. "He shot up off that back seat and was all like, 'I'm so sorry if my *face* hurt your stupid *fist*, Christian!'"

Recalling that story, Jennifer and I sat there on our couch and literally laughed until we cried.

The ability to make us all smile, regardless of the circumstances... it was a gift that Brant possessed so effortlessly.

Ethan, Brant and I, while being far from identical, looked enough alike that often times strangers would ask if we were triplets. Actually, the funny thing is that many times, with Ethan standing right next to us, people would ask if Brant and I were twins!

Brant's light blond hair and mop of loose curls set him apart from my more toned down, dirty blond look, but, in the face, there was no denying that we were brothers.

When we were dressed in identical jerseys, which was often the case, be it our high school game jerseys or the Alabama jerseys we wore on Saturdays, people tended to notice it more.

A typical game day experience at the University of Alabama usually went something like this. Brant was walking around outside the stadium wearing a crimson jersey, a crimson hat and khaki, cargo shorts with a crimson and white pom pom sticking out of his back pocket. Why was I walking several feet behind him, you might ask? That would be because my brother never met a stranger!

He was the type of guy who would watch the end of one game on a big screen at somebody's tailgate party and, five minutes later, score a hamburger from somebody else's tailgate party.

He could high-five half a capacity crowd prior to kickoff, and, by the time the game started, he was hugging strangers like he was their best friend.

I'm not gonna lie; he was fun to watch, but, as I noted, I looked enough like him that people knew we were together if I got close enough.

I mean, who goes to a college football game with their high ticket prices and outrageous food prices and ends up getting so much free junk by the end of the day that he probably made money in the exchange? That was my brother for you! He'd disappear for ten minutes while you were standing in the quad, and, all of a sudden, he'd show back up with a free, foot long, chili cheese dog!

I would get so worked up that I was a nervous wreck when watching close games.

Brant, on the other hand, just wanted on that field to rectify the situation. In his mind, he had a strategy; he had a plan, and if they would only do it his way… better yet, if they would just let him come out of the stands and take the ball… all would be well.

Brant had such a special eye for the game; he was an unbelievable quarterback, the most dynamic football player I have ever witnessed, but it was his ability to read the field, see things before they even happened, and instantly react that made him one of the best in the game.

My brother didn't live long enough to show the world just how smart and talented he truly was. His name is never going to come up in the conversation of greatest of all-time because he simply never had the opportunity to show exactly what he was made of on the biggest stage at the highest level.

Brant may have always had his eye on the pros, but my brother was a huge Alabama football fan. He may have worn his famous #13 on Friday nights, but he wore Alabama's famous #12 every Saturday.

Jordan says all the time that Brant's up there playing for Bear Bryant now, and, somehow, in my mind's eye I can totally picture it. I can see that legendary man in his houndstooth hat leaned up against the goalpost watching Brant play with all the greats who have left this Earth.

Dallas Cowboys coaching legend Tom Landry is there too, of course, in his equally famous fedora, his arms crossed in his signature fashion as he watches my brother, his biggest fan, do exactly what he does best.

I can see Brant, the stands full of angels, as he puts on a Heavenly display. Even in Heaven, amongst a host of angels, I imagine him standing out from the crowd.

Former Alabama quarterback, Jay Barker, told us once: "If you want to go to Heaven and walk the streets of gold, you've gotta know the password... Roll Tide Roll!"

Of course, he was only joking, and, so am I, but it makes me smile because I can *totally* imagine Brant McLachlan saying those exact words the night that amazing, funny kid met Jesus.

CHAPTER EIGHT

If Tomorrow Never Comes

Ben Smith

You hear all these stories about small towns, Southern football and kids growing up dreaming about following in the footsteps of their heroes. I can only speak for Cummins, Mississippi, but in the town that I've grown up in, our football team is most definitely the focal point of our town.

When I was a little kid, every boy in my class at school wanted to grow up to be Brant McLachlan, and the girls in my class at school all had a crush on him. They envied how close I was with him.

They may have gotten a high-five from him at the school pep rally and watched him play on Friday nights, but they all knew that I was the guy eating dinner with him after the game.

They may have seen him at church on Sundays; he may have even occasionally given them a piggyback ride from Sunday School into Big Church, but I was the one who was gonna get to ride home in his truck every week, sitting in between him and my sister.

My big sister had no idea how much she did for my elementary school social status by falling in love with the captain of our varsity team.

Brant always tried to teach me how to play football when I was a little kid; I love the game, and I play now, but I'm not that good. I play quarterback though because I want to be like Brant.

Coach McLachlan, as I had to adjust to calling Christian in front of the guys, is a really special coach, though I'm not sure he even knows it. Christian teaches us fundamentals of the game, and he makes us work hard, but my favorite part about him being my football coach is when he tells stories about Brant and Ethan and Tommy and things that happened on and off the field while those guys were winning four straight State Championships and building a North River Football dynasty.

On Friday nights, the kids I went to school with would watch in awe as Brant played rock star under those Friday night lights. His showmanship on the field easily elevated him to hero status in our town; the guy might as well have been wearing tights and a cape when he ran out onto the field because he was a superhero in my eyes. But, off the field, when Brant wasn't dancing around with the football making his opponents look silly, he was my real life hero.

Some people dream of finding a love like they read about in fairytales, but, as for me, I grew up in Cummins, Mississippi, so, when people ask me what I'm looking for in a soulmate, I smile and tell them I want a love like Brant and Jennifer had. Maybe if you're not from around here, you look at me like I'm crazy and try to recall which classic love story told the magical tale of protagonists by those names, but people in my hometown know exactly who I'm talking about.

When you saw Brant McLachlan, you saw a cocky, football star destined for glory; when you met Brant, he won your heart with his Southern charm, but, it wasn't until you witnessed the way that Brant looked at my sister that you truly knew what he was all about.

***

Jennifer McLachlan

Christian and I were helping clean out the garage at his parents' house one afternoon when I uncovered a dusty, black shoe box buried beneath old tackle boxes, crates of tools and other junk that had accumulated over the years.

"No way…" I gasped.

"What is that?" Christian laughed as I dug the box out of the spot that had been its hiding place for well over a decade.

"Christian, are you serious?" My mouth fell open. "You don't remember this box?"

Christian shrugged.

"Let me refresh your memory!" I exclaimed. "Me, you, Brant, Ethan and Tommy..."

"Yeah," Christian nodded sarcastically, "that pretty much covers every memory I've ever made in my life. Thanks for the hint, Jen!"

"I wasn't finished," I rolled my eyes, but I couldn't contain my excitement. "We were ten years old. It was New Year's Day..."

Christian grinned as he practically snatched the box from me. We both coughed playfully as he knocked dirt and dust off our old time capsule. "We wrote down where we wanted to be in the next ten years," he laughed. "We promised we wouldn't open this box until we turned twenty."

I swallowed, suddenly feeling overwhelmed. "Then on New Year's Day when we were twenty, we were supposed to all come together and see if our dreams had come true."

Christian put his arm around me. "We can throw it away... I'll toss it in the fire out back if you want me to."

"No," I shook my head after taking a second to consider his offer. I smiled. "I want to read them."

Christian grabbed my hand, and we ran with the box, down the driveway toward the giant oak tree in his parents' front yard... the very spot where, as ten-year-old kids, we had written these secret letters to our future selves.

"Do you remember what you wrote?" I giggled.

"No," he shook his head with a grin. He helped me and my growing, pregnant belly sit down in the grass. "Do you remember what *you* wrote?"

"Yeah, actually I do," I nodded slowly.

Christian opened the box and took out the first piece of paper. "How was Ethan's penmanship this good when we were ten?" he scoffed as he unfolded Ethan's letter.

"Dear Future Ethan,

I hope that you like all your college classes. You have a few more years before you become a doctor like Mom, but I'm sure you are on your way and making very good grades. One day when you get married, I hope that your wife is a lot like Jen.

Sincerely,
Ethan, age 10"

"Aww, Ethan, how sweet," I smiled as I reached for the next sheet of folded paper and recognized my own handwriting.

"When I grow up, I want to marry Brantley and have two babies named Morgan and Brandon. I hope that they look like Brant and have curly blond hair just like he does. I want to be a wife and a mom and love my family.

Jen Smith"

"I think your ten-year-old self pretty much nailed it," Christian smiled.

I puckered my lips, and he kissed me.

Christian opened his note to his future self and eyed his deplorable penmanship.

"My name is Christian McLachlan and when I am twenty years old I hope that I am a football player at Alabama. One day I want to be the coach at that school and make lots of money. It would be cool if me and my brothers all played pro ball one day but I want to be a coach like my dad too. I also might get married if I find a good girlfriend but only if she is as cute and nice and likes football like Jen."

I started laughing, and I couldn't stop. Christian made a face at me, and I covered my face with my hands. "*If I find a good girlfriend*," I repeated, my eyes watering as I laughed.

"Maybe one day I'll find one who doesn't laugh at me and my lonely ten-year-old love life." Christian stuck his tongue out at me.

I stuck my tongue out at him in return, and suddenly we *were* ten years old again.

"Oh my word!" I exclaimed as I unfolded Tommy's letter, read it to myself and practically flung it at Christian. "We were *ten*... shouldn't Tommy have known how to spell better than this by then?"

Christian rolled his eyes. "We all know that Tommy was essentially illiterate until high school."

> *"Tommy of the footure,*
>
> *I hope that you are tall and skiny and good looking. I hope that you didn't have to go to coledge and that Brant lets you live in his manchon with him and Jen.*
>
> *The End"*

"Well, he *is* tall," I shrugged.

"And he certainly didn't go to college," Christian added quickly.

"Oh, Tommy..." I sighed.

"Way to set those goals high, buddy!" Christian laughed.

Christian and I laughed until both our eyes fell on the shoebox where we had stored our dreams for all those years, and there was only one letter left inside.

"Do you want to read it, or do you want me to?" Christian asked as he took Brant's letter from the box. "Or should we just let it be?"

I swallowed hard, knowing that tears were inevitable. "You read it to me," I nodded hesitantly. "I want to know what he said. Where did Brant want to be when he was twenty?"

Christian cleared his throat, fully prepared for his voice to crack.

> *"My name is Brant McLachlan and when I'm twenty years old I hope that everybody already knows that!!!!!!"*

With one line, he had Christian and me laughing and crying.

> *"I want to win more Super Bowl rings than any quarterback in the history of the NFL. I want to play for the Cowboys and be famous. Most of all I want to marry Rocky so that she can live with me in Dallas because if she ain't there I don't really think I would like it that much.*
>
> *Brant #13"*

Christian was teary-eyed as he handed me Brant's letter, and I carefully folded it and hugged it close to my heart.

"You guys," I sighed. "That was so sweet; y'all bless my heart so much, every one of you. As ten-year-old boys… every day before that… and every day since."

Christian carefully packed the letters back into the shoebox, tucked our little treasure chest under his arm and helped me to my feet.

"You guys do so much for me," I smiled at my husband, "and I can't even tell y'all how much it means to me."

We stood there under that big oak tree, where we had played a million games of *Tag* and *Hide and Seek*, and Christian kissed my lips with such tender, loving appreciation that it made me weak in the knees. He stared at me with genuine affection and said, with a soft sincerity that made my heart swell, "maybe we're all just trying to repay you for the lifetime you've spent making us all better men."

CHAPTER NINE

Jennifer McLachlan

You didn't have to know Brant for very long to learn that he loved to sing or that he was a fan of country music. He knew every song Garth Brooks ever recorded; he didn't care where he was or who was listening, he would burst into song in that perfect pitch of his and leave onlookers amazed that one guy could be so talented.

We used to close the door to my childhood bedroom and pretend it was a recording studio. After Brant died, my many cassette tape recordings of Brant singing his favorite songs became some of my most treasured possessions.

> *It's Your Song, Rodeo, The Dance, In Lonesome Dove, Cowboys and Angels, If Tomorrow Never Comes, Against the Grain, It's Midnight Cinderella, Beaches of Cheyenne, Burning Bridges, That Summer, Shameless* ... I have them all and so many more.

Brant was a born performer, completely at home on any stage. He loved to put on a show; being an entertainer was as natural to him as breathing. It was when Brant wasn't performing for anyone, however, that I was truly touched by his talent.

He sang in a way that was heartfelt and often remarkable; he had the voice of an angel and the vocal control to really dig into a song. When he sang to me, that tough quarterback was my Cowboy.

That cheap, little tape recorder I used to record priceless moments when Brant was singing to me, and only me, has been a Godsend since I lost Brant.

Brant was an amazing singer who easily could have made a career out of music; I could carry a tune, but that was about it; yet, he loved for me to sing with him. It never seemed to bother him that I was pretty pitchy, and I simply couldn't hit the notes that he could; when he looked into my eyes, I had no doubt that I was his favorite duet partner.

The last tape I ever made was of Brant and me singing Tim McGraw and Faith Hill's duet *It's Your Love.* I wasn't about to be signed to a record label any time soon for my part in the rendition, in fact, it was pretty rough, but Brant's voice on that song grips my heart every time I hear it.

He had such a gift, such a beautiful instrument, and the sweet, sexy sound of his singing voice remains the soundtrack of my life.

After Brant passed away, an older gentleman from our church, a deacon I had known all my life, gave me a video tape he had recorded of Brant singing at a church picnic.

Christian took it and had it put on a DVD for us.

That single recording, filmed by a not always steady-handed old man, has been my saving grace.

Brant stood on that tiny, wooden stage with a microphone in hand; he was wearing blue jeans and a light blue, long sleeve, button-down shirt with his shirttail hanging out and the bill of his Dallas Cowboys cap tucked into his back pocket. He looked as handsome as ever as he grinned out at the crowd before closing his eyes and delivering the most moving, heartfelt, acoustic version of Michael English's arrangement of *In Christ Alone* that I have ever heard.

"Christ alone will I glory
Though I could pride myself
In battles won
For I've been blessed beyond measure
And by His strength alone, I overcome

Oh, I could stop and count successes
Like diamonds in my hands
But those trophies could not equal
To the grace by which I stand
In Christ alone
I place my trust
And find my glory
In the power of the cross
In every victory
Let it be said of me
My source of strength
My source of hope
Is Christ alone
Christ alone will I glory
For only by His grace
I am redeemed
And only His tender mercy
Could reach beyond my weakness
To my need
Now I seek no greater honor
Than just to know Him more
And to count my gains but losses
To the glory of my Lord
In Christ alone
I place my trust
And find my glory
In the power of the cross
In every victory
Let it be said of me
My source of strength
My source of hope
Is Christ alone
I place my trust
And find my glory
In the power of the cross
In every victory

Let it be said of me
My source of strength
My source of hope
Is Christ alone
My source of strength
My source of hope
Is Christ alone"

To hear Brant's voice so clear, so beautiful, so powerful and so sincere as he lifted up the name of his Lord and Savior brings tears to my eyes every single time. I can't even tell you the number of times I have played that DVD and how much comfort it has provided me over the years.

I always considered myself to be a girl who was mature in her faith, but it took losing Brant to make me realize that I needed to spend more time growing my faith because I knew enough to know that, in the dark days following my husband's murder, I could never get through it if I didn't believe wholeheartedly that "*my source of strength, my source of hope, is Christ alone.*"

I, by no means, claim that I no longer struggle. My emotions seem all too content to be in constant conflict.

I realize that I am not the first wife to lose her husband or the first person to lose their best friend, but most people have a time that they can go back to, a time before they befriended that person, a time before they met their future life partner. They can remember back and use that time as a starting point to find themselves again. They can gather all the memories of the time that they spent with the person they loved, take stock of the impact that person had on their life and readjust to life without that person. Don't get me wrong, I certainly don't suggest, in any way, that it makes things easier, but it seems sensible, like a starting point, a balance. I didn't have that. I didn't have a time that I could go back to and reclaim my identity. Brant had *always* been there, and now he wasn't.

I struggle daily, but, more often than not, I claim victory over my pain. And, as Brant's gorgeous voice so frequently reminds me, when I claim that victory, I give all the glory to my Lord.

If I believed that I would *never* see Brant again, I don't know that anything would be enough to pull me through. But, my God promises me that His children are guaranteed eternal life with Him in Heaven.

I go to the cemetery quite often and sit next to that headstone with Brant's name on it, placing flowers, decorating it for holidays and leaving mementos of The University of Alabama's recent string of National Championships, but I know that Brant isn't there. He's not in some box in the ground; he's singing for Jesus in a place so beautiful my mind can't even comprehend it.

Christian told me once, as we sat together in the church cemetery, that he found it strange that when a person dies there are two dates etched into their headstone, but all that really mattered was that dash in between.

Brant lived every moment to the fullest during his short time on Earth. We had a whole lifetime together, and one day when it's my time and God calls me home, I will see Brant again, and, through the love, mercy, grace and promise of our Lord and Savior, we will get the *forever* that we always dreamed of.

Thinking about the precious day that Brant stood before his Savior reminds me of another song that Brant used to sing. I hear his voice belting out: *"Surrounded by Your glory, what will my heart feel? Will I dance for You, Jesus? Or in awe of You be still? Will I stand in Your presence, or to my knees will I fall? Will I sing Hallelujah? Will I be able to speak at all? I can only imagine."* I can only imagine what that moment must have been like, but when I think about it, I actually smile… because I have a really good hunch that Jesus did too.

Christian and I struggled with defining our relationship for a very long time, but we both know the importance of making Christ the center of our marriage, the foundation of our family, and we are determined to put our trust in Him and His plan for our lives.

Morgan definitely got the music gene from his daddy. He loves to lie on his tummy on the floor with his ankles crossed in the air behind him and his chin resting on his hands, as I play my tapes of Brant singing all of Garth Brooks' songs. Morgan is drawn to the music and loves to try to sing along. His favorite toys for a long time have included a toy guitar and a little, red keyboard. There is a purity to Morgan's voice when he sings along with the radio from his car seat, and it blesses his mama's heart.

As long as I live, I will never forget the day that I overheard Morgan sitting in Christian's lap, pointing at a framed snapshot on our table. "Is that *me* in that picture, Daddy?" he asked.

Christian glanced at the picture of Brant and Brandon and shook his head. "That's Brandon," he told him with a smile.

Morgan looked around the living room and found another picture. "Is *that* me and my other daddy?" he asked curiously, again pointing to a framed picture of Brant and Brandon.

I knew that picture well… it was a true Kodak moment… a moment in time captured on film, so that, in the years to come, Brandon could reflect on the life of a man whose greatest achievement was not the confetti falling down in that stadium, the Super Bowl victory we were celebrating or the ring he had just won… but his willingness to be the man that Brandon needed him to be.

"That's Brandon too, buddy," Christian told Morgan.

"Brandon looks like me," Morgan fired back with a hilarious contortion of his lips and wrinkle of his nose, "just not as cute!" Those words from that little boy stopped me in my tracks. How was it that he could possibly embody the easy gestures, the perfect inflection, the playful cockiness, the bright personality of a man he had never met?

I smiled toward Heaven and just rolled my eyes at my child. Brant's mama had told me plenty of stories of raising such a little bundle of personality, and I proudly eyed Brant's mini-me and readied myself for the challenges that would no doubt be in my future as Morgan's mama.

"Let's find a picture of you," Christian said as he stood with Morgan in his arms and took a picture frame from its shelf. "Look, here's a picture of you and me! Look at those football jerseys!"

"Roll Tide!" Morgan grinned as he looked at the picture approvingly. Then his eyes moved back to Christian. "I like the pictures of me and you, Daddy," he said, as a precursor to what was coming next, "but where's the pictures of me and my other daddy? Like Brandon has…"

My breath caught, and, thankfully, Christian was more prepared for that inevitable moment than I was.

Christian didn't flinch. "Well," he told our son, "I wish that there were pictures of you and your daddy that I could show you. But do you know how baby Connor lives in Mommy's tummy, and, even though we can't see him yet, we can't wait for him to get here, so we can play with him and hold him and kiss him?"

Morgan nodded.

"When you were a baby, and you were still in Mommy's tummy," Christian continued, "your daddy couldn't wait to see you and hold you and kiss you and play with you. And I couldn't wait either because we all already loved you so much! But, while you were still in Mommy's tummy, Daddy had a bad accident…"

"And he went to Heaven," Morgan finished the story with an easy shrug.

"Yes, buddy, he did," Christian nodded.

As Christian's eyes filled with tears that he was desperately trying to hold back, Morgan threw his arms around him. "I'm sure glad *you* get to hold me, Daddy!" he said with childlike conviction.

Christian held our son close and rubbed his back as Morgan squeezed his neck. Christian kissed our precious little boy's cheek, tickled his tummy and set him back on his feet to run off and play.

Morgan ran over to me and pulled my shirt up to kiss my bare belly. As I tousled his hair, he gripped both sides of my baby bump and planted a big kiss on it.

As Morgan scampered happily toward the playroom, I slid my arm around Christian. "Thank you for that," I whispered. "You're an amazing daddy."

"Thanks, sweetie," he nodded as he kissed the side of my head. He thought for a moment as he picked up a framed picture of Brandon and Morgan. They were sitting in the rocking chair on our front porch, smiling sweetly for the camera. "I feel like God entrusted me with a pretty huge responsibility. It's a lot of pressure, but I know that if I do a really good job being Brandon and Morgan's daddy, and I teach them and guide them in the way that they should go… I'll raise sons who, when it's all said and done, get to spend eternity with the daddy they never got to know here."

CHAPTER TEN

It's Your Song

Jennifer McLachlan

It was just a little after midnight. My heart was pounding, and my head was spinning. There was no way this could be happening to me! "Christian, wake up," I cried, shaking his arm as I sat on the edge of our bed.

He woke easily, accustomed to finding me sobbing in the middle of the night.

"My water broke," I told him.

He jumped from our bed like a startled animal and flipped on the light. "Okay, I'm gonna call my mom to come stay with the boys; then I'm gonna grab the suitcase, and we're gonna get to the hospital," he said nervously checking off his mental, preparedness checklist as he stroked my hair and kissed my forehead.

I grabbed his hand, clinching it tightly. I started to speak, but my words were delayed by the onset of a painful contraction.

"Breathe," Christian coached.

"Please stop," I begged.

"Are you okay?" Christian gulped.

"No, I'm not okay! This has to stop; I can't have this baby today," I cried hysterically.

Christian looked at me as though I had lost my mind. His hair was messy from sleep, and his eyes were wide with panic. "Jen, what are you talking about?" he shook his head. "The baby's coming…"

"He's early; it wasn't supposed to happen like this," I sighed as I grabbed my lower back. "He's not due until next week."

I was being irrational… just a complete emotional wreck, and Christian looked confused.

"Do you know what today is?" I yelled at him, recalling how I had been unable to fall asleep in the hours leading up to midnight.

Christian thought for a moment, clearing the fog of sleep from his mind. "Oh," he gulped. He nodded slowly, understanding finally registering. "Yeah, sweetheart, I know what today is. I'm sorry; I wasn't thinking."

"I can't have our baby on the day that Brant died," I sobbed. "This isn't the way it is supposed to be."

Christian sat down next to me and put his arm around me. "I don't think that this baby coming today is an accident," he told me. "I think that it's about time you have something wonderful to focus on each year when this day rolls around."

"I don't want to forget about this day," I wailed. "I don't want anything to make me forget how awful this day was. I don't *want* to be happy today! I can't. I won't."

Christian tried his best to comfort me. "Jen, you're never going to forget the day you lost Brant, but won't it be nice, in years to come, that you can spend today celebrating life instead of mourning the loss of?"

"Our son cannot come today!" I shrieked at my husband, my hormones and my grief getting the best of me. "I can't do cupcakes and balloons on the day that Brant died, Christian!"

"I know it doesn't seem like it," Christian said earnestly. He kissed the side of my head. "You might not realize it, but you are the most amazing mother that any child could ever have. Your maternal instincts are always right on track, and I guarantee you that you'll step up to the plate every year for Connor's birthday."

There is something about hearing the man you love say his baby's name that melts a mother's heart. I rubbed my pregnant tummy, and I knew that my focus had to be on my baby.

As much as I might would have liked to reserve that day as my day of complete and utter misery, God had other plans for me, and, within the next few hours, the saddest day of my life also became one of my happiest.

As I held Connor in my arms, I couldn't stop crying, but they were tears of pure joy. There had been dark days when I never imagined I could ever again feel as blessed as I did in that moment.

The pride in Christian's eyes when he looked at our precious baby made my heart happy. He beamed at me like he couldn't believe that the two of us were capable of anything so miraculous.

I wish that, after experiencing the miracle of childbirth, every woman could feel the way that Christian made me feel as I cradled the life we had created. He looked at me with such admiration and appreciation that any anxiety I may have had subsided.

Brandon and Morgan were in awe of their little brother.

"He's so tiny," Brandon cooed.

Christian and I smiled at him, both thinking that Connor looked like a tank compared to what Brandon had looked like in his incubator the day he burst onto the scene two months before we were ready for him.

"I'll teach Connor how to play football," Morgan declared as he gently stroked his brother's little fingers. "Isn't that right, Daddy?" Then he addressed Connor directly to make sure that the terms of his offer were perfectly clear. "But, you can't be the quarterback because that's my job."

Christian lifted Morgan into his arms and nuzzled his cheek with a kiss. "Give Daddy a hug, buddy," he smiled, and Morgan flung his arms around Christian's neck and held on tight.

Tears streamed down Christian's face as he stared down at me and the baby. I knew exactly what he was thinking, and I reached my hand out and took his. I loved the tenderness of my husband's heart as he mourned, with a newfound understanding, the moment his brother had missed out on years earlier.

The day that Christian and I welcomed Morgan into the world while grieving the fact that Brant wasn't there to meet him, we never could have imagined that this day was in our future.

I looked around at my beautiful family, and I was overwhelmed by God's grace. Brandon cuddled next to me in bed. Morgan had one arm hooked around Christian's neck, and he grinned down at me with that smile that lit up his entire face. I kissed the top of Connor's baby blue cap, and I thanked God for my boys and for my husband.

***

David McLachlan

Connor McLachlan was a perfectly healthy, bouncing baby boy. As I held my newest grandson for the first time, I held his head close to my nose and inhaled that scent of sweet innocence.

His parents could not have been more deserving of such a perfect reflection of their love. My respect for Christian and Jennifer left me feeling proud that my grandson would be raised by two people who had each demonstrated such grace in the face of tragedy.

Christian might have been holding his firstborn child that day, but he had already proven himself to be an incredible daddy and an all-around good man.

I watched Christian struggle with his brother's death for a long time, but, in so many ways, he was the one who helped me learn to cope in a world without my boy.

Christian is solid, even when he thinks he's falling apart. He's such a great kid; he likes to tell me that he learned everything he knows from me, but the truth is… I have learned a lot about quiet strength and grown tremendously in my faith just by watching him. He's a first-class kid, and I'm proud he's mine.

Spending the morning awaiting Connor's birth was a welcome distraction from everything else that day brought with it.

I picked up the newspaper that day, knowing that I would find my son's smiling face staring back at me. There he was, right on the front page, wearing his football jersey, pointing and winking at the camera in a way that only he could. If I had ever tried to pull off something like that, I would have just ended up looking ridiculous, but it fit Brant somehow. I had actually never seen that particular picture, and, with the field and scoreboard behind him, it somehow captured Brant's personality perfectly. He was such a ham… such a shameless ham!

"Brant McLachlan's smile was like none other," I read. "He was pure sunshine, shining brightly on our little town."

"Forget the football prowess for a second, Brant had a spirit about him that was going to take him even farther than that cannon he had for a right arm."

"You hear people talk about having that *star* quality, and Brant McLachlan personified that. It didn't matter what he was doing… playing football, singing at a pep rally or just walking down the street; he was a *star*!"

My eyes glazed with tears as I read through neighbors' memories of my son.

"He would have loved this," I shook my head, pushing the newspaper aside, as my wife walked into our kitchen holding Morgan's hand.

I hid my tears as I smiled at Brant and Jennifer's beautiful baby boy. I helped him climb into my lap and kissed his curly head of hair as he cuddled next to me and rested against my chest. That precocious little boy is a handful at times, but he is always, always, always a heart full.

My grandchildren have no idea how often they are the thread PawPaw is holding on to.

They run to me when they want to be picked up; they hide behind me when they're scared; they call out for me when they need help, but what they don't know is how often I run to them, how I reach out for them when I'm scared, or how often I rely on help only they provide.

On days when the hole in my life feels too big to fill, God sends Brandon running into my arms; He puts Brantley's dimples on Morgan's face; He brings my darling Emily to visit, and, that day, he sent Connor to remind me that life goes on.

CHAPTER ELEVEN

Christian McLachlan

As a football fan, player and, now, coach, I have learned many lessons from my father.

As a young boy, he taught me about hard work and sportsmanship.

As a young man whose high school football career was an embarrassment of riches, he taught me humility.

Throughout my life, by his example, he taught me about love, loyalty and what's truly important when it's all said and done.

When I ask my dad for coaching advice, he always gives me his opinion and then quips, "but I don't know, Chris… maybe I never was that great of a coach… Brant just always made me look like it."

Brant had an uncanny way of making everybody he played with look better than we were and everybody he played against look worse than they were, so I smile at my dad's joke. However, the truth is that my dad's coaching, both in football and in life, have made me the man I am.

I learned that true, life lessons are learned, not through speeches or lectures, but by the example of parents who practice what they preach.

I will never forget the State Championship football game my senior year of high school. It would become the fourth and final State Championship win of my high school career. My graduating class achieved the highest honor, the biggest trophy at the end of each season of our four year tenure at North River High School.

Nevertheless, with so much glory on the line, we almost lost our final game; our streak almost ended that night… not because we weren't the best team… but because, for half of the State Championship game, our best player was sitting on the bench.

With our not-so-secret weapon on the sideline, my dad's coaching was being called into question by a mob of angry fans.

In a football game where winning meant everything, I witnessed my father put teaching honesty, integrity and self-control ahead of winning a football game.

I will admit that, at the time, as a teenager who just wanted to cap off his senior football season with the win he had been dreaming of, I wasn't sure that my dad's decision was the best, but, looking back at it now, I see a perfect example of what it means to be a father.

Even though it wasn't the popular decision or the most profitable decision, the only thing that mattered to my dad was that his son learned a hard lesson, one that would take him a lot farther in life than winning a football game.

The story of that game has become legend at North River High School; some people think it was Dad's plan all along, to stage a fantastically thrilling and intoxicating come-from-behind victory to capture that final trophy, but, as someone who was there, I assure you it had zero to do with dramatizing the highlight reel and everything to do with a coach raising his son to be a real man and not just another spoiled superstar doomed by his own hubris.

In raising my own children, I try to live up to the example that my father set for me. As I revere the job that he did in raising me and my brothers, I strive daily to create that kind of legacy for my own children.

When I was a little boy, I remember my dad teaching us to be tough. He didn't like whining, and he didn't stand for being lazy. He taught us to "shake it off" or "rub some dirt on it" as he would say.

But, under that gruff exterior, there was a man whose boys meant the world to him. He knew exactly when to push and exactly when to pick us up and dust us off.

My dad had a saying when I was a kid, and, the funny thing is, I didn't even realize it until one day when I heard myself say the same thing to my son.

Morgan had been playing in the yard one day when he came running toward me just bawling. I instinctively reached for him, scooped him into my arms and, out of habit, mimicked my dad's old adage, "point to the blood."

That day, as I bandaged the little fella's barely skinned elbow, I chuckled to myself over repeating my old man's familiar and poignant line. I had never even really thought about what it meant beyond the literal interpretation of telling him where it hurt.

"Point to the blood."

Suddenly, what had been a, mostly ignored, never analyzed, catchphrase of my youth was taking hold of my heart. I started hearing that odd instruction repeated inside my head in the strangest moments, until it clicked.

Point to the blood.

That was it.

That was the best advice my father had ever given me!

Through His shed blood on the cross, Jesus Christ paid the price for my sins. He gave me hope and a future in Him.

Point to the blood is an instruction I give myself often these days. When I face struggles in my marriage, roadblocks in my career or difficult moments in raising my children, I point to the blood and remind myself that my salvation is in Christ. My strength is in Him; only He can provide me the answers that I seek.

If there is one thing that I have learned through losing my brother and starting a romantic relationship with Jennifer, it is that while my humanity often fails me, He never will.

I grew up going to church every Sunday morning, Sunday night and Wednesday night, and I said my prayers before every meal and before bedtime, but when Brant died… that is when I *truly* learned to pray. Though my prayers had always been sincere, that was the first time in my life that I ever genuinely hit my knees and cried out for Him.

My marriage got off to a rocky start… or literally to a Rocky start if you will. Rocky was Brant's pet name for Jennifer. To this day, she is coy about the origin of that nickname. I have never referred to Jen as Rocky, and I have finally accepted that she doesn't ever want me to.

Every marriage takes dedication and commitment, no matter how much you love your partner. Marriage requires work and balance. It is a delicate give and take, even with someone you have been friends with your entire life. With Jennifer and me, there is a loyalty that was true long before we said our wedding vows, but it hasn't made marriage any easier.

The reality of our situation is… I'm Brant's brother… sometimes it is the reason that Jen and I work, and, sometimes, it is the reason we don't.

Marriage has taught me that *love* isn't always a feeling… it's a choice… one that Jen and I make every single day.

If Jennifer and I were the foundation of our own marriage, there is no doubt we would have become another sad marriage statistic by now, but, because our marriage is founded on our shared faith in Christ and not on our own understanding of the constant roller coaster of emotions we both seem to be on, we made a commitment that extends far beyond ourselves.

I am not saying it's easy; I'm not saying that there are not still times when I find myself getting angry at Jennifer for things beyond her control. As hard as it is to admit… sometimes I can still get jealous of the relationship my brother had with her. If she's being honest, there are times when she looks at me and wishes she saw her brother-in-law. We are all going to have bad days, but, in the difficult moments, Jen and I point to the blood.

I am not a perfect person, nor do I profess to be; I make a lot of mistakes in my relationship and in parenting, but because His love IS perfect, I AM forgiven.

Brant and Jen had this childhood bond that I will never be able to compete with… nor should I… because our love is not their love.

It's not a competition between my brother and me. We are two different people, at two very different times in our lives, who happened to fall in love with the same woman.

He got her first kiss, and I will get her last.

He was the boy she loved, and, God willing, I get to be the man she grows old with.

Either way, we both got a piece of her that the other never did.

Over time, my family has found a balance that works for us.

Some of my favorite moments are being out on my boat with my wife and my boys. I remember my dad teaching my brothers and me to fish when we were kids, and now I'm teaching my own boys.

I have so many wonderful memories of my childhood, and I love making memories for my kids. Though they don't realize it now, one day they will look back at days like this and wonder why they ever couldn't wait to grow up.

Whether we are fishing, playing football, camping out in our living room in tents made of covers or enjoying Jennifer's famous Dr. Pepper floats, I like to tell the boys stories about Brant. They giggle as I recount their daddy's childhood antics and listen wide-eyed as I give them the play-by-play of his football days.

Jennifer says that when I tell those stories, I make Brant larger than life for them. I guess I realize that I do that; maybe since they will never know him, I just want them to think of him as this superhero… or… maybe that's just how I see him… larger than life.

A sweet lady at our church, whose grandson plays on my team, made Brandon, Morgan and Connor these adorable, royal blue, football jerseys with *North River Football* on the front and their names and numbers on the back in white lettering.

One day as I was loading my team onto our team bus, my two older boys stood in one of the seats, their tiny hands gripping the back of the seat as they faced away from me. With their curly, blond hair and their blue football jerseys, they were picture perfect as the *1* on Brandon's back and the *3* on Morgan's back left me once again standing in awe of #13.

CHAPTER TWELVE

The Dance

Christian McLachlan

I will never forget the summer that we loaded into my mom's new van for its maiden voyage, and my dad drove us all to Disney World in Orlando, Florida. My brother Jordan was eighteen and starting college in the fall.

My dad was driving and Jennifer's dad rode in the passenger's seat next to him. Our moms rode in the middle seat, and, in the back, poor Jordan had been given the thankless task of sitting between Brant and me, since we couldn't seem to keep our hands off of one another.

I distinctly remember my arm stretched across Jordan, my finger dangling an inch from Brant's face, going, "I'm not touching you! I'm not touching you!" Brant snapped at my finger with his teeth, and I screamed to tattle on him as if I had been completely innocent in all of it.

We exhausted *I Spy*, and *Love Bug* turned *Punch Bug* was the reason Jordan ended up having to separate me and Brant to start with. We had looked for license plates from different states and played *The Quiet Game* at Mom's insistence, notably the only game that Brant didn't mind losing. Because, in that game, isn't losing really winning anyway?

"Are we there yet?" Ethan whined next to me.

"Five more minutes," Mom promised cheerfully, regardless of the fact that we were probably somewhere near Pensacola at the time.

On Jordan's right, Ethan and I shared a single lap belt, and on Jordan's left, Brant and Jennifer did the same. I rested my head against my big brother's arm, wondering if I was ever going to get out of that van and get to meet Mickey Mouse.

Once we arrived in Orlando and checked into our resort, Jennifer, my brothers and I were introduced to the Monorail. As far as we were concerned, we had just discovered the best ride that Disney World had to offer.

The next day, in the Magic Kingdom, Ethan, Brant, Jennifer and I were wild with excitement.

We were all holding hands, running toward the spinning teacups with Mickey Mouse-shaped water canteens hanging from around our necks and mouse ears atop our heads, when my Mickey Mouse ears blew from my head. We stopped running, and Jennifer, as is captured on video, ran to retrieve my hat. Her cheeks glowing and her ponytail swinging, she handed it back to me with a grin.

"Thanks, Jenny," I said, putting my ears back in place on my head.

"You can't lose your ears!" she exclaimed, her voice more high-pitched than I remember. "We're all a big, mouse family!"

"That's right, Jenny," my dad said from behind the camera as he videoed us with a camera big and heavy enough that it held a full-sized VHS. "Today our family is in the happiest place on Earth!"

We waved at the camera, blew it kisses, did some completely random ninja moves and made a series of funny faces.

Brant mugged for the camera like it was his job, but my favorite part of watching that video now is that, at the very end, right before my dad accidently filmed the pavement long enough that the battery died, Brant put his arms around Jennifer and me and stated emphatically, "we are the happiest people on Earth!"

"And I love you!" Jennifer exclaimed, as she squeezed him into a side hug. She pulled me into the mouse-eared group hug, "and I love you."

"I love y'all times a billion," my five-year-old self squeaked.

Brant looked right at the camera and, right before Dad stopped videoing us, he summed up our lives pretty well, when, with wide-eyed innocence, he simply declared, "there's a lot of love here, ladies and gentlemen!"

***

Ethan McLachlan

Childhood… it's that time in your life when you sit in the back seat of your parents' car on a rainy day watching two raindrops slide down the outside of your window, and, in your head, they are racing.

Childhood was when having a really good day meant that your mom let you buy Fruit by the Foot at the grocery store, pick up a roll of Bubble Tape in the check-out line or drink a SqueezeIt in the swimming pool.

Having a great day meant piling your friends into your mom's car and going to ShowBiz… having pizza, ice cream cake and a sing-along with Billy Bob and Mitzi… then enjoying some rambunctious fun in the giant ball pit and using your tokens to play enough Skee-ball and Whack-a-Mole to win massive amounts of tickets that ultimately scored you a neon, friendship bracelet, novelty eraser or bouncy ball that you lost before you left the parking lot.

During childhood the answers to life's great questions all seemed pretty obvious, or at least pretty easy to figure out. Some didn't even require a second thought.

Yes, they should sell boxes of Lucky Charms consisting of only marshmallows.

No, there is no lesson worth learning that the Berenstain Bears didn't already teach us.

Yes, we really do want to live inside a department store with Jodi, Jeff the mannequin and his magic hat, Sam the security guard and Muffy, the resident mouse.

No, we are not going to injure ourselves with a slap bracelet, and who are these children you have supposedly heard stories about, Mom?

Some life-altering questions required more experimentation.

Yes, Brant can run faster than Tommy even while using a jump rope to drag Christian behind him on a Roller Racer.

No, you can't stand downstairs holding Stretch Armstrong's feet while Brant stands upstairs holding his arms.

Yes, it is possible to make a blindfolded Jennifer cry by putting nutmeg from Mom's spice rack into her mouth during a classic game of Name that Mystery Food.

No, Tommy can't talk faster than the man in the MicroMachines commercial.

Yes, an Easy-Bake Oven really can burn you.

No, Tommy can't run five yards after five minutes on the Sit n Spin.

Yes, a Radio Flyer wagon carrying triplets can make it safely down a hill with Christian using the handle like a joystick to guide it.

No, a Radio Flyer wagon carrying triplets plus Tommy Jackson can't make it safely down the same hill.

Like all kids, my brothers and I couldn't wait to grow up. When you're little you just can't wait to be one of the grown-ups. Then when you reach adulthood and learn about all the responsibilities that come along with it, you realize that being a grown-up doesn't just mean that you can finally have that packet of Fun Dip for dinner if you so choose.

I absolutely loved going to the service station with my dad when my brothers and I were kids. I have no idea why it is such a vivid memory for me, but there was something about going in there with my brothers and rushing over to the branded, paint can full of Tongue Splashers Bubble Gum that takes me back to a simpler time.

As advertised, Tongue Splashers were pieces of bubble gum that would paint your tongue red, blue, green, orange or purple. At that time in American history, the red pieces were a hot commodity. Why? Because with the help of three, red Tongue Splashers, Christian, Brant and I could transform ourselves into Ax, Smash and Crush of the WWF tag-team known as Demolition.

In 1988, my brothers and I, along with Jennifer Smith and Tommy Jackson, were treated to our very first trip to the movie theatre in Meridian, Mississippi.

The movie was called *Mac and Me.* The plot revolved around wheelchair-bound Eric and his friend, a mysterious alien creature. It was my first time seeing a movie on the big screen, and, to me, it is a classic.

Sure, it may have been a rip-off of *ET*, but my friends and I had never seen *ET*.

Sure, I see now that it may have played like a long, really strange commercial for McDonald's and Coca-Cola (watch it back, and you'll see what I mean), but sitting in that theatre on the edge of my seat in 1988, as Eric's wheelchair raced down that hill and the brake ripped right off in his hand, I was having the time of my life.

Effects weren't in the 80's what they are today, but when Eric was caught up in an explosion at the gas station that very clearly didn't come anywhere close to touching him, my mouth still hung open in anticipation as strange music began to play and pot-bellied, papa alien wandered over looking all big eyed and creepy to lay his hands on Eric and heal him.

I mean, the plot may not read like a classic now, but, back then, when Mac and his family stood in that courtroom in their new, fancy, dress clothes being sworn in as American citizens before driving off in their pink Corvette… I may have shed a tear.

Driving home from that movie, reveling in our first trip to the theatre, we stopped by the gas station. Jennifer's mom let us each pick out a piece of candy inside the store, and, when we brought our selections to the register, Brant bought a blue raspberry Ring Pop.

Outside, next to the always romantic gas pump, he got down on one knee and presented it to Jennifer.

It was the first time I had ever seen my brother propose to Jen, but it wouldn't be the last, and I think I knew that even then.

She said *yes*, and Brant slid the Ring Pop engagement ring onto her finger. Because that left Brant without a piece of candy, Jennifer then traded him her pack of Bonkers.

That was that; we crawled into the car to go home, unfazed and happy as could be. I sorted through my Runts, picking out all of the bananas, Christian and Tommy shoved Big League Chew into their cheeks, and Jennifer ate her engagement ring.

***

Jennifer McLachlan

In 1992, in the hockey-deprived South, I was introduced to my very first celebrity crush, courtesy of *The Mighty Ducks* and team captain, Charlie Conway.

In 1993, the boys and I were all crushing pretty hard on Benny "The Jet" Rodriguez in *The Sandlot*. I mean, how cool was that guy?

That same year, Henry Rowengartner pitched for the Chicago Cubs in *Rookie of the Year*, and Brant dreamed of success in the big leagues.

Then in 1994, Becky "The Icebox" O'Shea and the *Little Giants*, spoke to the tomboy inside of me.

Brant, Christian, Ethan, Tommy and I watched all of those movies over and over. Those were the movies our parents were okay with us watching. There were television shows, however, that we were not allowed to watch growing up. I remember specifically that we *were not* allowed to watch them because other kids in our class *were* allowed to watch them, and that spurred our curiosity. The list of forbidden television viewing included: *Salute Your Shorts, Clarissa Explains It All* and *My So-Called Life*.

In the most rebellious act of my childhood, Brant, Christian and I snuck into Jordan's bedroom, turned his television on really low and caught an episode of *My So-Called Life* on MTV.

I was way too young and much too sheltered to understand the way that Jordan Catalano made me feel, but, whatever it was that he was doing to me with those gorgeous, blue eyes and that barely audible mumble, it scared me so badly that I never turned that show on again.

In a convenient twist of fate, Tommy *was* allowed to watch *Clarissa Explains It All*, and the triplets and I managed to nervously catch a couple episodes on Nickelodeon while playing at his house.

My parents needed not worry about that one. Sam climbing through Clarissa Darling's bedroom window didn't do much for me. Now, years later when Joey Potter first climbed that ladder into Dawson Leary's bedroom window… that was a different story. Dawson may have been the title character, but, when *Dawson's Creek* hit the WB, Charlie Conway re-entered my life as the lovable Pacey Witter.

That's right, my childhood crushes were a couple of cute brunettes, courtesy of actors Joshua Jackson and Jared Leto.

In real life, however, my only crush was the blond sitting next to me playing with Cabbage Patch Kids and Care Bears, petting Pound Puppies, dancing next to me, singing along to *The Right Stuff* by New Kids on the Block and plotting a *Double Dare* obstacle course that would have made Marc Summers jealous.

Looking back on memories I will never forget, I realize that I had the best childhood ever! From creating magical designs on the Lite Brite to watching my hero creating magic under the Friday night lights... from playing *Pretty Pretty Princess* to being named queen on homecoming night... from a blue raspberry Ring Pop to a sparkling diamond ring... reflecting on my childhood fills me with nostalgia for priceless memories of a time gone by.

***

Tommy Jackson

Brant hated to lose. I loved his competitive spirit; it didn't matter what he was doing... he HAD to win.

I remember playing Super Mario Bros. with him on the original Nintendo; if he wasn't going to beat the game, he'd restart it. He'd punch that reset button on the front of the console and act like something just hadn't been working correctly. It didn't matter that you were stuck being Luigi again and currently having the game of your life; if it wasn't going his way, that game was getting restarted.

For a long time, the only games we had were Super Mario Bros. and Duck Hunt, which included a Zapper Light Gun used to shoot ducks as they flew across the screen. I can't even tell you how many times Coach McLachlan scolded us for pressing that gun right up against the glass of his television set.

If you missed a duck while playing Duck Hunt, there was this awesome, laughing dog that would pop up and make fun of you. I would miss on purpose just to watch that feature. It was genius, and it cracked me up.

Brant hated that dog and his annoying snicker with a passion far beyond what Nintendo intended, I'm sure. The game didn't allow you to shoot the mascot dog, which I only know because Brant fired at him repeatedly. Then, you guessed it… restart!

Jen got the board game *CandyLand* for her birthday one year, and Brant hated it. It was all luck-of-the-draw, zero skill involved. You could be *just* about to win the game and then draw the dreaded Mr. Plum card and get sent right back to the start.

Brant wasn't a bad sport; he didn't throw a fit or quit the game; games of chance just weren't really Brant McLachlan's thing.

His detest of harmless games such as *CandyLand* might have been less tolerable if that fierce competitor wasn't your quarterback. I loved that Brant hated to lose. It meant that he put in the extra work to be the best. It meant that in a football game when our backs were against the wall, we could count on him to find a way.

It didn't matter if it was a preseason scrimmage or a State Championship game; I'm not sure he knew the difference. It was a competition, and he was going to win it.

Christian, Ethan, Brant and I played football together from our very first peewee football game, all the way through mine and Ethan's very last football game ever.

I loved being on the field with my best friends. I loved celebrating victories together, riding on the bus together, goofing off in the locker room and making memories that will last a lifetime. But, most of all, I loved being there with the most up-close and personal view possible as my best friend became… #13.

The stands were full of people cheering on their team… in love with their special quarterback and watching him lead our team and our town to victory after victory… but none of those people were on the field… none of them had the behind the scenes, front row seat that I had.

That grin in the huddle… that wink he'd give you right before he did something extraordinary… that nonchalance that had nothing to do with his focus and everything to do with his trademark style… that high-five and accompanying rebel yell that meant more to any of us who ever played with Brant than words ever could. If you did something wrong, he was going to spell it out for you; you'd better believe that… but, if he just screamed at you with no words, you knew you had your quarterback's seal of approval… you had done something right.

Brant was a force on the football field, blazing past defenses, making cuts so sharp that defenders fell at his feet.

Watching him run was poetry in motion… this graceful dance that was so precise that it looked choreographed at times.

He was king of the fake-out, juking left or right, spinning past you, his feet lightening fast as he skillfully worked his way through the fun, little maze somebody had been kind enough to set up for him to enjoy on his way to the end zone.

Sometimes I try to imagine where that handsome son of a gun would be today.

High school could have lasted forever as far as I'm concerned, and, in a way, it has because those days when we were the quintessential boys of fall will live with me forever.

I miss my friend, but it's like Garth Brooks' song says, "I'm glad I didn't know the way it all would end, the way it all would go. Our lives are better left to chance; I could have missed the pain, but I'd have had to miss the dance."

CHAPTER THIRTEEN

Jennifer McLachlan

There is a spot in the woods that I can lead you right to. Though my tree looks just like all the rest, I can take you right to the tree where Brant carved our initials with a pocket knife. I know exactly which fence to jump and which path to take, but I hadn't been back there since Brant died... not until the day I spontaneously grabbed Christian by the hand and took him running across a field, ready to visit my tree. To finally be in a place where memories like those are ones I can happily share with Christian is such a refreshing feeling.

As Christian and I stood under the tree, I put my hands on his face and pulled his lips to mine. As I kissed my husband, I was lost in the moment... until a pinecone fell right smack on top of our heads and startled us both so badly we screamed.

Then, suddenly, I was doubled over laughing. In my mind's eye, we were children, and I could see the whole scene unfold. The perfect throw... the mischievous grin. What once would have sent me spiraling into depression and left me riddled with guilt, now brought on the release of the most indescribable tears.

Christian picked up the pinecone and hurled it skyward with a grunt and a laugh.

It seems like a simple moment, but, for me and Christian, on our journey, it meant everything.

I don't want to be a fraud living behind my white picket fence; I think that is the real reason I wanted to tell my story. I try to put on a brave face, but the reality of profound loss is that it's a difficult journey through grief to acceptance, no matter how strong you are.

For so long, I felt like I needed Christian to save me; I was in love with him, so I couldn't figure out why, even wrapped in the safety of his arms, I still felt like I was drowning.

I had to get to a place where I realized that, while Christian was the answer to my prayers, only God could truly heal my heart.

I would be the first person to tell you… faith doesn't take away the pain… it doesn't make things easy; but, hallelujah, it does make them possible.

Loss is never easy. When I say that God's love has healed my heart, I don't mean to suggest that missing Brant doesn't still hurt, but there is a peace to my pain now.

Trust me, there are still bad days when the girl I was and the woman I've become struggle to coexist. Struggle is a part of life. My life wasn't struggle free with Brant, and I can't expect it to be struggle free now. The key for me is learning how to deal with the struggle in a way that is productive for me and for my family.

I'm blessed to be surrounded by people who know that, despite the tears in my eyes at the most inopportune times, I am a happy person who loves life, loves my husband and my children… and was lucky enough to be loved by someone who touched my heart so deeply that he will live in it forever.

I embrace the tomboy I was, the childhood friendship that contained within it the most innocent love, and the teenager who treasured a lifetime of love she shared with one boy.

And I'm no longer afraid to embrace the woman who literally lives behind a white picket fence on River Bend Road with a husband who is the most unselfish person I know. He is gracious, patient, compassionate and empathetic. Our shared pain may have catapulted Christian and me into each other's arms, but it is our love and respect for one another and our devotion to our God, our marriage and our children that keeps us standing by each other through good times and bad.

Christian and I often joke that I ended up married to Brant's mild-mannered alter-ego. And all I have to say about that is... I feel like there are a lot of girls out there holding out for Superman when Clark Kent is standing right in front of them.

When I got pregnant with our baby girl after three, rambunctious boys, Christian and I were ecstatic. Brandon, Morgan and Connor had each been named well before their arrivals; this would be the first time that Christian and I sat down to agree on a name for our child.

The decision was easy and instantly unanimous! We would name our daughter after Brant's three favorite football heroes, in no particular order, of course! *Wink! Wink!*

Born at a healthy 5lbs 13oz, we welcomed our only daughter into the world. From the moment we laid eyes on that perfect, brown-haired, brown-eyed beauty, our baby daughter, Bryant Landry McLachlan, had her mama, her daddy and her three, big brothers wrapped around her tiny, little fingers.

On the day that Bryant was born, Christian gently placed our tightly swaddled daughter into Brandon's eagerly waiting arms as he sat with Morgan and Connor flanked on either side of him.

Tears of absolute joy streamed down my face as I snapped a picture of those three, blond-headed boys staring so protectively at the brunette baby sister they so tenderly cradled.

Images from my own life flashed before my eyes, and I smiled for my daughter, knowing she would grow up feeling like the luckiest girl in the world.

Printed in the United States
By Bookmasters